THE COMET DOOM by Edmond Hamilton.
A colossal conspiracy from the depths of
space sends the Earth off orbit toward a
mysterious comet and a band of invading
aliens who must enslave the Earth or die ...

INTO THE SUN by Robert Duncan Milne.
A comet plunges into the sun, huge firestorms
redden the horizon, and the temperature on
Earth skyrockets while a pair of scientists
struggle to save themselves—and the world!

INSIDE THE COMET by Arthur C. Clarke.
Caught in the icy methane grip of a comet two
million light-years from Earth, a tiny band of
Earthmen's only hope lies in the sophisticated
navigational computer that the comet's
influence has rendered incapable of the
simplest arithmetic!

The Mysteries of Science from MENTOR

COMETS
Isaac Asimov's Wonderful Worlds of Science Fiction #4

—————— EDITED BY ——————

Isaac Asimov,
Martin H. Greenberg,
and Charles G. Waugh

A SIGNET BOOK

NEW AMERICAN LIBRARY

Acknowledgments

"The Comet Doom," by Edmond Hamilton. Copyright 1928; copyright
renewed © 1956 by Edmond Hamilton. Reprinted by permission of the agents
for the author's Estate, the Scott Meredith Literary Agency, Inc., 845 Third
Avenue, New York, NY 10022.

"Sunspot," by Hal Clement. Copyright © 1960 by Street and Smith Publications, Inc. Reprinted by permission of the author.

"Inside the Comet," by Arthur C. Clarke. Copyright © 1960 by Mercury
Press, Inc. From THE MAGAZINE OF FANTASY AND SCIENCE FIC-
TION. Reprinted by permission of the author and his agents, the Scott
Meredith Literary Agency, Inc., 845 Third Avenue, New York, NY 10022.

"Raindrop," by Hal Clement. Copyright © 1965 by Galaxy Publications, Inc.
Reprinted by permission of the author.

"Comet Wine," by Ray Russell. Copyright © 1967 by Ray Russell. Originally
appeared in PLAYBOY. Used by permission of the author.

"The Red Euphoric Bands," by Philip Latham. Copyright © 1967 by Galaxy
Publishing Corporation. Reprinted by permission of the Scott Meredith Literary Agency, Inc., 845 Third Avenue, New York, NY 10022.

"Throwback," by Sidney J. Bounds. Copyright © 1969 by Sydney J. Bounds.
Reprinted by permission of the author.

"Kindergarten," by James E. Gunn. Copyright © 1970 by Universal Publishing and Distributing Corporation. Reprinted by permission of the author.

"West Wind, Falling," by Gregory Benford and Gordon Eklund. Copyright ©
1971 by Terry Carr. Reprinted by permission of the authors.

"The Comet, the Cairn and the Capsule," by Duncan Lunan. Copyright ©
1972 by UPD Publishing Corporation. Reprinted by permission of the author.

"Some Joys Under the Star," by Frederick Pohl. Copyright © 1973 by UPD
Publishing Corporation. Reprinted by permission of the author.

"Future Forbidden," by Philip Latham. Copyright © 1973 by UPD Publishing
Corporation. Reprinted by permission of the Scott Meredith Literary Agency,
Inc., 845 Third Avenue, New York, NY 10022.

"The Death of Princes," by Fritz Leiber. Copyright © 1976 by the Ultimate
Publishing Company. Reprinted by permission of Richard Curtis Associates,
Inc.

"The Funhouse Effect," by John Varley. Copyright © 1976 by Mercury Press,
Inc. From THE MAGAZINE OF FANTASY AND SCIENCE FICTION.
Reprinted by permission of Kirby McCauley, Ltd.

The following page constitutes an extension of this copyright page.

SIGNET TRADEMARK REG. U.S. PAT. OFF. AND FOREIGN COUNTRIES
REGISTERED TRADEMARK—MARCA REGISTRADA
HECHO EN CHICAGO, U.S.A.

SIGNET, SIGNET CLASSIC, MENTOR, PLUME, MERIDIAN and NAL BOOKS
are published by New American Library,
1633 Broadway, New York, New York 10019

First Printing, February, 1986

1   2   3   4   5   6   7   8   9

PRINTED IN THE UNITED STATES OF AMERICA

CONTENTS

Introduction
C O M E T S

Isaac Asimov

From the time when human beings first began to gaze curiously at the night sky, comets must have been special. They were so different from everything else.

The stars were just dots of light which might have been decorations, perhaps, or simply an interesting background against which more important objects might be considered.

The stars were of only limited interest themselves. They did not move relative to each other (they were "fixed stars"), or change in any way. However, the moon shifted position against the stars dramatically from night to night and changed phases at the same time. From these changes, human beings developed a calendar to mark the passage of time and the shifting of the seasons. It was eventually found that the sun (which also shifted position against the stars, but more slowly than the moon did) produced a much better calendar.

There were five objects that looked like bright stars yet also shifted position, but in a much more complicated way than the sun and moon did. We know these five objects as Mercury, Venus, Mars, Jupiter, and Saturn. These, plus the sun and moon, were called "planets" (from a Greek word meaning "wanderers").

About five thousand years ago, early astronomers began to work out the pattern of movement for each of these seven bodies, and the heavens took on an orderly and predictable aspect. Since it seemed clear that the heavenly bodies influenced the earth (the sun's motions produced day and night, the moon's made the first calendar possible), the complicated motions of Mercury, Venus, Mars, Jupiter, and Saturn must also have meaning. It was that which gave rise to the silly nonsense we call "astrology."

The comets, however, were different. In the first place, they weren't sharp, bright dots of light like the stars and the dimmer planets. They weren't a bright circle of light like the sun, or the full moon. (When the moon changed shape, half its boundary was always a circular arc.) Comets, instead, were hazy objects of irregular shape. Most noticeably they possessed a long hazy tail, which seemed never exactly the same in different comets. Even during the lifetime of a single comet, the tail would change shape.

What's more, comets were unpredictable. They appeared in the sky unexpectedly, followed an unpredictable course, and then eventually faded and disappeared. It seemed fair to suppose that the planets in their stately and orderly minuet across the sky predicted the ordinary changes and vicissitudes of earthly affairs. Comets, however, unusual and unexpected, must predict something equally unusual and unexpected.

Since, in this sad world of ours, anything unusual seems much more likely to be disastrous than wonderful, leaden rather than golden, it was natural to suppose that comets brought a message of catastrophe. This was reinforced by the fact that the comet's tail looked like the unbound hair of a woman in mourning, hair that was streaming backward as she ran wailing behind the funeral procession of her child or lover. (The very word "comet" is from the Greek word for "hair.") Others saw the shape of the tail as that of a sword, which was an even more direct and unmistakable sign of death and destruction.

It is not surprising, then, that the appearance of a comet almost invariably created fear and consternation among people. In the Middle Ages, comets were greeted with virtual panic. Even nowadays, when we know quite well what comets are and know that their motions are predictable in principle and, in many cases, in actuality as well, the appearance of a bright comet stirs strong uneasiness, at the least. The last really bright appearance was that of Comet Halley (the most famous of all comets) in 1910, and it was greeted with a scarcely controlled hysteria by a surprisingly large percentage of the population in Europe and the

United States despite all the soothing statements that astronomers could make.

It was not surprising, then, that this fear of comets pervades modern science fiction. We know that Mars can't veer from its orbit and collide with Earth, but who knows for certain that some comet might not someday do so? (As a matter of fact, in the 1980s, evidence came unexpectedly to hand which seemed to indicate that it was possible that storms of comets might rain down upon the inner Solar system every 26,000,000 years or so, and that some might indeed strike Earth, creating terrible havoc. The disappearance of the dinosaurs may be accounted for by such a strike, 65,000,000 years ago.)

Or even if there was not a direct collision, harm could be imagined. A comet has a small nucleus at its center but is surrounded by a haze (the "coma") which contains various gases that we have, in recent years, identified. Some of the gases in the coma, and the tail as well, are poisonous. What if the comet nucleus misses us but comes so close that its gases mingle with the atmosphere? Might we not all be poisoned? Fortunately, the coma, and even more so the tail, of a comet is so rarefied that any poisonous gases present would at once be diluted to harmlessness by our much denser atmosphere. In 1910, Earth passed through the tail of Comet Halley and absolutely nothing happened, although some charlatans made tidy sums by selling "comet pills" to the gullible, prior to the comet's appearance, pills that were supposed to neutralize the poisons.

In 1986, Comet Halley is returning once more. Unfortunately it will pass at a considerable distance this time, so it won't be particularly bright in the sky. What's more, its position will be such that it will be much more easily seen from the southern hemisphere than from the northern. Nevertheless, it *is* coming, and that alone is once again arousing an interest (and once again a certain amount of fear) concerning comets.

Astronomers are interested in Comet Halley, too. Comets are thought to be samples of the early material out of which the solar system was built, material that has not been changed by nuclear or geologic processes, or by meteoric bombardment. Comets have existed more or less unchanged, so it is thought, for all the nearly five billion years our solar system has existed. For that reason, several probes are being sent out toward Comet Halley in order to study its structure and chemical composition. It is perhaps the only way we can learn about our own very early history.

Under these circumstances, then, it seems reasonable to collect some of the best science fiction stories we can find that deal with comets (in a few cases, rather glancingly) from a scientific, rather than a superstitious, standpoint—though the old habit of fear often remains, as you will see.

In the case of a few of the older stories, I will add afterwords, in which I will comment on the science contained in them. You don't have to read those if you don't wish to, however. You can, if you would rather, simply enjoy the stories on their own terms.

A BLAZING STARRE
SEENE IN THE WEST

A Blazing Starre seene/In The/West/At *Totneis* in *Devonshire*, on the foureteenth/of this instant *November*, 1642./Wherin is manifested how Master/*Ralph Ashley*, a deboyst Cavalier, attem-/ted to ravish a young Virgin, the/Daughter of Mr. *Adam Fisher*, in-/habiting neare the said Towne./Also how at that instant, a fearefull Comet/appeared, to the terrour and amazment of/all the Country thereabouts./Likewise declaring how he persisting/in his damnable attemt, was struck with/a flaming Sword, which issued from the/Comet, so that he dyed a fearefull ex-/ample to al his fellow Cavaliers./London./Printed for *Jonas Wright*, and *I. H.* 1642./

A Blazing Starre in the West, or fearefull Comet seene in the Aire at *Totneis* in *Devonshire*, on the fourteenth of this instant *November*, 1642.

SO IT happened on Munday the 14.th of this instant *November*, that a young Virgine, Daughter to Master *Adam Fisher*, inhabitant in *Devonshire*, within a mile of *Totneyes,* upon some particular occasions happened to go to the said Towne, where being busied, partly about her occasions, and partly in visiting some Friends and Kinsfolkes, she was belated, so that her Friends were importunate to have her stay all night, but she replyed, that her Father would be discontented if she should be absent without his leave, the times being so dangerous, and so many Cavaliers abroad, wherefore she was resolved hap what might hap, to goe home that night.

Notwithstanding all these reasons which she alledged, her Friend grew importunate to have her stay, telling her that there were many deboyst Cavaliers abroad, so that they could not passe securely in the day time, much lesse in the night, for all this she would not be perswaded, but replied, that God was above the Devill, and that she feared not, but that that God which shee trusted in, could, and would defend her from all her Enemies.

With this resolution she set forward, but before she could get the halfe of the way to her fathers house it grew very darke, so that she could scarce discerne her hand, thus she went on, sometime listening whether she could heare any Body, upon the way, on a sudden she heard the noyse of a Horse galloping towards her, at which she beganne to be affraid.

But at last she plucked up a good heart and went forward, till shee met with this Gentleman Mr. *Ralph Ashley*, a Gentleman which knew her well, and she knew him, meeting with this Gentleman, he asked her whether she was going so late, she told him home to her fathers, he demanded who that was, she told him Master *Adam Fisher*, with that he called to mind her beauty, and the Devill strait furnished him with a device to obtaine his wicked purpose, sweet heart quoth he I know thy father well, and for his sake J will see the safe at thy fathers House, for the times are dangerous, and but a little before there are souldiers which J have cause to suspect, will doe the some outrage, the maid hearing him say so, was wonne to condiscend to him, partly by her knowledge of his supposed friendship to her father, and partly by her desire to get home without any further danger, to be short, the maid being wonne by his specious pretences of love and friendship, applied her selfe to get up, he having her behind him rode cleane out of the Road, (pretending that he did so to avoid the souldiers) till he was got out of hearing of any inhabitant.

Where being arrived, he fained an excuse to light, with that she slipt off the horse backe, and he alighted, then presently he layed His hands on her, and began to woe her to grant his desire, but she denying him with unlimited resolution, he went about to ravish her, taking a grievous oath that no power in heaven or earth could save her from his lust, with that the poore virgin, with pittious shrikes and cries spake these words *O Lord God of*

Hosts, tis in thy power to deliver me, help Lord or J perish, in the meane time he continued cursing and swearing that her prayers were in vaine, for there was no power could redeeme her, the words were no sooner vttered, but immediatly a fearefull Commet burst out in the ayre, so that it was as light as at high noone, this sudden apparition struck him and all the inhabitants into a great feare, and the poore virgin was intranced, the wretch casting his eye about and seeing her lye upon the ground as if he had meant to dare damnation tooke a great oath swearing *God-Damme-him*, alive or dead he would jnjoy her.

And as he was going about to lay hands of her intranced Body, A streame of fire strucke from the Comet, in the perfect shape, and exact resemblance of a flaming Sword, so that he fell downe staggering, severall poore shepheards which were in the field, foulding their flockes, these being amazed, seeing the flame of the Comet strike at the Earth, as they conceived, made to the place as neere as they could, where they heard a man blaspheming, and belching forth many damnable imprecations, and comming to the place, demanding how he came so wounded, he voluntarily related his intention, and what had happened to him by the perversenesse of that Roundheaded-whore, so he died raving and blaspheming to the terrour and amazement of the beholders.

The men presently took up the Maid, supposing she had been dead, and carried her home to her fathers House, where they were entertained, though with great sorrow for their daughters supposed death, the maid having continued intranced thus almost all that night, at length she began to draw her breath, and when she came to her selfe, the very first words that she spake were these, *Lord thou art lust in thy Judgments and mercifull in the midest of thy justice, wherefore J beseech the let not this sinne be imputed to his Charge, in the day of Judgment.*

Reader heare is a president for all those that are customary blasphemers, and live after the lusts of their flesh, especially all those Cavaliers which esteem murder and rapine the chiefe Principalls of their religion, for doubtlesse this is but a beginning of Gods vengance for not onely he, but they, and we, and all of us, except we repent, we shall all likewise perish.

Afterword

This is a purportedly true account of a startling event in seventeenth-century England, which not only serves as an exciting tale but may also have been an effective propaganda weapon of the Puritans against the Anglican "Cavaliers."

With such supposed eyewitness accounts of what a comet can do, presented in such affecting detail, it is no wonder that comet panic, being constantly reinforced, continued over the centuries.

We dismiss such stories nowadays with a smile (those of us who have some minimal sophistication in these matters), but they have their uses. They should give us a clear notion of what the numerous circumstantial tales of "flying saucers," and other popular nonsense, may be worth.

ISAAC ASIMOV

INTO THE SUN

Robert Duncan Milne

Scene—San Francisco / Time—1883

"And so you think, doctor, that the comet which has just been reported from South America is the same as last year's comet—the one discovered first by Cruls at Rio Janeiro, I mean, and which was afterward so plainly visible to us here all through the month of October?"

"Judging from the statement in the papers regarding its general appearance, and the course in which it is traveling, I do not see to what other conclusion we can come. It is approaching the sun from the same quarter as last year's comet; it resembles it in appearance; its rate of motion is as great, if not greater; all these things are very strong arguments of identity."

"But, then, how do you account for so speedy a return? This is only the end of August, and last year's comet was computed to have passed its perihelion about the eighteenth of September—scarcely a year ago. Even Encke's and Biela's comets, which are denizens of our solar system, so to speak, have longer periods than that."

"I account for it simply on the hypothesis that this comet passes so close to the sun that its motion is retarded, and its course consequently changed after every such approach. I believe, with Mr. Proctor and Professor Boss, that this is the comet of 1843 and 1880; that it is moving in a succession of eccentric spirals, the curvatures of which have reduced its periods of revolution from perhaps many hundreds of years to—at its last

5

recorded return—thirty-seven years, then to two and a fraction, and now to less than one; and that its ultimate destination is to be precipitated into the sun.''

"This is certainly startling, supposing your hypothesis to be correct; and should such a casualty happen, what result would you anticipate?''

"That demands some consideration. Take another cigar, and we shall look into the matter.''

The foregoing conversation took place in the rooms of my friend Doctor Arkwright, upon Market Street; the time was about eleven o'clock at night; the date, the twenty-seventh of August; the interrogations had been mine and the answers the doctor's. I may add that the doctor was a chemist of no mean attainments, and took great interest in all scientific discussions and experiments.

"The effect of the collision of a comet with the sun,'' observed the doctor, as he lit his cigar, "would depend upon a good many conditions. It would depend primarily upon the mass, momentum, and velocity of the comet—something, too, upon its constitution. Let me see that paragraph again. Ah, here it is,'' and the doctor proceeded to read from the paper:

" 'RIO JANEIRO, August 18th. — The comet was again visible last evening, before and after sunset, about thirty degrees from the sun. Mr. Cruls pronounces it identical with the comet of last year. It is approaching the sun at the rate of two and a half degrees a day. R. A., at noon, yesterday, 178 degrees, 24 minutes; Dec. 83 degrees, 40 minutes, S.'

"Now this,'' he went on, "corresponds exactly with the position and motion of last year's comet. It came from a point nearly due south of the sun, consequently was invisible to the northern hemisphere before perihelion.''

"Pardon me,'' I interrupted, "but you remember the newspaper predictions regarding last year's comet were to the effect that it would speedily become invisible to us here, whereas it continued to adorn the morning skies for weeks, till it faded away in the remote distance.''

"That was because the nature of its orbit was not distinctly understood. The plane of the comet's orbit cut the plane of the earth's orbit nearly at right angles, but the major axis or general direction of this orbit in space, was also inclined some fifty degrees to our plane; and so it came about that while the approach of the comet was from a point somewhat east of south, its return journey into space was along a line some twenty degrees south of west, which threw its course nearly along the line of the celestial equator; consequently, last year's comet was visible in the early morning, not only to us, but to every inhabitant of the earth between the sixtieth parallel north and the south pole, until the vast distance caused it to disappear. But, as I was going to say when you interrupted me, if the distance of the comet from the sun was only thirty degrees when observed at Rio Janiero, nine days ago, and its speed was then two and a half degrees a day, it can not be far from perihelion now, especially as its speed increases as it approaches the sun.''

"Suppose it should strike the sun this time," said I. "What results would you predict?''

"A solid globe,'' replied the doctor, "of the size of our earth, if falling upon the sun with the momentum resulting from direct attraction from its present position in space, would engender sufficient heat to maintain the solar fires at their existing standard, without further supply, for about ninety years. This calculation does not involve great scientific or mathematical knowledge, but, on the contrary, is as simple as it is reliable, because we have positive data to go upon in the mass and momentum of our planet. But with a comet the case is different. We do not know what elements its nucleus is composed of. It is true we know the value of its momentum; but what does that tell us if we do not know its density or its mass? A momentum of four hundred miles a second—the estimated rate of speed of the present comet at perihelion—would undoubtedly engender fierce combustion were the comet a ponderable body. On the other hand, large bodies composed of fluid matter highly volatilized might collide with the sun without an appreciable effect.''

"Have we any data to go upon in this matter?'' I inquired.

"With regard to our own sun,'' replied the doctor, "we have not; but several suggestive circumstances have occurred in the case of other suns which lead us to infer that something similar might happen to our own. Some years ago, a star in the constellation Cygnus was observed to suddenly blaze out with extraordinary brilliancy, its luster increasing from that of a star of the sixth magnitude—but faintly distinguishable to the unaided eye—to that of a star of the first. This brilliancy was maintained for several days, when it resumed its original condition. Now, it is fair to infer that this great increase of light may have been caused by the precipitation of some large solid body—a planet, a comet, or perhaps another sun—upon the sun in question; and, as light and heat are now understood to be merely different modes or expressions of the same quality of motion, it is fair to infer further that the increment of heat corresponded to that of light.''

"What, then, do you suppose would be the natural effect upon ourselves here, on this planet, by some such catastrophe as you have just imagined happening to our own sun?'' I asked.

"The light and heat of our luminary might be increased a hundred fold, or a thousand fold, according to the nature of the collision. One can conceive of combustion so fierce as to evaporate all of our oceans in one short minute, or even to volatilize the solid matter of our planet in less than that time, like a globule of mercury in a hot-air chamber. 'Large' and 'small' are not absolute, but relative, terms in Nature's vocabulary; both are equally amenable to her laws,'' sententiously observed the doctor.

"A comforting reflection, certainly,'' I remarked. "Let us hope we shall not be favored with any such experience.''

"Who can tell?'' rejoined the doctor, as he rose from his seat. "Excuse me for a minute. You know there is a balloon ascension from Woodward's Gardens tomorrow, and there is a new ingredient I am going to introduce at the inflation. The stuff wants a little more mixing. Take another cigar. I won't be a minute.''

I sat back and meditated as I listened to the retreating footsteps of the doctor, as he passed into an adjoining room. I looked at the clock. It was half past eleven. It was a warm night for San Francisco in August—remarkably so, in fact. I got up to open the window, and as I did so the doctor entered the room again.

"What is that?'' I exclaimed involuntarily, as I threw up the sash. And the spectacle which met my gaze as I did so certainly warranted the exclamation.

Doctor Arkwright's rooms were on the north side of Market Street, and the inferior height of the buildings opposite afforded an uninterrupted view of the horizon to the south and east. Over the tops of the houses to the east could be seen a thin, livid line, marking the waters of the bay, and beyond it the serrated outline of the Alameda hills. All this was normal and just as I had seen it a hundred times before, but in the northeast the sky was lit up with a lurid, dull red glow, which extended northward along the horizon in a broadening arc, till the view was shut out by the street line to our left. This light resembled in all respects the *aurora borealis*, except that of color. Instead of the cold, clear radiance of the northern light, we were confronted with an angry, blood-red glare which ever and anon shot forks, and tongues, and streamers of fire upward toward the zenith. It was as if some vast conflagration were in progress to our north. But what, I asked myself, could produce so extensive, so powerful an illumination? Vast forest fires, or the burning of large cities, make themselves manifest by a sky-reflected glare for great distances, but they do not display the regularity—or the harmony, so to speak—which was apparent in the present instance. The conclusion was inevitable that the phenomenon was not local in its source.

As we looked out at the window we could see that the scene had arrested the attention of others besides ourselves. Little knots of people had collected on the sidewalk; larger knots at the street corners; and the passersby kept turning their heads to gaze at the strange spectacle. At the same time the air was growing heavier and more sultry every minute. There was not a breath stirring, but an ominous and preternatural calm seemed to brood over the city, like that which in some climates is the precursor of a storm, and which here is frequently known as "earthquake weather."

The doctor broke the silence.

"This is something quite out of the common run of events," he exclaimed. "That light in the north must have a cause. All the Sonoma and Mendocino redwoods, with the pineries of Oregon and Washington Territory thrown in, would not make such a blaze as that. Besides, that is not the sort of sky-reflection a forest fire would cause."

"Just my own idea," I asserted.

"Let us see if we can not connect it with a wider origin. It is now nearly midnight. That light is in the north. The sun's rays are now illuminating the other side of the globe. It is, therefore, sunrise on the Atlantic, noon in eastern Europe, and sunset in western Asia. When you came here, scarcely an hour ago, the heavens were clear, and the temperature normal. Whatever has given rise to this extraordinary phenomenon has done so within the last hour. Even since we began to look I see that the extremity of the illuminated arc has shifted further to the east. That light has its origin in the sun, but it altogether passes the bounds of experience."

"Might we not connect it with the comet we have just been speaking about?" I suggested. "It should now be near its perihelion point."

"That must be it," acquiesced the doctor. "Who knows but

that the fiery wanderer has actually come in contact with the sun? Let us go out.''

We put on our hats, and left the building. All along the sidewalks we came upon excited groups staring at the strange light, and speculating upon its cause. The general expression of opinion referred it to some vast forest fire, though there were not wanting religious enthusiasts who saw in it a manifestation of divine wrath, or a portent of the predicted consummation of all things; for in the uninformed human mind there is no middle ground between the grossly practical and the purely fanatical. We hurried along Market Street and turned down Kearny, where the crowds were even denser and more anxious-looking. Arrived at the *Chronicle* office. I noticed that a succession of messengers from the various telegraph offices were encountering each other on the stairs of the building.

"If you will wait a minute," I said to the doctor, "I will run upstairs and find out what is the matter.''

"Strange news from the East," said the telegraphic editor, hurriedly, in answer to my question, at the same time pointing to a little pile of dispatches. "These have been coming in for the last half hour from all points of the Union.''

I took up one, and read the contents:

NEW YORK, 3:15 A.M.—Extraordinary light just broke out over the eastern horizon. Very red and threatening. Seems to proceed from a great distance out at sea. People unable to assign cause.

Another ran as follows:

NEW ORLEANS, 4:10 A.M.—Vivid conflagration reflected in the sky, a little north of east. General sentiment that vast fires have sprung up in the cane-brakes. Population abroad and anxious.

"There are a score more," remarked the editor, "from Chicago, Memphis, Canada—everywhere, in fact—all to the same purpose. What do you make of it?''

"The phenomenon is evidently universal," I said. "It must have its origin in the sun. Do you notice how hot and stifling the air is getting? Have you any dispatches from Europe?''

"None yet. Ah, here is a cablegram repeated from New York," said the editor, taking a dispatch from the hand of a messenger who just then entered. "This may tell us something. Listen:

" 'LONDON, 7:45 A.M. — Five minutes ago sun's heat became overpowering. Business stopped. People falling dead in streets. Thermometer risen from 52 degrees to 113. Still rising. Message from Greenwich Observatory says —'

"The dispatch stops abruptly there," interpolated the editor, "and the New York operator goes on thus: 'Message cut short. Nothing more through cable. Intense alarm everywhere. Light and heat increasing.' "

"Well," said I, "it must be as Doctor Arkwright suggested. The comet observed again at Rio Janeiro, ten days ago, has fallen into the sun. Heaven only knows what we had better do."

"I shall edit these dispatches and get the paper out, at any rate," said the editor with determination. "Ah, here comes the ice for the printers," as half a dozen men filed past the door, each with a sack upon his shoulder. "The paper must come out if the earth burns for it. I fancy we can hold out until sunrise, and before then the worst may be over."

I left the office, rejoined the doctor in the street, and told him the news.

"There is no doubt about it," he remarked at once. "The comet of last year has fallen into the sun. All the telegraphic messages were nearly identical in time, as it is now just midnight here, and consequently about four o'clock in New York, and eight o'clock in England."

"What had we better do?" queried I.

"I do not think there is any cause for immediate alarm," replied the doctor. "We shall see whether the heat increases materially between now and sunrise, and take measures accordingly. Meanwhile, let us look about us."

The scenes of alarm were intensified in the streets as we passed along. It seemed as if half the population of the city had left their houses, and gathered in the most public places. Thousands of people were pushing and jostling each other in the neighborhood of the various newspaper offices in frantic endeavors to get a glimpse of the bulletin boards, where the substance of the various telegrams was posted up as fast as they came in. Multitudes of hacks and express wagons were driving hither and thither, crowded with family parties seemingly intent upon leaving the city, and probably without any definite aim or accurate comprehension of what they were doing or whither they were going.

As the hours wore on toward morning the angry red arch moved farther along the horizon, its outlines grew bolder and brighter, and its flaming crest towered higher in the heavens.

Nothing could be conceived more ominous or ghastly, more calculated to produce feelings of brutish terror, and to convince the spectator of his utter powerlessness to cope with an inevitable and inexorable event, than this blood-red arch of flame which spread over one fourth of the apparent horizon. The air, too, was momentarily growing heavier and more stifling. A glance at a thermometer in one of the hotels gave a temperature of 114 degrees.

Between two and three o'clock four successive alarms of fire were sounded from the lower quarters of the city. Two large wholesale houses and a liquor store, in three contiguous blocks, caught fire, evidently the work of incendiaries. Multitudes of the worst rabble collected, as if by concert, in the business quarters. Shops and warehouses were broken into and looted—the police force, though working vigorously, not being strong enough to arrest the work of pillage, backed as it was by the moral terrors of the night, and the general paralysis which unnerved the better class of citizens. Strange scenes were being enacted at every corner and on every street. Groups of women kneeling upon sidewalks, and rending the air with prayers and lamentations, were jostled aside by ruffians wild and furious with liquor. A procession of religious fanatics, chanting shrill and discordant hymns, and bearing lanterns in their hands, passed unheeded through the crowded streets, and we could afterward watch them threading their way up the steep side of Telegraph Hill. In short, the terrible and bizarre effects of that fearful night would overtax the pen of a Dante to describe, or the pencil of a Doré to portray.

"Let us go home," said the doctor, looking at his watch. "It is now half past three. The temperature of the atmosphere is evidently rising. The chances are that it will become unbearable after sunrise. We must consider what is best to do."

We pushed our way back through the crowded streets, past despairing and terror-stricken men and wailing women; but as we passed the bulletin boards at the corner of Bush and Kearny streets, it was encouraging to mark that at least one earthly industry would continue to go on till the mechanism could run no longer, and that the world would, at any rate, get full particulars of its approaching doom, so long as wires could transmit them, compositors set them in type, and pressmen print them. I felt that the power and grandeur of the press had never been more fully exemplified than in the regular and ceaseless pulsations of its machinery as the daily issue was being thrown off, with the news

that the other hemisphere was in conflagration, and that a few
short hours would in all probability witness the same catastrophe
in our own.

The last two wagons which had driven up with ice for the
employees had been boarded and sacked by the thirsty mob, and,
looking down into the press room as I entered the building, I
could see the pressmen stripped to the waist in that terrible
hot-air bath, while upstairs the telegraphic editor was in similar
deshabille, with the additional feature of a wet towel bound
round his temples. He motioned to the latest dispatch from New
York as I entered. I took it up and read as follows:

NEW YORK, 6 A.M. — Sun just risen. Heat terrible. Air
suffocating. People seeking shade. Thousands bathing off the
docks. Thousands killed by sunstroke.

"Almost a recapitulation of the London message of three
hours ago," I said, as I hurried out. "Three hours hence we may
expect the same here."

I rejoined the doctor in the street, and together we proceeded
to his apartments.

"Now," said he, as I told him the purport of the last message,
"there is only one thing to be done if we wish to save our lives.
It is a chance if even this plan will succeed, but at all events
there *is* a chance."

"What is it?" I asked eagerly.

"I take it," answered he, "that the increase of heat and light
which will accrue as soon as the sun rises above the horizon
must prove fatal to all animal life beneath the influence of his
beams. The population of Europe, and by this time, I doubt not,
of all this country east of the Mississippi, is next to annihilated.
With us it is but a question of time unless—"

"Unless what?" I exclaimed excitedly, as he paused medita-
tively.

"Unless we are willing to run a great risk," he added. "You
are a philosopher enough to know that heat and light are simply
modes of motion—expression, so to speak, of the same molecular action of the elements they pass through or agitate. They have
no intrinsic being in themselves, no entity, no existence, as it
were, independent of outside matter. In their case the two forms
of outside matter affected by them are the ether pervading space
and the atmosphere of our planet. Do you follow?"

"Certainly," I replied, impatiently, for I dreaded one of the
doctor's disquisitions at such a critical moment as this. "But my

dear sir, what is the practical application of your theorem? How
can we apply it to the case in point?''

"In this wise," he went on: "heat—that is, the heat we have
to do with now—is caused by the action of the sun's rays upon
our atmosphere. If we get beyond the limits of that atmosphere,
what then? Simply, we have no heat. Ascend to a sufficient
altitude, even under the cloudless rays of the vertical sun, and
you will freeze to death. The limit of perpetual snow is not an
extreme one.''

"I catch your idea perfectly," I assented. "I concede the
accuracy of your premises. But what does it avail us? The Sierra
Nevada mountains are practically as far off as the peaks of the
Himalayas.''

"There are other means," rejoined the doctor, "of attaining
the necessary altitude. A balloon ascension, as you are aware,
was to have taken place today from Woodward's Gardens. I was
going to assist at the inflation, to test a new method of generat-
ing gas. I now propose that we endeavor to gain possession of
the balloon and make the ascension. I do not think we shall be
anticipated or thwarted in doing so.

"We must remember that the risk of the balloon bursting,
through the expansion of the gas, is great; for we shall be
exposed, not only to its normal expansion, should we penetrate
the upper atmospheric strata, but to its abnormal expansion
through heat, should we fail to do so in time.''

"It is shaking the dice with Death in any case," I answered,
and proceeded to assist the doctor in packing the apparatus and
chemicals he had prepared overnight; and, having done so, we
left the building and hastened southward along Market Street.
The cars were not running, and the carriages we saw paid no
heed to our importunities; so the precious time seemed to fly
past, while we swiftly covered the mile which separated us from
the gardens. The gates were luckily open, and none of the
employees visible, so we made for the spot where the balloon,
half-inflated, lay like some slimy antediluvian monster in its lair.
We adjusted the apparatus and arranged the ropes as speedily as
possible, and waited anxiously while the great bag slowly swelled
and shook, rearing itself and falling back by turns, but gradually
assuming more and more spherical proportions.

Meanwhile, we had again opportunity to observe the condition
of the atmosphere and the heavens. It was already half past four,
and in less than an hour the sun would spring up in the east.

The pale, bluish tints of daybreak were beginning to assert themselves beside the lurid semicircle which flamed above them. This latter changed to a hard, coppery hue as daylight became stronger, but preserved its contour unchanged. The heat became more oppressive, the thermometer we had brought with us now registering 133 degrees. Strange sounds were wafted in from the city—meaningless, indeed, but rendered fearfully suggestive by the circumstances of the morning. The animals howled unceasingly from their cages, and we could hear their frantic struggles for liberty. One catlike form that had made good its escape shot past us in the gloom. Had the whole menagerie been set free at that moment, we should have had nothing to fear from them, so great is the influence elemental crises exert over the brute creation.

We had at last the satisfaction of seeing the great globe swing clear of the ground, though not yet full inflated, and tug at the ropes which moored it. We had already placed the ballast-bags and other necessary articles in the car, when, perspiring at every pore, we simultaneously cut the last ropes, and rose heavily into the air. There was not a breath of wind stirring, but our course was guided slightly east in the direction of the bay.

It was now broad daylight, and the upper limb of the sun appeared above the horizon as we estimated our altitude from surrounding objects at about a thousand feet. As the full orb appeared the heat became more intense, and by the doctor's direction we swathed our heads in flannel, sprinkled sparingly with a preparation of ether and alcohol, the swift evaporation of which imparted coolness for a short time. The sky had now assumed the appearance of a vast brazen dome, and the waters of the ocean to the west and the bay beneath us reflected the dull, dead, pitiless glare with horrible fidelity. We had taken the precaution to hang heavy blankets upon the ropes sustaining the car, and these we kept sparingly moistened with water. Our own thirst was as intense as our perspiration was profuse, and we had divested ourselves of everything but our woolen underclothing— wool being a nonconductor, and therefore as effective in excluding heat as retaining it. We were provided with a powerful ship telescope, and also a large binocular glass of long range, and so far as the discomforts of the situation would permit us we took observations of the prospect beneath. To the unaided eye the city simply presented a patch of little rectangles at the end of a brown peninsula, but through our glasses the streets and houses became surprisingly plain. Little squat black forms were to be seen moving, falling down, and lying in the streets. Down by the city front the wharves were seen to be lined with nude or seminude bodies, which dived into the water and remained submerged, with the exception of their heads, though these disappeared at short intervals below the surface. Thousands upon thousands of people were thus engaged. The spectacle would have been utterly absurd and ludicrous had it not been tremendous in its awful suggestiveness.

"The mortality will be terrible, I fear," said the doctor, "if things do not change for the better soon, and I see no prospect of that. Our thermometer already marks 147 degrees even at this altitude. We are in the *tepidarium* of a thrice-heated Turkish bath. And if this is the case at a barometric altitude of eleven thousand feet—nearly two perpendicular miles—what must it be down there? It it too terrible to contemplate!"

"It is only seven o'clock yet," I remarked, looking at my watch. "The sun is scarcely an hour high."

"We must throw out more ballast," said the doctor, "and reach the higher strata at all hazards." He threw out a forty-pound bag of sand.

We shot upward with tremendous velocity for several minutes, when our ascent again became regular. We now remarked, with intense relief, that the thermometer did not rise—that, in fact, it had fallen about two degrees; though this relief was counterbalanced by the extreme difficulty of breathing the rarefied air at this immense altitude, which we estimated by the barometer at twenty-five thousand feet, or nearly five perpendicular miles. We therefore opened the valve and discharged a quantity of gas, and presently descended into a stratum of dense fog. This fog reminded me of the steam which rises from tropical vegetation during the rainy season, and I mentioned the fact to the doctor.

"If these fogs," replied he, "would only rest upon the city, they might shield it from destruction, but in a case of this kind we have no meteorological data to go on. No one can estimate either the amount of heat or the meteorological results it is now producing on the surface of the earth five miles below us."

The stratum of fog in which we now were was dense and impenetrable. We lay in it as in a steam-bath, the balloon not seeming to drift, but swaying sluggishly from side to side, like a sail flapping idly against a mast in a calm.

Hour after hour passed like this, the temperature still ranging from 130 to 140 degrees Fahrenheit. The doctor preserved his wonted equanimity.

"I have grave apprehensions," he remarked impressively, as if in answer to my thoughts, "that the final fiery cataclysm, a foreboding of which has run through all systems of philosophies and religions through all ages, and which seems to be, as it were, ingrained in the inner consciousness of man, is now upon us. I am determined, however, not to fall a victim to the fiery energy that has been evoked, and shall anticipate such a fate by an easier and less disagreeable one," and as he spoke he motioned significantly toward his right hip.

"Do you think, then," said I, "that an act under such circumstances"—designedly employing a vague periphrasis on such an unpleasant topic—"is morally defensible?"

"What can it matter?" returned the doctor, with a shrug. "Of two alternatives, both leading to the same end, common sense accepts the easier. A refusal to touch the hemlock would not have saved Socrates."

In spite of the terrible forebodings which filled me, the exigencies of the situation seemed to render my brain preternaturally concentrated and abnormally active. The surrounding stillness, the lack of sound of any description, the dreamy warmth of the dense mist in which we lay, exercised a sedative influence, and rendered the mind peculiarly impressionable to action from within.

"We have no means, then, of calculating the probable intensity of the heat at the earth's surface?" I asked.

"None whatever," replied the doctor. "We are now at an indicated elevation, by barometrical pressure, of twenty-two thousand feet. We are probably actually much higher, as the steam in which we lie is acting on the barometer. Atmospheric conditions like the present, at such an altitude, are totally beyond the experience of science. They might be, and probably are, caused by the action of intense heat upon hotter surfaces below us. To the fact of their presence, however, we owe our existence. This atmosphere, though peculiarly favorable to the passage of heat rays through it, is incapable of retaining them."

"Supposing," I went on, in a wildly speculative mood, engendered by the excitement of the occasion, "supposing that the heat of the surface of the earth were sufficiently intense to melt metals—iron, for instance—the most refractory substances, in fact. Take a further flight: supposing that such heat were ten times intensified, what would be its effect upon our planet?"

"The solid portions—the crust with everything upon it—would be the first to experience the effects of such a catastrophe. Then the oceans would boil, and their surface waters, at any rate, be converted into steam."

"What then?" I continued.

"This steam would ascend to the upper regions of the atmosphere till it reached an equilibrium of rarefaction, when its expansion would cool it, upon which rapid condensation would follow, and it would descend to earth in the form of rain. The more sudden and energetic the heat, the sooner would this result be accomplished, and the more copious the precipitation of the succeeding rain. After the first terrible crisis, the grand compensation of natural law would come into play, and the face of the planet would be protected from further harm by the shield of humid vapor—the *vis medicatrix naturae*, so to speak. Equilibrium would be restored, but most organisms would meanwhile have perished."

"Most organisms, you say?" I repeated, inquiringly.

"It is possible," said the doctor, "that ocean infusoria, and even some of the comparatively higher forms of ocean life, might survive. It is also possible that terrestrial animals occupying high altitudes—mountaineers for example, whose homes are deep snows and glaciers, denizens of the frozen zone, and beings similarly situated—might escape. This would altogether depend upon the intensity and duration of the heat. We must remember that *size*, looked at from a universal point of view, is merely relative. If we consider our planet as a six-inch ball, our oceans, with their insignificant average depth of a few miles, would be aptly represented by a film of the finest writing paper. How long, think you, would a watery film, such as that, last a few feet from a suddenly stirred fire?"

I bowed acquiescence to the conclusion drawn from the simile, and the doctor proceeded:

"There can be no longer any doubt that the present elemental convulsion is due to the collision of the comet with the sun. Knowing what we do of its orbit from last year's computation, its precipitation upon the solar surface has taken place on the side farthest from our own position in space. We do not, therefore, experience so sudden and so fierce atmospherical excitement as would otherwise have followed. It now remains to be seen what the duration of the effect will be."

During the latter portion of our conversation a low moaning

sound, which had been heard for the past few minutes, was growing more pronounced and seemingly coming nearer. At the same time the barometer was observed to be falling rapidly.

"That is the sound of wind," I exclaimed. "I have heard it on tropical deserts and on tropical seas. I cannot be mistaken. It comes from the east."

"The hot air from the parched continent is approaching," said the doctor. "Scientifically speaking, atmospheric convection is taking place, and we shall bear the brunt of it."

As he spoke the balloon was seized with a violent tremor. It vibrated from apex to car, and the next moment was struck by the most terrific tornado it is possible to imagine. The blast was like the torrid breath of a furnace, and we involuntarily covered our heads with our blankets, and clutched convulsively to the frail bulwarks of the car, which was being dragged on at a tremendous velocity, and at a horribly acute angle, by the distended gas-bag which towered ahead of us. Luckily we had both clutched mechanically at the railing on the side whence the wind came, to let go which hold would have meant instant precipitation over the opposite side of the car into the yawning gulf beneath. For less than a minute, so far as my stricken and scattered senses could compute, we were borne on by this terrific simoom, when, suddenly, we found ourselves as before, in the midst of a preternatural calm. We had evidently drifted into an eddy of the cyclone; for I could hear its sullen and awful roar at some distance to our right. Hardly had we composed ourselves when the blast struck us again; this time on the opposite side of the car. Again we were hurled forward by the resistless elemental fury; but this time in a sensibly downward direction. The blast had struck us from above, and was hurling us before it—down, down, to inevitable destruction. Fortunately the comparative bulk of the balloon offered more resistance than the car to this downward progress. Down, down, we sped, till, of a sudden, we emerged from the cloud-strata and obtained a brief and abrupt glimpse of the scene below. The counterblasts of the past few minutes had apparently compensated each other's action, for we found ourselves just over the city.

The city? There was no city. I recognized, indeed, the contour of the peninsula, and the well-known outlines of the bay and islands, through casual rifts in the dense clouds of steam which rose in volumes from below. Well nigh stupefied and maddened as I was by the intense heat, a horrible curiosity seized me to peer into the dread mystery beneath, and while with one scorched and writhing hand I held the blankets, which had not yet parted with the moisture gathered from the clouds above, to my aching head and temples, with the other I raised the powerful binocular to my eyes. Through drifting rifts of the steam-clouds that obscured the scene, I caught glimpses which filled me with unutterable and nameless horror. Neither streets nor buildings were decipherable where the city once had been. The eye rested upon nothing but irregular and misshapen piles of vitrified slag and calcined ashes. Everything was as scarred in a ruinous silence as the ruined surface of the moon. There was neither flame nor fire to be seen. Things seemed to have long passed the stage of active combustion, as though all the elements necessary to sustain flame had already been abstracted from them. Here and there an ominous dark red glow showed, however, that the lava into which the fair city had been transformed was still incandescent. The sand dunes to the west shone like glaciers or dull mirrors through the steam fissures, and long shapeless masses of what resembled charred wood were strewn here and there over the surface of the bay. Less than five seconds served to reveal all that I have taken so long to describe. The binocular, too hot to hold, dropped from my hand. At the same moment the balloon was again struck by the cyclone, and dashed eastward with the same fury as before. The doctor caught convulsively at the railing of the car, missed his hold, and with a wild, despairing shriek, outstretched arms, and starting eyes fixed upon mine, disappeared headlong in the abyss.

I am alone in the balloon—perhaps alone in the world. My companion has been hurled to a fiery death below. His awful shriek still rings in my ears. It sounds over the sullen roar of the cyclone. I am whirled resistlessly onward.

The blast shifts. Again the balloon pauses in one of the strange eddies formed by this strange simoon. The wind dies away to a moan. It rises again. It writhes around the car like the convulsive struggles of some gigantic reptile in the throes of death. It seizes me again in its resistless clutch. The balloon is being whirled toward the earth.

I am falling. But no—it seems to me that the earth—the plutonic, igneous earth—is rising toward me. With lightning-like rapidity it seems to hurl itself up through the air to meet me. I hear the roar of flames mingling with the roar of the blast. I see the seething, bubbling waste of waters through rifts in the clouds of steam.

I am nearing the molten surface. My feeling has changed. I am conscious that it has ceased to seem to rise. I feel that I am falling now—falling into the fiery depths below. Nearer—nearer yet; scorched and blackened by the awful heat as I approach—I fall—down—down—down—

Afterword

There were five exceedingly bright comets in the sky during the course of the nineteenth century: 1811, 1843, 1858, 1861, and 1882. In addition, Comet Halley made its appearance in 1835. By the end of the century, then, people had been fed to surfeit with comets. (Since 1882 there has been only one really impressive, naked-eye comet, and that was Comet Halley in 1910.)

Milne's story is one that would naturally occur to a writer in 1882, the year in which "Into the Sun" was written. What if a comet were to spiral inward and strike the sun? The suggestion in the story that comets skimming the sun are slowed (presumably by passing through the solar atmosphere) and would therefore return at quickening intervals is not entirely impossible. However, all the nineteenth-century comets were separate and distinct, and none except Comet Halley will appear again not just for "many hundreds of years" but for a million years, perhaps.

As for the catastrophic results of a comet striking the sun, it was quite clear even a hundred years ago that comets had insignificant masses. They never disturbed any object they approached. One comet had even passed through Jupiter's satellite system without disturbing anything, showing that its gravitational pull was insignificant and that its mass was therefore very small.

Still, the word "comet" was sometimes used for any astronomical object, however massive, which possessed a very elongated orbit, or which came from interstellar space. Thus, in

the seventeenth century, the French naturalist Buffon specu-
lated that the planets had come into being when a "comet"
struck the sun long, long ago and knocked pieces of it into
orbit. Buffon meant an interstellar visitor with a mass comparable to that of the sun itself—that is, another star. His use of the
word "comet," however, set a fashion among fiction writers.

As a matter of fact, comets must indeed strike the sun once
in a while, and in recent years, astronomers have obtained
photographs actually showing such an event. However, considering the mass of actual comets, it is not surprising that astronomers only became aware of it thanks to the advanced nature
of contemporary astronomical instruments. To the general public, there wasn't the slightest hint of anything untoward happening. (If a comet were to strike the earth, however, it might not
much affect the inanimate planet itself, but it could produce
catastrophic effects that might wipe out much of life.)

Still, it is reasonable to allow Milne his nineteenth-century
view and to read his successful evocation of a dying earth on
its own terms. You will find the description horribly effective.
And you have noted, I am sure, that it is one of the very small
group of stories in which the first-person narrator dies at the
end.

ISAAC ASIMOV

CAPTAIN STORMFIELD'S VISIT TO HEAVEN [EXTRACT]

Mark Twain

Foreword

Captain Stormfield's Visit to Heaven was first published in 1907, but I suspect it was written earlier. It is, in essence, a jovial satire of Heaven as it was imagined to be by Protestant Fundamentalists—the sort of thing young Sam Clemens was brought up to believe in, except that it didn't take.

It is not, in my opinion, very good Mark Twain, and I think Mark Twain may have believed that, too, for it was never finished. However, the first part of Chapter III is the best part. In it, Captain Stormfield, who has died, is speeding his way to Heaven, which is pictured as located somewhere in ordinary space many light-years from Earth. Pick it up at that point.

ISAAC ASIMOV

Well, when I had been dead about thirty years, I begun to get a little anxious. Mind you, I had been whizzing through space all that time, like a comet. *Like* a comet! Why, Peters, I laid over the lot of them! Of course there warn't any of them going my way, as a steady thing, you know, because they travel in a long circle like the loop of a lasso, whereas I was pointed as straight

23

as a dart for Hereafter; but I happened on one every now and then that was going my way for an hour or so, and then we had a bit of a brush together. But it was generally pretty one-sided, because I sailed by them the same as if they were standing still. An ordinary comet don't make more than about 200,000 miles a minute. Of course when I came across one of that sort—like Encke's and Halley's comets, for instance—it warn't anything but just a flash and a vanish, you see. You couldn't rightly call it a race. It was as if the comet was a gravel-train and I was a telegraph despatch. But after I got outside of our astronomical system, I used to flush a comet occasionally that was something *like*. We haven't got any such comets—ours don't begin. One night I was swinging along at a good round gait, everything taut and trim, and the wind in my favor—I judged I was going about a million miles a minute—it might have been more, it couldn't have been less—when I flushed a most uncommonly big one about three points off my starboard bow. By his stern lights I judged he was bearing about northeast-and-by-north-half-east. Well, it was so near my course that I wouldn't throw away the chance; so I fell off a point, steadied my helm, and went for him. You should have heard me whiz, and seen the electric fur fly! In about a minute and a half I was fringed out with an electrical nimbus that flamed around for miles and miles and lit up all space like broad day. The comet was burning blue in the distance, like a sickly torch, when I first sighted him, but he begun to grow bigger and bigger as I crept up on him. I slipped up on him so fast that when I had gone about 150,000,000 miles I was close enough to be swallowed up in the phosphorescent glory of his wake, and I couldn't see anything for the glare. Thinks I, it won't do to run into him, so I shunted to one side and tore along. By and by I closed up abreast of his tail. Do you know what it was like? It was like a gnat closing up on the continent of America. I forged along. By and by I had sailed along his coast for a little upwards of a hundred and fifty million miles and then I could see by the shape of him that I hadn't even got up to his waistband yet. Why, Peters, *we* don't know anything about comets, down here. If you want to see comets that *are* comets, you've got to go outside of our solar system—where there's room for them, you understand. My friend, I've seen comets out there that couldn't even lay down inside the *orbits* of our noblest comets without their tails hanging over.

Well, I boomed along another hundred and fifty million miles, and got up abreast his shoulder, as you may say. I was feeling pretty fine, I tell you; but just then I noticed the officer of the deck come to the side and hoist his glass in my direction. Straight off I heard him sing out—

"Below there, ahoy! Shake her up, shake her up! Heave on a hundred million billion tons of brimstone!"

"Ay—ay, sir!"

"Pipe the stabboard watch! All hands on deck!"

"Ay—ay, sir!"

"Send two hundred thousand million men aloft to shake out royals and sky-scrapers!"

"Ay—ay, sir!"

"Hand the stuns'ls! Hang out every rag you've got! Clothe her from stem to rudder-post!"

"Ay-ay, sir!"

In about a second I begun to see I'd woke up a pretty ugly customer, Peters. In less than ten seconds that comet was just a blazing cloud of red-hot canvas. It was piled up into the heavens clean out of sight—the old thing seemed to swell out and occupy all space; the sulphur smoke from the furnaces—oh, well, nobody can describe the way it rolled and tumbled up into the skies, and nobody can half describe the way it smelt. Neither can anybody begin to describe the way the monstrous craft begun to crash along. And such another powwow—thousands of bo's'n's whistles screaming at once, and a crew like the populations of a hundred thousand worlds like ours all swearing at once. Well, I never heard the like of it before.

We roared and thundered along side by side, both doing our level best, because I'd never struck a comet before that could lay over me, and so I was bound to beat this one or break something. I judged I had some reputation in space, and I calculated to keep it. I noticed I wasn't gaining as fast, now, as I was before, but still I was gaining. There was a power of excitement on board the comet. Upwards of a hundred billion passengers swarmed up from below and rushed to the side and begun to bet on the race. Of course this careened her and damaged her speed. My, but wasn't the mate mad! He jumped at the crowd, with his trumpet in his hand, and sung out—

"Amidships! amidships, you——! or I'll brain the last idiot of you!"

Well, sir, I gained and gained, little by little, till at last I went skimming sweetly by the magnificent old conflagration's nose. By this time the captain of the comet had been rousted out, and he stood there in the red glare for'ard, by the mate, in his shirt-sleeves and slippers, his hair all rats' nests and one suspender hanging, and how sick those two men did look! I just simply couldn't help putting my thumb to my nose as I glided away and singing out:

"Ta-ta! ta-ta! Any word to send to your family?"

Peters, it was a mistake. Yes, sir, I've often regretted that—it was a mistake. You see, the captain had given up the race, but that remark was too tedious for him—he couldn't stand it. He turned to the mate, and says he—

"Have we got brimstone enough of our own to make the trip?"

"Yes, sir."

"Sure?"

"Yes, sir, more than enough."

"How much have we got in cargo for Satan?"

"Eighteen hundred thousand billion quintillions of kazarks."

"Very well, then, let his boarders freeze till the next comet comes. Lighten ship! Lively, now, lively, men! Heave the whole cargo overboard!"

Peters, look me in the eye, and be calm. I found out, over there, that a kazark is exactly the bulk of a *hundred and sixty-nine worlds like ours!* They hove all that load overboard. When it fell it wiped out a considerable raft of stars just as clean as if they'd been candles and somebody blowed them out. As for the race, that was at an end. The minute she was lightened the comet swung along by me the same as if I was anchored. The captain stood on the stern, by the afterdavits, and put his thumb to his nose and sung out—

"Ta-ta! ta-ta! Maybe *you've* got some message to send your friends in the Everlasting Tropics!"

Then he hove up on his other suspender and started for'ard, and inside of three-quarters of an hour his craft was only a pale torch again in the distance. Yes, it was a mistake, Peters—that remark of mine. I don't reckon I'll ever get over being sorry about it. I'd 'a' beat the bully of the firmament if I'd kept my mouth shut.

*   *   *

But I've wandered a little off the track of my tale; I'll get back on my course again. Now you see what kind of speed I was making. So, as I said, when I had been tearing along this way about thirty years I begun to get uneasy. Oh, it was pleasant enough, with a good deal to find out, but then it was kind of lonesome, you know. Besides, I wanted to get somewhere. I hadn't shipped with the idea of cruising forever. First off, I liked the delay, because I judged I was going with its fire and its glare—light enough then, of course, but towards the last I begun to feel that I'd rather go to—well, most any place, so as to finish up the uncertainty.

Well, one night—it was always night, except when I was rushing by some star that was occupying the whole universe with its fire and its glare—light enough then, of course, but I necessarily left it behind in a minute or two and plunged into a solid week of darkness again. The stars ain't so close together as they look to be. Where was I? Oh yes; one night I was sailing along, when I discovered a tremendous long row of blinking lights away on the horizon ahead. As I approached, they begun to tower and swell and look like giant furnaces.

"By George, I've arrived at last—and at the wrong place, just as I expected!"

Then I fainted. I don't know how long I was insensible, but it must have been a good while, for, when I came to, the darkness was all gone and there was the loveliest sunshine and the balmiest, fragrantest air in its place. And there was such a marvellous world spread out before me—such a glowing, beautiful, bewitching country. The things I took for furnaces were gates, miles high, made all of flashing jewels, and they pierced a wall of solid gold that you couldn't see the top of, nor yet the end of, in either direction. I was pointed straight for one of these gates, and a-coming like a house afire. Now I noticed that the skies were black with millions of people, pointed for those gates. What a roar they made, rushing through the air! The ground was as thick as ants with people, too—billions of them, I judge.

I lit. I drifted up to a gate with a swarm of people, and when it was my turn the head clerk says, in a businesslike way—

"Well, quick! Where are you from?"

"San Francisco," says I.

"San Fran—*what?*" says he.

"San Francisco."

He scratched his head and looked puzzled, then he says—
"Is it a planet?"

By George, Peters, think of it! *"Planet?"* says I, "it's a city.
And moreover, it's one of the biggest and finest and—"

"There, there!" says he, "no time for conversation. We don't
deal in cities here. Where are you from in a *general* way?"

"Oh," I says, "I beg your pardon. Put me down for
California."

I had him *again*, Peters! He puzzled a second, then he says,
sharp and irritable—

"I don't know any such planet—is it a constellation?"

"Oh, my goodness!" says I. "Constellation, says you? No—
it's a State."

"Man, we don't deal in States here. *Will* you tell me where
you are from *in general—at large*, don't you understand?"

"Oh, now I get your idea," I says. "I'm from America—the
United States of America."

Peters, do you know I had him *again?* If I hadn't I'm a clam!
His face was as blank as a target after a militia shooting-match.
He turned to an under clerk and says—

"Where is America? *What* is America?"

The under clerk answered up prompt and says—

"There ain't any such orb."

"Orb?" says I. "Why, what are you talking about, young
man? It ain't an orb; it's a country; it's a continent. Columbus
discovered it; I reckon likely you've heard of *him*, anyway.
America—why, sir, America—"

"Silence!" says the head clerk. "Once for all, where—are—
you—*from?"*

"Well," says I, "I don't know anything more to say—unless
I lump things, and just say I'm from the world."

"Ah," says he, brightening up, "now that's something like!
What world?"

Peters, he had *me*, that time. I looked at him, puzzled, he
looked at me, worried. Then he burst out—

"Come, come, what world?"

Says I, "Why *the* world, of course."

"The world!" he says. "H'm! there's billions of them! . . .
Next!"

That meant for me to stand aside. I done so, and a skyblue
man with seven heads and only one leg hopped into my place. I
took a walk. It just occurred to me, then, that all the myriads I

had seen swarming to that gate, up to this time, were just like that creature. I tried to run across somebody I was acquainted with, but they were out of acquaintances of mine just then. So I thought the thing all over and finally sidled back there pretty meek and feeling rather stumped, as you may say.

"Well?" said the head clerk.

"Well, sir," I says, pretty humble, "I don't seem to make out which world it is I'm from. But you may know it from this—it's the one the Saviour saved."

He bent his head at the Name. Then he says, gently—

"The worlds He has saved are like to the gates of heaven in number—none can count them. What astronomical system is your world in?—perhaps that may assist."

"It's the one that has the sun in it—and the moon—and Mars"—he shook his head at each name—hadn't ever heard of them, you see—"and Neptune—and Uranus—and Jupiter—"

"Hold on!" says he—"hold on a minute! Jupiter . . . Jupiter . . . Seems we had a man from there eight or nine hundred years ago—but people from that system very seldom enter by this gate." All of a sudden he begun to look me so straight in the eye that I thought he was going to bore through me. Then he says, very deliberate, "Did you come *straight here* from your system?"

"Yes, sir," I says—but I blushed the least little bit in the world when I said it.

He looked at me very stern, and says—

"That is not true, and this is not the place for prevarication. You wandered from your course. How did that happen?"

Says I, blushing again—

"I'm sorry, and I take back what I said, and confess. I raced a little with a comet one day—only just the least little bit—only the tiniest lit—"

"So—so," says he—and without any sugar in his voice to speak of.

I went on, and says—

"But I only fell off just a bare point, and I went right back on my course again the minute the race was over."

"No matter—that divergence has made all this trouble. It has brought you to a gate that is billions of leagues from the right one. If you had gone to your own gate they would have known all about your world at once and there would have been no delay. But we will try to accommodate you." He turned to an under clerk and says—

"What system is Jupiter in?"

"I don't remember, sir, but I think there is such a planet in one of the little new systems away out in one of the thinly worlded corners of the universe. I will see."

He got a balloon and sailed up and up and up, in front of a map that was as big as Rhode Island. He went on till he was out of sight, and by and by he came down and got something to eat and went up again. To cut a long story short, he kept on doing this for a day or two, and finally he came down and said he thought he had found that solar system, but it might be fly-specks. So he got a microscope and went back. It turned out better than he feared. He had rousted out our system, sure enough. He got me to describe our planet and its distance from the sun, and then he says to his chief—

"Oh, I know the one he means now, sir. It is on the map. It is called the Wart."

Says I to myself, "Young man, it wouldn't be wholesome for you to go down *there* and call it the Wart."

Well, they let me in, then, and told me I was safe forever and wouldn't have any more trouble.

Afterword

Mark Twain makes no effort to stick to astronomical facts, of course. Aside from the fact that he is no expert in astronomy, his fictional character, Captain Stormfield, is pictured as a traditional spinner of yarns, one who exaggerates wildly as a matter of course.

Thus, Stormfield says that "an ordinary comet don't make more than about 200,000 miles a minute."

Actually, a comet that is orbiting a star like our sun never goes much more than 1 percent of that speed, and through most of its orbit it goes very slowly indeed. As for interstellar comets, of the type Mark Twain is dealing with, we don't really know that they exist, but even if they do (and it is not very outlandish to suppose that) they probably loaf along at very small speeds relative to the galaxy generally.

Captain Stormfield's own speed is "about a million miles per minute." This is about 1/11 the speed of light and is pretty good. Earlier in the story, the captain describes himself as moving along at the actual speed of light, which is even better. It is clear, though, that Mark Twain sets no limits and is quite prepared to have objects race at many times the speed of light. He must be forgiven this. Einstein established the speed of light in a vacuum as an absolute maximum in 1905, but it may well be that Twain hadn't yet heard that—and Captain Stormfield *certainly* hadn't.

Mark Twain playfully exaggerates the size of interstellar comets (supposing there to be any). He says some are as big as the *orbits* of those we know. There are indeed objects in space that are as voluminous as our entire solar system out to the farthest comets, and even much more voluminous. These are interstellar clouds of dust and gas, which are rather related to comets in general composition, but are *not* comets by any reasonable definition.

In describing Captain Stormfield's race with the comet, Mark Twain calmly treats the comet as an inconceivably giant riverboat. He has the comet gain speed by heaving its "ballast" overboard, all "eighteen hundred thousand billion quintillions of kazarks" of it. That is, in scientific notation, 1.8×10^{29} kazarks. One kazark is defined as equal to the mass of 169 Earths, or just about 10^{27} kilograms.

The total mass of the ballast, therefore, is 1.8×10^{56} kilograms. This is just about ten times what the mass of the entire universe would be if it were at the threshold of being "closed." We certainly can't complain of Stormfield's being conservative in his exaggerations.

ISAAC ASIMOV

THE COMET DOOM

Edmond Hamilton

Destiny.

We know, now. Destiny, from the first. Out in the depths of space the colossal conspiracy came into being. Across the miles and years, it sped toward its climax. Flashed toward our earth, toward that last supreme moment when a world stood at the edge of doom. Then—fate spoke.

Circling planet, blazing sun, far-flung star, these things but the turning wheels of fate's machinery. And that other thing, that supernally beautiful, supernally dreadful thing that flamed across the heavens in a glory of living light, that too but a part of the master-mechanism. Destiny, all of it, from the beginning. And that beginning—

The story, as we know it, is Marlin's story, and the beginning, to him, was always that June evening when he first came to the Ohio village of Garnton, just at sunset. He had trudged up over the ridge of a long hill, when the place burst suddenly upon his vision.

Before him, sweeping away to the misty horizon, lay the steel-blue expanse of Lake Erie, smoke-plumes far out on its surface marking the passage of steamers. In the west the setting sun glowed redly, its level rays tipping the drifting clouds with flame. And just below him, stretched along the lake shore, lay Garnton, a straggling assemblage of neat, white-painted buildings.

The sight was a grateful one to Marlin's eyes, and he contemplated it for a few moments from the ridge, inhaling great breaths of the sweet, cold air. A plump little man of middle age, dressed in stained khaki clothes and crush hat, rucksack on back, his blue eyes surveying the scene below with evident pleasure. A large white building beside the lake caught his eye, and he gazed at it with sudden intentness.

"Hotel," he muttered to himself, with conviction. And then, in a tone rich with anticipation—"Supper!"

The thought spurred him to renewed action, and hitching his knapsack higher on his shoulders, he began to tramp down toward the village. For though Marlin had so far yielded to the gypsy lure of the open road as to spend his vacation in a walking-tour, he was as yet not at all insensible to the civilized comforts that might be obtained at hotels. It was with quickened speed that he trudged on toward the village, over a rutted dirt road. Even so, twilight was darkening by the time he entered the dim, quiet hotel in quest of room and supper.

Complete darkness had descended on the world, and complete contentment on Marlin, by the time he sauntered out of the big dining-room and inspected his surroundings. He wandered into the lobby but found it uninviting. A few magazines of the type associated with dentists' waiting-rooms, and the only newspaper in sight in the joint possession of three oldsters who were fiercely arguing a question of local politics. When Marlin ventured to interject a remark, they regarded him with cold suspicion, and somewhat abashed he retreated to the wide veranda.

It was quite dark on the veranda, but he managed to stumble into a chair. Then, a moment later, he discovered that the chair beside him was occupied by the proprietor of the hotel, a very fat man who sat in silence like a contemplative Buddha, hands clasped across his stomach, chewing tobacco and gazing out into the darkness. His attitude was of such calm dignity that Marlin hesitated to disturb him with foolish speech, but, unexpectedly, the Buddha spoke.

"Tourist?" he asked, without turning, speaking in a deep, rumbling voice, like that of a questioning judge.

"Hiking," Marlin answered; "I've walked half-way around the lake, from my home-town over in Ontario. I guess I'll rest here for a day or two, and then get a boat back."

The fat man spat over the veranda-rail, accurately, and then uttered a grunt of acquiescence. He offered no further remark, and the two sat on in silence.

Looking out over the lake, Marlin absorbed with quickening interest all the beauty of the scene. There was no moon, but stars powdered the heavens like diamond-dust on black velvet, shedding a thin white light on the dark, tossing surface of the lake. To Marlin, gazing into that vista of cool, limitless night, the whole world seemed shrouded in quiet peace.

Abruptly, at the eastern horizon, a ghostly green radiance began to pour up from behind the distant waters. It pulsated, gathered, grew stronger and stronger. Then, seeming to clear the horizon with a single bound, there leaped up into the sky a disk of brilliant green light, as large as the absent moon. Like a huge, glowing emerald of fire it was, and from it there streamed a great green trail of light, stretching gigantically across the heavens.

The fat man, too, was regarding it.

"It gets bigger each night," he commented.

Marlin agreed. "It certainly does. You can see the difference from one night to the next. It says in the papers that it's coming millions of miles closer each night."

"They say it ain't going to hit us, though," remarked the other.

"No danger of that," Marlin assured him; "on the 14th— that's three nights from now—it will pass closest to earth, they say. But even then it'll be millions of miles away, and after that it'll be going further away all the time."

The fat man became oracular. "A comet's a queer thing," he stated, his eyes on that green splendor of light.

Marlin nodded assent. "This one's queer enough, I guess. What with its green color, and all. They say no one knows where it came from or where it's going. Just comes out of space, rushes down toward the sun and around it, and then rushes back into space, like it's doing now. Like a big tramp, wandering around among the stars."

The hotel-proprietor regarded him with new respect. "You must know a good bit about them," he said.

Flattered, Marlin yet deprecated the compliment. "Oh, I just read the papers a good bit. And there's been a lot in them about the comet since they first discovered its presence in the sky."

"But what's it made of?" asked the other. "Is it solid, like the earth?"

The smaller man shook his head. "I don't know. Some say it's solid at the nucleus—that's the bright spot in its head—and some say that the whole comet's nothing but light and gas. Nobody knows for sure, I guess.''

Together they stared up at the shining thing. The fat one shook his head in slow doubt.

"I don't like the looks of it," he asserted. "It's too big—and bright."

"No harm in it," Marlin assured him; "it won't come near enough to hurt *us* any. They've got it all calculated, you know, all worked out. These professors—''

Unconvinced, the other continued to stare up at the brilliant comet. And Marlin too regarded it, chin in hand, fantastic thoughts passing through his brain.

Many another chance watcher was gazing up toward the comet that night. The thief prowling in the shadows looked over his shoulder at it, muttering curses against its green, revealing light. The hospital-patient, lying unsleeping in his dim-lit chamber, watched it through his window with sick eyes. The policeman, sauntering through darkened streets, spared it a casual glance.

And in the darkened observatories, others, hurrying, excited men, worked unceasingly with lens and spectroscope and photographic plate. With a myriad delicate instruments they sought for data on the nearing comet, for this great green wanderer from outer space, known to be the largest and speediest comet ever to enter the solar system, was swinging out again from the sun on its outward journey into space. There remained but a few nights more before it would have attained its nearest position to earth, and after that it would flash out into the void, perhaps to reappear thousands of years hence, perhaps never to return. From its first appearance as a far, tiny speck of light, their telescopes had watched it, and would watch it until it had receded again into the infinity of interstellar space. Data!—that was their cry. Later all could be examined, marshaled, correlated; but now, if ever, data must be obtained and recorded.

Yet they had found time, from the first, to send out reassuring messages to the world. The comet would not come within millions of miles of earth, for all its size and brilliance, and it was impossible for it to collide with or bring any harm to the earth. Though no man could know what lay hidden at the nucleus, the comet's heart, it was known that the great, awesome coma and tail were nothing but light and electrical force and tenuous gases, with hardly more mass than the aurora borealis, and as harmless. There was nothing to be feared from its passing.

With that calm reassurement, few indeed felt any anxiety concerning the thing. And with that reassurement in mind, Marlin could repeat to the doubting man beside him—"It won't affect us any. The thing's been all worked out."

But to that his host made no answer, and for a time they sat in thoughtful silence.

Abruptly there drifted across their vision, some distance out on the lake, but seeming quite near, a great, high-built boat, its four decks ablaze with yellow light. Very clearly, over the water, they could hear the sound of its paddles, and could hear, too, a faint, far sound of singing, and a ghostly thrumming of ukuleles and guitars.

The fat man nodded toward it. "Excursion-boat from Cleveland," he pronounced.

As it came nearer, the sounds from it came more distinctly to their ears, borne on a little breeze. Clear young voices, singing a popular melody of the day. Tuneful young voices and throbbing music, drifting across the summer night. Fascinated, Marlin watched it. And over in the eastern sky, the flaming orb seemed to be watching also, like a great malignant eye, green, baleful, immense. . . .

It was on the next morning that there appeared in the newspapers the first dispatch from the Buell Observatory. It has sometimes been stated that that first dispatch "aroused widespread interest," but such an assertion is quite untrue, as even a casual inspection of the newspapers for that date will disclose. Only a few of them printed the item at all, and those who did so, assigned it inconspicuous positions.

The message itself was signed by Lorrow, the head of the Buell institution, and stated simply that a slight increase in the earth's orbital speed had been detected during the last twenty-four hours. It added that while this apparent increase might be due to erratic instruments, it was being given further attention. A few hours later a second message announced that the increase had been definitely confirmed, and that it was somewhat greater than had been at first believed.

To astronomers, the news was startling enough, for to them this sudden acceleration of the earth's speed seemed quite inexplicable. Their calculations assured them that it could not be due to the influence of any known heavenly body, but what, then, was its cause? They attacked the problem with exasperated interest.

Outside of astronomical circles, though, it is doubtful if there were a thousand people who gave any serious attention to those first two statements. In science, as in all else, the public's attention is centred always upon the spectacular, and it took but little interest in this matter of fractional differences in speed. The only reference to it in the newspapers that evening was a short message from the Washington Observatory, which confirmed Lorrow's discovery and stated the exact amount of speed-increase, with a staggering array of fractions, decimals and symbols. It also stated that this acceleration was only momentary, and would disappear within the next twenty-four hours.

So the few puzzled over the matter, and the many shrugged their shoulders at mention of it, while the sun sank down into the west and darkness stole across the world. And then the night was split by the rising comet, driving up above the horizon and soaring toward the zenith. It flashed across the heavens in green glory and then it too rocketed down toward the west, while in the east there crept up the gray light of dawn. It was then that there came to the world Lorrow's third message.

It sped along a thousand humming wires, roared from the presses in a thousand cities, was carried shouting through ten thousand sleeping streets. Men woke, and read, and wondered, and stared at each other in strange, dawning fear. For instead of returning to its normal speed, they learned the earth was moving faster and faster through the heavens, and already, as a consequence of this increased speed, was beginning to veer outward a little from its accustomed orbit.

"If this inexplicable acceleration continues," Lorrow wrote, "and the earth veers still further outward, it will be brought uncomfortably close to the head of the passing comet."

A sudden doubt, a moment of chilling fear, oppressed the world as those first words of warning were flashed around it. Had Lorrow's message been allowed to stand uncontradicted, it might well have precipitated a panic then and there. But it was not allowed to do so, for before many minutes had passed, there came from a score of observatories indignant denials of Lorrow's statements.

They admitted that the unexplained acceleration of the earth's speed was apparently continuing, but they denied that the planet had swerved from its orbit, and poured scorn upon the idea that it might collide with the nearing comet. Such a thing was impossible, they asserted, and quoted innumerable authorities to prove that the earth would not come within millions of miles of the comet. Lorrow they denounced as a cheap alarmist who sought to gain publicity for himself at the expense of the world's fear. There was no danger. They repeated it, they insisted upon it. There was no danger.

Such statements were effective, and by means of them the first fears of the public were soon calmed. Here and there one might read with knitted brow and look up in sudden apprehension, and here and there in observatories men might glance at each other with startled eyes, but in the main, the currents of life pulsed through their accustomed channels, and through that long June day men walked their ways as always.

It is with a stilled, incredulous wonder that we now look back upon that day. Knowing what was to happen, what was happening even then, we see that day as the last of an era, the final hour of the world's doom. But at the time, it must have seemed like any other day in early June.

Children released from long months of school would be running and shouting, no doubt. There would be men gazing out of office windows, their thoughts on green links and winding roads. And women chatting in the markets. And sleepy cats, on porches, sprawling in the sunshine. . . .

The newspapers that evening announced that the comet would be larger when it rose that night, and explained that this increase in size was due to the fact that the great green wanderer was still steadily nearing earth, on its way out of the solar system. On the next night it would reach its closest position to earth, they stated, and thereafter would soon grow smaller until it vanished from sight entirely. It was believed that when the comet departed from the solar system, the mysterious acceleration of the earth's speed would disappear also. In any case, they repeated, there was no danger. . . .

Night came, and almost at once the eastern heavens flamed ghastly green. Across the sky streamed brilliant trails of emerald light, obscuring the familiar stars, tarnishing their glory. The radiance in the east condensed, dazzled, and then there flamed up above the horizon—the comet.

It rose that night like a great green sun, immeasurably increased in size and splendor, flooding the earth with its throbbing radiance. The tremendous coma, the brilliant nucleus, the vast tail—they flared in the heavens like a new green Milky

Way. And across the millions who watched, there sped whispers of awe.

For millions there were who watched the comet rise that night. From the roofs and windows and streets and parks of great cities, they watched it. Savages in deep jungles prostrated themselves before it, uttering weird cries of fear. Sailors far out at sea looked up toward it and spoke of ancient superstitions and old beliefs. Men in prison gazed up at it through barred windows, with dim wonder. Fearful men pointed toward it and spoke of the wrath of God.

Yet even then, for all the millions who watched in awe, there were tens of millions who merely glanced at it as one might at an interesting spectacle, who discussed it weightily, or gibed at the fears of the timid, or who paid it no attention at all, going about their good or evil business unheeding. And as the hours marched on, fearful and indifferent alike sought sleep, while over forests and fields and seas and steepled cities, the giant meteor soared across the heavens. Almost it seemed to grow greater with the passing of each hour, and the whole west flared with livid light as it sank down toward the horizon there.

From a window perched high above the canyoned streets of New York City, a single man watched the setting of the comet. Through the night the news of Amsterdam and Hong Kong and Valparaiso had passed through his ears and brain and fingers, from clicking telegraph or clicking typewriter, to be circulated by the presses in the building beneath him. Now, as he leaned beside the open window, the cigarette in his hand drooped listlessly, and beneath the green eyeshade his eyes were very tired.

A sudden metallic chattering at the other side of the room aroused him, and instantly he turned and hastened toward the operating table. With a swift, automatic movement he slid fresh paper into his typewriter and began tapping out a copy of the message. As the instrument beside him clicked on, however, his body tensed in the chair, and he struck the typewriter-keys with a sudden clumsiness. When the sounder's chattering had ceased, he sat motionless, staring at the words he had written, then rose, trembling, and walked with dragging steps toward the window.

Around and beneath him the city slept, silent beneath the first gray light of dawn. Westward, the Jersey heights loomed darkly against the sky, and low above them spun the gigantic comet, its splendor dulling a little in the pallid light of dawn. It was the comet that the man at the window was watching, his face white, his lips working.

"It is doom!" he whispered.

From far below came a sudden whistling of tugboats, clamorous, strident. It ceased, and a faint echo of his words murmured mockingly in his ears.

"Doom!"

He turned suddenly and reached for a telephone, pressing a button at its base. When he spoke into the instrument, his voice was dry and level.

"Collins?" he asked. "This is Brent, first night-operator. Take a bulletin that just came through. Ready?"

Washington, D. C., June 14th. Special Bulletin. (All papers copy.) Astronomers at the Washington Observatory have just discovered that as a result of its mysterious acceleration in speed, the earth has left its proper orbit and is moving headlong through space toward the head of the oncoming comet. The latest spectroscopic observations reveal the presence of vast quantities of poisonous gases in the coma and tail of the comet, so if the earth continues in its present course and passes into the comet's head, the result will be the swift asphyxiation of all life on this planet. It is estimated that before midnight tonight the earth will have definitely passed inside the gravitational grip of the comet, and after that it will be only a matter of hours until the end.

That night, when the giant comet again rose in the east, it blazed in the sky like a great sea of green fire, its whirling coma filling half the heavens, its brilliant nucleus shining with an intolerable radiance. And its light fell down across a world gone mad with fear.

The shouts of men, the sobbing of women, the crying of children; the ringing of bells and screaming of whistles that heralded the terror across the earth; the chanting voices of crowds that kneeled in tearful prayer, the hoarse voices that called for them to repent; the roar of automobiles that fled north and south and east and west, in a blind effort to find escape where there was no escape; all of these sounds and ten thousand others combined to form one vast cry of utter terror that leaped from the world as from a single voice.

But as the inexorable hours marched on, and the sea of fire

above grew greater and greater, nearer and nearer, a strange stillness seized the world. The mad shouting and the mumbled prayers died away, the fear-crazed figures in the streets sank down and sprawled in an apathy of hopeless terror. It was the end. For earth, and for man, and for all the works of man, the end. Thus sunken in a lassitude of dull despair, silent as a planet peopled by the dead, the world drove on toward its doom.

At the very moment when the Washington Observatory's fateful message was being flashed around the earth, Marlin was leaving Garnton, heading north across the lake toward the Ontario shore. And while the world writhed beneath the panic caused by that message, he remained entirely ignorant of it. During the two days which he had spent at Garnton, he had read Lorrow's first dispatches regarding the earth's sudden speeding up, but in common with most of the world, had paid them but little attention. When he left the village that morning, nothing was further from his mind.

It was a in a small fishing-cruiser that he left, a dilapidated, noisy-motored little boat whose aroma strongly proclaimed its calling. By chance Marlin had discovered that the boat's owner, a tall, silent and weather-beaten fisherman, intended to cross the lake at dawn that morning, and had prevailed upon him to take a passenger. So when the little craft headed out from shore at sunrise, Marlin sat at its bow, gazing into the gray banks of fog that spread over the surface of the lake.

Steadily the cruiser chugged onward, through lifting veils of mist. By the time the fog cleared, the land behind had dwindled to a thin, purple line. Then that too had vanished, so that they seemed to move upon a boundless waste of waters.

The sun, lifting higher in the east, flooded the world with its golden light, and as they forged onward, Marlin whistled cheerfully. The world seemed to him just then an extravagantly bright and friendly place.

For two hours the little boat crept north across the sunlit waters, and must have traversed at least half of the lake's width, Marlin estimated, when an island swung up above the horizon ahead, a black spot that grew swiftly into a low, dark mass as they moved on toward it. Marlin eyed it with lively curiosity, and then turned toward his taciturn companion at the helm.

"What island's that?" he asked, jerking a thumb toward it.

The steersman peered ahead for a moment with keen eyes, and then turned back to Marlin.

"That'll be Logan Island," he told him. "Don't pass it very often."

"Wild-lookin' place," commented his passenger. "Anybody live there?"

The other pursed his lips and shook his head. "Not that I ever heard of. There's lots of little islands like that scattered around this end of the lake, with nobody on 'em."

They were swinging closer to the island by then, passing it at a distance of a quarter-mile. It was a long, low mass of land, a rough oblong in shape, and some three miles in length, its greater dimension. Thick forests appeared to cover it completely, extending to the water's edge, but broken here and there along the shoreline by expanses of sandy beach. Marlin could detect no sign or sound of human presence.

It was while he stared at the place, there in the brilliant morning sunlight, that there rushed upon them—the inexplicable.

A high, thin buzzing sound struck his ears, and at the same moment a flexible, swaying rod of gray-gleaming metal thrust itself up above the trees at the island's center, rearing swiftly into the air like an uncoiling snake. At its top was a round gray ball which appeared to be slowly revolving.

Marlin's jaw dropped in sheer surprise, and he heard a startled exclamation from his companion. The rod had ceased its upward climb, and abruptly, from the ball at its top, there flashed forth a narrow, dazzling ray of white light, brilliant even in the morning sunshine. It cut slantwise down across the waters and struck the little cruiser's stern.

The next few seconds remained in Marlin's memory always as a confused moment of blind, instinctive action. As the ray struck the boat, he saw the figure of his companion outlined for a second in living light, and then the whole rear end of the cruiser had vanished, steersman, deck and cabin being whiffed out of existence in a single instant. Immediately the deck beneath Marlin's feet tilted sharply, and he felt himself catapulted into the lake. The cold waters swirled around him, over him, as he sank beneath the surface. He struggled frantically for a moment, and then was shooting up again, his head popping up into the open air.

A few pieces of floating wreckage were all that remained of the cruiser. Hiding his head as much as possible behind one of these, he peered toward the island. The ray had ceased, and he glimpsed the high, swaying rod sinking down again behind the tree-tops. In a moment the buzzing sound ceased also.

Marlin swallowed hard, and his pounding heart quieted a little. He listened tensely but could hear no further sound from the island. There was only the washing of the waters around him, and the continual whisper of the wind. Then, slowly and fearfully, he began to paddle toward the island, still clinging to his piece of wreckage, and hiding as much as possible behind it.

For a time that seemed hours to his dazed brain, he crept across the waters toward the island, heading for its northern end. The sun blazed down upon him with ever-increasing heat as he struggled on, and the mass of land ahead seemed remote and mirage-like. Twice he heard sounds from the island's center, sharp, rattling sounds, and each time he cowered down in sudden fear and then crept on again. When at last he pulled himself from the water, he stumbled across a narrow beach and into the forest, flinging himself into a thicket of underbrush and lying there in a stupor of exhaustion.

For minutes he lay thus, breathing in great sobs, and then was abruptly roused by the realization that something was tugging at his shoulder. He sat up quickly, and instantly felt himself gripped from behind, while a strong hand clamped across his mouth and smothered the instinctive exclamation which he had been on the point of uttering. A voice sounded in his ear, low and tense.

"Quiet!" it rasped.

For a space of seconds he lay motionless, held by his unseen companion. He heard the distant rattling sounds again, murmuring faintly through the forest from the south. Suddenly they ceased. Then the grip around him relaxed, and he turned to face the one who had held him.

Crouched beside him was a hatless and coatless young man of twenty-five or twenty-six, his clothing stained and torn, his hair disheveled. He gazed into Marlin's face with quick, bright eyes, and when he spoke it was in a whisper.

"You were one of the men in the boat," he said, gesturing toward the lake. "I saw—from the shore."

"What was it?" whispered Marlin. "My God, man, what's on this island? That ray—"

The other raised a hand in quick warning, and for a moment they were tensely silent. Again came that far rattling and clanging, hardly to be heard, dying away in a few seconds. Marlin's companion was speaking again.

"Have you any weapon?" he asked. "A pistol—" but Marlin shook his head. Abruptly the other agonized.

"No weapons!" he whispered hoarsely. "Only our bare hands. And they—"

Marlin caught his arm. "For God's sake, what's going on here?" he asked. "Who are *they*?"

The other gripped himself, and then spoke in level tones. "I will explain," he said dully, passing his hands wearily over his eyes. "I need your help—God knows I need more help than yours!—but first—"

He gazed somberly into the forest for minutes before speaking again.

"Coburn's my name, Walter Coburn. I'm an entomologist—a bug-chaser—working out of the Ferson Museum, in New York. You've heard of it? Well, I've been there three years, ever since I got my degree. Not much salary to it, but the work is interesting enough. It was with that work partly in mind that I came to this island.

"You know, or you may not know, that some of these little islands have an extraordinary profusion of insect-life. I was on the track of an hitherto unclassified wood-tick, and had an idea that it might be found on some such island as this. So when Hanley suggested that we spend our vacation camping here, I jumped at the chance.

"Hanley was the closest friend I had. We were about the same age, and had got acquainted at the university, where we took many of the same courses. We shared a small apartment in New York, where he had been grubbing along teaching biology in a preparatory-school, and as we couldn't spend much on our vacation, he had conceived the idea of camping on one of these islands for a couple of months. He knew about them from having cruised over the lake with a friend, some years before, and as lots of the islets were uninhabited, they would make ideal camping-places. It would be a little lonely, but far better than a hot little apartment in New York, so he put it up to me and we decided to try it.

"It was this particular island—Logan Island, they call it—which he had in mind. We came to Cleveland, bought some second-hand camping equipment and some supplies, and loaded the whole outfit into a leaky old tub of a motorboat which we had rented for the next few months. Then we headed out to the island.

"We got here all right, and spent a day exploring the place. Back from the shore, at the island's center, we found a little green plateau, slightly raised above the rest of the island, which was quite bare and treeless and on the edge of which stood an old log-cabin. The cabin was in pretty good shape, except for a leaky roof, so we decided to stay in it, and spread our tent over the roof as an additional protection. It took us only a day to clean the place up and install our simple outfit, and then we were all fixed. That was just three weeks ago.

"In the days that followed, we thoroughly enjoyed ourselves, fishing, swimming or just loafing. Now and then I beat around the island in search of the elusive wood-tick, and every few days we went over to the mainland, so it wasn't as lonely as we'd expected. After three years of New York, the quietness of the place was soothing. And then, twelve days after our first coming to the island, the lightning struck.

"The thing was like a bolt from a clear sky. On that particular night Hanley and I were sitting up late, smoking and discussing the new green comet, which was getting nearer and was beginning to fill the newspapers with astronomical articles. Sprawled out in front of the cabin, and looking up into the star-scattered heavens, we were talking of the comet when Hanley suddenly stopped short in the middle of a sentence and jumped to his feet. He turned to me with a queer expression on his face. 'Do you hear it?' he asked.

"I listened, but could hear no unusual sounds, and then, in a moment, I got it too. It was a deep, powerful droning sound, something like the whirring of a great machine, and it seemed to come from directly over our heads. Every moment it was getting louder, nearer.

"I turned to Hanley. 'A plane?' I suggested, but he shook his head, listening with frowning interest. I knew that he was right, for the sound was unlike that of any airplane-motor, but what it was I could not guess. Then I saw, almost directly above us, a little circle of blackness, a round black circle that hid the stars behind it, and that was *growing*.

"It was growing very swiftly, expanding out and obscuring star after star, and the droning sound was becoming terrific. Had it not been for that sound, I would have thought the thing a balloon or parachute coming down toward us, but it was clearly not that. Whatever it was, it was descending toward us with very great speed, and as it continued to do so, a vague, instinctive fear shot through me. I stepped back, hastily, toward the cabin. Then I heard an exclamation from Hanley, and turned around again, just in time to see the thing itself descending upon the plateau.

"It was a cone, a gigantic cone of smooth metal, which shot swiftly down and came to rest on its great base without a jar, its apex still pointing skyward. It must have been fifty feet in height, from base to apex, and its sides were smooth and unbroken by any opening. The great droning sound had suddenly ceased.

"Hanley took a quick step toward the thing, his face alight with interest. I shouted to him to come back, and ran toward him. Then the whole scene was cut short in a fraction of a second. There was a click from the side of the great cone, and a flash of intense white light leapt toward us. It struck me with stunning force, like a blow from a great club, and all went black before me.

"When I came back to consciousness, my head was still aching from that blow, and bright morning sunlight was falling on my face. My first glance around showed me that I was lying on the floor of the cabin, and Hanley lay beside me, still unconscious. And in a moment I discovered that we were both shackled to the cabin-wall, by means of short metal chains and metal anklets that were fitted around our right legs.

"From the plateau outside, there came to my ears sounds of prolonged activity, hammering and tapping and clanging, with now and then a loud hissing as of some escaping force. For the moment, though, I paid no attention to them, bending my energies toward reviving my friend. After a few crude restorative measures on my part, he opened his eyes, and with my help, sat up. His eyes widened as they took in the chains that bound us to the wall, and as the enigmatic sounds from outside came to his ears. He turned back to me and for a moment we crouched there and stared at each other, a little wildly, I think. Then, before we could speak, the cabin-door swung suddenly open, admitting a single figure.

"We turned our eyes toward that figure, and then gasped. For the thing that stood framed in the open doorway was so grotesque, so incredible, that for a moment I felt myself in the depths of some hideous nightmare. I heard Hanley whisper, 'God!'

"Imagine a man whose body, or trunk, is of smooth black metal instead of flesh, just a round, thick cylinder of glossy metal, whose two legs have been replaced by four spider-like metal limbs, and whose two arms have been supplanted by four twisting metal tentacles, like those of an octopus. This creature was like that, not much exceeding the average man's height, and instead of a head there was set on top of its cylindrical body a small square box, or cube, which it could turn at will in any direction. Inset on each of this cube's four sides was a single circle of soft glowing white light.

"My first thought was that the thing was an intricate machine of some sort, but its quick, intelligent movements soon disproved that theory. A swift tentacle whipped up from it as it stood there, and closed the door behind it. It poised for a moment, seeming to contemplate us, and then came closer, gliding smoothly toward us on its spiderlike limbs. It halted a few feet away; seemed to be examining us.

"I shrank back in utter fear, yet I could not take my eyes from the thing. It was, I saw then, entirely metallic. A vague notion that this was some living creature armored in metal was driven from my mind when I saw that there was no trace of flesh, or even clothing, about it. I noted, too, that one tentacle held a daggerlike object which I guessed to be a weapon of some sort.

"For only a moment the thing stood there, but in that moment I sensed that the strange glowing circles in the head were eyes of some sort, and that they were regarding us intently. Then, silent as ever, the thing glided back and out of the cabin, closing the door behind it. And again we faced each other in the silent little room.

"It was Hanley who broke the silence first. 'They've got us,' he said dully. 'That thing—'

" 'But what was it?' I asked him desperately. 'Metal—and yet moving—like that.'

" 'God knows,' he answered. 'It was alive, and intelligent, I think. A high order of intelligence, too. That cone—the ray that stunned us—' He was talking more to himself than to me. Suddenly he jumped to his feet and stepped over to the window, dragging the short chain with him. He gazed out of the dirty, cracked glass in the opening, and watching, I saw something of astonishment and fear fall upon his face.

"In a moment I was by his side, peering out also. Before me lay the sunlit, green plateau, a scene of incredible activity. The first thing which I glimpsed was a row of four metal cones, similar to the one we had already seen, which rested on their bases at the further edge of the clearing. Wide sections of their sides had swung aside, however, and in and out of the cones and across the pleateau were swarming dozens of grotesque, metallic figures like the one which had already visited us in the cabin. All seemed the same, in appearance, and except for a few who appeared to direct and watch the efforts of the others, all were busy at some task or another.

"Some were removing masses of tools and small machines from the cones, while others were busy assembling and testing other mechanisms, in the open clearing. We glimpsed machines and tools, the purposes of which we could not guess. What struck me most was that all of these hundred or more figures in the clearing worked in utter silence. There was no speech of any sort between them, and except for an occasional changing of tools, or a buzzing and hissing of machines, their work was quite noiseless. Yet each went about his particular task without the slightest confusion.

"For perhaps a half-hour we watched the things, whose activities never ceased, and only left the window when we saw three of their number approaching the cabin. We stepped away from the wall at once; in a moment the door swung open and the three entered.

"They were of the same appearance as the one who had first visited us; indeed, he may have been of these three, for there was no distinguishing one from another. They came toward us, and I saw that one was holding a small, square tablet of smooth white material like stone, and a long metal pencil in a tentacle. The other two carried the daggerlike weapons which we had already seen.

"The one with the tablet came closer and held the tablet up to our view, then began to sketch swiftly upon it with the pencil. 'Evidently trying to communicate with us,' muttered Hanley, and I nodded. In a moment the sketching ceased, and the creature held up the tablet for us to see. On it he had drawn a number of circles, one very large circle being at the center, while around it and at various distances from it were placed other circles of differing size, but all much smaller than the central one. With the pencil, the sketcher pointed to the central circle and then up through the open door. We stared at him blankly, and he repeated the gesture. Suddenly Hanley understood.

" 'The sun!' he exclaimed. 'He means the sun, Coburn. He's drawn a diagram of the solar system.'

"To show our comprehension, Hanley pointed also to the central circle on the tablet, and then up toward the sun. Satisfied that we understood, the creature then pointed to one of the smaller circles, the third in distance from the central one, and then pointed to us. This time his meaning was clear enough. He was indicating earth on the diagram, and pointing to us as if to say that we were earth-men, and that this was earth. Again Hanley repeated his gesture, to show our understanding, and then the thing began to draw again on the tablet. In a moment he held it up for us to see.

"He had drawn a curious little design on the white surface, some distance away from the central suncircle. It was a large circle, from which there streamed backward a number of long, straight lines. He held it for us to see, then pointed first to the new design and then to himself and his two companions. For a moment we did not understand, and then an exclamation broke from Hanley.

" 'The comet!' he cried. 'He's drawn the comet—he means that they are from the comet!'

"Something of awe fell upon us as we looked at the creature. He pointed again to the comet-sign on the tablet, then toward the four cones on the plateau, and then to himself again. With that, the three turned from us and glided out of the cabin, again fastening the door behind them. The meaning of that last gesture had been clear enough to us. The things had come from the comet to earth, in those four great cones. But *why?*

For hours we discussed the thing, while from outside came the clanking and hissing of the invaders' enigmatic machines. Why had they come to earth? It was plain that this was no invading party, for however advanced their science, a hundred of them could not conquer and hold a world. Yet why, then, had they come? We knew that the comet was at that time racing around the sun, and that it would come close to the earth on its way out of the solar system. Could it be that they were establishing a base on the island, so that when the comet came closer, the others on it could pour down on earth? It was possible. But why had they spared us, and kept us prisoners, instead of killing us?

And above all, what *were* these comet-people? Living, intelligent, yet with bodies and limbs of metal?

"For all the rest of that day we lay in the cabin, discussing those questions in awed whispers, returning now and then to the window for further glimpses of the activities outside. We saw that escape was impossible, for the shackles and chains that bound us were strong and tightly fastened to the wall-logs, while every weapon and tool of any sort had been removed from the cabin before we regained consciousness. Even if we had been unfettered, there would have been no chance for escape, for all around the cabin there swarmed the metal figures, their activity never ceasing.

"The day waned, and when night came, the invaders set into action great flood-lights from the cones, which lit up the whole plateau like day. And beneath this light they went on working. I could not see a single one who stopped to rest. Always they labored, and beneath their swift tentacle-arms there grew up a great, half-formed machine of some sort, the foundation of which was already finished. Dully, I wondered what its purpose might be.

"A day passed—another—while we remained prisoners in the cabin. We had been left our own food, and water was brought to us, but we were not permitted to leave the cabin. Gradually we lost interest in the activities of the creatures outside, who went on with their building and testing and assembling almost unobserved by us. Then, on the afternoon of the second day, there came to us again one with a tablet and pencil, who gave us to understand, by various signs, that he wished to learn our written language. We agreed to teach him, and within an incredibly short time, he had mastered the reading and writing of English. We would point to an object and write down its name, and so on until his vocabulary was complete. His memory must have been almost perfect, for he could look at a word once and use it thereafter without hesitation. Within two days he could converse with us at ease, through the writing tablet. And it was then that we learned, from him, the purpose of their invasion.

"As we had guessed, they came from the great comet which was sweeping through the solar system. At the nucleus of that comet, we learned, there was a solid core formed eons ago by long accumulations of meteoric material. There was air and water upon that core, though little of either, and it was lighted by the intrinsic light of the surrounding coma, and heated more or less by electrical radiation also from the coma. The vast clouds of deadly gases in the comet's tail and head did not touch the solid core, and on that core life had sprung up. That was but natural, given a setting fit for the propagation of life. The theory of Arrhenius, according to which life-spores constantly traverse the universe and evolve into living creatures on whatever planet they strike, applies equally well to the comet's solid core. The life-spores had fallen there, also, and had grown through ages of evolutionary change into a race of intelligent active creatures. They were not men, not human in form, but their science was more than human.

"They devoted this superhuman scientific knowledge of theirs to the task of making life easier on their own comet-world. Every living thing must have food in order to live, and it was hard to produce food of any kind on the barren core of the comet. And this set their scientists to thinking. For a long time these comet-people had depended more and more on machines to do their work, and less and less on their own bodily strength. It is the same with the races of man today, who are beginning to forsake manual labor for machine labor. On the comet that process was very far advanced. Machines performed every needed action for its inhabitants, and they rarely made use of their own strength. It is not hard to understand what finally happened.

"They began to say to themselves in effect—'It is our brain, our intelligence, that is the vital part of us; we would be rid of this handicap of the body forever.'

"With this idea in mind, their scientists worked together and finally produced a body of metal, a body-machine which was driven by atomic force, like all of their machines, and which needed only the slight, occasional care which is given to any machine. Inside that body had been arranged an electrical nerve-system, the controls of which led up into the square metal head. In that head, also, had been placed a small super-radio by which silent, constant communication could be had from metal body to metal body. Nerves, sense-organs, muscles, they were all there, and all were artificial, inorganic. The metal body lacked only a brain.

"It was then that one of their scientists performed his greatest achievement, and brought success to their plan. From the living body of one of their number he removed the living brain, as their consummate art in super-surgery enabled him to do. This living brain was then placed within a specially prepared brain chamber of a metal body, inside its cubical head.

"Of course you know that the human brain is fed from the bloodstream of the human body. To replace this, they placed the brain in a special solution, having all the properties of nourishing the brain cells. This solution is usually renewed once a week, so it is always fresh, and therefore the brain never really ages.

"Elaborate precautions are taken that no germs shall ever enter the brain chamber, as it was soon found that results were disastrous, wherever sufficient care had not been exercised.

"The brain chamber is formed of a platinum-like metal, which never oxidizes, and lasts practically forever, unless damaged by blows or other unusual accidents.

"When the brain is finally placed in its platinum chamber, the surgeon carefully connects the nerve ends of the brains with the electrical nerve connections of the metal body. Then an apparent miracle is accomplished. The body lives, can move, and can walk. The brain or intelligence of the one who had gone under the knife is now actuating the lifeless metal frame, directing it and controlling it. And that intelligence is now forever free from the demands of its former body of flesh, residing as it does now in the untiring metal body which requires neither food nor sleep.

"The experiment was thus a complete success, and at once it was duplicated on a big scale. Within a short time every living being on the comet-world had been treated likewise, so that his brain reposed in a similar body of metal. And so, for ages, the comet-people lived, undying brains cased in bodies of metal. When a body was worn out, it was a simple matter to remove the brain from it and place it in a new body. Thus they had achieved immortality. Ages rolled on while their strange world drove across the heavens, and flashed from star to star.

"At last, though, there came a time when the world of the comet-people seemed threatened with downfall. Their metal bodies, like all of their machines, were actuated by atomic force, force produced through the accelerated disintegration of certain radio-active elements. As time went on, however, their supply of these elements became smaller and smaller. It became plain that within a short time, as they measured time, they were doomed to extinction, for without the force to run their machines and bodies, those bodies must become inert and useless, and the brain inside of each must die. It would take long, but it would be sure, and in the end they would all be gone. They must find new sources of such elements, or die.

"In this extremity, their astronomers made an important announcement. They had charted the course which their comet-world was following, and had discovered that soon it would pass through a star-system with eight planets. On its way through this system, they stated, the comet woud pass close to one of these planets, the one which is our earth. Their spectroscopic instruments assured them that this planet, earth, held great stores of the radioactive elements they needed, so they conceived the gigantic plan of stealing earth from the solar system, of drawing it into the comet and carrying it out into space with them. If they could do this, it would furnish them an endless supply of the materials they needed, and would also give them new lands inside the comet. So they set to work and formulated their great conspiracy. A conspiracy to steal a world!

When the comet had entered the solar system, a hundred of the comet-people set out in four great cones, or space-ships, to establish themselves upon earth and carry out their plan. These cones were driven through space by light-pressure, the possibities of which force they had long utilized. Even on earth, we know that this force exists and understand a few of its manifestations; though only a few. We know that it is the pressure of the sun's light that causes a comet's tail to swing always away from the sun. It drove their cones through space at will. The same principle is used in their destroying white ray. In that ray, light-pressure could be used of such power as to disintegrate the molecules of any object, or it could be used merely to strike a powerful blow, as when Hanley and I had been stunned by it. By means of this force the cones of the comet-people rose from their world and drove headlong out through the great coma, across the solar system to the earth.

"They knew earth was inhabited and planned, on reaching the planet, to find some secluded spot where they could work without fear of interruption. For this reason they had approached earth at night, finally landing upon the dark silent island. Surprised there by the presence of Hanley and myself, they had instantly stunned us with the light-ray, but had refrained from killing us for their own reasons. They wished to learn as much as possible about our world, and for that reason had spared us and had taken the trouble to get into communication with us.

"It was thus that we learned the method which they intended to use in pulling our planet into the passing comet. You know that the earth, whirling around the sun, is exactly like a hand swinging a ball around and around at the end of a long cord. The sun is the hand, the earth is the ball, and the power of the sun's gravitation is the cord. If it were not for the earth's motion, its centrifugal force, it would fall into the sun, pulled there by the latter's gravitational power. And similarly, if it were not for the pull of the sun's gravity, the earth's centrifugal force would cause it to fly off into space at a tangent, just as the swinging ball would fly off if someone suddenly cut the cord.

"That was just what the comet-people meant to do. They meant to cut the cord. They were setting up an apparatus that would neutralize the sun's gravitational power on the earth. They had learned that the emanations of gravitational force from any body have a measurable wavelength, and that this wavelength is different in the case of each different body. The vibrations of gravitational force from the sun are thus different in wavelength from those of earth, and it is the same always; the wavelengths of no two emanations are the same. Thus the invaders could neutralize the sun's gravitational power on earth without affecting the power of the earth itself, or of any other body. They would set up a wave-plant, or vibration machine, to send out vibrations equal in wavelength to the sun's gravitational emanations; these would meet and oppose and neutralize the gravitational force of the sun. In that way, the sun would no longer pull earth, and the earth, therefore, would fly off into space at a tangent.

"It was the plan of the invaders to do this at a time when the comet was nearing the earth, so that when the planet did fly off from its orbit, it would do so just as the comet was passing, and would thus be brought inside the gravitational grip of the great comet itself. That done, the rest would be easy. The grip of the comet would pull the earth down through the coma to the nucleus, where it would be received so as to cause it to revolve about the nucleus. Of course the earth's moon would accompany its mother-planet when it left its orbit, and would be carried into the comet likewise. All life on earth would be annihilated when it passed through the coma by the dense and deadly gases there, and thus earth and moon would be at the disposal of the comet-people. And thus the earth would be carried out of the solar system inside the great comet for all time, and its riches of minerals and materials would form a great supply base for the comet-people, and another world for them to inhabit.

"This much Hanley and I learned in our written conversations with the leader of the invaders, for it was the leader, we learned, who was communicating with us. And we were dazed with horror. Soon the invaders would have finished that great machine by which they meant to cut off the sun's pull, and when the comet drew near earth, the planet would go hurtling out toward its doom. We alone knew the peril that hung over earth, and we could do nothing, fettered and imprisoned as we were. Nor was there chance of outside help, for the invaders kept a close watch on the waters around the island, and twice used the light-ray to annihilate small boats that came too near. There was no chance for escape or for help from outside, and we must remain helpless witnesses of the world's doom.

"It was then that the leader revealed to us the purpose for which we had been saved, and made to us an amazing proposal, which filled me with horror. He proposed that we cast in our lot with the comet-people, become one of them and help them in their plans. He had learned that we were both scientists, and knew that after the earth had been drawn into the comet, we would be of invaluable aid in helping them exploit its resources. So he informed us that if we would do so, if we would agree to help them, he would confer immortality on us by removing our brains from our own bodies and placing them in metal bodies like their own. If we refused—death.

"The thought filled me with loathing—the idea of our living brains enduring through centuries in metal bodies. We had been given a few days in which to decide, and as I knew that I would never accept, I saw death ahead. But to my horror and dismay, Hanley began to lean toward the idea. As a biologist, I think, he had long been interested in the idea of achieving immortality, of preserving the intelligence beyond the death of the body, and now that he saw the thing within his grasp, he was disposed to accept it. I argued with him for hours, trying to make him feel the utter horror of the whole business, invoking every argument I could think of to shake him, but all to no purpose, for he was sullen and unyielding to all my words. He pointed out that we would die in any case, and that the peoples of earth were doomed, so that our refusal would in no way help us or anyone else. So to all of my entreaties he turned a deaf ear, and when the time came, he informed the leader of the invaders that he was willing to accept their proposition and become one of them.

"That afternoon they did the thing. God, what a sight it was! Through the window I watched them. Nearby they set up a folding metal table on the plateau, and stretched Hanley upon it, then they applied their anesthetics. Close by lay the metal body which they had prepared for him. It was the same as their own, except for one feature. Instead of four tentacle-arms and four legs, it had only two of each. That puzzled me for a time, but it occurred to me that this was so because there were no nerve-ends in Hanley's brain with which to control an extra pair of arms and legs. Therefore, his metal body had been provided with just two of each.

"I saw their instruments, then flashing in the sunlight, and when the moment came, they lifted Hanley's living brain from his skull and placed it in that metal frame, inside the cubical head. A flash of the light-ray, and his own dead body vanished, while the invaders clustered around the metal body, twisting, turning, connecting.

"At last they stepped back, and a sick horror came over me as I saw that metal body standing erect, moving, walking, obeying the commands of Hanley's brain, inside it.

"From that time on, Hanley was one of the comet-people. Like them, he worked unceasingly on the great machine, directed by the leader, no doubt, and like them, he never seemed to rest, his brain ever driving that tireless metal body. He paid no attention whatever to me, never came near the cabin. He may have been ordered to stay away from it, of course. But I could always distinguish him from the other metal figures, even at a distance, because of the difference in the number of his limbs.

"I had expected death when they finished with Hanley, but I soon learned that a fate far worse lay ahead. The leader visited me once more, and told me, out of sheer cruelty, I think, that when their work on earth was finished, they would take me back with them. Living creatures were very rare on their own world, except for themselves, and I would be a valuable subject for experimentation. Even that news hardly altered the dull despair that filled me.

"The days dragged by slowly, and the great machine outside neared completion. It looked much like a battery of great turbines, a long row of dark, squat cylindrical mechanisms which were joined to each other by an intricate web of connections.

Over all of them had been placed a great cover of shining metal, protecting the mechanisms beneath from rain and dew, and inset on the front of this cover was the switchboard which controlled the great machine. It was a square tablet of black metal, covered by a mass of intricate adjustments and controls, switches, knobs and levers. At the center was a single shining lever much larger than the others, which swung around a graduated dial.

"At the very edge of the plateau, not far from the cabin, the invaders had erected another mechanism, which puzzled me for a time. It was a large upright screen of ground-glass, or a similar material, behind which was attached some smaller mechanisms, which I only glimpsed. This screen was, in fact, a great chart, a chart of the heavens, on which was presented the comet and the earth. The comet was a great disk of green light, and around this central disk was a thin green circle, which represented the limits of the comet's gravitational grip. Any object inside that thin green line was inside the comet's grasp, and would inevitably be drawn down into the coma, while so long as it lay outside of that line, it was in the power of the sun's gravity. In other words, that line was the "neutral" between the two zones of gravitational force.

"The earth was represented on the chart by a small disk of white light. Both the tiny white disk and the great green one moved on the screen in exact proportions to the movements of the earth and comet in the heavens. How this was accomplished I could not conjecture, but supposed that the mechanism behind the screen caught a moving picture of the actual movements of comet and earth, by means of light-rays or electrical radiations, and reproduced it in miniature on the screen. The purpose of the chart was clear enough. It would enable them to time their operations with accuracy, so that the earth would leave its orbit at the exact moment when its outward flight would bring it inside of that thin green line, and within the comet's gravitational power. Tensely I watched that chart, and each day I saw the comet and the earth drawing nearer, nearer, as the green wanderer sped out of the solar system.

"By then the work of the invaders was slackening, for the great machine appeared to be finished. At last came the time, just four nights ago, when they finally put it into operation. I saw them gathered around the switchboard, Hanley among them. The leader stood ready, a tentacle grasping the large central lever. Others were watching the great chart, calculating the positions of earth and comet. I knew that the whole operation must be timed to an incredible nicety, if it were to succeed at all, and I waited, as anxiously as they. At last, there was a sudden stir among those at the chart, and I divined that the signal had been given, speeding silently and swiftly from brain to brain. And I was right, for at the same moment the leader, at the switchboard, swung the big lever around the dial, slowly and carefully. He had reason to be careful. The difference in wavelength of the different gravitational emanations must be extremely minute, and if he had accidentally neutralized the earth's gravity instead of the sun's, if only for an instant, there is no telling what tremendous cataclysm might not have occurred. But that did not happen, for when he had swung the lever to a certain position on the dial, there rose from the great machine a low humming, a sound so deep as to be scarcely audible. Instantly the leader stepped back.

"The machine had been started. I knew that at that moment it was sending forth its own powerful vibrations to meet and oppose and neutralize those of the sun's gravitational force. The cord had been cut!

"For a time, though, nothing seemed changed. Like the metal figures on the plateau, I watched the great chart for all the rest of that night, but it was only toward morning that any change became apparent. Even that change was so small that it could hardly be noted. It was only that the little white earth-circle on the chart was moving a little faster, was leaping toward the green comet a little more quickly.

"And as the hours went by, it moved faster and faster, until by that night I could see plainly that the earth was already a little out of its orbit, veering out a little bit toward the nearing comet. Gathered around the chart and the great vibration-mechanism, the invaders watched the result of their work. And fettered there in the little cabin I, too, watched and waited.

"But that night, when I had all but reached the blackest depths of despair, I stumbled on something that gave me a ray of hope. Much of the time I spent in the cabin I occupied myself in searching endlessly for some sort of tool or weapon, but always without avail, for as I have said, every object that would serve for either had been taken away. But at last, that night, I came across a tiny point of metal that projected a bit from the dirt floor of the cabin, in one of the dark corners. In a moment I was digging away at the thing, and inside a minute had unearthed a long, rusty file, which had been buried beneath the floor, with only the tip projecting through the dirt. It was so badly rusted that it appeared almost useless, but the very possession of the thing gave me new life, and after cleaning it as well as I could, I set to work on the shackle around my leg, muffling the grate of the file by wrapping it with cloths while I worked.

"All through that night I sawed away at the shackle, and when morning came I was disheartened by the little I had accomplished. The rusty file had made only a shallow notch in the hard metal of the shackle. Yet, I knew that it was my only chance, and kept steadily at it, now and then glancing out of the window to make sure that I was unobserved.

"Weariness overcame me, and I slept for several hours, waking shortly after noon. That was yesterday. And when I glanced out of the window at the great chart, I saw that earth had traveled half the distance between itself and the comet, and was approaching perilously near to the thin green line that marked the limits of the comet's grip. I knew that once it passed inside that line it was the end, for no power in the universe could then release it from the comet. The machine must be smashed or turned off before that happened. Frantically I worked at the shackle, through all of that long, hot afternoon.

"Night came, and the comet flared overheard in awful splendor, waxing tremendously in size and brilliance, its green light falling through my window and clashing with the white brilliance of the floodlights on the plateau. Out on that plateau, the invaders were still gathered in motionless groups, still watching the tiny earth-circle on the chart, which hurtled toward the comet now with terrifying speed. From its rate of progress I estimated that it would have passed inside the comet's grip by the next night and knew that after it had done so, the invaders would enter their cones and leave for their own world at the comet's center, while earth passed to its doom in the deadly coma. I must escape that night, if ever.

"At last, shortly before midnight, I had sawed the shackle half through, and with a muffled blow, managed to break it. I crept to the window, then, and cautiously looked out.

"Under the dazzling lights, the metal figures outside were gathered together in two masses, around the chart and the machine, sprawled on the ground. None of them seemed to be watching the cabin at the moment, but the little building had only two windows, and both of them faced toward the plateau. The forest lay only a few yards behind the cabin, and once inside it I would be comparatively safe, but to get there I must creep from the building in full view of the invaders on the plateau, and beneath the dazzling glare of their flood-lights.

"There was no other course for me to follow, though, so without hesitating further, I gently pried the window open and as quietly as possible slid through it, dropping at once to the ground and lying still for a tense moment. There were no sudden sounds or movements from the metal figures around the two mechanisms, so as stealthily as possible I began to crawl around the base of the cabin, and in a few moments had reached the welcome shadows behind it. I then rose to my feet, and took a swift step toward the forest, a few yards away. And I stopped short. Fifty feet to the right of me a single metal figure had suddenly stepped into view, confronting me, a light-ray tube held in its tentacle and pointing toward me. And it was Hanley!

"Hanley, or what had once been Hanley's brain and soul, cased in that body of metal. I recognized him at once, by reason of his two tentacles and limbs, and the bitterness of death came over me, for I had failed. Instinctively, though, even at that moment, I staggered toward the trees ahead, waiting for the death from behind. In a moment the ray would flash, then death.

"But it did not come! With a sudden thrill of hope I began to run, and within a few seconds had passed into the dense darkness of the forest. I had escaped, though for the moment I could hardly credit my escape. I glanced back toward the plateau, and saw the figure of Hanley still standing there, silent, unmoving, the deadly ray-tube still held in his grasp. He had let me go!

"Before I could understand what had happened, there came a sudden flurry of movement across the plateau, a little stir of excitement there, and over my shoulder, I saw a dozen or so dark shapes gliding smoothly across the clearing on my track. They had discovered my escape, and were after me.

"Frantic as some hunted creature of the wild, I raced through the forest, stumbling on projecting roots, hurling myself through patches of briars with mad haste. And swift on my trail came that inexorable pursuit, drawing nearer and nearer toward me, turn and twist as I might, I was soon out of breath and knew I could not long compete in speed or endurance with the tireless metal bodies behind me. At last I saw the ripple of water ahead, and a plan, a last expedient, flashed into my mind.

"I stumbled on until I had reached the water's edge, where the thick forest extended right down to the island's shore. Swiftly I searched the ground around me, and in a moment had found what I needed—a large, thick section of deadwood. Grasping this, I threw myself behind a clump of bushes a few yards away, and waited for my pursuers.

"In a few seconds they came, crashing through the underbrush on my track. I waited a moment longer, until they had almost reached me, then hurled my section of wood out into the water, and at once flattened myself again behind my screen of bushes.

"The piece of wood splashed into the water at the exact moment when my pursuers, some five or six in number, reached the water's edge, not ten feet away from me. At the sound of the splash, the brilliant light-ray instantly flashed forth from their weapons, churning the waters of the lake with its disintegrating force. For perhaps a minute this continued, and then they snapped off the ray and waited. There was silence, except for the washing of the troubled waters.

"I crouched lower behind my flimsy shelter, holding my breath, but after a long moment the metal figures turned away, and I heard them retracing their way through the forest. My trick had worked.

"For half an hour I lay there, a little dazed by the swift action I had just passed through. Then I rose and began to make my way stealthily along the shore. It was my thought to get to our little motorboat, which we had kept in a tiny cove, and to make for the mainland in it. If I could do that, I might be able to obtain help and return to the island, make an effort to destroy these invaders and smash their machine. But when I got to the cove I found only a few fragments of the boat. It had been destroyed by the invaders!

"To me, that seemed the end—the end, to all our earth. There was no chance left to give warning now, for I knew that by the next night earth would have passed inside the comet's grip forever, and it would all be over. Through the rest of the night, our last night, I wandered over the island, a little mad, I think, and when this morning finally came it found me at the island's northern end. I lay there, trying to plan some last course of action, when the chugging of a boat roused me. I hurried to the shore, just in time to see your boat destroyed by the light-ray from the plateau, and your companion killed. I saw that you had escaped—though the watchers did not—and waited until you got to shore. And that is all.

"And that is all. Over there on the plateau stands the great machine which is sending earth hurtling into the comet, while the invaders there watch and wait. A little longer, a little nearer, and earth will have passed inside the comet's grip, and then it will be hours only until the end. The comet overhead growing larger and larger, nearer and nearer, and then the deadly gases of the coma, bringing swift death to all on earth. And at the last, the comet racing out of the solar system with the earth inside it, flashing out into space, never to return, plunging across the universe for all time with its stolen, captive world!"

The hoarse whisper of Coburn's voice ceased, and for minutes the two men sat in silence. The whole island seemed unutterably silent, at that moment, except for the wind gently rustling the leaves around them, and the drowsy hum of insects. Through the foliage above, the sunlight slanted down in bars of bright gold.

Marlin was the first to speak.

"The earth!" he whispered chokingly; "The whole earth! What can we do—we two—"

Coburn was staring into the forest, scarcely listening. When he spoke, his voice was deadened, toneless. "Nothing, now," he said. "We must wait—until tonight—" A little flame of hope leaped into his eyes, and he turned quickly to Marlin.

"Tonight there is a chance," he whispered. "A chance in ten million, but—a chance. If we could get to that machine—"

"Smash it?" asked Marlin. "Turn it off?"

Coburn nodded slowly. "We'll try," he said. "Tonight, when it's darker. If I had a single moment at that switchboard—"

He broke off suddenly as once more there came through the forest the clanging rattle of metal against metal. His eyes held Marlin's. "Getting ready," he whispered. "Getting ready to leave, tonight. They'll wait till earth has passed that neutral line, until it's in the comet's grip, and then they'll destroy the machine and leave in the cones."

Crouched there, they listened, silent, white-faced, tense. . . .

Always afterward the remaining hours of the day were to Marlin a vague, half-remembered time. Hot, hungry and very thirsty, he lay beside Coburn, speaking little and that in whispers, listening fearfully to the sounds that drifted to their ears from the south. As the day waned, the events through which he had just passed, the things which he had just been told, became blurred and confused in his brain. Once or twice he caught himself wondering why he lay thus in hiding, and brought himself back to reality only with a sharp effort.

A few hours more, and the sunset flamed low in the west, painting the sky there with a riot of brilliant colors. Marlin strove to remember a sunset which he had once seen, with a great blue lake and a neat white village in the foreground. How long ago had that been? Days, months, years?

While he struggled with that thought, the gold and orange and crimson were fading from the sky above, and they awaited only the darkening of the long June twilight. Its gray deepened to a darker gray, and then to black. Then, up from the eastern horizon, there soared colossal bars and banners of viridescent light, sweeping across the heavens like an aurora of blinding green. Prepared as he had been for the sight, Marlin gasped when the comet wheeled into the heavens, a single vast ocean of green fire, that crept smoothly westward across the firmament, dripping down a ghastly, throbbing radiance upon the world. It was as if the whole sky were boiling with emerald flame.

Coburn stood up, his burning eyes fixed upon the comet, his face deathlike beneath the green unearthly light. He turned to Marlin, who had risen beside him.

"I am going ahead to reconnoiter first," he explained swiftly, "and I want you to stay here while I'm gone. We have a few hours at least, I think, and before we can plan any course of action I must know what is happening on the plateau."

"You won't be long?" whispered Marlin, and the other shook his head. "Not more than a half-hour. But don't leave this spot until I come back."

Marlin whispered his assent, sinking to the ground again, while Coburn glanced quickly around, then moved stealthily into the forest, toward the south. In a moment he had been swallowed up by the shadows.

Left alone, Marlin resumed his prone position on the ground, not venturing any movement. Except for the steady chirping of crickets, and the deep croaking of distant frogs, the forest around him was very silent. He turned, after a moment, and gazed up into the flaming heavens, until his eyes were dazzled by the splendor of the waxing comet. There came to him, dimly, some realization of what that flaming thing above must be doing to the world of men, of the pit of fear into which it must have precipitated all earth. The thought steadied him a little, and his jaw tightened.

Abruptly Marlin realized that Coburn had been gone for a longer time than he had mentioned, and swift anxiety and fear chilled him. Where was Coburn? Had he been captured? Killed? He tried to reassure himself, to force down his misgivings, but with the passing of every minute his fear deepened. When an hour had passed he rose at last to his feet, looking anxiously around. He hesitated for a moment, then uttered a low call.

"Coburn!"

No answer came back to him, except for a rustling echo of his own voice. A ray of green light from the wheeling comet overhead struck down through the canopy of restless leaves and fell upon his white, anxious face.

"Coburn!"

Again he had called, and louder, but again his cry went unanswered. Marlin could endure the suspense no longer, and suddenly crept from his hiding place and began to make his way southward through the forest, as silently as possible.

Slowly he moved forward through the dark forest, a forest pillared here and there by shafts of green radiance from the comet overhead. He stumbled across green-lit clearings, and over tiny, gurgling brooks, and through dense thickets of brush and briars. Twice he crossed steep little ridges, and once he blundered across a soggy patch of swamp, where his feet sank deeply into the treacherous ground, and where snakes rustled away from him through the grass on either side. Still he stumbled on, breath almost gone, heart near to bursting. It seemed to him now that he must be very near to the plateau at the island's center.

But as he emerged from a dense little tangle of brush, and took in the sight ahead of him, something like a sob came from him, and he slumped to the ground in sheer exhaustion. He was standing at the edge of a narrow, sandy beach, and beyond it there stretched away the rippling, green-lit lake. Instead of heading toward the island's center, he had lost his way, and had lost more than an hour blundering across the island in the wrong direction. He dropped to the ground, half-dazed by his efforts, striving to get his bearings.

He thought of calling to Coburn again, but dared not do so, for he could not know how close he might be to the plateau. Nor could he know where the plateau lay, there on the strange dark island. If he were to return to where Coburn had left him, then he might be able—

Clang!

It rang across the island, loud and clear, a single short, metallic note. Marlin started to his feet. He stood motionless, listening intently. In a moment came another sound, a deep, powerful droning, that waxed in intensity for a moment, then continued without change. At once Marlin moved off again into the forest, heading unhesitatingly to the left. The sound, which could come only from the plateau, had given him his bearings.

Hastily he pushed on, his weariness forgotten for the moment, his throat tight with excitement. Far ahead he made out a thin white light that filtered feebly through the forest, a pale light very different from the green radiance of the comet overhead. And as Marlin pressed on toward it, the droning sound came to his ears louder and louder, nearer and nearer. He slackened his pace a little, moving more stealthily.

Clang!

Again it came, that single ringing note, sounding louder in his ears than the first, as he drew nearer to the plateau. And again, following it, there rose the deep droning sound, combining with the first to fill the air with a terrific humming, as of ten thousand dynamos.

The white light ahead grew stronger and stronger, until at last there rose before Marlin a steep little slope, at the top of which the forest ended, and from beyond which came the white radiance. He flattened himself on the ground, crawled stealthily up the slope, and paused at its edge, behind a slight thicket of bushes. Cautiously he parted the bushes and peered forward.

Before him lay the plateau, a broad, grassy surface perhaps a quarter-mile across. Some fifty feet above its center there hung in the air two great shapes from which came the droning sound, two gigantic cones of metal. Attached to these were flood-lights that drenched all on the plateau with their white light, which even there was pale in comparison with the throbbing radiance from the comet overhead.

At the center of the plateau two similar cones rested on the ground, in the side of each of which was an oval opening. Even as Marlin first glimpsed these, the opening in one of them closed, with the loud clanging note he had twice heard, and then, with a powerful droning roar, the cone rose smoothly into the air to hang beside the two others there.

On the plateau was left the single great cone. Beside it there stood a long, low structure, shining brilliantly beneath the double illumination from cones and comet, and bearing on its face a black tablet covered with knobs and levers, with a single large lever and dial at its center. It was the neutralizing-machine, Marlin knew, the machine that was cutting off the sun's pull, that was sending the earth hurtling out toward its doom in the comet. Around this machine were grouped a score of grotesque, metallic figures, figures strangely spiderlike with their multiple tentacles and limbs, and with square, unhuman heads of metal on which were set the glowing circles that were their eyes. A deep, shuddering hatred shook Marlin as he saw them for the first time.

He turned his gaze to the right and saw, at the edge of the plateau there, the low, rough cabin, and beyond it the great chart which Coburn had described to him, a large ground-glass screen on which moved the small white disk that was earth and the great green disk that was the comet, the latter encircled by the thin green line that marked the limits of its gravitational grip. And as Marlin's eyes fell upon it, his heart leaped uncontrollably. For the earth-disk on the chart was only a few inches from the thin green line around the comet, the neutral between its gravitation and the sun's. And swiftly that tiny gap was closing.

For the first time the significance of the hovering cones above struck Marlin. The invaders were leaving, their work accomplished. In a few moments earth would have passed forever inside the comet's grasp, and they could destroy the great machine with a flash of the light-ray, and speed off in their cones, leaving earth to its doom. It was the end.

Marlin's brain was whirling, his hands trembling, but he hesitated only for a second, then crawled slowly forward from behind his flimsy shelter. Out over the plateau, beneath the glaring light from above, he crawled on toward the machine, half-hidden by the tall grasses that covered the plateau. For ten yards he crept forward, then stopped, and ventured to raise his head a little and look ahead.

The last of the metal figures on the plateau were trooping into the remaining cone, through the opening in its side. There remained only four or five who were standing beside the great machine, beside the switchboard. And in the moment that Marlin saw these, they discovered him. He saw them turning and evidently gazing straight toward him. A moment Marlin crouched there, petrified, and then he rose to his feet with a mad shout and raced straight across the plateau toward the switchboard of the great machine.

Even as he rose to his feet two of the little group at the machine flashed toward him, with incredible speed, and before he had covered a dozen paces they were upon him. He felt himself gripped by cold coiling tentacles, grasped and thrown to the ground. For a moment he struggled frantically, then heard a hoarse cry, and wrenched his head up to see a dark shape speeding across the plateau from the opposite edge. It was Coburn!

Twisting in the remorseless grip of the two with whom he battled, he had a flashing glimpse of Coburn racing towards the machine, and then he uttered a cry of agony. From one of the hovering cones above, a shaft of the light-ray had flashed down and it struck Coburn squarely. A moment he was visible, aureoled in a halo of blinding light, and then he had vanished. Marlin closed his eyes, ceased his struggles. He felt himself jerked to his feet by his two captors.

He opened his eyes, then, and stared dazedly over toward the great chart. The earth-disk there was less than an inch from the green neutral-line. It was all over. He and Coburn had shot their feeble bolt and failed. He felt himself being jerked forward toward the last cone, sagging between his captors in dull despair.

But what was that sudden crash of metal at the machine, that rush of movement there? Marlin's head snapped up with sudden hope. A single metal figure had sprung out of the group beside the machine, a figure oddly manlike, with only two tentacles and two limbs, that leaped toward the switchboard of the great machine.

"Hanley!"

He screamed aloud, and at the same moment was released, thrown to the ground, by his two guards, who also raced toward the switchboard. From the cone on the ground there poured forth a stream of metal figures, and the droning giants above dropped swiftly down toward the machine. Hanley was beside the switchboard, had reached up with a swift tentacle and grasped the great lever at its center. From cones above and metal figures below, a dozen shafts of the brilliant light-ray flashed toward him. But in the fraction of a second before they reached him, he had wrenched the great lever far around the dial, and the next moment a titanic explosion rocked the island to its foundation. Marlin was knocked backward by a terrific gust of force, and had only a single flashing glimpse of all at the center of the plateau, machine and metal figures and hovering cones, shooting skyward at lightning speed.

He staggered to his feet, dazed, half-blind, reeled drunkenly forward and then stopped short. For at the center of the plateau there yawned a terrific gulf, a vast pit torn from the earth in a single instant. Cones and machine and invaders had vanished utterly in that tremendous cataclysm, blown off into space when Hanley had swung the lever, and had neutralized earth's gravity, for that single moment and at that single spot, instead of the gravity of the sun.

Marlin staggered along the edge of that mighty abyss, toward the great chart-screen at the plateau's edge. It had been twisted and bent by that tremendous detonation, but it still functioned, and on it there moved still the two disks, the earth and comet symbols. Marlin stumbled closer, his whole soul fixed upon the screen. The tiny earth-disk there was still creeping forward toward the green neutral-line around the comet, moving slower and slower, but still moving. Slower, slower, it moved. Now it was just a half-inch from the line, a quarter, an eighth. By then it was hardly moving. It had touched the line, now, hovered at its edge. Hovered as the earth was hovering, at that moment, on the neutral between sun and comet, hesitating, tottering— And then Marlin cried aloud.

For the white disk was moving back!

Slowly at first, and then faster and faster, the earth-disk was falling back from that thin line, swinging back into its usual orbit, pulled back again by the sun's far-reaching power, pulled back from the very edge of doom.

Marlin raised his tear-stained face toward the great comet above, a single vast sea of green flame, immense, titanic. It was passing, now, passing out of the solar system for all time, its one chance of stealing our earth gone forever. He shook his fist toward it in mad defiance. "You lost!" he screamed, in insane rage and triumph. "Damn you, you lost!"

*   *   *

It was twilight of the next day when Marlin left the island, paddling slowly out from it on the crude little log-raft which he had fashioned. Shadows of dusk were falling upon the world, deepening into darkness. In the west there trembled forth a star. Still he crept on.

Night, and up from the east there rose again the comet. Marlin lapsed in his progress at that, gazing toward it. Small and shrunken and harmless, it seemed now, its evil glory fast waning as it thundered out into space on its appointed course. He wondered, momentarily, what frenzies of thanksgiving were shaking the peoples of earth to see it thus receding, to see themselves thus snatched back from the very gates of death.

He turned, for a moment, looking back toward the island. It seemed dark and small, now, a low, black mass of land that stood out indistinctly against the pale-lit waters. Only a tiny speck of land, there in the great lake, and yet on it had been decided the fate of a planet. On it the comet-people had played their great game, with a world as the stake, and on it they had lost, their vast conspiracy smashed, in the end, by Hanley. Hanley, whose human brain, human intelligence, human soul, had lived on in a body of metal, to shatter the invaders' colossal plan at the last, remorseful moment.

Marlin paddled on, a dull ache filling his heart. Coburn, Hanley—they had died for the world, for him, while he still lived on. Yet even now, he could give them something, however little, in return. The homage and the gratitude of a world, when that world learned who had saved it. He could give them that, at least.

Afterword

This story, first published in 1927, is an excellent example of magazine science fiction as written before the editorial influence of John W. Campbell had made itself felt. Allowing for the old-fashioned writing technique, we can still respond to the excitement of the story.

I must explain, though, that in this story, Ed Hamilton does something I have seen him do in other stories. He seems under the impression that if a planet is pulled out of its orbit by some technological means, destroying the machinery that produces the effect will cause the planet to return, spontaneously, to its original orbit.

This is a total misunderstanding of celestial mechanics. It is like supposing that if a sailing ship is blown off course by a gale, the cessation of that gale will cause the ship to return, spontaneously, to its original course.

I'll forgive Ed for the sake of the story, but I can't allow the unwary reader to be misled by Ed's misunderstanding.

ISAAC ASIMOV

SUNSPOT

Hal Clement

Ron Sacco's hand reached gently toward his switch, and paused. He glanced over at the commander, saw the latter's eyes on him, and took a quick look at the clock. Welland turned his own face away—to hide a smile?—and Sacco almost angrily thumbed the switch.

Only one of the watchers could follow the consequences in real detail. To most, the closing of the circuit was marked a split second later by a meaningless pattern on an oscilloscope screen; to "Grumpy" Ries, who had built and installed the instrument, a great deal more occurred between the two events. His mind's eye could see the snapping of relays, the pulsing of electrical energy into the transducers in the ice outside and the hurrying sound waves radiating out through the frozen material; he could visualize their trip, and the equally hasty return as they echoed back from the vacuum that bounded the flying iceberg. He could follow them step by step back through the electronic gear, and interpret the oscilloscope picture almost as well as Sacco. He saw it, and turned away. The others kept their eyes on the physicist.

Sacco said nothing for a moment. He had moved several manual pointers to the limits of the weird shadow on the screen, and was using his slide rule on the resulting numbers. Several seconds passed before he nodded and put the instrument back in its case.

"Well?" sounded several voices at once.

"We're not boiling off uniformly. The maximum loss is at the south pole, as you'd expect; it's about sixty centimeters since the last reading. It decreases almost uniformly to zero at about fifteen degrees north; any loss north of that has been too small for this gear to measure. You'll have to go out and use one of Grumpy's stakes if you want a reading there."

No one answered this directly; the dozen scientists drifting in the air of the instrument room had already started arguments with each other. Most of them bristled with the phrase "I told you—" The commander was listening intently now; it was this sort of thing which had led him, days before, to schedule the radius measurements only once in twelve hours. He had been tempted to stop them altogether, but realized that it would be both impolite and impractical. Men riding a snowball into a blast furnace may not be any better off for knowing how fast the snowball is melting, but being men they *have to know*.

Sacco turned from his panel and called across the room.

"What are the odds now?"

"Just what they were before," snapped Ries. "How could they have changed? We've buried ourselves, changed the orbit of this overgrown ice cake until the astronomers were happy, and then spent our time shoveling snow until the exhaust tunnels were full so that we couldn't change course again if we wanted to. Our chances have been nailed down ever since the last second the motors operated, and you know it as well as I do."

"I stand . . . pardon me, float . . . corrected. May I ask what our *knowledge* of the odds is now?" Ries grimaced, and jerked his head toward the commander.

"Probably classified information. You'd better ask the chief executive of Earth's first manned comet how long he expects his command to last."

Welland managed to maintain his unperturbed expression, though this was as close to outright insolence as Ries had come yet. The instrument man was a malcontent by nature, at least as far as speech went; Welland, who was something of a psychologist, was fairly sure that the matter went no deeper. He was rather glad of Ries' presence, which served to bring into the open a lot of worrying which might otherwise have simmered under cover, but that didn't mean that he liked the fellow; few people did. "Grumpy" Ries had earned his nickname well. Welland, on the present occasion, didn't wait for Sacco to repeat the question; he answered it as though Ries had asked him directly—and politely.

"We'll make it," he said calmly. "We knew that long ago, and none of the measures have changed the fact. This comet is over two miles in diameter, and even after our using a good deal of it for reaction mass it still contains over thirty billion tons of ice. I may be no physicist, but I can integrate, and I know how much radiant heat this iceberg is going to intercept in the next week. It's not enough, by a good big factor, to boil off any thirty billion tons of the stuff around us. You all know that—you've been wasting time making a book on how much we'd still have around us after perihelion, and not one of you has figured that we lose more than three or four hundred meters from the outside. If that's not a safe margin, I don't know what is."

"You don't know, and neither do I," retorted Ries. "We're supposed to pass something like a hundred thousand miles from the photosphere. You know as well as I do that the only comet ever to do that came away from the sun as two comets. Nobody ever claimed that it *boiled* away."

"You knew that when you signed up. No one blackmailed you. No one would—at least, no one who's here now." The commander regretted that remark the instant he had made it, but saw no way to retract it. He was afraid for a moment that Ries might make a retort which he couldn't possibly ignore, and was relieved when the instrument man reached for a handhold and propelled himself out of the room. A moment later he forgot the whole incident as a physicist at one of the panels suddenly called out.

"On your toes, all of you! X-ray count is going up—maybe a flare. Anyone who cares, get his gear grinding!" For a moment there was a scene of confusion. Some of the men were drifting free, out of reach of handholds; it took these some seconds to get swimming. Others, more skilled in weightless maneuvering, had kicked off from the nearest wall in the direction of whatever piece of recording machinery they most cherished, but not all of these had made due allowance for the traffic. By the time everyone was strapped in his proper place, Ries was back in the room, his face as expressionless as though nothing had been said a few moments before. His eyes kept swiveling from one station to another; if anyone had been looking at him, they would have supposed he was just waiting for something to break down. He was.

To his surprise, nothing did. The flare ran its course, with instruments humming and clicking serenely and no word of complaint from their attendants. Ries seemed almost disappointed; at least Pawlak, the power plant engineer who was about the only man on board who really liked the instrument specialist, suspected that he was.

"C'mon, Grump," was this individual's remark when everything seemed to have settled down once more. "Let's go outside and bring in the magazine from the monitor camera. Maybe something will have gone wrong with *it*; you said you didn't trust that remote-control system."

Ries almost brightened.

"All right. These astronomers will probably be howling for pictures in five minutes anyway, so they can tell each other they predicted everything correctly. Suit up." They left the room together with no one but the commander noting their departure.

There was little space outside the ship's air lock. The rocket had been brought as close to the center of the comet as measurement would permit, through a tunnel just barely big enough for the purpose. Five more smaller tunnels had been drilled, along three mutually perpendicular axes, to let out the exhaust of the fusion-powered reaction motors which were to use the comet's own mass to change its course. One other passageway, deliberately and carefully zigzagged, had been cut for personnel. Once the sunward course had been established all the tunnels except the last had been filled with "snow"—crushed comet material from near the ship. The cavern left by the removal of this and the exhaust mass was the only open space near the vessel, and even that was not too near. No one had dared weaken the structure of the big iceberg *too* close to the rocket; after all, one comet *had* been seen to divide as it passed the sun.

The monitor camera was some distance from the mouth of the tunnel—necessarily; the passage had been located very carefully. It opened in the "northern" hemisphere, as determined by direction of rotation, so that the camera could be placed at its mouth during perihelion passage and get continuous coverage. This meant, however, that in the comet's present orbital position the sun did not rise at all at the tunnel mouth. Since pictures had to be taken anyway, the camera was at the moment in the southern hemisphere, about a mile from the tunnel mouth.

Some care was needed in reaching it. A space-suited man with a mass of two hundred fifty pounds weighed something like a quarter of an ounce at the comet's surface, and could step away at several times the local escape velocity if he wished—or, for that matter, if he merely forgot himself. A dropped tool, given only the slightest accidental shove sideways, could easily go into orbit about the comet—or leave it permanently. That problem had been solved, though, after a fashion. Ries and Pawlak attached their suits together with a snap-ended coiled length of cable; then they picked up the end of something resembling a length of fine-linked chain which extended off to the southwest and disappeared quickly over the near horizon—or was it around the corner? Was the comet's surface below them, or beside or above? There was not enough weight to give a man the comforting sensation of a definite "up" and "down." The chain had a loop at the end, and both men put one arm through this. Then Ries waved his free arm three times as a signal, and they jumped straight up together on the third wave.

It was not such a ridiculous maneuver if one remembered the chain. This remained tight as the men rose, and pulled them gradually into an arc toward the southwest.

Partway up, they emerged from the comet's shadow, the metal suits glowing like miniature suns themselves. The great, gaseous envelope of a comet looks impressive from outside, seen against a background of black space; but it means exactly nothing as protection from sunlight even at Earth's distance from the sun. At twenty million miles it is much less, if such a thing is possible. The suits were excellent reflectors, but as a necessary consequence they were very poor radiators. Their temperature climbed more slowly than that of the proverbial black body, but it would climb much higher if given time. There would be perhaps thirty minutes before the suits would be too hot for life; and that, of course, was the reason for the leap.

A one-mile walk on the surface of the comet would take far more than half an hour if one intended to stay below circular velocity; swinging to their goal as the bobs on an inverted pendulum, speed limited only by the strength of their legs, should take between ten and twelve minutes. There were rockets on their suits which could have cut even that time down by quite a factor, but neither man thought of using them. They were for *emergency;* if the line holding them to the comet were to part, for example, the motors would come in handy. Not until.

* * *

They reached the peak of their arc, the chain pointing straight "down" toward the comet. Their goal had been visible for several minutes, and they had been trying to judge how close to it they would land. A direct hit was nearly impossible; even if they had been good enough to jump exactly straight up, the problem was complicated by the comet's rotation. As it turned out, the error was about two hundred yards, fairly small as such things went.

The landing maneuver was complicated-looking but logical. Half a minute before touchdown, Ries braced his feet against Pawlak and pushed. The engineer kept his grip on the chain and stayed in "orbit" while his companion left him in an apparently straight line. About fifteen seconds sufficed to separate them by the full length of the connecting snap line; the elasticity of this promptly started them back together, though at a much lower speed than they had moved apart. Just before they touched the surface, Ries noted which side of the camera the snap line was about to land on, and deliberately whipped it so that it fell on the other side; then, when both men took up slack, it snubbed against the camera mounting. Even though both men bounced on landing—it was nearly impossible to take up exactly the right amount of energy by muscle control alone—they were secure. Ries sent a couple more loops rippling down the line and around the camera mount—a trick which had taken some practice to perfect, where there was no gravity to help—and the two men pulled themselves over to their goal. The tendency to whip around it like a mishandled yo-yo as they drew closer was a nuisance but not a catastrophe; both were perfectly familiar with the conservation of angular momentum.

Ries quickly opened the camera, removed the exposed part of the film in its take-up cartridge and replaced and re-threaded another, checked the mounting for several seconds, and the job was done. The trip back was like that out, except for the complication that their landing spot was not in sunlight and control was harder. Five minutes after getting their rope around the pole at the tunnel mouth, they were in the ship. There was no speed limit *inside* the comet.

Once they were inside the air lock, Ries' prophecy was promptly fulfilled. Someone called for pictures before his suit had been off for two minutes. Pawlak watched his friend's blood pressure start up, and after a moment's calculation decided that intervention was in order—Grumpy couldn't be allowed *too* many fights.

"Go develop the stuff," he said. "I'll calm this idiot down."

For a moment it looked as though Ries would rather do his own arguing; then he relaxed, and vanished toward the instrument shop. Pawlak homed on the voice of the complaining astrophysicist, and in the three minutes it took Ries to process the film managed to make the fellow feel properly apologetic. This state of affairs lasted for about ten seconds after the film was delivered.

A group of six or seven scientists were waiting eagerly and had it in a projector almost instantly. For a few seconds after the run started there was silence; then a babble of expostulating voices arose. The general theme seemed to be, "Where's that instrument maker?"

Ries had not gone far, and when he appeared did not seem surprised. He didn't wait to be asked any questions, but took advantage of the instant silence which greeted his entrance.

"Didn't get your flare, did you? I didn't think so. That camera has a half-degree field, and the sun is over two degrees wide seen from here—"

"We know that!" Sacco and two or three others spoke almost together. "But the camera was supposed to scan the whole sun automatically whenever it was turned on from here, and keep doing it until we turned it off!"

"I know. And it didn't scan. I thought it hadn't when I was getting the film—"

"How could you tell? Why didn't you fix it? Or did you? What was wrong, anyway? Why didn't you set it up right in the first place?"

"I could tell that there hadn't been enough film exposed for the time it was supposed to be on. As for fixing it out there, or even finding out what was wrong—don't sound any more idiotic than you can help. It'll have to be brought into the shop. I can't promise how long it'll take to fix it until I know what's wrong."

The expostulation rose almost to a roar at this last remark. The commander, who alone of the group had been silent until now, made a gesture which stilled the others.

"I know it's hard to promise, but please remember one thing," he said. "We're twenty million miles from the sun; we'll be at perihelion in sixty-seven hours. If we pass it without that camera, we'll be missing our principal means of correlating any new observations with the old ones. I don't say that without the camera we might as well not be here, but—''

"I know it," growled Ries. "All right. I knew we should have laid down a walk cable between here and the blasted thing when we first set it up, but with people talking about time and shortage of anchoring pins and all that tripe—''

"I think that last was one of your own points," interjected the commander. "However, we have better things to do than fix blame. Tell us what help you need in getting the camera back to the ship."

An hour later, the device came in through the air lock. Its mass had demanded a slight modification in travel technique; if the chain had broken during a "swing" the rockets would not have been able to return men and camera both to the comet, in all likelihood. Instead of swinging, therefore, the workers had pulled straight along the chain, building up speed until they reached its anchorage and then slowing down on the other side by applying friction to the chain as it unwound behind them. An extra man with a line at the tunnel mouth had simplified the stopping problem on the return trip with the camera.

Four hours later still, Ries had taken the camera completely apart and put it together again, and was in a position to say that there had been nothing wrong with it. He was not happy about this discovery, and the scientists who heard his report were less so. They were rather abusive about it; and that, of course, detonated the instrument man's temper.

"All right, *you* tell *me* what's wrong!" he snapped at last. "I can say flatly that nothing is broken or out of adjustment, and it works perfectly in here. Any genius who's about to tell me that *in here* isn't *out there* can save his breath. I know it, and I know that the next thing to do is take it back out and see if it still works. That's what I'm doing, if I can spare the time from listening to your helpful comments." He departed abruptly, donned his suit, and went outside with the instrument but without Pawlak. He had no intention of returning to the original camera site, and needed no help. The tunnel mouth was "outside" enough, he felt.

It took several more hours to prove that he was right. At first, the trouble refused to show itself. The camera tracked beautifully over any sized square of sky that Ries chose to set into its control. Then after half an hour or more, the size of the square began to grow smaller no matter what he did with the controls. Eventually it reached zero. This led him into its interior, as well as he could penetrate it in a spacesuit, but no information was forthcoming. Then, just to be tantalizing, the thing started to work again. On its own, as far as Ries could tell. He was some time longer in figuring out why.

Eventually he came storming back into the ship, fulminating against anyone who had had anything to do either with designing or selecting the device. He was a little happier, since the trouble was demonstrably not his own fault, but not much. He made this very clear to the waiting group as soon as his helmet was off.

"I don't know what genius indulged his yen for subminiaturization," he began, "but he carried it too far. I suppose using a balanced resistance circuit in a control is sensible enough; it'll work at regular temperatures, and it'll work at comet temperatures. The trouble is it won't work unless the different segments are near the *same* temperature; otherwise the resistors can't possibly balance. When I first took the thing outside, it worked fine; it was at ship's temperature. Then it began to leak heat into the comet, and went crazy. Later on, with the whole thing cooled down to comet temperature, it worked again. Nice design!"

"But it had been outside for days before—" began someone, and stopped as he realized what had happened. Ries pounced on him just the same.

"Sure—outside *in the sunlight*. Picking up radiant heat on one side, doing its best to get to equilibrium at a couple of hundred degrees. Conducting heat out into the ice four or five hundred degrees colder on the other side. Nice, uniform—aach!"

"Can't a substitute control be devised?" cut in the commander mildly. "That's your field, after all. Surely you can put something together—"

"Oh, sure. In a minute. We're just loaded with spare parts and gear; rockets always are. While I'm at it I'll try to make the thing wristwatch size so it will fit in the available space— all we need is a research lab's machine shop. I'll do what I can, but you won't like it. Neither will I." He stormed out to his own shop.

"I'll buy his last remark, anyway," muttered someone. Agreement was general but not too loud.

At fifteen million miles from the sun, with another meter or so boiled off the comet's sunlit surface, Ries emerged with his makeshift. He was plainly in need of sleep, and in even worse temper than usual. He had only one question to ask before getting into his suit.

"Shouldn't the sun be starting to show near the tunnel mouth by now?"

"One of the astronomers did a little mental arithmetic.

"Yes," he answered. "You won't need to travel anywhere to test the thing. Do you need any help?"

"What for?" growled Ries in his usual pleasant fashion, and disappeared again. The astronomer shrugged. By the time conversation had gotten back to normal the instrument specialist and his camera were in the air lock.

Taking the heavy device out through the tunnel offered only one danger, and that only in the last section—the usual one of going too fast and leaving the comet permanently. To forestall the risk of forcing people to pay final respects to him and regret the camera, he made full use of the loops of safety cable which had been anchored in the tunnel wall. He propped the instrument at the tunnel mouth facing roughly north, and waited for sunrise. This came soon enough. It was the display characteristic of an airless world, since the coma was not dense enough to scatter any light to speak of. The zodiacal light brightened near the horizon; then it merged into pearly corona; then a brilliant crimson eruptive arch prominence appeared, which seemed worth a picture or two to the nonprofessional; and finally came the glaring photosphere on which the test had to be made. It was here that another minor problem developed.

The photosphere, area for angular area, was of course no brighter than when seen from just above Earth's atmosphere; but it was no fainter either, and Ries could not look at it to aim his camera. The only finder on the latter was a direct-view collimating sight, since it was designed for automatic control. After a moment's thought, Ries decided that he could handle this situation too, but, since his solution would probably take longer than the sun would be above the horizon, he simply ran the camera through a few scanning cycles, aiming it by the shape of its own shadow. Then he anchored the machine in the tunnel mouth and made his way back to the ship.

Here he found what he wanted with little difficulty—a three-inch-square interference filter. It was not of the tunable sort, though of course its transmission depended on the angle of incidence of the light striking it, but it was designed for sixty-five hundred Angstroms and would do perfectly well for what he had in mind.

Before he could use it, though, another problem had to be solved. Almost certainly the lining up of the camera and its new control—that is, making sure that the center of its sweep field agreed with the line laid down by the collimator sight—would take quite a while. At fifteen million miles from the sun, one simply doesn't work for long with only a spacesuit as protection. The expedition had, of course, been carefully planned so that no one would have to do any such thing; but the plans had just graduated from history to mythology. Grumpy Ries was either going to work undisturbed in full sunlight, probably for one or two whole hours, or spend twenty minutes cooling off in the tunnel for every ten he spent warming up outside it; and that last would add hours and hours to the job time—with the heating period growing shorter with each hour that passed. A parabolic orbit has one very marked feature; its downhill half is very *steeply* downhill, and speed builds up far too quickly for comfort. It seemed that some means of working outside, if one could be found, would pay for itself. Ries thought he could find one.

He was an artisan rather than a scientist, but he was a good artisan. A painter knows pigments and surfaces, a sculptor knows metal and stone; Ries knew basic physics. He used his knowledge.

Limited as the spare supplies were, they included a number of large rolls of aluminum foil and many spools of wire. He put these to use, and in an hour was ready with a six-foot-square shield of foil, made in two layers a couple of inches apart, the space between them stuffed with pulverized ice from the cavern. In its center was mounted the filter, and beside this a hole big enough to take the camera barrel. The distance between the two openings had been measured carefully; the filter would be in front of the camera sight.

Characteristically, he showed the device to no one. He made most of it outside the ship, as a matter of fact; and when it was done he towed it rather awkwardly up the tunnel to the place where the camera was stored. Incredibly, twenty minutes later the new control was aligned, the camera mounted firmly on its planned second base at the tunnel mouth, and a control line was being run down the tunnel to the ship. With his usual curtness he reported completion of the job; when the control system had been tested from inside, and the method Ries had used to accomplish the task wormed out of him, the reaction of the scientists almost had him smiling.

Almost; but a hardened grouch doesn't change all at once—if ever.

Ten million miles from Sol's center. Twenty-one hours to go—people were not yet counting minutes. The sun was climbing a little higher above the northern horizon as seen from the tunnel mouth, and remaining correspondingly longer in view each time it rose. Some really good pictures were being obtained; nothing yet which couldn't have been taken from one of the orbital stations near Earth.

Five million miles. Ten hours and fifty minutes. Ries stayed inside, now, and tried to sleep. No one else had time to. Going outside, even to the mouth of the tunnel, was presumed impossible, though the instrument maker had made several more shields. Technically, they were within the corona of the sun, though only of its most tenuous outlying zones—there is, of course, a school of thought that considers the corona as extending well past the earth's orbit. None of the physicists were wasting time trying to decide what was essentially a matter of definition; they were simply reading and recording every instrument whose field of sensitivity seemed to have the slightest bearing on their current environment, and a good many which seemed unlikely to be useful, but who could tell?

Ries was awake again when they reached the ninety degree point—one quarter of the way around the sun from perihelion. The angular distance the earth travels in three months. Slightly over one million miles from the sun's center. Six hundred thousand miles from the photosphere. Well within *anyone's* definition of the corona; within reach of a really healthy eruptive prominence, had any been in the way. One hour and eighteen minutes from their closest approach—or deepest penetration, if one preferred to put it that way. Few did.

They were hurtling, at some three hundred ten miles per second, into a region where the spectroscope claimed temperatures above two million degrees to exist, where ions of iron and nickel and calcium wandered about with a dozen and more of their electrons stripped away, and where the electrons themselves formed almost a gas in their own right, albeit a highly tenuous one.

It was that lack of density on which the men were counting. A single ion at a "temperature" of two million degrees means nothing; there isn't a human being alive who hasn't been struck by vast numbers of far more energetic particles. No one expected to pick up any serious amount of heat from the corona itself.

The photosphere was another matter. It was an opaque, if still gaseous, "surface" which they would approach within one hundred fifty thousand miles—less than its own diameter by a healthy factor. It had a radiation equilibrium temperature of some six thousand degrees, and would fill a large solid angle of sky; this meant that black-body equilibrium temperature at their location would not be much below the same value. The comet, of course, was not a black body—and did not retain even the heat which it failed to reflect. The moment a portion of its surface was warmed seriously, that portion evaporated, taking the newly acquired heat energy with it. A new layer, still only a few degrees above absolute zero, was exposed in its turn to the flood of radiation.

That flood was inconceivably intense, of course; careless, nonquantitative thought could picture the comet's vanishing under that bombardment like a snowball in a blast furnace—but the flood wasn't infinite. A definite, measurable amount of energy struck the giant snowball; a definite amount was reflected; a definite, measurable amount was absorbed and warmed up and boiled away the ices of water and ammonia and methane that made it up.

And there was a lot to boil away. Thrust-acceleration ratios had long ago given the scientists the mass of their shelter, and even at a hundred and fifty thousand miles a two-and-a-half-mile-thick bar of sunlight will take some time to evaporate thirty-five billion tons of ice. The comet would spend only a little over twenty-one hours within five million miles of the sun, and unless several physicists had misplaced the same decimal point, it should last with plenty to spare. The twelve-hour rule on Sacco's echo sounder had been canceled now, and its readings were common knowledge; but none of them caused anxiety.

In they drove. No one could see out, of course; there was nothing like the awed watching of an approaching prominence or gazing into the deceptively pitlike area of a sunspot of which many of them had unthinkingly dreamed. If they could have seen a sunspot at all, it would have been as blinding as the rest of the photosphere—human eyes couldn't discriminate between the two orders of overload. For all any of them knew, they might be going through a prominence at any given second; they wouldn't be able to tell until the instrument records were developed and reduced. The only people who could "see" in any sense at all were the ones whose instruments gave visible as well as recorded readings. Photometers and radiometers did convey a picture to those who understood them; magnetometers and ionization gauges and particle counters meant almost as much; but spectrographs and interferometers and cameras hummed and clicked and whirred without giving any clues to the nature of the meals they were digesting. The accelerometers claimed their share of watchful eyes—if there were any noticeable drag to the medium outside, all bets on the comet's future and their own were off—but nothing had shown so far.

They were nineteen minutes from perihelion when a growing sense of complacency was rudely shattered. There was no warning—one could hardly be expected at three hundred twenty-five miles a second.

One instant they were floating at their instruments, doing their allotted work, at peace with the universe; the next there was a violent jolt, sparks flew from exposed metal terminals, and every remote indicator in the vessel went dead.

For a moment there was silence; the phenomenon ended as abruptly as it had started. Then there was a mixed chorus of yells, mostly of surprise and dismay, a few of pain. Some of the men had been burned by spark discharges. One had also been knocked out by an electric shock, and it was fortunate that the emergency lights had not been affected; they sprang automatically to life as the main ones failed, and order was quickly restored. One of the engineers applied mouth-to-mouth respiration to the shock victim—aesthetic or not, it is the only sort practical in the weightless condition—and each of the scientists began trouble shooting.

None of the remote gear registered in any way, but much of the apparatus inside the ship was still functioning, and a tentative explanation was quickly reached.

"Magnetic field," was Mallion's terse comment, "size impossible to tell, just as impossible to tell what formed or maintained it. We went through it at three hundred twenty miles a second, plus. If this ship had been metal, it would probably have exploded; as it was, this general sort of thing was a considered possibility and there are no long conducting paths anywhere in the ship—except the instrument controls. The field intensity was between ten and a hundred Gauss. We've taken all the outside readings we're going to, I'm afraid.''

"But we can't stop now!" howled Donegan. "We need pictures—hundreds more of them. How do we correlate all the stuff we have, and the things that will still show on the inside instruments we can still use, unless there are pictures—it's fine to say that this or that or the other thing comes from a prominence, or a flare, or what have you, but we won't *know* it does, or anything about the size of the flare. . . .''

"I understand, sympathize, and agree; but what do you propose to do about it? I'd bet a small but significant sum that the cable coming in through the access tunnel *did* explode. Something certainly stopped the current surge before all the instruments here burned up.''

"Come on, Dr. Donegan. Get your suit.'' It was Ries, of course. The physicist looked at him, must have read his mind, and leaped toward his locker.

"What are you madmen up to?'' shouted Mallion. "You can't go out to that camera—you'd be a couple of moths in a candle flame, to put it mildly!''

"Use your brain, not your thalamus, Doc,'' Ries called over his shoulder. Welland said nothing. Two minutes later the pair of madmen were in the air lock, and sixty seconds after that were floating as rapidly as they dared out the tunnel.

The lights were out, but seeing was easy. There was plenty of illumination from the mouth of the tunnel, crooked as the passage was; and the two had to use the filters on their face plates long before they reached the opening. By that time, the very snow around them seemed to be glowing—and may very well have been doing just that, since light must have filtered for some distance in through the packed crystalloids as well as bounced its way around the tunnel bends.

Ries had left his foil shelters at the first bend. There was some loose snow still on hand from his earlier experiments, and they stuffed as much of this as they could between the thin metal layers, and took several of the sandwiched slabs with them as they gingerly approached the opening. They held one of the larger of these—about four feet square—ahead of them as they went; but it proved insufficient when they got within a few yards of the mouth. The trouble was not that the shield failed, but that it wasn't big enough; no matter how close to the opening they came, the entire sky remained a sea of flame. They retreated a little way and Ries rapidly altered the foil armor, bending the sheets and wiring them together until he had a beehive-shaped affair large enough to shield a man. He used the last of their snow in this assembly.

Covered almost completely, he went alone to the tunnel mouth, and this time he had no trouble. He was able to use a loop of control wire as a safety, and by hooking his toes under this reached the instrument. It had settled quite a bit—its case and mounting had transmitted heat as planned to the broad silver feet, and these had maintained good surface contact. Naturally a good deal of comet material had boiled away from under them, and the whole installation was in a pit over two feet deep and eight in width. The general lowering of the comet's surface was less obvious.

The vanes of the legs were faintly well sunk into the surface, but with gravity as it was, the only difficulty in freeing them was the perennial one—the risk of giving too much upward momentum. Ries avoided this, got camera and mounting loose, and as quickly as possible brought them back into the tunnel. There was no need to disconnect the control wire from the main cable; as Mallion had predicted, both had disappeared. Their explosion had scarred a deep groove along the tunnel wall at several points where they had been close to the side. Ries regretted their loss; without them he had some difficulty getting himself and his burden started downward, and he wanted the camera into the tunnel's relative shelter as quickly as possible. With its heat-shedding "feet" out of contact with the ground, it would not take long to heat up dangerously. Also, with the comet now whipping closer and closer to perihelion, there was already an annoyingly large gap in the photographic record.

Back in the tunnel, Ries improvised another set of shields for the camera and its operator, and checked the one he had used to see how much snow remained in it. There was some, but discouragingly little. He placed his helmet against that of Donegan and spoke—the radios were useless in the Sun's static.

"You can't go out until we get more snow for this thing, and you'll have to come back every few minutes for a refill. I'd do the photography, but you know better than I what has to be taken. I hope you can make out what you need to see through the sixty-five hundred filter in the shield I made for the finder. I'll be back."

He started back down the tunnel, but at the second turn met another suited figure coming out—with a large bag of snow. He recognized Pawlak by the number on the suit, since the face of the occupant was invisible behind the filter. Ries took the bag and gestured his thanks; Pawlak indicated that he would go back and bring more, and started on this errand. Ries reappeared at the camera soon enough to surprise his companion, but the physicist wasted no time in questions. The two men restuffed the shields with snow, and Donegan went back to the tunnel mouth to do his job.

Through the filter, the angry surface of the sun blazed a fiery orange. Features were clear enough, though not always easy to interpret. Individual "rice grains" were clearly visible; a small spot, badly foreshortened, showed far to one side. By moving his head as far as the shield allowed, the observer could see well away from the camera's line of sight; doing this, of course, blued the sun as the ray path difference between the reflecting layers in the filter was shortened. He could not tell exactly what wavelength he was using at any given angle, but he quickly learned to make use of the rather crude "tuning" that angle change afforded. He began shooting, first the spot and its neighborhood, altering the camera filter wavelength regularly as he did so. Then he found something that might have been a calcium flocculus and took a series around it; then feature after feature caught his eye, and he shot and shot, trying to get each field through the full wavelength range of the camera at about fifty Angstrom intervals plus definite lengths which he knew should be there—the various series lines of hydrogen and of neutral and ionized helium particularly, though he did not neglect such metals as calcium and sodium.

He was distracted by a pull on his armored foot; Ries had come up, inadequately protected by the single remaining sheet of "parasol," to warn him to recharge his own shield. Reluctantly he did so, grudging the time. Ries packed snow against the feet of the camera mounting while Donegan stuffed it between the foil layers of his shield as rapidly as his space-suited hands could work. The moment this was done he headed back to the tunnel mouth, now not so far away as it had been, and resumed operations.

They must have been almost exactly at perihelion then. Donegan neither knew nor cared. He knew that the camera held film enough to let him take one picture a second for about ninety minutes, and he intended to use all of it if he could. He simply scanned the sun as completely as his eyesight, the protecting filter, and his own knowledge permitted, and recorded as completely as possible everything even slightly out of the ordinary that he saw. He knew that many instruments were still at work in the ship, even though many were not, and he knew that some of the devices on the comet's surface would function—or should function—automatically even though remote control was gone; and he intended that there should be a complete record in pictures of everything which might be responsible for whatever those machines recorded. He did a good job.

Not too many—in fact, as time went on, too few—yards below him Ries also worked. If being an instrument maintenance specialist involved moving snow, and in this part of the universe it seemed to involve little else, then he would move snow. He had plenty of it; Pawlak kept bringing more and more bags of the stuff. Also, on his second trip, the engineer produced a lengthy coil of wire; and at the first opportunity Ries fastened one end of this to Donegan's ankle. It served two purposes—it was no longer necessary to go out to let the fellow know by physical contact that his time was getting short, and it let the observer get back to work more quickly. Since he was belayed to Ries, who could brace himself against the tunnel walls beyond the bend, there was no worry of going back to the surface too rapidly and being unable to stop.

Ries kept busy. No one ever knew whether he did it silently or not, since the radios were unavailable. It was generally taken for granted that he grumbled as usual, and he may very well have done just that, or even surpassed himself. Hanging weightless in a white-glowing tunnel, trying to read a watch through the heaviest solar filter made for space helmets, holding one end of a line whose other end was keeping a man and a fantastically valuable camera from drifting away and becoming part of the solar corona, all the while trying to organize a number of large plastic sacks of pulverized frozen water, ammonia, and methane which persistently gathered around him would have driven a more self-controlled man than Ries to bad language.

Of course, Donegan didn't map the whole surface. This would take quite a while, using a camera with a half-degree field on a surface over ninety-five degrees across, even when the surface in question is partly hidden by the local horizon. It was made even more impossible by their rate of motion; parabolic velocity at a distance of five hundred eighty thousand miles from Sol's center is just about three hundred thirty miles per second, and that produced noticeable relative motion even against a background a hundred and fifty thousand miles away. Features were disappearing below the solar horizon, sometimes, before Donegan could get around to them. Even Ries could think of no solution to this difficulty, when the physicist complained of it on one of his trips for more snow.

At this point, the sun's apparent motion in latitude was more rapid than that in longitude—the comet was changing its direction from the sun more rapidly than it was rotating. The resultant motion across the sky was a little hard to predict, but the physicist knew that the center of the solar disk would set permanently at the latitude of the tunnel mouth an hour and three-quarters after perihelion. The angular size of the disk being what it was, there would be *some* observing after that, but how much depended on what might be called the local time of day, and he had not attempted to figure that out. He simply observed and photographed, except when Ries dragged him forcibly back to get his shield recharged.

Gradually the gigantic disk shrank. It never was far above the local horizon, so there was always something with which to compare it, and the shrinking could be noticed. Also, Ries could tell as time went on that there was a little more snow left in Donegan's shield each time it came back for refilling. Evidently they were past the worst.

But the sun had taken its toll. The mouth of the tunnel was much closer to the ship than it had been; several times Ries had been forced back to another section of tunnel with his snow bags, and each resumption of observation by Donegan had involved a shorter trip than before to the surface. Ries, Donegan, and Pawlak were the only members of the expedition to know just how far the evaporation was progressing, since the echo-sounder had been wrecked by the magnetic field; they were never sure afterward whether this was good or not. Those inside were sustained, presumably, by their faith in mathematics. For the physicists this was adequate, but it might not have been for Ries if he had been with them. In any case, he didn't worry much about the fate of the comet after perihelion had been passed; he had too many other troubles, even though his activity had quickly become routine. This left him free to complain—strictly to himself.

Donegan was furious when he finally realized that the sun was going to set at his observing station while it was still close enough to photograph. Like Ries, however, he had no way of expressing his annoyance so that anyone could hear him; and as it turned out, it would have been wasted breath. Observation was cut even shorter by something else.

They had been driven down to what had been originally the third bend in the tunnel, and at this point the passage ran horizontally for a time. Pawlak had just come to the other end of this straight stretch with what he hoped would be his last load of snow when something settled gently through its roof between him and Ries. He leaped toward it, dropping his burden, and discovered that it was one of the instruments which had been on the surface. Its silver cover was slightly corroded, and the feet of its mounting badly so. Apparently its reflecting powers had been lowered by the surface change, and it was absorbing more energy than an equivalent area of comet; so its temperature had gone up accordingly, and it had melted its way below the rest of the surface.

Low as the sun was, it was shining into the hole left by the instrument; evidently the pit it had made was very broad and shallow. Pawlak made his way around the piece of gear and up to Ries, whose attention was directed elsewhere, and reported what had happened. The instrument man looked back down the tunnel and began to haul in on the line attached to Donegan. The physicist was furious when he arrived, and the fact became evident when the three helmets were brought together.

"What in blazes is going on here?" he fulminated. "You can't make me believe my shield had boiled dry again—I haven't been out five minutes, and the loads are lasting longer now. We're losing the sun, you idiot; I can't come back because someone has a brainstorm or can't read a watch—"

Pawlak interrupted by repeating his report. It did not affect Donegan.

"So what?" he blazed. "We expected that. All the gear around the tunnel mouth has sunk—we're in a big pit now anyway. That's making things still worse—we'll lose sight of the sun that much sooner. Now let me get back and work!"

"Go back and work if you want, provided you can do anything with the naked eye," retorted Ries, "but the camera's going back to the ship pronto. That's one thing we forgot—or maybe it was just assumed that gaseous ammonia in this concentration and at this temperature wouldn't do anything to silver. Maybe it isn't the ammonia, for all I know; maybe it's something we've been picking up from the corona; but look at that camera of yours! The polish is gone; it's picking up heat much faster than it was expected to, and not getting rid of it any quicker. If that magazine of exposed film you have in there gets too hot, you'll have wasted a lot of work. Now come on, or else let me take the camera back." Ries started along the tunnel without further words, and the physicist followed reluctantly.

Inside, Donegan disappeared with his precious film magazine, without taking time to thank Ries.

"Self-centered character," Pawlak muttered. "Not a word to anyone—just off to develop his film before somebody opens the cartridge, I suppose."

"You can't blame him," Ries said mildly. "He did a lot of work for it."

"*He* did a lot of work? How about us? How about you; it was all your idea in the first place—"

"Careful, Joe, or they'll be taking my nickname away from me and giving it to you. Come on; I want to see Doc Sonne. My feet hurt." He made his way to the main deck, and Pawlak drifted after him, grumbling. By the time the engineer arrived, the rest of the group was overwhelming Ries with compliments, and the fellow was grinning broadly. It began to look as though the name "Grumpy" *would* have to find a new owner.

But habit is hard to break. The doctor approached, and without removing his patient's shoes dredged a tube of ointment out of his equipment bag.

"Burn ointment," the doctor replied. "It'll probably be enough; you shouldn't have taken too bad a dose. I'll have you patched up in a minute. Let's get those shoes off."

"Now wouldn't you know it," said Ries aloud. "Not even the doctor around here can do the right thing at the right time. Physicists who want A's gear fixed on B's time—won't let a man go out to do a job in the only way it can be done—won't give a person time to rest—and now," it was the old Grumpy back again, "a man spends two hours or so swimming around among sacks of frozen methane, which melts at about a hundred and eighty-five degrees Centigrade below zero—that's about two hundred and ninety below Fahrenheit, doctor—and the doctor wants to use *burn ointment*. Break out the frostbite remedy, will you, please? My feet hurt.''

buried inactivity began to assert itself, his doctor
came to his bedside, saying "Wake up, the trouble's off,
you please...". My feet hurt...

INSIDE THE COMET

Arthur C. Clarke

"I don't know why I'm recording this," said George Takeo Pickett slowly into the hovering microphone. "There's no chance that anyone will ever hear it. They say the comet will bring us back to the neighborhood of Earth in about two million years, when it makes its next turn around the Sun. I wonder if mankind will still be in existence then, and whether the comet will put on as good a display for our descendants as it did for us. Maybe they'll launch an expedition, just as we have done, to see what they can find. And they'll find us. . . .

"For the ship will still be in perfect condition, even after all those ages. There'll be fuel in the tanks, maybe even plenty of air, for our food will give out first, and we'll starve before we suffocate. But I guess we won't wait for that; it will be quicker to open the airlock and get it all over.

"When I was a kid, I read a book on polar exploration called *Winter Amid the Ice*. Well, that's what we're facing now. There's ice all around us, floating in great porous bergs. *Challenger's* in the middle of a cluster of them, orbiting around one another so slowly that you have to wait several minutes before you're certain they've moved. But no expedition to Earth's poles ever faced *our* winter. During most of that two million years, the temperature will be four hundred and fifty below zero. We'll be so far away from the sun that it'll give about as much heat as the

93

stars. And who ever tried to warm his hands by Sirius on a cold winter night?

That absurd image, coming suddenly into his mind, broke him up completely. He could not speak for memories of moonlight upon snowfields, of Christmas chimes ringing across a land already fifty million miles away. Suddenly he was weeping like a child, his self-control dissolved by the remembrance of all the familiar, disregarded beauties of the Earth he had forever lost.

And everything had begun so well, in such a blaze of excitement and adventure. He could recall (was it only six months ago?) the very first time he had gone out to look for the comet, soon after eighteen-year-old Jimmy Randall had found it in his homemade telescope and sent his famous telegram to Mount Stromlo Observatory. In those early days, it had been only a faint pollywog of mist, moving slowly through the constellation of Eridanus, just south of the Equator. It was still far beyond Mars, sweeping sunwards along its immensely elongated orbit. When it had last shone in the skies of Earth, there were no men to see it, and there might be none when it appeared again. The human race was seeing Randall's Comet for the first and perhaps the only time.

As it approached the sun, it grew, blasting out plumes and jets, the smallest of which was larger than a hundred Earths. Like a great pennant streaming down some cosmic breeze, the comet's tail was already forty million miles long when it raced past the orbit of Mars. It was then that the astronomers realized that this might be the most spectacular sight ever to appear in the heavens; the display put on by Halley's Comet, back in 1986, would be nothing in comparison. And it was then that the administrators of the International Astrophysical Decade decided to send the research ship *Challenger* chasing after it, if she could be fitted out in time; for here was a chance that might not come again in a thousand years.

For weeks on end, in the hours before dawn, the comet sprawled across the sky like a second, but far brighter, Milky Way. As it approached the Sun, and felt again the fires it had not known since the mammoths shook the Earth, it became steadily more active. Gouts of luminous gas erupted from its core, forming great fans which turned like slowly swinging searchlights across the stars. The tail, now a hundred million miles long, divided into intricate bands and streamers which changed their patterns completely in the course of a single night. Always they pointed away from the Sun, as if driven starwards by a great wind blowing forever outwards from the heart of the Solar System.

When the *Challenger* assignment had been given to him, George Pickett could hardly believe his luck. Nothing like this had happened to any reporter since William Laurence and the Atom Bomb. The facts that he had a science degree, was unmarried, in good health, weighed less than one hundred and twenty pounds, and had no appendix undoubtedly helped. But there must have been many others equally qualified; well, their envy would soon turn to relief.

As the skimpy payload of *Challenger* could not accommodate a mere reporter, Pickett had had to double up in his spare time as Executive Officer. This meant, in practice, that he had to write up the Log, act as Captain's secretary, keep track of stores, and balance the accounts. It was very fortunate, he often thought, that in the weightless world of space one needed only three hours' sleep in every twenty-four.

Keeping his two duties separate had required a great deal of tact. When he was not writing in his closet-sized office, or checking the thousands of items stacked away in Stores, he would go on the prowl with his recorder. He had been careful, at one time or another, to interview every one of the twenty scientists and engineers who manned *Challenger*. Not all the recordings had been radioed back to Earth; some had been too technical, some too inarticulate, and others too much the reverse. But at least he had played no favorites and, as far as he knew, had trodden on no toes. Not that it mattered now.

He wondered how Dr. Martens was taking it; the astronomer had been one of his most difficult subjects, yet the one who could give most information. On a sudden impulse, Pickett located the earliest of the Martens tapes, and inserted it in the recorder. He knew that he was trying to escape from the present by retreating into the past, but the only effect of that self-knowledge was to make him hope the experiment would succeed.

He still had vivid memories of that first interview, for the weightless microphone, wavering only slightly in the draft of air from the ventilators, had almost hypnotized him into incoherence. Yet no one would have guessed: his voice had its normal, professional smoothness.

They had been twenty million miles behind the comet, but swiftly overtaking it, when he had trapped Martens in the observatory and thrown that opening question at him.

"Dr. Martens," he began, "just what *is* Randall's Comet made of?"

"Quite a mixture," the astronomer had answered. "And it's changing all the time as we move away from the sun. But the tail's mostly ammonia, methane, carbon dioxide, water vapour, cyanogen—"

"Cyanogen? Isn't that a poison gas? What would happen if the Earth ran into it?"

"Not a thing. Though it looks so spectacular, by our normal standards a comet's tail is a pretty good vacuum. A volume as big as Earth contains about as much gas as a matchbox full of air."

"And yet this thin stuff puts on such a wonderful display!"

"So does the equally thin gas in an electric sign, and for the same reason. A comet's tail glows because the Sun bombards it with electrically charged particles. It's a cosmic sky-sign; one day, I'm afraid, the advertising people will wake up to this, and find a way of writing slogans across the Solar System."

"That's a depressing thought—though I suppose someone will claim it's a triumph of applied science. But let's leave the tail; how soon will we get into the heart of the comet—the nucleus, I believe you call it?"

"Since a stern chase always takes a long time, it will be another two weeks before we enter the nucleus. We'll be plowing deeper and deeper into the tail, taking a cross-section through the comet as we catch up with it. But though the nucleus is still twenty million miles ahead, we've already learned a good deal about it. For one thing, it's extremely small—less than fifty miles across. And even that's not solid, but probably consists of thousands of smaller bodies, all milling around in a cloud."

"Will we be able to go into the nucleus?"

"We'll know when we get there. Maybe we'll play safe and study it through our telescopes from a few thousand miles away. But personally, I'll be disappointed unless we go right inside. Won't you?"

Pickett switched off the recorder. Yes, Martens had been right. He *would* have been disappointed, especially as there had seemed no possible source of danger. Nor was there, as far as the comet was concerned. The danger had come from within.

They had sailed through one after another of the huge but unimaginably tenuous curtains of gas that Randall's Comet was still ejecting as it raced away from the Sun. Yet even now, though they were approaching the densest regions of the nucleus, they were for all practical purposes in a perfect vacuum. The luminous fog that stretched round *Challenger* for so many millions of miles scarcely dimmed the stars; but directly ahead, where lay the comet's core, there was a brilliant patch of hazy light, luring them onwards like a will-of-the-wisp.

The electrical disturbances now taking place around them with ever-increasing violence had almost completely cut their link with Earth. The ship's main radio transmitter could just get a signal through, but for the last few days they had been reduced to sending "O.K." messages in Morse. When they broke away from the comet and headed for home, normal communication would be resumed; but now they were almost as isolated as explorers had been in the days before radio. It was inconvenient, but that was all. Indeed, Pickett rather welcomed this state of affairs; it gave him more time to get on with his clerical duties. Though *Challenger* was sailing into the heart of a comet, on a course that no captain could have dreamed of before the twentieth century, someone still had to check the provisions and count the stores.

Very slowly and cautiously, her radar probing the whole sphere of space around her, *Challenger* crept into the nucleus of the comet. And there she came to rest—amid the ice.

Back in the 1940s, Whipple of Harvard had guessed the truth, but it was hard to believe it even when the evidence was before one's eyes. The comet's relatively tiny core was a loose cluster of icebergs, drifting and turning around one another as they moved along their orbit. But unlike the bergs that floated in polar seas, they were not a dazzling white, nor were they made of water. They were a dirty gray, and very porous, like partly thawed snow. And they were riddled with pockets of methane and frozen ammonia, which erupted from time to time in gigantic gas jets as they absorbed the heat of the sun. It was a wonderful display, but Pickett had little time to admire it, at first. Now he had far too much.

He had been doing his routine check of the ship's stores when he came face to face with disaster—though it was some time before he realized it. For the supply situation had been perfectly satisfactory; they had ample stocks for the return to earth. He had checked that with his own eyes, and now had merely to confirm the balances recorded in the pinhead-sized section of the ship's electronic memory which stored all the accounts.

When the first crazy figures flashed on the screen, Pickett assumed that he had pressed the wrong key. He cleared the totals, and fed the information into the computer once more.

60 cases of pressed meat to start with; 17 consumed so far; quantity left: 99999943.

He tried again, and again, with no better result. Then, feeling annoyed but not particularly alarmed, he went in search of Dr. Martens.

He found the astronomer in the Torture Chamber—the tiny gym, squeezed between the Technical Stores and the bulkhead of the main propellant tank. Each member of the crew had to exercise here for an hour a day, lest his muscles waste away in his gravityless environment. Martens was wrestling with a set of powerful springs, an expression of grim determination on his face. It became much grimmer when Pickett gave his report.

A few tests on the main input board quickly told them the worst. "The computer's insane," said Martens. "It can't even add or subtract."

"But surely we can fix it!"

Martens shook his head. He had lost all his usual cocky self-confidence; he looked, Pickett told himself, like an inflated rubber doll that had started to leak.

"Not even the builders could do that. It's a solid mass of microcircuits, packed as tightly as the human brain. The memory units are still operating, but the computing section's utterly useless. It just scrambles the figures you feed into it."

"And where does that leave us?" Pickett asked.

"It means that we're all dead," Martens answered flatly. "Without the computer, we're done for. It's impossible to calculate an orbit back to Earth. It could take an army of mathematicians weeks to work it out on paper."

"That's ridiculous! The ship's in perfect condition, we've plenty of food and fuel—and you tell me we're all going to die just because we can't do a few sums."

"A *few* sums!" retorted Martens, with a trace of his old spirit. "A major navigational change, like the one needed to break away from the comet and put us on an orbit to Earth, involves about a hundred thousand separate calculations. Even the computer needs several minutes for the job."

Pickett was no mathematician, but he knew enough of astronautics to understand the situation. A ship coasting through space was under the influence of many bodies. The main force controlling it was the gravity of the Sun, which kept all the planets firmly chained in their orbits. But the planets themselves also tugged it this way and that, though with much feebler strength. To allow for all these conflicting tugs and pulls—above all, to take advantage of them to reach at the right moment a desired goal scores of millions of miles away—was a problem of fantastic complexity. He could appreciate Martens' despair; no man could work without the tools of his trade, and no trade needed more elaborate tools than this one.

Even after the Captain's announcement, and that first emergency conference when the entire crew had gathered to discuss the situation, it had taken hours for the facts to sink home. The end was still so many months away that the mind could not grasp it; they were under sentence of death, but there was no hurry about the execution. And the view was still superb. . . .

Beyond the glowing mists that enveloped them—and which would be their celestial monument to the end of time—they could see the great beacon of Jupiter, brighter than all the stars. Some of them might still be alive, if the others were willing to sacrifice themselves, when the ship went past the mightiest of the Sun's children. Would the extra weeks of life be worth it, Pickett asked himself, to see with your own eyes the sight that Galileo had first glimpsed through his crude telescope four centuries ago—the satellites of Jupiter, shuttling back and forth like beads upon an invisible wire?

Beads upon a wire. With that thought, an all-but-forgotten childhood memory exploded out of his subconscious. It must have been there for days, struggling upwards into the light. Now at last it had forced itself upon his waiting mind.

"No!" he cried aloud. "It's ridiculous! They'll laugh at me!"

So what? said the other half of his mind. You've nothing to lose; if it does no more, it will keep everyone busy while the food and the oxygen dwindle away. Even the faintest hope is better than none at all. . . .

He stopped fidgeting with the recorder; the mood of maudlin self-pity was over. Releasing the elastic webbing that held him to his seat, he set off for the Technical Stores in search of the material he needed.

"This," said Dr. Martens three days later, "isn't my idea of a joke." He gave a contemptuous glance at the flimsy structure of wire and wood that Pickett was holding in his hand.

"I guessed you'd say that," Pickett replied, keeping his temper under control. "But please listen to me for a minute. My grandmother was Japanese, and when I was a kid she told me a story that I'd completely forgotten until this week. I think it may save our lives.

"Sometime after the Second World War, there was a contest between an American with an electric desk calculator, and a Japanese using an abacus like this. The abacus won."

"Then it must have been a poor desk machine, or an incompetent operator."

"They used the best in the U.S. Army. But let's stop arguing. Give me a test—say a couple of three-figure numbers to multiply."

"Oh—856 times 437."

Pickett's fingers danced over the beads, sliding them up and down the wires with lightning speed. There were twelve wires in all, so that the abacus could handle numbers up to 999999999-999—or could be divided into separate sections where several independent calculations could be carried out simultaneously.

"374072," said Pickett, after an incredibly brief interval of time, "Now see how long *you* take to do it, with pencil and paper."

There was a much longer delay before Martens, who like most mathematicians was poor at arithmetic, called out "375072." A hasty check soon confirmed that Martens had taken at least three times as long as Pickett to arrive at the wrong answer.

The astronomer's face was a study in mingled chagrin, astonishment and curiosity.

"Where did you learn that trick?" he asked. "I thought those things could only add and subtract?"

"Well—multiplication's only repeated addition, isn't it? All I did was to add 856 seven times in the tens column, and four times in the hundreds column. You do the same thing when you use pencil and paper. Of course, there are some short cuts, but if you think *I'm* fast you should have seen my granduncle. He used to work in a Yokohama bank, and you couldn't see his fingers when he was going at speed. He taught me some of the tricks, but I've forgotten most of them in the last twenty years. I've only been practicing for a couple of days, so I'm still pretty slow. All the same, I hope I've convinced you that there's something in my argument."

"You certainly have: I'm quite impressed. Can you divide just as quickly?"

"Very nearly, when you've had enough experience."

Martens picked up the abacus, and started flicking the beads back and forth. Then he sighed.

"Ingenious—but it doesn't really help us. Even if it's ten times as fast as a man with pencil and paper—which it isn't—the computer was a million times faster."

"I've thought of that," answered Pickett, a little impatiently. (Martens had no guts—he gave up too easily. How did he think astronomers managed a hundred years ago, before there were any computers?)

"This is what I propose—tell me if you can see any flaws in it. . . ."

Carefully and earnestly he detailed his plan. As he did so, Martens slowly relaxed, and presently he gave the first laugh that Pickett had heard aboard *Challenger* for days. •

"I want to see the skipper's face," said the astronomer, "when you tell him that we're all going back to the nursery to start playing with beads."

There was skepticism at first, but it vanished swiftly when Pickett gave a few demonstrations. To men who had grown up in a world of electronics, the fact that a simple structure of wire and beads could perform such apparent miracles was a revelation. It was also a challenge, and because their lives depended upon it they responded eagerly.

As soon as the engineering staff had built enough smoothly operating copies of Pickett's crude prototype, the classes began. It took only a few minutes to explain the basic principles; what required time was practice—hour after hour of it, until the fingers flew automatically across the wires and flicked the beads into the right positions without any need for conscious thought. There were some members of the crew who never acquired both accuracy and speed, even after a week of constant practice: but there were others who quickly outdistanced Pickett himself.

They dreamed counters and columns, and flicked beads in their sleep. As soon as they had passed beyond the elementary stage they were divided into teams which then competed fiercely against each other, until they had reached still higher standards of proficiency. In the end, there were men aboard *Challenger* who could multiply four-figure numbers on the abacus in fifteen seconds, and keep it up hour after hour.

Such work was purely mechanical; it required skill, but no

intelligence. The really difficult job was Martens', and there was little that anyone could do to help him. He had to forget all the machine-based techniques he had taken for granted, and re-arrange his calculations so that they could be carried out automatically by men who had no idea of the meaning of the figures they were manipulating. He would feed them the basic data, and then they would follow the program he had laid down. After a few hours of patient routine work, the answer would emerge from the end of the mathematical production line—provided that no mistakes had been made. And the way to guard against that was to have two independent teams working, cross-checking results regularly.

"What we've done," said Pickett into his recorder, when at last he had time to think of the audience he had never expected to speak to again, "is to build a computer out of human beings instead of electronic circuits. It's a few thousand times slower, can't handle many digits, and gets tired easily—but it's doing the job. Not the whole job of navigating to Earth—that's far too complicated—but the simpler one of giving us an orbit that will bring us back into radio range. Once we've escaped from the electrical interference around us, we can radio our position and the big computers on Earth can tell us what to do next.

"We've already broken away from the comet and are no longer heading out of the Solar System. Our new orbit checks with the calculations, to the accuracy that can be expected. We're still inside the comet's tail, but the nucleus is a million miles away and we won't see those ammonia icebergs again. They're racing on towards the stars into the freezing night between the suns, while we are coming home. . . .

"Hello, Earth . . . hello, Earth This is *Challenger* calling, *Challenger* calling. Signal back as soon as you receive us—we'd like you to check our arithmetic—before we work our fingers to the bone!"

RAINDROP

Hal Clement

I

"It's not very comfortable footing, but at least you can't fall off."

Even through the helmet phones, Silbert's voice carried an edge that Bresnahan felt sure was amused contempt. The younger man saw no point in trying to hide his fear; he was no veteran of space and knew that it would be silly to pretend otherwise.

"My mind admits that, but my stomach isn't so sure," he replied. "It can't decide whether things will be better when I can't see so far, or whether I should just give up and take a running dive back there."

His metal-clad arm gestured toward the station and its comfortable spin hanging half a mile away. Technically the wheel-shaped structure in its synchronous orbit was above the two men, but it took careful observing to decide which way was really "up."

"You wouldn't make it," Silbert replied. "If you had solid footing for a jump you might get that far, since twenty feet a second would take you away from here permanently. But speed and velocity are two different animals. I wouldn't trust even myself to make such a jump in the right direction—and I know the vectors better than you do by a long shot. Which way would you jump? Right at the station? Or ahead of it, or behind it? And which is ahead and which is behind? Do you know?"

"I know which is ahead, since I can see it move against the star background, but I wouldn't know which way to jump. I *think* it should be ahead, since the rotation of this overgrown raindrop gives us less linear speed than the station's orbit; but I wouldn't know how far ahead," Silbert said.

"Good for you." Bresnahan noted what he hoped was approval in the spaceman's tone as well as in his words. "You're right as far as you committed yourself, and I wouldn't dare go any farther myself. In any case, jumping off this stuff is a losing game."

"I can believe that. Just walking on it makes me feel as though I were usurping a Biblical prerogative."

The computerman's arm waved again, this time at the surface underfoot, and he tried to stamp on it at the same moment. The latter gesture produced odd results. The material, which looked a little like clear jelly, gave under the boot but bulged upward all around it. The bulge moved outward very slowly in all directions, the star patterns reflected in the surface writhing as it passed. As the bulge's radius increased, its height lessened, as with a ripple spreading on a pond. It might have been an ultra-slow motion picture of such a ripple, except that it did not travel far enough. It died out less than two yards from Bresnahan's foot, though it took well over a minute to get that far.

"Yeah, I know what you mean. Walking on water was kind of a divine gift, wasn't it? Well, you can always remember we're not right on the water. There's the pressure film, even if you can't see it."

"That's so. Well, let's get on to the lock. Being inside this thing can't be much worse than walking around on its surface, and I have a report to make up." Silbert started walking again at this request, though the jellylike response of the water to his footfalls made the resulting gait rather odd. He kept talking as he led the way.

"How come that friend of yours can't come down from the station and look things over for himself? Why should you have to give the dope to him secondhand? Can't he take weightlessness?"

"Better than I can, I suspect," replied Bresnahan, "but he's not my friend. He's my boss, and pays the bills. Mine not to reason why, mine but to act or fry. He already knows as much as most people do about Raindrop, here. What more he expects to get from me I'm not sure. I just hope that what I can find to tell him makes him happy. I take it this is the lock.''

They had reached a disk of metal some thirty feet in diameter, projecting about two feet from the surface of the satellite. It continued below the surface for a distance which refraction made hard to estimate.

Its water line was marked by a ring of black, rubbery-looking material where the pressure film adhered to it. The men had been quite close to it when they landed on Raindrop's surface a few minutes before, but it is hard to make out landscape details on a water surface under a black, starfilled sky; the reflection underfoot is not very different from the original above. A five-mile radius of curvature puts the reflected images far enough down so that human depth perception is no help.

Waves betrayed themselves, of course, and might have shown the lock's location—but under a gravitational acceleration of about a tenth of an inch per second squared, the surface waves raised by spacesuit boots traveled much more slowly than the men who wore them. And with their high internal energy losses they didn't get far enough to be useful.

As a result, Bresnahan had not realized that the lock was at hand until they were almost upon it. Even Silbert, who had known about where they would land and could orient himself with Raindrop's rotation axis by celestial reference features, did not actually see it until it was only a few yards away.

"This is the place, all right," he acknowledged. "That little plate near the edge is the control panel. We'll use the manhole; no need to open the main hatch as we do when it's a matter of cargo."

He bent over—slowly enough to keep his feet on the metal— and punched one of the buttons on the panel he had pointed out. A tiny light promptly flashed green, and he punched a second button.

A yard-square trap opened inward, revealing the top of a ladder. Silbert seized the highest rung and pulled himself through the opening head first—when a man weighs less than an ounce in full space panoply it makes little real difference when he elects to traverse a ladder head downward. Bresnahan followed and found himself in a cylindrical chamber which took up most of the inside of the lock structure. It could now be seen that this must extend some forty feet into the body of Raindrop.

At the inner end of the compartment, where curved and flat walls met, a smaller chamber was partitioned off. Silbert drove in this direction.

"This is a personnel lock," he remarked. "We'll use it; it saves flooding the whole chamber."

"We can use ordinary spacesuits?"

"Might as well. If we were going to stay long enough for real work, we'd change—there is local equipment in those cabinets along the wall. Spacesuits are safe enough, but pretty clumsy when it comes to fine manipulation."

"For me, they're clumsy for anything at all."

"Well, we can change if you want; but I understood that this was to be a fairly quick visit, and that you were to get a report back pronto. Or did I misread the tone your friend Weisanen was using?"

"I guess you didn't, at that. We'll go as we are. It still sounds queer to go swimming in a spacesuit."

"No queerer than walking on water. Come on, the little lock will hold both of us."

The spaceman opened the door manually—there seemed to be no power controls involved—and the two entered a room some five feet square and seven high. Operation of the lock seemed simple; Silbert closed the door they had just used and turned a latch to secure it, then opened another manual valve on the other side of the chamber. A jet of water squirted in and filled the space in half a minute. Then he simply opened a door in the same wall with the valve, and the spacesuited figures swam out.

This was not as bad as walking on what had seemed like nothingness. Bresnahan was a good swimmer and experienced free diver, and was used to being suspended in a medium where one couldn't see very far.

The water was clear, though not as clear as that sometimes found in Earth's tropical seas. There was no easy way to tell just how far vision could reach, since nothing familiar and of known size was in view except for the lock they had just quitted. There were no fishes—Raindrop's owners were still debating the advisability of establishing them there—and none of the plant life was familiar, at least to Bresnahan. He knew that the big sphere of water had been seeded by "artificial" life forms—algae and bacteria whose genetic patterns had been altered to let them live in a "sea" so different from Earth's.

II

Raindrop was composed of the nuclei of several small comets or rather what was left of those nuclei after some of their mass had been used in reaction motors to put them into orbit about the earth. They had been encased in a polymer film sprayed on to form a pressure seal, and then melted by solar energy, concentrated by giant foil mirrors.

Traces of the original wrapping were still around, but its function had been replaced by one of the first tailored life forms to be established after the mass was liquid. This was a modification of one of the gelatin-capsule algae, which now encased all of Raindrop in a microscopically thin film able to heal itself after small meteoroid punctures, and strong enough to maintain about a quarter of an atmosphere's pressure on the contents. The biological engineer who had done that tailoring job still regarded it as his professional masterpiece.

The methane present in the original comet material had been oxidized by other bacteria to water and carbon dioxide, the oxygen of course coming from normal photosynthesis. A good deal of the ammonia was still present, and furnished the principal reason why genetic tailoring was still necessary on life forms being transplanted to the weightless aquarium.

The men were drifting very slowly away from the lock, though they had stopped swimming, and the younger one asked, "How do we find our way back here if we get out of sight?"

"The best trick is not to get out of sight. Unless you want to examine the core, which I've never done, you'll see everything there is to see right here. There is sonic and magnetic gear—homing equipment—in your suit if you need it, though I haven't checked you out on its use. You'd better stay with me. I can probably show you what's needed. Just what points do you think Weisanen wants covered?"

"Well, he knows the general physical setup—temperature, rotation, general current pattern, the nature of the skin. He knows what's been planted here at various times; but it's hard to keep up to date on what's evolved since. These tailored life forms aren't very stable toward mutation influences, and a new-stocked aquarium isn't a very stable ecological environment. He'll want to know what's here now in the way of usable plants,

I suppose. You know the Agency sold Raindrop to a private concern after the last election. The new owners seem willing to grant the importance of basic research, but they would sort of like a profit to report to the stockholders as well.''

"Amen. I'm a stockholder."

"Oh? Well, it does cost something to keep supply ships coming up here, and—''

"True enough. Then this Weisanen character represents the new owners? I wonder if I should think of him as my boss or my employee."

"I think he is one of them."

"Hmph. No wonder."

"No wonder what?"

"He and his wife are the first people I ever knew to treat a spaceflight like a run in a private yacht. I suppose that someone who could buy Raindrop wouldn't be bothered by a little expense like a private Phoenix rocket.''

"I suppose not. Of course, it isn't as bad as it was in the days of chemical motors, when it took a big commercial concern or a fair-sized government to launch a manned spaceship.''

"Maybe not; but with fourteen billion people living on Earth, it's a little unusual to find a really rich individual, in the old Ford-Carnegie tradition. Most big concerns are owned by several million people like me.''

"Well, I guess Weisanen owns a bigger piece of Raindrop than you do. Anyway, he's my boss, whether he's yours or not, and he wants a report from me, and I can't see much to report on. What life is there in this place besides the stuff forming the surface skin?''

"Oh, lots. You just aren't looking carefully enough. A lot of it is microscopic, of course; there are fairly ordinary varieties of pond-scum drifting all around us. They're the main reason we can see only a couple of hundred yards, and they carry on most of the photosynthesis. There are lots of nonphotosynthetic organisms—bacteria—producing carbon dioxide just as in any balanced ecology on Earth, though this place is a long way from being balanced. Sometimes the algae get so thick you can't see twenty feet, sometimes the bacteria get the upper hand. The balance keeps hunting around even when no new forms are appearing or being introduced. We probably brought a few new bacteria in with us on our suits just now; whether any of them can survive with the ammonia content of Raindrop this high I don't know, but if so the ecology will get another nudge.

"There are lots of larger plants, too—mostly modifications of the big seaweeds of Earth's oceans. The lock behind us is overgrown with them, as you can see—you can look more closely as we go back—and a lot of them grow in contact with the outer skin, where the light is best. Quite a few are free-floating, but of course selection works fast on those. There are slow convection currents, because of Raindrop's size and rotation, which exchange water between the illuminated outer regions and the darkness inside. Free-floating weeds either adapt to long periods of darkness or die out fast. Since there is a good deal of hard radiation near the surface, there is also quite a lot of unplanned mutation over and above the regular gene-tailoring products we are constantly adding to the pot. And since most of the organisms here have short life spans, evolution goes on rapidly."

"Weisanen knows all that perfectly well," replied Bresnahan. "What he seems to want is a snapshot—a report on just what the present spectrum of life forms is like."

"I've summed it up. Anything more detailed would be wrong next week. You can look at the stuff around us—there. Those filaments which just tangled themselves on your equipment clip are a good example, and there are some bigger ones if you want *there*—just in reach. It would take microscopic study to show how they differ from the ones you'd have gotten a week ago or a year ago, but they're different. There will be no spectacular change unless so much growth builds up inside the surface film that the sunlight is cut down seriously. Then the selection factors will change and a radically new batch—probably of scavenger fungi—will develop and spread. It's happened before. We've gone through at least four cycles of that sort in the three years I've worked here."

Bresnahan frowned thoughtfully, though the facial gesture was not very meaningful inside a space helmet.

"I can see where this isn't going to be much of a report," he remarked.

"It would have made more sense if you'd brought a plankton net and some vacuum jars and brought up specimens for him to look over himself," replied Silbert. "Or wouldn't they mean anything to him? Is he a biologist or just a manager?"

"I couldn't say."

"How come? How can you work for him and not know that much?"

"Working for him is something new. I've worked for Raindrop ever since I started working, but I didn't meet Weisanen until three weeks ago. I haven't been with him more than two or three hours' total time since. I haven't talked with him during those hours; I've listened while he told me what to do."

"You mean he's one of those high-handed types? What's your job, anyway?"

"There's nothing tough or unpleasant about him; he's just the boss. I'm a computer specialist—programming and maintenance, or was until he picked me to come up here to Raindrop with him and his wife. What my job here will be, you'll have to get from him. There are computers in the station, I noticed, but nothing calling for full-time work from anyone. Why he picked me I can't guess. I should think, though, that he'd have asked you rather than me to make this report, since whatever I am I'm no biologist."

"Well, neither am I. I just work here."

Bresnahan stared in astonishment.

"Not a biologist? But aren't you in charge of this place? Haven't you been the local director for three years, in charge of planting the new life forms that were sent up, and reporting what happened to them, and how Raindrop was holding together, and all?"

"All is right. I'm the bo's'n tight and the midshipmite and the crew of the captain's gig. I'm the boss because I'm the only one here full-time; but that doesn't make me a biologist. I got this job because I have a decently high zero-gee tolerance and had had experience in space. I was a space-station handyman before I came here."

"Then what sort of flumdiddle is going on? Isn't there a professional anywhere in this organization? I've heard stories of the army using biochemists for painters and bricklayers for clerks, but I never really believed them. Besides, Raindrop doesn't belong to an army—it isn't even a government outfit anymore. It's being run by a private outfit which I assumed was hoping to make a profit out of it. Why in blazes is there no biologist at what has always been supposed to be a biological research station, devoted to finding new ways of making fourteen billion people like what little there is to eat?"

Silbert's shrug was just discernible from outside his suit.

"No one ever confided in me," he replied. "I was given a pretty good briefing on the job when I first took it over, but that didn't include an extension course in biology or biophysics. As far as I can tell they've been satisfied with what I've done. Whatever they wanted out of Raindrop doesn't seem to call for high-caliber professionals on the spot. I inspect to make sure no leaks too big for the algae to handle show up, I plant any new life forms they send up to be established here, and I collect regularly and send back to Earth the samples of what life there is. The last general sampling was nearly a month ago, and another is due in a few days. Maybe your boss could make do with that data—or if you like I can offer to make the regular sampling run right away instead of at the scheduled time. After all, he may be my boss too instead of the other way around, so I should be reporting to him."

Bresnahan thought for a moment.

"All right," he said. "I'm in no position to make either a decent collection or a decent report, as things stand. Let's go back to the station, tell him what's what, and let him decide what he does want. Maybe it's just a case of a new boss not knowing the ropes and trying to find out."

"I'd question that, somehow, but can't think of anything better to do. Come on."

Silbert swam back toward the lock from which they had emerged only a few minutes before. They had drifted far enough from it in that time so that its details had faded to a greenish blur, but there was no trouble locating the big cylinder. The door they had used was still open.

Silbert pulled himself through, lent Bresnahan a hand in doing likewise, closed the portal, and started a small pump. The pressure head was only the quarter atmosphere maintained by the tension of the alga skin, and emptying the chamber of water did not take long. The principal delay was caused by Bresnahan's failure to stand perfectly still; with gravity only a little over one five-thousandths Earth normal, it didn't take much disturbance to slosh some water away from the bottom of the lock where the pump intake was located.

Silbert waited for some of it to settle, but lacked the patience to wait for it all. When he opened the door into the larger lock chamber, the men were accompanied through it by several large globules of boiling liquid.

"Wasteful, but helps a bit," remarked the spaceman as he opened the outside portal and the two were wafted through it by the escaping vapor. "Watch out—hang on there. You don't have escape velocity, but you'd be quite a while getting back to the surface if you let yourself blow away." He seized a convenient limb of Bresnahan's space armor as the younger man drifted by, and since he was well anchored himself to the top rung of the ladder was able to arrest the other's flight. Carefully they stepped away from the hatch, Silbert touching the closing button with one toe as he passed it, and looked for the orbiting station.

This, of course, was directly overhead. The same temptation which Bresnahan had felt earlier to make a jump for it came back with some force; but Silbert had a safer technique.

He took a small tube equipped with peep-sights from the equipment clip at his side and aimed it very carefully at the projecting hub of the wheel-shaped station—the only part of the hub visible, since the station's equator was parallel to that of Raindrop and the structure was therefore edge-on to them. A bright yellow glow from the target produced a grunt of satisfaction from Silbert, and he fingered a button on the tube. The laser beam, invisible in the surrounding vacuum, flicked on and off in a precisely timed signal pattern which was reported faithfully by the source-return mirror at the target. Another response was almost as quick.

III

A faintly glowing object emerged from the hub and drifted rapidly toward Raindrop, though not quite toward the men. Its details were not clear at first, but as it approached it began to look more and more like a luminous cobweb.

"Just a lattice of thin rods, doped with luminous paint for spotting and launched from the station by a spring gun," explained Silbert. "The line connecting it with the station isn't painted, and is just long enough to stop the grid about fifty feet from the water. It's launched with a small backward component relative to the station's orbit, and when the line stops it it will drift toward us. Jump for it when I give the word; you can't miss."

Bresnahan was not as certain about the last statement as his companion seemed to be, but braced himself anyway. As the glowing spiderweb approached, however, he saw it was over a hundred feet across and realized that even he could jump straight enough to make contact. When Silbert gave the word, he sprang without hesitation.

He had the usual moment of nausea and disorientation as he crossed the few yards to his target. Lacking experience, he had not "balanced" his jump perfectly and as a result made a couple of somersaults en route. This caused him to lose track of his visual reference points, and with gravity already lacking he suffered the moment of near-panic which so many student pilots had experienced before him. Contact with one of the thin rods restored him, however; he gripped it frantically and was himself again.

Silbert arrived a split second later and took charge of the remaining maneuvers. These consisted of collapsing the "spiderweb"—a matter of half a minute, in spite of its apparent complexity, because of the ingenuity of its jointing—and then starting his companion hand-over-hand along the nearly invisible cord leading back to the station. The climb called for more coordination than was at first evident; the spaceman had to catch his less experienced companion twice as the latter missed his grip for the line.

Had Silbert been going first the situation might have been serious. As it was, an extra tug on the rope enabled him to catch up each time with the helpless victim of basic physics. After the second accident, the guide spoke.

"All right, don't climb anymore. We're going a little too fast as it is. Just hold on to the rope now and to me when I give the word. The closing maneuver is a bit tricky, and it wouldn't be practical to try to teach you the tricks on the spot and first time around."

Silbert did have quite a problem. The initial velocities of the two men in their jumps for the spiderweb had not, of course, been the correct ones to intercept the station—if it had been practical to count on their being so, the web would have been superfluous. The web's own mass was less than fifty pounds, which had not done much to the sum of those vectors as it absorbed its share of the men's momentum. Consequently, the men had an angular velocity with respect to the station, and they were *approaching* the latter.

* * *

To a seventeenth-century mathematician, conversation of angular momentum may have been an abstract concept, but to Silbert it was an item of very real, practical, everyday experience—just as the orbit of a comet is little more than a set of numbers to an astronomer while the orbit of a baseball is something quite different to an outfielder. The problem this time was even worse than usual, partly because of Bresnahan's mass and still more because of his inexperience.

As the two approached the station their sidewise motion became evident even to Bresnahan. He judged that they would strike near the rim of the spinning structure, if they hit it at all, but Silbert had other ideas.

Changing the direction of the spin axis by landing at the hub was one thing—a very minor one. Changing the *rate* of spin by meeting the edge could be a major nuisance, since much of the apparatus inside was built on and for Earth and had Earth's gravity taken for granted in its operation. Silbert therefore had no intention of making contact anywhere but at one of the "poles" of the station. He was rather in the situation of a yo-yo whose string is winding up on the operator's finger; but he could exercise a little control by climbing as rapidly as possible "up" the cord toward the structure or allowing himself to slide "down" away from it.

He had had plenty of experience, but he was several minutes playing them into a final collision with the entry valve, so close to the center of mass of the station that the impact could produce only a tiny precession effect. Most of its result was a change in the wheel's orbit about Raindrop, and the whole maneuver had taken such a small fraction of an orbital period that this effect nearly offset that produced when they had started up the rope.

"Every so often," remarked the spaceman as he opened the air lock, "we have to make a small correction in the station orbit; the disturbances set up by entering and leaving get it out of step with Raindrop's rotation. Sometimes I wonder whether it's worth the trouble to keep the two synchronized."

"If the station drifted very far from the lock below, you'd have to jump from the liquid surface, which might be awkward," pointed out the younger man as the closing hatch cut off the starlight.

"That's true," admitted the other as he snapped a switch and air started hissing into the small lock chamber. "I suppose there's something to be said for tradition at that. There's the safety light''—as a green spot suddenly glowed on the wall—''so you can open up your suit whenever you like. Lockers are in the next room. But you arrived through this lock, didn't you?''

"Right. I know my way from here.''

Five minutes later the two men, divested of space suits, had "descended'' to the rim of the station where weight was normal. Most of this part of the structure was devoted to living space which had never been used, though there were laboratory and communication rooms as well. The living space had explained to Bresnahan, when he first saw it, why Silbert was willing to spend three quarters of his time alone at a rather boring job a hundred thousand miles from the nearest company. Earth was badly crowded; not one man in a million had either as much space or as much privacy.

Weisanen and his wife had taken over a set of equally sumptuous rooms on the opposite side of the rim, and had been in the process of setting up housekeeping when the two employees had descended to Raindrop's surface a short time before. This had been less than an hour after their arrival with Bresnahan on the shuttle from Earth; Weisanen had wasted no time in issuing his first orders. The two men were prepared to find every sign of disorder when the door to the "headquarters'' section opened in response to Silbert's touch on the annunciator, but they had reckoned without Mrs. Weisanen.

At their employer's invitation, they entered a room which might have been lived in for a year instead of an hour. The furniture was good, comfortable, well arranged, and present in quantity which would have meant a visible bulge in a nation's space research budget just for the fuel to lift it away from the earth in the chemical fuel days.

Either the Weisanens felt strongly about maintaining the home atmosphere even when visiting, or they planned to stay on the station for quite a while.

The official himself was surprisingly young, according to both Bresnahan's and Silbert's preconceived notions of a magnate. He could hardly have been thirty, and might have been five years younger. He matched Bresnahan's five feet ten of height and looked about the same weight; but while the computerman regarded himself as being in good physical shape, he had to admit the other was far more muscular. Even Silbert's six feet five of

height and far from insignificant frame seemed somehow inade-
quate beside Weisanen's.

"Come in, gentlemen. We felt your return a few minutes ago!
I take it you have something to report, Mr. Bresnahan. We did
not expect you back quite so soon." Weisanen drew further back
from the door and waved the others past him. "What can you
tell us?" He closed the door and indicated armchairs. Bresnahan
remained on his feet, uneasy at the incompleteness of his report;
Silbert sank into the nearest chair. The official also remained
standing. "Well, Mr. Bresnahan?"

"I have little—practically nothing—to report, as far as detailed, quantitative information is concerned," the computerman
took the plunge.

"We stayed inside the Raindrop only a few minutes, and it
was evident that most of the detailed search for life specimens
would have to be made with a microscope. I hadn't planned the
trip at all effectively. I now understand that there is plankton-
collecting apparatus here which Mr. Silbert uses regularly and
which should have been taken along if I were to get anything
worth showing to you."

Weisanen's face showed no change in its expression of courteous interest. "That is quite all right," he said. "I should have
made clear that I wanted, not a detailed biological report, but a
physical description by a nonspecialist of what it is like subjec-
tively down there. I should imagine that you received an adequate impression even during your short stay. Can you give such
a description?"

Bresnahan's worried expression disappeared, and he nodded
affirmatively.

"Yes, sir. I'm not a literary expert, but I can tell what I saw."

"Good. One moment, please," Weisanen turned toward another door and raised his voice. "Brenda, will you come in here,
please? You should hear this."

Silbert got to his feet just as the woman entered, and both men
acknowledged her greeting.

Brenda Weisanen was a full head shorter than her husband.
She was wearing a robe of the sort which might have been seen
on any housewife expecting company; neither man was compe-
tent to guess whether it was worth fifty dollars or ten times that.
The garment tended to focus attention on her face, which would
have received it anyway. Her hair and eyebrows were jet black,
the eyes themselves gray, and rounded cheeks and chin made the

features look almost childish, though she was actually little younger than her husband. She seated herself promptly, saying no more than convention demanded, and the men followed suit.

"Please go on, Mr. Bresnahan," Weisanen said. " My wife and I are both greatly interested, for reasons which will be clear shortly."

Bresnahan had a good visual memory, and it was easy for him to comply. He gave a good verbal picture of the greenish, sunlit haze that had surrounded him—sunlight differing from that seen under an Earthly lake, which ripples and dances as the waves above refract it. He spoke of the silence, which had moved him to keep talking because it was the "quietest" silence he had known, and "didn't sound right."

He was interrupted by Silbert at this point; the spaceman explained that Raindrop was not always that quiet. Even a grain-of-dust meteoroid striking the skin set up a shock wave audible throughout the great sphere; and if one was close enough to the site of collision, the hiss of water boiling out through the hole for the minute or two needed for the skin to heal could also be heard. It was rather unusual to be able to spend even the short time they had just had inside the satellite without hearing either of these sounds.

Bresnahan nodded thanks as the other fell silent, and took up the thread of his own description once more. He closed with the only real feature he had seen to describe—the weed-grown cylinder of the water-to-space lock, hanging in greenish emptiness above the dead-black void which reached down to Raindrop's core. He was almost poetical in spots.

The Weisanens listened in flattering silence until he had done, and remained silent for some seconds thereafter. Then the man spoke.

"Thank you, Mr. Bresnahan. That was just what we wanted." He turned to his wife. "How does that sound to you, dear?"

The dark head nodded slowly, its gray eyes fastened on some point far beyond the metal walls.

"It's fascinating," she said slowly. "Not just the way we pictured it, of course, and there will be changes anyway, but certainly worth seeing. Of course they didn't go down to the core, and wouldn't have seen much if they had. I suppose there is no life, and certainly no natural light, down there."

"There is life," replied Silbert. "Nonphotosynthetic, of course, but bacteria and larger fungi which live on organic matter swept there from the sunlit parts. I don't know whether anything is actually growing *on* the core, since I've never gone in that far, but free-floating varieties get carried up to my nets. A good many of those have gone to Earth, along with their descriptions, in my regular reports."

"I know. I've read those reports very carefully, Mr. Silbert," replied Weisanen.

"Just the same, one of our first jobs must be to survey that core," his wife said thoughtfully. "Much of what has to be done will depend on conditions down there."

"Right." Her husband stood up. "We thank you gentlemen for your word pictures; they have helped a lot. I'm not yet sure of the relation between your station time and that of the Terrestrial time zones, but I have the impression that it's quite late in the working day. Tomorrow we will all visit Raindrop and make a very thorough and more technical examination—my wife and I doing the work, Mr. Bresnahan assisting us, and Mr. Silbert guiding. Until then—it has been a pleasure, gentlemen."

Bresnahan took the hint and got to his feet, but Silbert hesitated. There was a troubled expression on his face, but he seemed unable or unwilling to speak. Weisanen noticed it.

"What's the matter, Mr. Silbert? Is there some reason why Raindrop's owners, or their representatives, shouldn't look it over closely? I realize that you are virtually the only person to visit it in the last three years, but I assure you that your job is in no danger."

Silbert's face cleared a trifle.

"It isn't that," he said slowly. "I know you're the boss, and I wasn't worried about my job anyway. There's just one point—of course you may know all about it, but I'd rather be safe, and embarrassed, than responsible for something unfortunate later on. I don't mean to butt into anyone's private business, but Raindrop is essentially weightless."

"I know that."

"Do you also know that unless you are quite certain that Mrs. Weisanen is not pregnant, she should not expose herself to weightlessness for more than a few minutes at a time?"

Both Weisanens smiled.

"We know, thank you, Mr. Silbert. We will see you tomorrow, in spacesuits, at the big cargo lock. There is much equipment to be taken down to Raindrop."

IV

That closing remark proved to be no exaggeration.

As the four began moving articles through the lock the next morning, Silbert decided at first that the Weisanen's furniture had been a very minor item in the load brought up from Earth the day before, and wondered why it had been brought into the station at all if it was to be transferred to Raindrop so soon. Then he began to realize that most of the material he was moving had been around much longer. It had come up bit by bit on the regular supply shuttle over a period of several months. Evidently whatever was going on represented long and careful planning—and furthermore, whatever was going on represented a major change from the origin᷐ plans for Raindrop.

This worried him, since Silbert had become firmly attached to the notion that the Raindrop plan was an essential step to keeping the human race fed, and he had as good an appetite as anyone.

He knew, as did any reasonably objective and well-read adult, how barely the advent of fusion power and gene tailoring had bypassed the first critical point in the human population explosion, by making it literally possible to use the entire surface of the planet either for living space or the production of food. As might have been expected, mankind had expanded to fill even that fairly generous limit in a few generations.

A second critical point was now coming up, obviously enough to those willing to face the fact. Most of Earth's fourteen billion people lived on floating islands of gene-tailored vegetation scattered over the planet's seas, and the number of these islands was reaching the point where the total sunlight reaching the surface was low enough to threaten collapse of the entire food chain. Theoretically, fusion power was adequate to provide synthetic food for all; but it had been learned the hard way that man's selfishness could be raised to the violence point almost as easily by a threat to his "right" to eat natural—and tasty—food as by a threat to his "right" to reproduce without limit. As a matter of fact, the people whom Silbert regarded as more civilized tended to react more strongly to the first danger.

Raindrop had been the proposed answer. As soon as useful, edible life forms could be tailored to live in its environment it was to be broken up into a million or so smaller units which could receive sunlight throughout their bulks, and use these as "farms."

But power units, lights, and what looked like prefabricated living quarters sufficient for many families did not fit with the idea of breaking Raindrop up. In fact, they did not fit with any sensible idea at all.

No one could live on Raindrop, or in it, permanently; there was not enough weight to keep human metabolism balanced. Silbert was very conscious of that factor. He never spent more than a day at a time on his sampling trips, and after each of these he always remained in the normal-weight part of the station for the full number of days specified on the AGT tables.

It was all very puzzling.

And as the day wore on, and more and more material was taken from the low-weight storage section of the station and netted together for the trip to Raindrop, the spaceman grew more puzzled still. He said nothing, however, since he didn't feel quite ready to question the Weisanens on the subject and it was impossible to speak privately to Bresnahan with all the spacesuit radios on the same frequency.

All the items moved were, of course, marked with their masses, but Silbert made no great effort to keep track of the total tonnage. It was not necessary, since each cargo net was loaded as nearly as possible to an even one thousand pounds and it was easy enough to count the nets when the job was done. There were twenty-two nets.

A more ticklish task was installing on each bundle a five-hundred-pound-second solid-fuel thrust cartridge, which had to be set so that its axis pointed reasonably close to the center of mass of the loaded net and firmly enough fastened to maintain its orientation during firing. It was not advisable to get rid of the orbital speed of the loads by "pushing off" from the station; the latter's orbit would have been too greatly altered by absorbing the momentum of eleven tons of material. The rockets had to be used.

Silbert, in loading the nets, had made sure that each was spinning slowly on an axis parallel to that of Raindrop. He had also attached each cartridge at the "equator" of its net. As a result, when the time came to fire it was only necessary to wait beside each load until its rocket was pointing "forward" along the station's orbit, and touch off the fuel.

The resulting velocity change did not, in general, exactly offset the orbital speed, but it came close enough for the purpose. The new orbit of each bundle now intersected the surface of Raindrop—a target which was, after all, ten miles in diameter and only half a mile away. It made no great difference if the luggage was scattered along sixty degrees of the satellite's equatorial zone; moving the bundles to the lock by hand would be no great problem where each one weighed about three and a half ounces.

With the last net drifting toward the glistening surface of Raindrop, Weisanen turned to the spaceman.

"What's the best technique to send us after them? Just jump off?"

Silbert frowned, though the expression was not obvious through his face plate.

"The best technique, according to the AGT Safety Tables, is to go back to the rim of the station and spend a couple of days getting our personal chemistry back in balance. We've been weightless for nearly ten hours, with only one short break when we ate."

Weisanen made a gesture of impatience which was much more visible than Silbert's frown.

"Nonsense!" he exclaimed. "People have remained weightless for a couple of weeks at a time without permanent damage."

"Without having their bones actually turn to rubber, I grant. I don't concede there was no more subtle damage done. I'm no biophysicist, I just believe the tables; they were worked out on the basis of knowledge gained the hard way. I admit they have a big safety factor, and if you consider it really necessary I won't object to staying out for four or five days. But you haven't given us any idea so far why this should be considered an emergency situation."

"Hmmm. So I haven't. All right, will you stay out long enough to show Brenda and me how to work the locks below, so we can get the stuff inside?"

"Why—of course—if it's that important we'll stay and do the work too. But I didn't—"

Silbert fell silent as it dawned on him that Weisanen's choice of words meant that he had no intention of explaining just yet what the "emergency" was. Both newcomers must have read the spaceman's mind quite accurately at that point, since even Bresnahan was able to, but neither of them said anything.

Conversation for the next few minutes consisted entirely of Silbert's instructions for shoving off in the proper direction to reach Raindrop, and how to walk on its not-quite-zero-gravity, jellylike surface after they reached it. The trip itself was made without incident.

Because fast movement on the surface was impossible, several hours were spent collecting the scattered bundles and stacking them by the lock. The material could not be placed inside, as most of it had to be assembled before it could go underwater; so for the moment the lesson in lock management was postponed. Weisanen, after some hesitation, agreed to Silbert's second request that they return to the station for food and rest. He and his wife watched with interest the technique of getting back to it.

With four people instead of two, the velocity-matching problem might have been worse, but this turned out not to be the case. Silbert wondered whether it were strictly luck, or whether the Weisanens actually had the skill to plan their jumps properly. He was beginning to suspect that both of them had had previous space experience, and both were certainly well-coordinated physical specimens.

According to the tables which had been guiding Silbert's life, the party should have remained in the high-weight part of the station for at least eighty hours after their session of zero-gee, but his life was now being run by Weisanen rather than the tables. The group was back on the water twelve hours after leaving it.

Bresnahan still had his feeling of discomfort, with star-studded emptiness on one side and its reflection on the other, but he was given little time to brood about it.

The first material to go into the lock consisted of half a dozen yard-wide plastic bubbles of water. Silbert noted with interest that all contained animal life, ranging from barely visible crustacea to herring-sized fish.

"So we're starting animal life here at last," remarked the spaceman. "I thought it was a major bone of contention whether we ever would."

"The question was settled at the first meeting of the new board," replied Weisanen. "Life forms able to live here—or presumably able to live here—have been ready for several years. Please be careful in putting those in the lock—just the odd-numbered ones first, please, first. The evens contain predators, and the others should be given a few hours to scatter before they are turned loose.''

"Right. Any special techniques for opening? Or just get the bubbles through the second lock and cut them open?''

"That will do. I assume that a few hours in the currents inside, plus their own swimming abilities, will scatter them through a good part of the drop.''

"It should. I suppose they'll tend to stay pretty close to the skin because of the light; I trust they can take a certain amount of hard radiation.''

"That matter has been considered. There will be some loss, damage, and genetic change, of course, but we think the cultures will gain in spite of that. If they change, it is no great matter. We expect rapid evolution in an environment like this, of course. It's certainly been happening so far.''

Bresnahan helped push the proper spheres into the lock at the vacuum end and out of it at the other, and watched with interest as each was punctured with a knife and squeezed to expel the contents.

"I should have asked about waiting for temperatures to match,'' remarked Silbert as the cloud of barely visible, jerkily moving specks spread from the last of the containers, "but it doesn't seem to be bothering them.''

"The containers were lying on Raindrop's surface all night, and the satellite is in radiative equilibrium,'' pointed out Bresnahan. "The temperatures shouldn't be very different anyway. Let's get back outside and see what's going on next. Either these water-bugs are all right, or they're beyond our help.''

"Right.'' Silbert followed the suggestion, and the newly released animals were left to their own devices.

Outside, another job was under way. The largest single items of cargo had been a set of curved segments of metal, apparently blue-anodized aluminum. In the few minutes that Silbert and Bresnahan had been inside, the Weisanens had sorted these out from the rest of the material and were now fitting them together.

Each section attached to its neighbor by a set of positive-acting snap fasteners which could be set almost instantly, and within a very few minutes it became evident that they formed a sphere some twenty feet in diameter. A transparent dome of smaller radius was set in one pole, and a cylindrical structure with trap doors in the flat ends marked the other. With the assembly complete, the Weisanens carefully sprayed everything, inside and out, from cylinders which Silbert recognized as containing one of the standard fluorocarbon polymers used for sealing unfindable leaks in spaceships.

Then both Weisanens went inside.

Either the metallic appearance of the sphere was deceptive or there were antennae concealed in its structure, because orders came through the wall on the suit-radio frequency without noticeable loss. In response to these, Bresnahan and the spaceman began handing the rest of the equipment in through the cylindrical structure, which had now revealed itself as a minute air lock. As each item was received it was snapped down on a spot evidently prepared to receive it, and in less than two hours almost all the loose gear had vanished from the vicinity of Raindrop's entry lock. The little that was left also found a home as Weisanen emerged once more and fastened it to racks on the sphere's outer surface, clustered around the air lock.

The official went back inside, and, at his orders, Silbert and the computerman lifted the whole sphere onto the top of the cylindrical cargo lock of the satellite. Either could have handled the three-pound weight alone, but its shape and size made it awkward to handle and both men felt that it would be inadvisable to roll it.

"Good. Now open this big hatch and let us settle into the lock chamber." directed Weisanen. "Then close up, and let in the water."

It was the first time Silbert had caught his boss in a slip, and he was disproportionately pleased. The hatch opened outward, and it was necessary to lift the sphere off again before the order could be obeyed.

Once it was open, the two men had no trouble tossing the big globe into the yawning, nearly dark hole—the sun was just rising locally and did not shine into the chamber—but they had to wait over a minute for Raindrop's feeble gravity to drag the machine entirely inside. They could not push it any faster, because it was not possible to get a good grip on sphere and lock edge simultaneously; and pushing down on the sphere without good anchorage would have done much more to the pusher than to the sphere.

However, it was finally possible to close the big trap. After making sure that it was tightly latched—it was seldom used, and

Silbert did not trust its mechanism unreservedly—he and Bresnahan entered the lock through the smaller portal.

"Aren't there special suits for use inside Raindrop, a lot more comfortable than this space armor?" asked Weisanen.

"Yes, sir," replied the spaceman, "though the relative comfort is a matter of opinion. There are only three, and two of them haven't been used since I came. They'll need a careful checkout."

"All right. Bring them in here, and then let the water into this lock." Silbert found the suits and handed them to Bresnahan to carry out the first part of the order, while he went to the controls to execute the second.

"All ready?" he asked.

"All set. Both lock doors here are shut, and the three of us are inside. Let the flood descend."

"Wrong verb," muttered Silbert to himself.

He very cautiously cracked the main inner hatch; opening it would have been asking for disaster. Even at a mere quarter atmosphere's pressure the wall of water would have slammed into the evacuated lock violently enough to tear the outer portal away and eject sphere and occupants at a speed well above Raindrop's escape value. There was a small Phoenix rocket in the station for emergency use, but Silbert had no wish to create a genuine excuse for using it. Also, since he was in the lock himself, he would probably be in no condition to get or pilot it.

V

The water sprayed in violently enough through the narrow opening he permitted, bouncing the sphere against the outer hatch and making a deafening clamor even for the spacesuited trio inside. However, nothing gave way, and in a minute it was safe to open the main hatch completely.

Silbert did so. Through the clear dome which formed the sphere's only observation window he could see Weisanen fingering controls inside. Water jets from almost invisible ports in the outer surface came into action, and for the first time it became evident that the sphere was actually a vehicle. It was certainly not built for speed, but showed signs of being one of the most maneuverable ever built.

After watching for a moment as it worked its way out of the lock, Silbert decided that Weisanen had had little chance to practice handling it. But no catastrophe occurred, and finally the globe was hanging in the greenish void outside the weed-grown bulk of the lock. The spaceman closed the big hatch, emerged through the personnel lock himself, and swam over to the vehicle's entrance.

The outer door of the tiny air lock opened manually. Thirty seconds later he was inside the rather crowded sphere removing his helmet—some time during the last few minutes Weisanen had filled the vehicle with air.

The others had already unhelmeted and were examining the "diving" suits which Bresnahan had brought inside. These were simple enough affairs; plastic form-fitting coveralls with an air-cycler on the chest and an outsized, transparent helmet which permitted far more freedom of head movement than most similar gear. Since there was no buoyance in this virtually weight-free environment, the helmet's volume did not create the problem it would have on Earth. Silbert was able to explain everything necessary about the equipment in a minute or two.

Neither of the Weisanens needed to have any point repeated, and if Bresnahan was unsure about anything he failed to admit it.

"All right." Raindrop's owner nodded briskly as the lesson ended. "We seem to be ready. I started us down as soon as Mr. Silbert came aboard, but it will take the best part of an hour to reach the core. When we get there a regular ecological sampling run will be made. You can do that, Mr. Silbert, using your regular equipment and techniques; the former is aboard, whether you noticed it being loaded or not. Brenda and I will make a physical, and physiographical, examination of the core itself, with a view to finding just what will have to be done to set up living quarters there and where will be the best place to build them."

Silbert's reaction to this remark may have been expected; both Weisanens had been watching him with slight smiles on their faces. He did not disappoint them.

"*Living* quarters? That's ridiculous! There's no weight to speak of even at Raindrop's surface, and even less at the core. A person would lose the calcium from his skeleton in a few weeks, and go unbalanced in I don't know how many other chemical ways—"

"Fourteen known so far, Mr. Silbert. We know all about that, or as much as anyone does. It was a shame to tease you, but my husband and I couldn't resist. Also, some of the factors involved are not yet public knowledge, and we have reasons for not wanting them too widely circulated for a while yet." Brenda Weisanen's interruption was saved from rudeness by the smile on her face. "I would invite you to sit down to listen, but sitting means nothing here—I'll get used to that eventually, no doubt.

"The fact you just mentioned about people leaching calcium out of their skeletons after a few days or weeks of weightlessness was learned long ago—even before long manned spaceflights had been made; the information was gained from flotation experiments. Strictly speaking, it is not an effect of weightlessness *per se*, but a feedback phenomenon involving relative muscular effort—something which might have been predicted, and for all I know may actually have been predicted, from the fact that the ankle bones in a growing child ossify much more rapidly than the wrist bones. A very minor genetic factor is involved; after all, animals as similar to us as dolphins which *do* spend all their time afloat grow perfectly adequate skeletons.

"A much more subtle set of chemical problems were noticed the hard way when manned space stations were set up, as you well know. A lot of work was done on these, as you might expect, and we now are quite sure that all which will produce detectable results in less than five years of continuous weightlessness are known. There are fourteen specific factors—chemical and genetic keys to the log jam, if you like to think of it that way.

"You have the ordinary educated adult's knowledge of gene tailoring, Mr. Silbert. What was the logical thing to do?"

"Since gene tailoring on human beings is flagrantly illegal, for good and sufficient reasons, the logical thing to do was and is to avoid weightlessness," Silbert replied. "With Phoenix rockets, we can make interplanetary flight at a continuous one-gravity acceleration, while space stations can be and are centrifuged."

Brenda Weisanen's smile did not change, but her husband looked annoyed. He took up the discussion.

"Illegal or not, for good or bad reasons, it was perfectly reasonable to consider modifying human genetic patterns so that some people at least could live and work normally and indefinitely in a weightless environment. Whether it shocks you or not, the thing was tried over seventy years ago, and over five hundred people now alive have this modification—and are not, as I suppose you would put it, fully human.''

Bresnahan interrupted. "I would *not* put it that way!" he snapped. "As anyone who has taken work in permutation and combination knows perfectly well, there is no such thing as a fully human being if you define the term relative to some precise, specific idealized gene pattern. Mutations are occurring all the time from radiation, thermal effects, and just plain quantum jumping of protons in the genetic molecules. The sort of phenomenon is used as example material in elementary programming courses, and one of the first things you learn when you run such a problem is that no one is completely without such modifications. If, as I suppose you are about to say, you and Mrs. Weisanen are genetically different enough to take weightlessness, I can't see why it makes you less human. I happen to be immune to four varieties of leukemia virus and sixteen of the organisms usually responsible for the common cold, according to one analysis of my own gene pattern. If Bert's had ever been checked we'd find at least as many peculiarities about his—and I refuse to admit that either of us is less human than anyone else we've ever met.''

"Thank you, Mr. Bresnahan," Brenda Weisanen took up the thread of the discussion once more. "The usual prejudice against people who are known to be significantly different tends to make some of us a little self-conscious. In any case, my husband and I can stand weightlessness indefinitely, as far as it is now possible to tell, and we plan to stay here permanently. More of us will be coming up later for the same purpose.''

"But why? Not that it's any of my business. I like Raindrop, but it's not the most stimulating environment and in any case I'm known to be the sort of oddball who prefers being alone with a collection of books to most other activities.''

The woman glanced at her husband before answering. He shrugged.

"You have already touched on the point, Mr. Silbert. Modifying the human genetic pattern involves the same complication which plagued medicine when hormones became available for use in treatment. Any one action is likely to produce several others as an unplanned, and commonly unwanted, by-product. Our own modification is not without its disadvantages. What our various defects may be I would not presume to list in toto—any more than Mr. Bresnahan would care to list his—but one of them strikes very close to home just now. Aino and I are expecting a child, and about nine times out of ten when a woman of our type remains in normal gravity any child she conceives is lost during the fifth or sixth month. The precise cause is not known; it involves the mother's physique rather than the child's, but that leaves a lot still to be learned. Therefore, I am staying here until my baby is born, at the very least. We expect to live here. We did not ask to be modified to fit space, but if it turns out that we can live better here—so be it."

"Then Raindrop is going to be turned into a—a—maternity hospital?"

"I think a fairer term would be 'colony,' Mr. Silbert," interjected Weisanen. "There are a good many of us, and most if not all of us are considering making this place our permanent home."

"Which means that breaking it up according to the original plan to supply farming volume is no longer on the books."

"Precisely."

"How do you expect to get away with that? This whole project was planned and paid for as a new source of food."

"That was when it was a government project. As you know, it became a private concern recently; the government was paid full value for Raindrop, the station, and the shuttle which keeps it supplied. As of course you do not know, over eighty percent of the stock of that corporation is owned by people like myself. What we propose to do is perfectly legal, however unpopular it may make us with a few people."

"More than a few, I would say. And how can you afford to be really unpopular, living in something as fragile as Raindrop?" queried Bresnahan. "There are lots of spaceships available. Even if no official action were or could be taken, anyone who happened to have access to one and disliked you sufficiently could wreck the skin of this tank so thoroughly in five minutes that you'd have to start all over again even if you yourselves lived through it. All the life you'd established would freeze before repairs could be made complete enough to stop the water from boiling away."

"That is true, and is a problem we haven't entirely solved," admitted the other. "Of course, the nasty laws against the publication of possible mob-rousing statements which were found necessary as Earth's population grew should operate to help us. Nowadays many people react so negatively to any unsupported statement that the word would have trouble getting around. In any case, we don't intend to broadcast the details and comparatively few people know much about the Raindrop project at all. I don't think that many will feel cheated.''

Silbert's reaction to the last sentence was the urge to cry out, "But they *are* being cheated!" However, it was beginning to dawn on him that he was not in the best possible position to argue with Weisanen.

He subsided. He himself had been living with the Raindrop project for three years, had become closely identified with it, and the change of policy bothered him for deeper reasons than his intelligence alone could recognize.

Bresnahan was also bothered, though he was not as deeply in love with the project as the spaceman. He was less impressed by Weisanen's conviction that there would be no trouble; but he had nothing useful to say about the matter. He was developing ideas, but they ran along the line of wondering when he could get to a computer keyboard to set the whole situation up as a problem. His background and training had left him with some doubt of any human being's ability—including his own—to handle all facets of a complex problem.

Neither of the Weisanens seemed to have any more to say, either, so the sphere drifted downward in silence.

VI

They had quickly passed the limit which sunlight could reach, and were surrounded by blackness, which the sphere's own interior lights seemed only to accentuate.

With neither gravity nor outside reference points, the sphere was of course being navigated by instrument. Sonar equipment kept the pilot informed of the distance to the nearest point of the skin, the distance and direction of the lock through which they had entered, and the distance and direction of the core. Interpretation of the echoes was complicated by the fact that Raindrop's outer skin was so sharply curved, but Weisanen seemed to have that problem well in hand as he drove the vehicle downward.

Pressure, of course, did not change significantly with depth.

The thirty percent increase from skin to core meant nothing to healthy people. There was not even an instrument to register this factor, as far as Silbert could see. He was not too happy about that; his spaceman's prejudices made him feel that there should be independent instrumentation to back up the sonar gear.

As they neared the core, however, instruments proved less necessary than expected.

To the mild surprise of the Weisanens and the blank astonishment of Silbert—Bresnahan knew too little to expect anything, either way—the central region of the satellite was not completely dark. The light was so faint that it would not have been noticed if they had not been turning off the sphere's lamps every few minutes, but it was quite bright enough to be seen, when they were a hundred yards or so from the core, without waiting for eyes to become dark-adapted.

"None of your samples ever included luminous bacteria," remarked the official. "I wonder why none of them ever got close enough to the skin for you to pick up."

"I certainly don't know," replied Silbert. "Are you sure it's caused by bacteria?"

"Not exactly by a long shot; it just seems the best starting guess. I'm certain it's not heat or radioactivity, and offhand I can't think of any other possibilities. Can you?"

"No, I can't. But maybe whatever is producing the light is attached to the core—growing on it, if it's alive. So it wouldn't have reached the surface."

"That's possible, though I hope you didn't think I was criticizing your sampling techniques. It was one of my friends who planned them, not you. We'll go on down; we're almost in contact with the core now, according to the fathometer."

Weisanen left the lights off, except for the tiny fluorescent sparks on the controls themselves, so the other three crowded against the bulge of the viewing port to see what was coming. Weightlessness made this easier than it might have been; they didn't have to "stand" at the same spot to have their heads close together.

For a minute or so, nothing was perceptible in the way of motion. There was just the clear, faintly luminous water outside the port. Then a set of slender, tentacular filaments as big around as a human thumb seemed to writhe past the port as the sphere sank by them; and the eyes which followed their length could suddenly see their point of attachment.

"There!" muttered Brenda Weisanen softly. "Slowly, dear—only a few yards."

"There's no other way this thing can travel," pointed out her husband. "Don't worry about our hitting anything too hard."

"I'm not—but look! It's beautiful! Let's get anchored and go outside."

"In good time. It will stay there, and anyway I'm going out before you do—long enough before to, at least, make reasonably certain it's safe."

The wife looked for a moment as though she were about to argue this point, if her facial expression could be read accurately in the faint light, but she said nothing. Bresnahan and Silbert had the intelligence to keep quiet as well; more could be learned by looking than by getting into the middle of a husband-wife disagreement, and now there plenty to look at.

The core was visible for at least two hundred yards in all directions, as the sphere spun slowly under Weisanen's control. The light definitely came from the life forms which matted its surface.

Presumably these were fungi, since photosynthetic forms could hardly have grown in such an environment, but they were fungi which bore little resemblance to their Terrestrial ancestors. Some were ribbonlike, some featherlike, some snaky—even patches of what looked like smoothly mown lawn were visible. The greenish light was evidently not pure color, since other shades were visible; red, purple, and yellow forms stood out here and there in eye-catching contrast to grays and browns. Some forms were even green, though it seemed unlikely that this was due to chlorophyll. Practically all seemed to emit the vague light which bathed the entire scene—so uniformly that outlines would have been hard to distinguish were it not for a few specimens which were much brighter than the others. These types bore what might have been spore pods; brilliantly luminous knobs ranging from fist to grapefruit size, raised "above" the rest of the surface, as much as eight or ten feet on slender stalks. These cast shadows which helped distinguish relief.

The woman was right; weird it might be, but the scene was beautiful.

Weisanen cut off the water jets and waited for a minute or two. The vehicle drifted slowly but perceptibly away from the surface; evidently there was some current.

"We'll have to anchor," he remarked. "Bren, stay inside

until we've checked. I'll go out to see what we can fasten ourselves to; there's no information at all on what sort of surface
there may be. A fair-sized stony meteoroid—really an asteroid—
was used as the original core, but the solids from the comets
would be very fine dust. There could be yards of mud too fine to
hold any sort of anchor surrounding the solid part. You gentlemen will please get into the other suits and come with me. If
nothing has happened to any of us in half an hour, Bren, you
may join us."

"There are only three suits," his wife pointed out.

"True. Well, your spacesuit will do; or if you prefer, one of us
will use his and let you have the diving gear. In any case, that
problem is low-priority. If you gentlemen are ready we'll go. I'll
start; this is strictly a one-man airlock."

All three had been climbing out of their spacesuits as Weisanen
was talking. The other garments were easy enough to get into,
though Bresnahan found the huge helmet unwieldy even with no
weight. Weisanen was through the lock before either of the
others was ready to follow; Silbert was slowed by his space-born
habit of double-checking every bit of the breathing apparatus,
and Bresnahan by his inexperience. They could see their employer through the window as they finished, swimming slowly
and carefully toward the weedy boundary of Raindrop's core.

Both men stayed where they were for the moment, to see what
would happen when he reached it. Brenda Weisanen watched
even more closely; there was no obvious reason to be afraid, but
her breath was coming unevenly and her fists tightly clenched as
her husband approached the plants and reached out to touch the
nearest.

Nothing spectacular happened. It yielded to his touch; when
he seized it and pulled, it broke.

"Either the plants are awfully fragile or there is fairly firm
ground anchoring them," remarked Silbert. "Let's go outside.
You're checked out on the controls of this thing, aren't you,
Mrs. Weisanen?"

"Not in great detail," was the reply. "I know which switches
handle lights and main power for the lock pump, and which
control bank deals with the jets; but I've had no practice in
actually handling it. Aino hadn't, either, until we started this
trip an hour ago. Go ahead, though; I won't have to do anything
anyway. Aino is anchoring us now."

She gestured toward the port. Her husband could now be seen through it carrying something like a harpoon, with a length of fine line attached to it. A couple of yards from the surface he poised himself and hurled the object, javelin-style—or as nearly to that style as anyone can manage in water—into the mass of vegetation.

The shaft buried itself completely. Weisanen gave a tug on the line, whose far end was attached to the sphere. He seemed satisfied and turned to look at the vehicle. Seeing the men still inside, he gestured impatiently. Bresnahan followed Silbert through the tiny air lock as rapidly as its cycling time would permit, leaving the woman alone in the sphere.

Outside, Weisanen was several yards away, still beckoning imperiously.

"You can talk, sir," remarked Silbert in ordinary tones. "There's no need for sign language."

"Oh. Thanks; I didn't see any radio equipment in these helmets."

"There isn't any. The helmets themselves aren't just molded plastic; they're a multilayered arrangement that acts as an impedance matcher between the air inside and the water outside. Sound goes through water well enough; it's the air-water interface that makes conversation difficult. This stuff gets the sound across the boundary."

"All right; good. Let's get to work. If the figures for the size of the original nucleus still mean anything, we have nearly twenty million square feet to check up on. Right now we won't try to do it all; stay in sight of the sphere. Get test rods and plankton gear from that rack by the air lock. Mr. Silbert, use the nets and collectors as you usually do. Mr. Bresnahan, you and I will use the rods; simply poke them into the surface every few yards. The idea is to get general knowledge of the firmness of the underlying surface, and to find the best places to build—or attach—permanent structures. If you should happen to notice any connection between the type of vegetation and the kind of ground it grows on, so much the better; surveying by eye will be a lot faster than by touch. If any sort of trouble comes up, yell. I don't see why there should be any, but I don't want Brenda out here until we're a little more certain."

The men fell to their rather monotonous tasks. The plant cover, it developed, ranged from an inch or two to over a yard in thickness, not counting the scattered forms which extended their tendrils scores of feet out toward the darkness. At no point was the underlying "ground" visible.

Where the growing cover was pushed or dug away, the core seemed to be made of a stiff, brownish clay, which reached at least as deep as the test prods could be pushed by hand. This rather surprised Silbert, who had expected either solid rock or oozy mud. He was not geochemist enough to guess at the reactions which might have formed what they actually found, and was too sensible to worry about it before actual analyses had been made.

If Weisanen had any opinions, he kept them to himself.

Bresnahan was not worried about the scientific aspect of the situation at all. He simply poked away with his test bar because he had been told to, devoting only a fraction of his attention to the task. His thoughts were elsewhere.

Specifically, he was following through the implications of the information the Weisanens had furnished during the trip down. He admitted to himself that in the other's position he would probably be doing the same thing; but it seemed as though some compromise should be possible which would salvage the original purpose of Raindrop.

Bresnahan did not, of course, expect to eat as well as the average man of the mid-twentieth century. He never had, and didn't know what he was missing. He did know, however, that at his present age of twenty-five there was a smaller variety of foodstuffs available than he could remember from his childhood, and he didn't want that process to go any farther. Breaking up Raindrop according to the original plan seemed to him the obvious thing to do. If land and sea farming areas were disappearing under the population flood, the logical answer was farming areas in the sky. This should be as important to the Weisanens as to anyone else.

He felt a little uneasy about bringing the matter up again, however. Somehow, he had a certain awe of Weisanen which he didn't think was entirely due to the fact that the latter was his employer.

Several times their paths came close together as the two plied their test bars, but Bresnahan was unable to wind his courage up to the necessary pitch for some time—not, in fact, until they had been exploring the region uneventfully for over half an hour and

Weisanen had finally, with some hesitation, decided that it was safe for his wife to join them.

There was some slight rivalry between Silbert and Bresnahan over who should give up his diving gear to the woman and resume his spacesuit. If Bresnahan had won, a good deal of subsequent trouble might have been avoided; but when all four were finally outside, Silbert was wearing space armor. He had pointed out quite logically that he was the most used to it and would work better than any of the others in its restrictions.

VII

The key to the subsequent trouble was that one of the restrictions involved communication. If Silbert had been able to hear clearly, he might have understood what was developing before it had gone too far; but he couldn't. His space helmet lacked the impedance-matching feature of the diving gear, and the latter equipment had no radios.

Some sound did get through his helmet both from and into the water, but not much; for real conversation he had to bring the helmet into physical contact with that of the other party. He therefore knew little of what went on during the next few minutes. He spent them continuing his ecology sample, and paid little attention to anything else.

With Mrs. Weisanen present, some of Bresnahan's unease in her husband's presence left him, and he brought up at last the point which had occurred to him.

"I've been wondering, sir," he opened, "why it wouldn't be possible to break up Raindrop just as was planned, and still use the smaller drops as homes for people like yourselves. I can't see that it would be very different from your present plan."

Weisanen did not seem annoyed, but answered in a straightforward fashion. "Aside from the fact that we would prefer to be in a single city rather than a lot of detached houses which would require us to visit our neighbors by spaceship, the smaller drops will have the radiation problem. Here we have nearly five miles of water shielding us."

"Hmph. I never thought of that."

"No reason why you should have. It was never your problem."

"But still—what do we do about food? Conditions on Earth

are getting worse all the time. Starting another Raindrop project would take years. Couldn't you at least compromise? Permit the small drops to be skimmed off the surface of this one while you are living here, and while another Raindrop is set up?''

"I don't like the idea. Can you imagine what it will be like here with shock waves from exploding steam bubbles echoing all through the globe every time the skin is opened for a new farm lot?''

"Why should they break the skin? I should think they'd want to draw off the water through the lock, or other locks which might be built, anyway; otherwise there'd be a lot of waste from boiling. I should think—''

Weisanen's annoyance suddenly boiled over, though no sign of it had been visible before.

"Mr. Bresnahan, it matters very little what you think when you forget that Raindrop is now, legally and properly, private property. I dislike to sound selfish and misanthropic, but I belong to a group which has gone to a great deal of thought and labor to get for itself, legally and without violence, an environment which it needs and which no one else—including the people responsible for our existence—was willing to provide. In addition, if you would think with your brain instead of your stomach you'd realize that the whole original project was pure nonsense. The only possible way mankind can keep himself adequately fed is to limit his population. If you'll pardon the pun, the whole idiotic project was a drop in the bucket. It might have put the day of reckoning back five years, conceivably ten or fifteen, but then we'd have been right back where we started. Even with fusion energy there's a limit to the number of space farms which could be built in a given time, and the way Earth's population grows it would soon be impossible just to make new farms fast enough, let alone operate them. Cheating people? Nonsense! We're doing the rest of mankind a favor by forcing them to face facts while there are a few billion less of them to argue with each other. One group has had to exercise the same sort of control the rest of mankind should be using for a good half century. We didn't *dare* have children except when it was practicable to keep the mother in orbit for the best part of a year. Why should we be particularly sympathetic with the rest of you?''

"I see your point," admitted Bresnahan, "but you've forgotten one other thing. The food problem is yours, too. What will you do as *your* food supply shrinks like everyone else's? Or worse, when people decide not to send any food at all up here, since you won't send any down? Raindrop is a long way yet from being self-supporting, you know."

A grin, clearly visible in the light from a nearby plant knob, appeared on Weisanen's face; but his irritation remained.

"Slight mistake, my young friend. There is another minor modification in our structure; our saliva glands produce an enzyme you lack. We can digest cellulose." He waved his hand at the plants around them.

"How do you know these plants contain cellulose?"

"All plants do; but that's a side issue. The weeds near the surface were analyzed long ago, and proved to contain all the essentials for human life—in form which we can extract with our own digestive apparatus. Raindrop, as it now is, could support all of us there are now and there are likely to be for a couple of generations. Now, please get back to checking this little world of ours. Brenda and I want to decide where to build our house."

Bresnahan was silent, but made no move to get back to work. He floated for a minute or so, thinking furiously; Weisanen made no effort to repeat or enforce his order.

At last the computerman spoke slowly—and made his worst mistake.

"You may be right in your legal standing. You may be right in your opinion about the value of Raindrop and what the rest of the human race should do—personally, I want a family someday. You may even be right about your safety from general attack because the communication laws will keep down the number of people who know about the business. But, right or wrong, if even a single person with access to a spaceship *does* find out, then you—and your wife—and your baby—are all in danger. Doesn't that suggest to you that some sort of compromise is in order?"

Weisanen's expression darkened and his muscles tensed. His wife, looking at him, opened her mouth and made a little gesture of protest even before he started to speak; but if she made a sound it was drowned out.

"It certainly suggests something, young fellow," snapped the official. "I was hoping the matter wouldn't descend to this level, but remember that while we can live here indefinitely, you cannot. A few weeks of weightlessness will do damage which your bodies can never repair. There is no regular food down here. And we control the transportation back to the station and weight.''

"Aino—no!'' His wife laid a hand on his arm and spoke urgently. ''Wait, dear. If you threaten at all, it's too close to a threat of death. I don't want to kill anyone, and don't want to think of your doing so. It wouldn't be worth it.''

''You and the little one *are* worth it. Worth anything! I won't listen to argument on that.''

''But argument isn't needed. There is time. Mr. Bresnahan and his friend will certainly wait and think before risking the consequences of a mob-raising rumor. He wants a compromise, not—''

''His compromise endangers you and the others. I won't have it. Mr. Bresnahan, I will not ask you for a promise to keep quiet; you might be the idealistic type which can justify breaking its word for what it considers a good cause. Also, I will not endanger your life and health more than I can help. Brenda is right to some extent; I don't want a killing on my conscience either, regardless of the cause. Therefore, you and Mr. Silbert will remain here at the core until Brenda and I have returned to the station and made sure that no communication gear will function without our knowledge and consent. That may be a few days, which may be more than your health should risk. I'm sorry, but I'm balancing that risk to you against one to us.''

''Why should it take days? An hour to the surface, a few minutes to the station—''

''And Heaven knows how long to find and take care of all the radios. Neither of us is an expert in that field, and we'll be a long time making sure we have left no loopholes.''

''Will you at least stop to find out whether the air renewers in these diving suits are indefinite-time ones, like the spacesuit equipment? And if they aren't, let me change back into my spacesuit?''

''Of course. Change anyway. It will save my trying to get the substance of this conversation across to Mr. Silbert. You can tell him on radio while we are on the way. Come with me back to the sphere and change. Brenda, stay here.''

''But, dearest—this isn't right. You know—''

''I know what I'm doing and why I'm doing it. I'm willing to follow your lead in a lot of things, Bren, but this is not one of them.''

''But—''

''No buts. Come, Mr. Bresnahan. Follow me.''

The wife fell silent, but her gaze was troubled as she watched the two men vanish through the tiny lock. Bresnahan wondered what she would do. It was because he felt sure she would do something that he hadn't simply defied Weisanen.

The woman's face was no happier when the computerman emerged alone and swam back to a point beside her. Her husband was visible through the port, outsized helmet removed, beckoning to her.

For a moment Bresnahan had the hope that she would refuse to go. This faded as she swam slowly toward the sphere, occasionally looking back, removed the anchor in response to a gesture from the man inside, and disappeared through the lock. The vehicle began to drift upward, vegetation near it swirling in the water jets. Within a minute it had faded from view into the darkness.

"Just what's going on here?" Silbert's voice was clear enough; the suit radios carried for a short distance through water. "Where are they going, and why?"

"You didn't hear any of my talk with Weisanen?"

"No. I was busy, and it's hard to get sound through this helmet anyway. What happened? Did you argue with him?"

"In a way." Bresnahan gave the story as concisely as he could. His friend's whistle sounded eerily in the confines of his helmet.

"This—is—really—something. Just for the record, young pal, we are in a serious jam, I hope you realize."

"I don't think so. His wife is against the idea, and he'll let himself get talked out of it—he's a little afraid of the results already."

"Not the point. It doesn't matter if the whole thing was a practical joke on his part. They're out of sight, in a medium where no current charts exist and the only navigation aids are that sphere's own sonar units. He could find his way back to the core, but how could he find *us*?"

"Aren't we right under the lock and the station? We came straight down."

"Don't bet on that. I told you—there are currents. If we made a straight track on the trip down here I'll be the most surprised man inside Luna's orbit. There are twenty million square feet on this mudball. We'd be visible from a radius of maybe two hundred—visible and recognizable, that is, with our lights on.

That means they have something like two hundred search blocks, if my mental arithmetic is right, without even a means of knowing when they cover a given one a second time. There is a chance they'd find us, but not a good one—not a good enough one so that we should bet your chance of dodging a couple of weeks of weightlessness on it. When that nut went out of sight, he disposed of us once and for all."

"I wouldn't call him a nut," Bresnahan said.

"Why not? Anyone who would leave a couple people to starve or get loaded with zero-gee symptoms on the odd chance that they might blab his favorite scheme to the public—"

"He's a little unbalanced at the moment, but not a real nut. I'm sure he didn't realize he'd passed the point of no return. Make allowances, Bert; I can. Some of my best friends are married, and I've seen 'em when they first learned a kid was on the way. It's just that they don't usually have this good a chance to get other people in trouble; they're all off the beam for a little while."

"You're the most tolerant and civilized character I've met, and you've just convinced me that there can be too much of even the best of things. For my money the guy is a raving nut. More to the point, unless we can get ourselves out of the jam he's dropped us into, we're worse than nuts. We're dead."

"Maybe he'll realize the situation and go back to the station and call for help."

"There can be such a thing as too much optimism, too. My young friend, he's not going to get to the station."

"What? Why not?"

"Because the only laser tube not already in the station able to trigger the cobweb launchers is right here on my equipment clip. That's another reason I think he's a nut. He should have thought of that and pried it away from me somehow."

"Maybe it just means he wasn't serious about the whole thing."

"Never mind what it means about him. Whatever his intentions, I'd be willing to wait for him to come back to us with his tail between his legs if I thought he could find us. Since I don't think he can, we'd better get going ourselves."

"Huh? How?"

"Swim. How else?"

"But how do we navigate? Once we're out of sight of the core we'd be there in the dark with absolutely nothing to guide us. These little lights on our suits aren't—"

"I know they aren't. That wasn't the idea. Don't worry; I may not be able to swim in a straight line, but I can get us to the surface eventually. Come on; five miles is a long swim."

Silbert started away from the glow, and Bresnahan followed uneasily. He was not happy at the prospect of weightlessness and darkness combined; the doses on the trip down, when at least the sphere had been present for some sort of orientation, had been more than sufficient.

The glow of the core faded slowly behind them, but before it was too difficult to see Silbert stopped.

"All right, put your light on. I'll do the same; stay close to me." Bresnahan obeyed both orders gladly. "Now, watch."

The spaceman manipulated valves on his suit, and carefully ejected a bubble of air about two feet in diameter. "You noticed that waste gas from the electrolyzers in the diving suits didn't stay with us to be a nuisance. The bubbles drifted away, even when we were at the core," he pointed out. Bresnahan hadn't noticed, since he wasn't used to paying attention to the fate of the air he exhaled, but was able to remember the fact once it was mentioned.

"That of course, was not due to buoyancy, so close to the core. The regular convection currents started by solar heat at the skin must be responsible. Therefore, those currents must extend all the way between skin and core. We'll follow this bubble."

"If the current goes all the way, why not just drift?"

"For two reasons. One is that the currents are slow—judging by their speed near the skin, the cycle must take over a day. Once we get away from the core, the buoyancy of this bubble will help; we can swim after it.

"The other reason is that if we simply drift we might start down again with the current before we got close enough to the skin to see daylight.

"Another trick we might try if this takes too long is to have one of us drift while the other follows the bubble to the limit of vision. That would establish the up-down line, and we could swim in that direction for a while and then repeat. I'm afraid we probably couldn't hold swimming direction for long enough to be useful, though, and it would be hard on the reserve air supply. We'd have to make a new bubble each time we checked. These suits have recyclers, but a spacesuit isn't built to get its oxygen from the surrounding water the way that diving gear is."

"Let's just follow this bubble," Bresnahan said fervently.

At first, of course, the two merely drifted. There simply was no detectable buoyancy near the core. However, in a surprisingly short time the shimmering globule of gas began to show a tendency to drift away from them.

The direction of drift was seldom the one which Bresnahan was thinking of as "up" at the moment, but the spaceman nodded approval and carefully followed their only guide. Bresnahan wished that his training had given him more confidence in instrument readings as opposed to his own senses, but followed Silbert hopefully.

IX

The fourteen hours he spent drifting weightless in the dark made an experience Bresnahan was never to forget, and his friends were never to ignore. He always liked crowds afterward, and preferred to be in cities or at least buildings where straight, clearly outlined walls, windows, and doors marked an unequivocal up-and-down direction.

Even Silbert was bothered. He was more used to weightlessness, but the darkness he was used to seeing around him at such times was normally pocked with stars which provided orientation. The depths of Raindrop provided *nothing*. Both men were almost too far gone to believe their senses when they finally realized that the bubble they were still following could be seen by a glow not from their suit lights.

It was a faintly blue-green illumination, still impossible to define as to source, but unmistakably sunlight filtered through hundreds of feet of water. Only minutes later their helmets met the tough, elastic skin of the satellite.

It took Silbert only a few moments to orient himself. The sun and the station were both visible—at least they had not come out on the opposite side of the satellite—and he knew the time. The first and last factors were merely checks; all that was really necessary to find the lock was to swim toward the point under the orbiting station.

"I don't want to use the sonar locater unless I have to," he pointed out. "There is sonar gear on the sphere. I should be able to get us close enough by sighting on the station so that the magnetic compass will work. Judging by where the station seems to be, we have four or five miles to swim. Let's get going."

"And let's follow the great circle course," added Bresnahan. "Never mind cutting across inside just because it's shorter. I've had all I ever want of swimming in the dark."

"My feeling exactly. Come on."

The distance was considerably greater than Silbert had estimated, since he was not used to doing his sighting from under water and had not allowed for refraction; but finally the needle of the gimbaled compass showed signs of making up its mind, and with nothing wrong that food and sleep would not repair the two men came at last in sight of the big lock cylinder.

For a moment, Silbert wondered whether they should try to make their approach secretly. Then he decided that if the Weisanens were there waiting for them the effort would be impractical, and if they weren't it would be futile.

He simply swam up to the small hatch followed by Bresnahan, and they entered the big chamber together. It proved to be full of water, but the sphere was nowhere in sight. With no words they headed for the outer personnel lock, entered it, pumped back the water, and emerged on Raindrop's surface. Silbert used his laser, and ten minutes later they were inside the station. Bresnahan's jump had been a little more skillful than before.

"Now let's get on the radio!" snapped Silbert as he shed his space helmet.

"Why? Whom would you call, and what would you tell them? Remember that our normal Earth-end contacts are part of the same group the Weisanens belong to, and you can't issue a general broadcast to the universe at large screaming about a plot against mankind in the hope that someone will take you seriously. Someone might."

"But—"

"My turn, Bert. You've turned what I still think was just a potentially tragic mistake of Weisanen's into something almost funny, and incidentally saved both our lives. Now will you follow my lead? Things could still be serious if we don't follow up properly."

"But what are you going to do?"

"You'll see. Take it from me, compromise is still possible. It will take a little time; Aino Weisanen will have to learn something I can't teach him myself. Tell me, is there any way to monitor what goes on in Raindrop? For example, can you tell from here when the lock down there is opened, so we would know when they come back?''

"No.''

"Then we'll just have to watch for them. I assume that if we see them, we can call them from here on regular radio.''

"Of course.''

"Then let's eat, sleep, and wait. They'll be back after a while, and when they come Aino will listen to reason, believe me. But we can sleep right now, I'm sure; it will be a while yet before they show up. They should still be looking for us—getting more worried by the minute.''

"Why should they appear at all? They must have found out long ago that they can't get back to the station on their own. They obviously haven't found us, and won't. Maybe they've simply decided they're already fugitive murderers and have settled down to a permanent life in Raindrop.''

"That's possible, I suppose. Well, if we don't see them in a couple of weeks, we can go back down and give them a call in some fashion. I'd rather they came to us, though, and not too soon.

"But let's forget that; I'm starved. What's in your culture tanks besides liver?''

X

It did not take two weeks. Nine days and eight hours after the men had returned to the station, Silbert saw two spacesuited figures standing on the lock half a mile away, and called his companion's attention to them.

"They must be desperate by this time,'' remarked Bresnahan. "We'd better call them before they decide to risk the jump anyway.'' He activated the transmitter which Silbert indicated, and spoke.

"Hello, Mr. and Mrs. Weisanen. Do you want us to send the cobweb down?''

The voice that answered was female.

"Thank God you're there! Yes, please. We'd like to come up for a while.'' Silbert expected some qualifying remarks from her husband, but none were forthcoming. At Bresnahan's gesture, he activated the spring gun which launched the web toward the satellite.

"Maybe you'd better suit up and go meet them," suggested the computerman. "I don't suppose either of them is very good at folding the web, to say nothing of killing angular speed."

"I'm not sure I care whether they go off on their own orbit anyway," growled the spaceman, rising with some reluctance to his feet.

"Still bitter? And both of them?" queried Bresnahan.

"Well—I suppose not. And it would take forever to repair the web if it hit the station unfolded. I'll be back." Silbert vanished toward the hub, and the younger man turned back to watch his employers make the leap from Raindrop. He was not too surprised to see them hold hands as they did so, with the natural result that they spun madly on the way to the web and came close to missing it altogether.

When his own stomach had stopped whirling in sympathy, he decided that maybe the incident was for the best. Anything which tended to cut down Weisanen's self-assurance should be helpful, even though there was good reason to suspect that the battle was already won. He wondered whether he should summon the pair to his and Silbert's quarters for the interview which was about to ensue, but decided that there was such a thing as going too far.

He awaited the invitation to the Weisanens' rooms with eagerness.

It came within minutes of the couple's arrival at the air lock. When Bresnahan arrived he found Silbert already in the room where they had first reported on their brief visit to Raindrop. All three were still in spacesuits; they had removed only the helmets.

"We're going back down as soon as possible, Mr. Bresnahan," Weisanen began without preliminary. "I have a rather lengthy set of messages here which I would like you and Mr. Silbert to transmit as soon as possible. You will note that they contain my urgent recommendation for a policy change. Your suggestion of starting construction of smaller farms from Raindrop's outer layers is sound, and I think the Company will follow it. I am also advising that material be collected from the vicinity of the giant planets—Saturn's rings seem a likely source—for constructing additional satellites like Raindrop as private undertakings. Financing can be worked out. There should be enough profit from the farms, and that's the logical direction for some of it to flow.

"Once other sources of farm material are available, Raindrop will not be used further for the purpose. It will serve as Company headquarters—it will be more convenient to have that in orbit anyway. The closest possible commercial relations are to be maintained with Earth."

"I'm glad you feel that way, sir," replied Bresnahan. "We'll get the messages off as soon as possible. I take it that more of the Company's officials will be coming up here to live, then?"

"Probably all of them, within the next two years or so. Brenda and I will go back and resume surveying now, as soon as we stock up with some food. I'll be back occasionally, but I'd rather she kept away from high weight for the next few months, as you know."

"Yes, sir." Bresnahan managed, by a heroic effort, to control his smile—almost. Weisanen saw the flicker of his lip, and froze for a moment. Then his own sober features loosened into a broad grin.

"Maybe another hour won't hurt Brenda," he remarked. "Let's have a meal together before we go back."

He paused, and added almost diffidently. "Sorry about what happened. We're human, you know."

"I know," replied Bresnahan. "That's what I was counting on."

"And that," remarked Silbert as he shed his helmet, "is that. They're aboard and bound for the core again, happy as clams. And speaking of clams, if you don't tell me why that stubborn Finn changed his mind, and why you were so sure he'd do it, there'll be mayhem around here. Don't try to make me believe that he got scared about what he'd nearly done to us. I know his wife was on our side, basically, but she wasn't about to wage open war for us. She was as worried about their kid as he was. Come on; make with the words, chum."

"Simple enough. Didn't you notice what he wanted before going back to Raindrop?"

"Not particularly—oh; food. So what? He could live on the food down there—or couldn't he? Don't you believe what he said?"

"Sure I believe him. He and his wife can digest cellulose,

Heaven help them, and they can live off Raindrop's seaweed. As I remarked to him, though—you heard me, and he understood me—they're human. I can digest kale and cauliflower, too, and could probably live off them as well as that pair could live off the weeds. But did you ever stop to think what the stuff must taste like? Neither did they. I knew they'd be back with open mouths—and open minds. Let's eat—anything but liver!''

COMET WINE

Ray Russell

I'm a bloodhound. Ask anyone who knows me and they'll tell you I'm a meticulous researcher, an untiring zealot, a ruthless bloodhound when pursuing facts. I'm not a professional musician, granted; not even a gifted amateur; but my fondness for music can't be disputed and my personal fund of musical and musicological knowledge happens to be huge. All the more remarkable (wouldn't you say?) that no catalog, no concert program, no newspaper file, no encyclopedia, no dictionary, no memoir, no interview, no history of music, no grave marker has rewarded my efforts by surrendering the name V. I. Cholodenko.

Such a person, it would seem, never existed. Or, if he did exist, became an Orwellian unperson who was whisked from this world as completely as were Ambrose Bierce, Judge Crater, or the passengers and crew of the *Marie Celeste*. I'm well aware of the transliteration problems regarding Russian names, and I've doggedly searched under the spellings Tcholodenko, Tscholodenko, Shcholodenko and even Zholodenko, but to no avail. True, I haven't had access to archives within the Soviet Union (my letters to Shostakovich and Khachaturian appear to have gone astray), but I've queried Russian musicians on tour in the United States, and to none of them is it a familiar name.

Its exclusive appearance is in a ribbon-tied bunch of old letters, crisp and desiccated, purchased last year by me, along with items of furniture and art, at a private auction of the effects of the late Beverly Hills attorney Francis Cargrave. They had belonged to his grandfather, Sir Robert Cargrave, an eminent London physician, to whom they are addressed, and all were written, in elegant if somewhat epicene prose, by Lord Henry Stanton, a fashionable beau and minor poet of the period.

The curiosity, the enigma, lies in the fact that all the people mentioned in the three pertinent letters are real people, who lived, whose names and achievements are well-known—all, that is, but the name and achievements of Cholodenko. Even the briefly mentioned Colonel Spalding existed, as will be noted later. Down to the most insignificant details—such as the color of his famous host's eyeglasses—Lord Stanton's letters can be substantiated (the only exceptions, again, being the references to the elusive Cholodenko).

Is the man a fabrication? Was Stanton the perpetrator of an elaborate hoax? If so, I can't in all honesty understand why. The letters were written to his closest friend, a presumably sober pillar of the medical profession and knight of the British Empire. Both men were no longer youngsters, and undergraduate pranks strike me as uncharacteristic of them.

But if it was not a prank, how can we explain the way Cholodenko has been ripped from history, his music not even a fading echo but a silence, a vacuum, completely forgotten, as totally unknown as the song the Sirens sang?

I don't presume to solve the mystery. I merely present the three letters "for what they're worth," and invite other bloodhounds to make what they will of them. Such bloodhounds will sniff out, as I did, a glaring discrepancy, for the very survival of these letters seems to discredit Lord Henry's colorful insinuations—but he would probably counter our incredulity, if he were here, by urbanely pointing out that if God proverbially moves in mysterious ways His wonders to perform, might not His Adversary do the same? For reasons of scholarship and accuracy, I haven't condensed or edited the letters in any way (except to eliminate the redundant addresses in all but the first), preferring to let even irrelevant or trivial observations stand, in the hope that they may contain clues which eluded me. I've also kept Stanton's not always standard, though phonetically accurate, transliterations. In a few places, I've inserted short bracketed notes of my own, in italics. The letters bear month and dates, but no year. Stanton being English, I assume these dates conform to the Gregorian calendar familiar to us, rather than to the old

Julian calendar, which was still in use in Russia at the time. On the basis of internal evidence, such as the first performance of *Eugene Onegin*, I believe the letters to have been written in 1879.

•   •   •

5 April

Sir Robert Cargrave
Harley Street
London, England

My dear Bobbie,

No, do not scold me! I know full well that I have been a renegade and most delinquent comrade. If I seem to have avoided your home these many months; if I have neglected you, your dear Maude, and your brood of cherubim—one of whom, young Jamey, must be quite ripe for Oxford by now!—then ascribe it, I pray you, not to a cooling of our friendship's fires nor to a crusty bachelor's disdain for the familial hearthstone, but, rather, to my persistent vice, travel.

I have set foot on divers shores since last I sipped your sherry, old cohort, and I write to you from St. Petersburg. Yes, I am cosily hugged by "the rugged Russian bear," a cryptic creature, I assure you, warm and greathearted, quick to laugh, and just as quick to plunge into pits of black *toská*—a word that haughtily defies translation, hovering mystically, as it does, somewhere between melancholy and despair. Neither melancholy nor despair, however, have dogged my steps here in this strange land. I have been most cheerful. There are wondrous sights to bend one's gaze upon; exotic food and drink to quicken and quench the appetite; fascinating people with whom to talk. To your sly and silent question, my reply is Yes!—there are indeed ladies here, lovely ones, with flared bright eyes and sable voices; lambent ladies, recondite and rare. There are amusing soirees, as well (I will tell you of one in a moment), and there are evenings of brilliance at the ballet and the opera.

The opera here would particularly captivate both you and your Maude, I am certain, for I know of your deep love of the form. How enviously, then, will you receive the news that just last month, in Moscow, I attended the premiere of a dazzling new *opus theatricum* by the composer Pyotr Chaikovsky. It was a work of lapidary excellence, entitled *Yevgeny Onyégin* (I transliterate as best I can from the spiky Cyrillic original), derived from a poem of that name by a certain Pushkin, a prosodist now dead for decades, who—my friend, Colonel Spalding, tells me—enjoys a classical reputation here, but of whom I had not hitherto heard, since his works have not been translated into English, an error the colonel is now busy putting right. [*Lieutenant Colonel Henry Spalding's English translation, transliterated as "Eugene Onéguine," was published in London in 1881*] The opera is a shimmering tapestry of sound, brocaded with waltzes and polonaises.

But St. Petersburg, I find, is richer in cultural life than even Moscow: I have been awed by the art treasures of The Hermitage, humbled by the baroque majesty of the Aleksandr Nevsky Cathedral, chastened by the mighty gloom of the Peter Paul fortress and properly impressed by the Smolny monastery and the Winter Palace. Apropos of winter, I have also been chilled to the marrow by the fiercest cold I have ever known. "Winter in April?" I can hear you say. Yes, the severe season stretches from November to April in this place, and the River Neva, which I can see, moonlit, from my window as I write, is frozen over, and has been thus, I am told, for the past six months! It is a great gleaming broadsword of ice, cleaving the city in two.

As for music: Just last night, thanks to a letter of introduction from Spalding, I was received at a famous apartment in the Zagoredny Prospekt—nothing ostentatious, a small drawing room, a few chairs, a grand piano, a table in the dining room loaded with the simplest food and drink . . . but what exceptional people were crowded, shoulder to shoulder, in that place. It was the apartment of Rimsky-Korsakov, who, I was pleased to discover, is not only a gifted and amiable gentleman but speaks excellent English—an accomplishment not shared by many of his compatriots, whose social conversations are customarily couched in (or, at least, liberally laced with) French. The guests, myself excluded, were, to a man, composers and performers, some (I later learned) being members of a *koochka*, or clan, of musicians of which Rimsky-Korsakov is the nucleus.

You will laugh when I tell you that, not five minutes after being welcomed into the *salon*, I committed a *faux pas*. Wishing to take part in the musical discussion, I minutely described and lavishly praised the Chaikovsky opera I had enjoyed so recently at the Moscow Conservatorium. My tall host's gentle eyes grew cold behind his blue-tinted spectacles (which he wears because of ailing sight) and I felt a distinct frost. The awkward moment soon passed, however, and a dark young man took me aside to dryly inform me that "Our esteemed Nikolai Andreyvich considers Chaikovsky's music to be in abominable taste."

"Do you share that opinion?" I asked.

"Not precisely, but I do feel Chaikovsky is not a truly Russian composer. He has let himself be influenced by bad French models—Massenet, Bizet, Gounod, and so on."

We were joined by a bloated, wild-haired, red-nosed, bleary-eyed but very courteous fellow who, after addressing me most deferentially, asked eagerly about the Chaikovsky work: "It is good, then, you think? Ah! Splendid! An excellent subject, *Onyégin*. I once thought of setting it myself, but it's not my sort of thing—Pyotr Ilyich is the man for it, there's no doubt. Don't you agree, Vassily Ivanovich?" he added, turning to my companion.

That intense young man shrugged. "I suppose so—but to tell the truth, I am growing weary of these operatic obeisances to Pushkin. One cannot blame a composer of the old school, such as Glinka, for setting *Ruslan and Lyudmila*, but what are we to think when Dargomizhsky sets not one but three Pushkin subjects—*Russalka*, *The Triumph of Bacchus* and *The Stone Guest*; when you joined the *cortège* five years ago with your own opera; and when Chaikovsky now follows the pattern with *Onyégin*?" He threw up his hands. "May that be the last!" he sighed.

"There is still *The Queen of Spades*," said the unkempt man, mischievously. "Perhaps you will undertake that one yourself?"

"Thank you, no," snapped the other (rather irritably, I thought). "I leave that to you."

"I may just do it," was the smiling reply, "unless Chaikovsky is too quick for me!" [*He was: Tchaikovsky's setting of* The Queen of Spades *or* Pique-Dame *was presented in 1890. And, later, Rimsky-Korsakov drew upon Pushkin for his operas* Le Coq d'Or *and* Mozart and Salieri; *and Rachmaninoff also turned to Pushkin for his* Aleko.] Elaborately excusing himself, the wild-haired man left us and began chatting with another group.

"Talented," my young friend said in appraisal of him after he left, "but he lacks technique. His scores are crude, grotesque, his instrumentation a disgrace. Of course, he isn't well. An epileptic. And, as you may have noted, he drinks heavily. Still, somehow, he goes on writing music. There is a tavern in Morskaia Street, called Maly Yaroslavets—any night you will see him there, drinking vodka, scribbling music on napkins, menus, the margins of newspapers, feverishly, almost as if—'' He broke off.

"As if possessed?" I said.

"A somewhat lurid allusion, don't you think? No, I was about to say, 'almost as if his life depended on it'—as I suppose it does, for his interest in music is probably the only thing keeping him alive. To look at him now, Lord Henry, would you ever guess he was once an impeccably groomed Guards officer, of refined breeding, a wit, a ladies' man?" He shook his head dolorously. "Poor Mussorgsky," he sighed.

Looking slowly about the *salon*, he then said, "The *koochka* is not what it was, sir. Do you see that pathetic creature sitting in the corner?" The gentleman indicated was indeed pathetic, a wraith who looked with glazed eye upon all who passed before him, responding feebly and mechanically to greetings, like an old man (although he was not old), then sinking back into motionless apathy. "That is, or was, the *koochka*'s vital force, its spine, its heart, its tingling blood. It was in *his* apartment we were wont to meet, he who held the group together, his hands that firmly gripped the reins, his whip that goaded us to frenzied effort. No man was more steeped in the classical scores, no memory was so vast as his. Now look at him. A coffin. His mind blighted by a mysterious malady. There he sits. His *Tamara* languishes unfinished. Music has ceased to interest him, he who breathed exotic harmonies every minute of the day."

We had been walking toward this pitiful wreckage, and now my guide leaned close and spoke to him: "Mily Alekseyevich! How is it with you?" The man looked up and blinked vapidly; it was quite obvious he did not recognize the speaker. "It is I, Vassily Ivanovich," he was forced to add.

"Vas . . . sily . . . 'Van . . . ovich . . ." A small, crooked smile of recognition twisted the poor man's face for a moment, although the eyes did not kindle.

"Allow me to present an honoured guest from England, Lord Henry Stanton. Lord Henry, Mily Balakirev."

The wretched fellow offered me a limp, dead hand, which I briefly shook; and then we left him, staring vacantly into empty air again. "Tragic," my Virgil murmured; "and the final offense is that poor Mily, who once was the most vociferous of scoffers, now mumbles prayers and bends his knee to ikons."

"I hope you are not an unbeliever," I said lightly.

"I believe," he said—a reply that would have satisfied me,

had it not been for its dark colour, which seemed to imply meanings beyond the simple words.

"Surely," I asked him, "such ruination of body or mind is not typical of your group?"

"Mussorgsky and Balakirev are possibly extreme examples," he agreed. "But there, at the table, stuffing himself with *zakuski*," he said, indicating a man in the uniform of a lieutenant general of engineers, "is Cui, who suffers from the worst disease of all: poverty of talent. And Rimsky, whose soul is corroded by his envy of Chaikovsky."

The music of Chaikovsky's *Yevgeny Onyégin* still rang in my memory and I was therefore reminded of the poet on whose work the opera was founded. "You spoke of Pushkin some moments ago," I said. "I have been told he was an extraordinary poet. Why do you hold him in low esteem?"

"I do not," he replied. "Pushkin was a genius. But suppose your English musicians persisted in setting only the plays and verses of Shakespeare, ignoring today's English writers? This preoccupation with the past is stagnating most of Russian culture, and the music itself is as dated as its subject matter. Even Mussorgsky, whose crudeness is sometimes redeemed by flashes of daring, is being obtunded and made 'inoffensive' by Rimsky—a pedant who gets sick to the stomach at the sound of a consecutive fifth!"

Does it strike you, Bobbie, that this chap was annoyingly critical of his illustrious colleagues? It so struck me, and a little later in the evening I had an opportunity to challenge him—but at this precise moment in our conversation, we were joined by our host.

My initial "offense" regarding the music of Chaikovsky was now, happily, forgotten, and Rimsky's eyes were warm behind the blue lenses. "Ah, Lord Henry," he said, "I see you have met our young firebrand. Has he been telling you what old fogeys we are, the slaves of tradition, and so on? Dear boy, for shame: our English visitor will carry away a bad impression of us."

"No, no," I said, "his views are refreshing."

"He is our gadfly," Rimsky said, with a diplomatic smile. "But we must all suspend our conversations—refreshing though they may be—and turn our attention to some music a few of our friends have consented to play for us."

We all found chairs, and a feast of sound was served.

Mussorgsky provided accompaniment for a song sung by a basso they called Fyodr [*Not Chaliapin, of course, who was only six years old at the time; but possibly Fyodr Stravinsky, the singer-father of Igor*]; after which a chemist named Borodin played pungent excerpts from an uncompleted opera ("He's been at it for fifteen years," whispered my young companion. "Keeps interrupting it to work on symphonies. A chaotic man, disorganized. Bastard son of a prince."). Next, Rimsky-Korsakov himself played a lyrical piece I found charming, but which my self-appointed commentator deprecated as "conventional, unadventurous."

I had, by this time, had a surfeit of his vicious carping. Taking advantage of a lull in the musical offerings, I now turned to him and, with as much courtesy as I could summon and in a voice distinct enough to be heard by all, said, "Surely a man of such austere judgment will condescend to provide an example of his ideal? Will *you* not take your place at the keyboard, sir, so that others may play as critic?"

He proffered me a strange look and an ambiguous smile. A profound hush fell upon the room. Our host cleared his throat nervously. My heart sank as I realized that somehow, in a way quite unknown to me, I had committed another and possibly more enormous *faux pas*!

But I see the dawn has begun to tint the sky, and I have not yet been to bed. I will dispatch these pages to you at once, Bobbie, and resume my little chronicle at the very next opportunity.

Your peripatetic friend,
Harry

•   •   •

8 April

My dear Bobbie,

I left off, if I remember rightly, at the moment in Rimsky-Korsakov's apartment when I committed some manner of gauche blunder merely by suggesting that a rather unpleasant young man, who had been so superciliously critical of his colleagues, play something of his own composition for the assembled guests. The embarrassed silence that fell upon the room thoroughly discomfited me. What had I said? In what way was my suggestion awkward or indelicate? Was the young man bitterly hated by our famous host? Unlikely, for he was a guest. Did the poor fellow have no hands? Not so: for, even now, he held wineglass and biscuit in long, slender fingers. I was bemused; I may have blushed. Only a moment passed, but it seemed an hour. Finally, the young man, still wearing the smirk with which he had greeted my challenge, replied, "Thank you, Lord Henry. I *shall* play something of my own, if our host gives me leave?" He cocked an eyebrow toward Rimsky.

Recovering his aplomb, Rimsky said hurriedly, "My dear fellow, of course. The keyboard is yours." And so, raking the room's occupants with an arrogant look, the young man swaggered to the piano and was seated.

He studied the keyboard for a moment, then looked up at us. "I am in the midst of composing an opera," he said. "Its source, you may be surprised to learn, is not a poem by the indispensable Pushkin or an old Slavonic tale. It is a modern novel, a book still in the writing, a work of revolutionary brilliance. It rips the mask of pretence and hypocrisy from our decadent society, and will cause an uproar when it is published. I was privileged to see it in manuscript—the author resides here in St. Petersburg. It is called *The Brothers Karamazov*. And this," he concluded, flexing his spidery fingers, "is the prelude to the first act of my operatic setting."

His hands fell upon the keys and a dissonant chord impaled our ears. Rimsky-Korsakov winced. Mussorgsky's bleared eyes went suddenly wide. Borodin's jaws, with a caviar savoury half-masticated, stopped chewing. The chord hung in the air, its life prolonged by the pedal, then, as the long fingers moved among the keys, the dissonance was resolved, an arresting modulation took place, a theme of great power was stated in octaves, and then that theme was developed, with a wealth of architectural ingenuity. The theme took wing, climbed, soared, was burnished with rich harmony, took on a glittering texture, yet not effete but with an underlying firmness and strength. The *koochka* and the other guests were transfixed, myself among them; Balakirev alone seemed unthrilled. Cascades of bracing sound poured from the piano. When the prelude reached its magnificent conclusion and the last breath-taking chord thundered into eternity, there was an instant of profound silence—followed by a din of applause and congratulatory cries.

The composer was immediately engulfed by his colleagues, who shook his hand, slapped his shoulders, plied him with questions about the opera. If I were pressed to find one word to best describe the general feeling exuded by these men, the word would be *surprise*. It was plain to me that they were stunned not only by the vigor and beauty of the music but by its source, the young gadfly. I wondered why.

My unvoiced question must have been written on my face, for at that moment Rimsky-Korsakov drew me aside and said, "You appear to be puzzled, Lord Henry. Permit me to enlighten you— although, I confess, I am extremely puzzled myself. The fact is, you see, that this is the very first time young Cholodenko has shown even the dimmest glimmer of musical talent!"

"What? But that prelude—"

"Astonishing, I agree. Daring, original, moving, soundly constructed. A little too dissonant for my taste, perhaps, but I have no hesitation in calling it a work of genius."

"Then how . . ." Incredulous, more baffled than ever, I stammered out my disbelief: "That is to say, a man does not become a genius overnight! His gifts must ripen and grow, his masterworks must be foreshadowed by smaller but promising efforts . . ."

Rimsky nodded. "Exactly. That is why we are all so surprised. That is why I am so puzzled. And that, you see, is why we were so uncomfortable when you asked Cholodenko to play. Hitherto, his attempts have been painfully inept, devoid of any creative spark, colourless, derivative, drab. And his piano playing! The awkward thumpings of an ape!"

"You exaggerate, surely."

"Only a little. The poor boy himself was aware of his shortcomings—shamefully aware. We tried to be polite, we tried to encourage him, we searched for compliments to pay him, but he saw through us and declined to play at these soirees."

"Yet he attends them."

"Yes, although his very presence has been a discomfort to himself and the rest of us. Music has a kind of insidious attraction for him; he is goaded by it as by a demon; he behaves almost as if . . ." He searched for words.

"As if possessed?" I said, for the second time that evening.

"As if it were food and drink to him. And yet, for some time now, he has been merely an observer."

"And a critic!"

"A caustic critic. He has been an embarrassment, an annoyance, but we tolerated him, we pitied him . . ."

"And now, suddenly . . ."

"Yes," said Rimsky. "Suddenly." The eyes narrowed behind their cool blue panes as he gazed across the room at the triumphant Cholodenko. "Suddenly he is a keyboard virtuoso and the creator of a masterpiece. There is a mystery here, Lord Henry."

And, at that, I burst out laughing!

Rimsky said, "You are amused?"

"Amused and appreciative," I replied. "It is a very good joke—you have my admiration, sir."

"Joke?"

"You had me completely gulled. An absolutely inspired hoax!"

Rimsky's brow now creased in an Olympian frown. "I do not waste time with hoaxes," he said with dignity, and walked stiffly away.

Determined not to be daunted by this, I pushed my way through to Cholodenko and shook his hand. "I am only a profane listener," I said, "and have no real knowledge of music, but my congratulations are sincere."

"Thank you, Lord Henry. You are most kind." His demeanour had undergone a subtle change: Victory and praise had softened the prickly edges of his character. How wrong, Bobbie, is the axiom of our mutual friend, Acton [*Obviously, John Emerich Edward Dalberg Acton, Eighth Baronet and First Baron, 1834–1902*]. "Power corrupts," he says; "absolute power corrupts absolutely." This is bosh, and I've often told him so: It would be much truer to say "Lack of power corrupts; absolute lack of power corrupts absolutely."

The soiree was nearing its end. As the guests began to leave, my curiosity impelled me to seek out Cholodenko and accompany him into the street.

The cold hit me like a cannon ball. Nevertheless, I strolled at Cholodenko's side, along the banks of the frozen Neva (the embankments, of Finnish grey and pink marble, were iridescent under the moon). Both of us were buried in enormous greatcoats of fur, but I was still cold.

"Be patient but a few more days," said my companion, "and you will see spring split open the land. Our Russian spring is sudden, like a beautiful explosion."

"I shall try to live that long," I said, shivering.

"You need a fire and some wine," he laughed. "Come—my apartment is only a few more steps . . ."

I was eager to learn more about this man, although custom

urged me to make a token demur: "No, no, it is late—I should be returning to my quarters."

"Please," he said. "I am wide awake from this evening's triumph—I should not like to celebrate it alone."

"But I am a stranger. Surely your friends—"

Cholodenko snarled bitterly, "Those vultures? They condescended to me when they felt me their inferior; soon they will hate me for being their superior. Here is my door—I entreat you—"

My face felt brittle as glass from the cold. With chattering teeth, I replied, "Very well, for a little while." We went inside.

His apartment was small. Dominating it was a grand piano of concert size. Scores and manuscript paper were piled everywhere. Cholodenko built a fire. "And now," he said, producing a dust-filmed bottle, "we will warm ourselves with comet wine."

His strong thumbs deftly pushed out the cork and the frothing elixir spewed out into the goblets in a curving scintillant jet, a white arc that brought to mind, indeed, a comet's tail.

"Comet wine?" I repeated.

He nodded. "A famed and heady vintage from the year of the comet, 1811. This is a very rare bottle, one of the last in the world. Your health, Lord Henry."

We drank. The wine was unlike any I have ever tasted—akin to champagne, but somehow spicy, richer; dry, yet with a honeyed aftertaste. I drained the goblet and he poured again.

"A potent potation," I said with a smile.

"It makes the mind luminous," he averred.

I said, "That heavenly wanderer, for which it is named, imbued it with astral powers, perhaps?"

"Perhaps. Drink, sir. And then I will tell you a little story, a flight of fancy of which I would value your opinion. If you find it strange, so much the better! For, surely, one must not tell mundane stories between draughts of comet wine?"

Of that story, and of its effect on me, I will write soon.

Your friend,
Harry

*   *   *

12 April

My dear Bobbie,

Forgive the palsied look of my handwriting—I scribble this missive on the train that carries me from St. Petersburg, and the jiggling motion of the conveyance is to blame. Yes, I take my leave of this vast country, will spend some time in Budapest, and will return to London in time to celebrate your birthday. Meanwhile, I have a narrative to conclude—if this confounded train will let me!

The scene, you may recall, was the St. Petersburg apartment of Vassily Ivanovich Cholodenko. The characters, that enigmatic young man and your faithful correspondent. My head was light and bright with comet wine, my perceptions sharpened, as my host lifted a thick mass of music manuscript from the piano and weighed it in his hands. "The score of *The Brothers Karamazov*," he said. "It needs but the final ensemble. When it is finished, Lord Henry, all the impresarios in the country, in the world, will beg me for the privilege of presenting it on their stages!"

"I can well believe it," I rejoined.

"After that, other operas, symphonies, concerti . . ." His voice glowed with enthusiasm. "There is a book that created a scandal when it was published three years ago—*Anna Karenyina*—what an opera I will make of it!"

"My dear Vassily," I said, only half in jest, "I see a receptacle for discarded paper there in the corner. May I not take away with me one of those abandoned scraps? In a few short years, an authentic Cholondenko holograph may be priceless!"

He laughed. "I can do better than wastepaper," he said, handing me a double sheet of music manuscript from a stack on the piano. It was sprinkled with black showers of notes in his bold calligraphy. "This is Alyosha's aria from the second act of *Karamazov*. I have since transposed it to a more singable key—this is the old copy—I have no further use of it."

I thanked him, then said, "This story you wish to tell . . . what is it?"

"No more than a notion, really. Something I may one day fashion into a libretto—it would lend itself to music, I think. I would like your thoughts, as a man of letters, a poet."

"A very minor poet, I fear, but I will gladly listen."

He poured more wine, saying, "I have in mind a Faustian theme. The Faust, in this case, would possibly be a painter. But it would be patently clear to the audience from the opening moments of the first act—for his canvases would be visibly deployed about his studio—that he is a painter without gift, a maker of wretched daubs. In a poignant aria—baritone, I think—he pours out his misery and his yearnings. He aspires to greatness, but a cruel Deity has let him be born bereft of greatness. He rails, curses God, the aria ends in a crashing blasphemy. Effective, yes?''

"Please go on," I said, my curiosity quickened.

"Enter Lucifer. And here I would smash tradition and make him not the usual booming basso but a lyric tenor with a seductive voice of refined gold—the Fallen Angel, you see, a tragic figure. A bargain is reached. The Adversary will grant the painter the gift of genius—for seven years, let us say, or five, or ten—and then will claim both his body and his immortal soul. The painter agrees, the curtain falls, and when it rises on the next scene, we are immediately aware of a startling transformation—the canvases in the painter's studio are stunning, masterful! A theatrical stroke, don't you agree?''

I nodded, and drank avidly from my goblet, for my throat was unaccountably dry. I felt somewhat dizzy—was it only the heady wine?—and my heart was beating faster. "Most theatrical," I replied. "What follows?"

Cholodenko sighed. "That is my dilemma. I do not know what follows. I had hoped you could offer something . . ."

My brain was crowded with questions, fears, wild conjectures. I told myself that a composer was merely seeking my aid in devising an opera libretto—nothing more. I said, "It is a fascinating premise, but of course it cannot end there. It needs complication, development, reversal. Possibly, a young lady? . . . No, that's banal . . ."

Suddenly, a face was in my mind. The remembrance of it, and the new implications it now carried, I found disturbing. The eyes in this face were dead, as blank as the brain behind them; the smile was vacuous and vapid: It was the face of that living corpse, Balakirev. My thoughts were racing, my head swam. I set down my goblet with a hand that, I now saw, was trembling.

Cholodenko's solicitous voice reached me as if through a mist: "Are you well, Lord Henry?"

"What? . . ."

"You are so very pale! As if you had seen—"

I looked up at him. I peered deep into the eyes of this man. *They* were not dead, those eyes! They were dark, yes, the darkest eyes I have ever seen, and deep-set in the gaunt face, but they were alive, they burned with fanatic fire. At length, I found my voice. "I am quite all right. A drop too much, I fear . . ."

"Comet wine is unpredictable. Are you sure—"

"Yes, yes. Don't concern yourself." I inhaled deeply. "Now then, this opera story of yours . . ."

"You must not feel obligated to—"

"Suppose," I said guardedly, "that you invent another character. A fellow painter—but a man immensely gifted and acclaimed. You introduce him in Act One, prior to the appearance of Lucifer . . ."

"Yes?" said Cholodenko quickly.

"As the opera progresses, we watch an uncanny transferral . . . we see the gifts of this great painter dim, in direct proportion to the rate with which your Faustian painter is infused with talent, until the great artist is an empty shell and his opposite number is a man of refulgent genius."

Cholodenko smiled sardonically. "The Devil robs Peter to pay Paul, is that it?"

"That is precisely it. What do you think of the idea?"

"It is arousing," he said, his dark eyes watching my face intently. "It is very clever." Then, waxing casual again, he asked, "But is it enough?"

"No, of course not," I said, rising and pacing. His eyes followed me, flickering from left to right and back again. "There must be the obligatory finale, wherein Lucifer returns after the stipulated time, and drags the condemned painter to fiery perdition. Quite a scene, that! Think what you could make of it."

"It's trite," he snapped. "The weary old bourgeois idea of retribution. I detest it."

I stared at him, mouth agape. "My dear boy, you needn't bite my head off. It's merely an opera . . . isn't it?"

He mumbled, "I apologize. But that scene has been done before—Mozart, Gounod, Dargomizhsky . . ."

I shrugged. "Then we will change it."

"Yes, yes," he said, almost desperately. "We *must* . . . change it."

"What would you suggest? That your Faust be spared?"

"Why may he not be spared? Must he be punished because he wished to bring the world great art? . . ."

"No," I said slowly, "not for that."

"Then for what? Why must he be damned for all eternity? *Why*, Lord Henry?"

We were facing each other across the piano. He was leaning forward, his hands gripping the instrument's lid, his nails digging into the very wood. When I answered him, my voice was even and low:

"Because," I said, "of the man who was drained of his God-given genius to satisfy the cravings of your Faust. The man who was sucked dry and thrown aside. For that, someone must pay. For that, your Faust must burn in Hell."

"No!"

The syllable was torn from his depths. It rang in the room. "Why must he burn for that? He had no way of knowing whence that talent came! Even if, later, he began to suspect the truth, if he saw the great master wane as his own star ascended, there was nothing he could do, no way he could stop it, the pact had been sealed! The Fiend had tricked him! Comprehend, if you can, the horror he would feel, the guilt, the shame, as he watched that blazing talent become cold ashes, sacrificed on the altar of his own ambition! He would hate and disgust himself, he would loathe himself far more than one would loathe a vampire—for a vampire drains only the blood of his victim, whereas *he . . .*"

Cholodenko's voice stopped, throttled by emotion. His face was a mask of anguish. Then he took a shuddering breath, straightened, and summoned the shadow of a laugh. "But what a very good story this must be, indeed, to sting us to such passion. I fear we are taking it too seriously."

"Are we?"

"Of course we are! Come, hand me your glass . . ."

"I have had enough, thank you. Perhaps we both have."

"You may be right. It has made us irritable. I'm sorry I burdened you with my problems."

"Not at all. It is stimulating to collaborate with a fellow artist. But it is really very late, and I must go."

I reached for my greatcoat, but he gripped my arm. "No, please, Lord Henry. Stay. I beseech you. Do not leave me here . . . alone."

I smiled courteously, and gently extricated my arm from his grasp. I put on my coat. At the door, I turned and spoke. "That final scene," I said. "You wish something different from the usual plunge to Hell. Here is something that might prove piquant, and is certainly theatrical . . ."

Although he did not respond, I continued:

"Lucifer drags your Faust down to The Pit, but the opera does not end, not quite. There is a little epilogue. In it, those lustrous

paintings fade before the audience's eyes and become empty
canvases—I suppose that might be done chemically, or by a trick
of lighting? And the poor chap whose gifts were stolen is restored to his former glory. As for your Faust—it is as if he never
lived; even the memory of him is swallowed in Hell. How does
that strike you?''

I do not know if he heard me. He was staring into the fire. I
waited for a reply, but he said nothing and did not look at me.
After a moment, I left.

Please pass on to Maude the enclosure you will find herein. It
is the piece of music Cholodenko gave me—Alyosha's aria from
Karamazov. Bid her play it (I am sure it is beautiful) and you
will be the envy of London: the first of your circle to be granted
a foretaste of a bold new opera that is certain to be greeted as a
masterpiece.

Your friend,
Harry

•   •   •

Lord Henry Stanton's account of his Russian sojourn ends
there. The other letters of his in the packet purchased at the
Beverly Hills auction are interesting enough to possibly justify
future publication, but all the material bearing upon what I may
call The Great Cholodenko Mystery is contained in the three
letters you have just read. To them, I can add nothing about
Cholodenko, although I can supply some peripheral data available to any researcher willing to spend a little time digging into
the history of Russian music:

In the years following Lord Henry's visit to Russia, Mily
Balakirev enjoyed a miraculous recovery. He returned to his
abandoned *Tamara*, completed it, and in 1882 saw it produced to
acclaim so tremendous that it secured for him, in the following
year, a coveted appointment as Director of the Court Chapel. He
again became an active host, filling his home with musicians and
others eager for his friendship and guidance. He composed his
second symphony and his piano concerto. He conducted. He
organized festivals in homage to Chopin and Glinka. He personally prepared a new edition of Glinka's works. He energetically
composed and edited music even into his retirement years, and
outlived the other members of the *koochka* (with the single exception of Cui), dying in 1910 at the age of 73.

A final curiosity: A yellowing sheet of music paper, presumably the one Lord Henry mentioned, the page he said contained Alyosha's aria from *The Brothers Karamazov* in Cholodenko's own hand, actually is folded into his April 12th letter—but, except for the printer's mark and the orderly rows of staves, it is blank.

Afterword

You may wonder what the phrase "comet wine" refers to.

In 1811, a huge comet appeared in the sky and remained visible for a year and a half. During that period, it was very bright for many weeks, and created the usual fears and apprehensions.

As it happened, Portugal produced a very good vintage of port wine while this comet was in the sky. The comet had no connection whatever with the wine, but, with a shrewd sense of business, the winemakers publicized it as "comet wine," and sold it at premium prices for over half a century.

The story, as you see, has nothing to do with comets as physical entities, but its use of "comet wine" to cast another shade of mystery over the story is an important reflection of the psychological influence of comets on a fearful human race.

Ordinarily I might think that the comet connection in this story was too weak to allow it entry into the anthology, but I liked the story so much that I couldn't bear to omit it.

ISAAC ASIMOV

THE RED EUPHORIC BANDS

Philip Latham

After some hesitation I've decided to present this material pretty much as I originally wrote it, instead of recasting it in the formal type suitable for scientific publication. The trouble with scientific papers today is that they all sound as if they were written by the same person, an omnipotent individual who proceeds step by step, never faltering, to the logical outcome of his researches. But scientists are human beings; they make mistakes, act on impulses, and play their hunches, even as you and I. Certainly in my own case it would be downright dishonest to pretend otherwise, as the record will show. So without further apology here is the story of Paul Finch. (From his soup-stained diary of 1995.)

1994, Dec. 19

I feel terrible. Thoroughly depressed and tired of life.

The regular end-of-the-year letter from the bursar arrived this morning. According to the disembodied personality who writes these missives ". . . Van Buren University is happy to inform you of your reappointment as Associate Professor of Astronomy at the same honorarium as in the previous year."

What makes this annual insult especially irritating is the cozy language in which it is couched. Why should they be "happy" to inform me of my reappointment? When I know only perfectly well they'd be only too glad to get rid of me. Why an "Associate" Professor? I don't "associate" with anybody, not if I can help it at least. Why do they persist in referring my miserable little salary as an "honorarium"? Where does the "honor" come in?

Oh, well, I didn't expect a raise anyhow. I suppose I should be grateful for the privilege of being allowed to continue withering on the vine till my enforced retirement at 65. Only six more years to go now. To go *where*? With another world war practically here.

I'll bet Peabody and Wadstrom both got healthy raises. I can tell from the smug look on their homely faces. Furthermore, *I* know that *they* know that I didn't get a raise.

I might as well admit it—I'm in a rut. God! If I could only uncover something big again. Not much chance working on parallaxes and proper motions. Had all my luck right at the start.

I'm the discoverer of Finch 17, the nearest star to the Earth. Nobody can take that away from me. Stumbled on it by pure dumb luck. Red dwarf about 2 ly's away, half the distance of Alpha Centauri.* Created a sensation at the time. *Fortune* magazine voted me one of America's ten scientists under thirty most likely to succeed. And I believed it! Never done much of anything since. Tried hard though. Still my proper motion catalogue will be out soon, a good solid piece of work. Better than that theoretical stuff Wadstrom keeps turning out by the bale.

Jan. 11

Situation has deteriorated till war looks inevitable now. Experts predict it'll be all over in about thirty minutes. Curious thing is nobody wants war, nobody's mad at anybody else. Everybody's for love and peace. Yet we go right ahead getting ready for war.

You might expect speeches denouncing the warmongers, draft-card burning parties, protest marches, etc., like back in the '60s. Nothing like that today. Instead hopelessness and apathy prevail. People go around as if they're in a trance. I think Peabody's cracking up. He came in yesterday looking completely shattered.

"Finch, do me a favor, will you? Take my Astronomy 1 class this afternoon."

---

*Finch 17, p = 1'.'670, corresponding to distance of 0.599 parsecs or 1.953 ly's. Second nearest star is Alpha Centauri, a binary, distant 4.3 ly's, with 3rd member of system, *Proxima,* believed slightly nearer.

Since his lecture schedule is lighter than mine this semester I wasn't too enthusiastic.

"Something wrong?" I inquired.

"It's the students."

"What's the matter with 'em?"

"Haven't you noticed? They're so quiet lately. Sit there all through the hour . . . not moving . . . staring straight ahead—"

"Is that bad?"

"—with that bewildered wide-eyed expression you see on the faces of those dummies they use for crash-testing buses and airplanes."

"Probably on some new kind of dope. Watermelon rind or pumpkin seeds."

"Finch, you're way behind the times. All that psychedelic stuff went out long ago. Never really helped. Kids had to find it out the hard way. I think that's where the trouble comes."

"Afraid I don't follow."

"If war comes they're sure to be killed. They know they'll be killed. There's no escape. They can't even escape for a little while in their minds any more."

Peabody bent closer.

"You know what I call them?"

"Haven't the foggiest notion."

"Reverse zombies," he said, in a hoarse whisper. "They're live people who think they're dead."

"Well, all right," I told him, "if it's that bad I'll take over these zombies of yours."

I thought he was going to fall on my neck.

"Thanks a million, Finch, old boy. Do the same for you sometime."

He was off like a shot but I caught him at the door.

"By the way, what are you on right now?"

His face went blank.

"Let's see . . . what *are* we on now? Can't remember. Give 'em the moon . . . Kepler's laws . . . *anything.*"

A neurotic personality if I ever saw one.

Feb. 18

You can avoid this mass somnambulism if you keep yourself busy.

Just started a program on this new Comet Ikegawa. The orbit

people have appealed for observations so I thought I'd lend a hand. Remarkable object. Discovered out around the orbit of Saturn at 10 au. Can't recall any comet being picked up so far from perihelion before.

The astronomy department's a shambles. Peabody is home enjoying a nervous breakdown. Had to cancel all his classes. Wadstrom's always running around with a letter and a grim expression. How could Van Buren U survive without him?

June 19

Working at the telescope on Comet Ikegawa has brought back old times, when I was still fairly young and the world comparatively peaceful. Although the war was shaping up even then if we'd had the sense to see it.

Been giving the comet 90 minutes on these new 113pan-Q plates. Had to catch it in the early morning sky. So calm and peaceful nights. Looking up through the dome it's hard to believe a bomb might come hurtling out of those stars.

Ninety minutes seem forever when you're working alone. You think of all sort of things: your first date . . . the difference between a moth and butterfly . . . how the eggplant is allied to the potato. One thing especially my mind keeps going back to again and again is that report of the American Biological Society last year in Chicago. The biologists' committee on extraterrestrial life issued a report you could really understand, a rare event in scientific annals. The words stick in my memory.

". . . the development of a brain and central nervous system of such enormous complexity as ours was an event of fantastic improbability. It could not happen twice. In our opinion the Earth is the only place in the universe where life exists."

Think of it! Our miserable little Earth—*the only place in the universe where life exists*.

June 23

Comet Ikegawa is brightening so fast, got a look at it in the dawn sky this morning. You can make it out even after sunrise if you know exactly where to look. Although much closer to us the increase in luminosity is due principally to the sun. We'd better do all the looking while we can, for this comet will never be back. It's a retrogade object moving in a parabolic or possibly slightly hyperbolic orbit. A ''sun grazer'' similar to 1965f (Ikeya-Seki), but definitely not a member of that comet group. Comet Ikegawa will encounter the Earth twice, early in September and again on November 7. It'll miss by 21 million miles in September, but the one on Nov. 7 will be real close, although just how close is hard to say. Orbit isn't too reliable. Still got some residuals exceeding a minute of arc.

July 7

Comet Ikegawa is a splendid naked-eye object now. Head shines up there in full daylight twice the size of the moon and you can follow the tail out more than 3°, if you block off the sun with the tower on the library building.

A bright comet is an impressive sight all right. No wonder ignorant people in the middle ages were filled with superstitious fear. Looking at Comet Ikegawa I feel kind of awestruck myself.

August 1

If I had my way all comets would be below naked-eye visibility. Since the comet flared up so bright everybody is out gawking at it now. Some of their thinking is positively medieval! In fact, I'm beginning to wonder if we ever got out of the Dark Ages. One thing the comet has done which I would never have believed possible. It's snapped us out of our trance.

Under the constant threat of instant annihilation our lives had ceased to have any meaning. Only the present had any reality. Things happened to us. But they happened as in a dream, we moved from one event to another without purpose or conscious volition on our part.

But the comet is for real. You can see it. You can watch it move from hour to hour. It *must* mean *something*. Otherwise why is it there? First we were going to be smashed to bits. Then it was death by suffocation from poison gas. Result is we're pestered all day by phone calls from hysterical old dames wanting to know when they're going to be asphyxiated.

August 3

Wadstrom has honored me with his presence. He had a yellow slip in his hand.

"Seen this telegram about the comet?" he said.

I shook my head. "I was working on the comet late last night. Didn't get here till after lunch."

His face assumed a disapproving expression as if sitting up all night with a telescope was no excuse for not being on the job bright and early next morning.

"The Poulkovo Observatory reports presence of cyanogen and

carbon monoxide in the spectrum of the head and tail,'' he said. ''Also, unidentified bands in the red and infrared.''

Wadstrom always attaches tremendous importance to the spectrum of anything, probably because it's a subject he doesn't know anything about. He's an authority on tidal evolution and wouldn't know the G band from a gonorrhea smear.

''You understand this information must remain strictly confidential,'' he said, replacing the telegram in his coat pocket.

''Why is that the case, hmm?''

''If word leaked out about poison gas in the comet all hell would break loose.''

''How awful!''

''Remember—not a word.''

''My lips are sealed.''

With this burden off his mind he was able to relax a little.

''There's been a press conference on the comet scheduled for this afternoon,'' he said. ''Public's invited too. I hope we can scotch some of these wild rumors flying around.''

''Good luck.''

''Finch, it would be a big help if you could put a diagram on the board showing the relative positions of Earth and comet.''

''When's this meeting scheduled?''

''Four sharp in Hildegarde Hall.''

''All right,'' I told him. ''I guess I can manage it.''

''I'd appreciate it if you could.'' He glanced at his watch. ''Don't forget, that's four sharp.''

The diagram turned out to be kind of fun. So far I'd been interested chiefly in the comet's position relative to the Earth and sun and hadn't paid much attention to its orbital elements. Now for the first time I had to give the elements a good hard look. I copied them down on the same card along with the orbit.

It was ten till four when I reached Hildegarde Hall. Wadstrom or somebody had badly underestimated our drawing power. The auditorium was jam-packed, with hundreds more clamoring for admission. By the time they'd set up some loudspeakers out on the lawn and got a few other things under control, it was nearly five. After a few introductory remarks by the president, the meeting was thrown open to questions.

''Is this a big comet?''

Wadstrom took this one.

"Yes, I think we are justified in describing Comet Ikegawa as a 'big one,' " he replied. "Comets seldom are bright enough to be discovered until within the orbit of Jupiter. This one was discovered slightly behind the orbit of Saturn."

"Where do comets come from?"

Wadstrom shook his head regretfully.

"There is an old theory that comets are born of volcanic eruptions from Jupiter or possibly its giant satellites. Another has them originating in a vast comet cloud surrounding the solar system. It was once thought that comets reached us from the realm of the stars, but that idea is now generally rejected. The truth of the matter is we don't know where comets come from."

"How close is Comet Ikegawa coming to the Earth?"

"Within only about twenty million miles at the first encounter this month on the 23rd. The second encounter on November 7, however, will be very close."

One of the newspaper men had a question. "How close is 'very close'?"

Wadstrom looked grave.

"Unfortunately no definite answer is possible yet. The orbit still requires improvement. Let us say . . . within the distance of the moon."

"How does it happen the comet makes *two* close approaches to the Earth?"

"An interesting question," was Wadstrom's comment. "I believe that my colleague, Dr. Finch, can enlighten us on that point."

I went to the blackboard and began fumbling for my card. To my consternation I couldn't find it. I located it finally, but it gave me a bad scare.

"This represents the orbit of the Earth," I said, drawing a wobbly circle on the board. "This line here points to the vernal equinox, from which we measure directions in space. When the sun reaches the vernal equinox about March 21, then spring is here." This was meant to be funny, but nobody laughed.

"To draw in the comet we first have to know how its orbit is oriented in space. We do this, from the longitude of perihelion, the point on the orbit nearest the sun."

Ordinarily I would have the sense to skip such technicalities; but I was nervous, and talking out loud to myself helped steady me.

"Starting at the vernal equinox, we measure off the longitude of the ascending node around this way,'' I informed my uncomprehending audience. ''And then since this is a retrograde comet, we set off the argument of perihelion the other way. Which fixes perihelion for us here, in longitude 186°.''

I remained mute staring at the number. There was something familiar about it I should know. Now what was it? It was right here on the tip of my tongue. . . . Got it! Of course!

I'm not very clear about the rest of the meeting. My mind was too busy elsewhere. It seems to me the reporters worked us around into a corner with their questions. After a while we were answering them all the same way, ''Nobody knows.''

Sept. 12

Life for me has become intensely interesting.

It happened when I blanked out at the blackboard trying to locate that comet's perihelion. Only it wasn't perihelion that interested me. It was the direction of the point opposite that caught my attention. For it is this point that tells us the direction in space from which the comet came. I was sure I recognized it. The direction was the same as Finch 17, in Cetus.

Now comets approach the sun from all directions in space. Comet Ikegawa could have come in from Cetus as well as any other old constellation. Cetus occupies quite a bit of territory. If it had merely been the same constellation. I'd never have given it a moment's thought. Just a coincidence. But was it a coincidence when this direction fell within 5 minutes of my star?

Could star and comet be associated in some way?

I've done a lot of thinking about it since then. It is a very tempting hypothesis. Without independent evidence to back it up, however, I am compelled to reject it.

Oct. 2

The story about finding carbon monoxide and cyanogen in Comet Ikegawa was all over the front page this morning. Wish I could have seen Wadstrom's face. Nothing secret about $CO+$ and CN being in a comet anyhow. It's something we've known for about a hundred years.

Actually the spectrum hasn't been too exciting so far, the usual bright bands on a solar type background. Interest is centered chiefly in the weak emission features in the red around 6400 A, which don't seem to match with anything in the ARCS.* But

---

Atlas of Representative Cometary Spectrum.

identification is next to impossible on the low dispersion spectra they've got now, 100A/mm. Maybe the bands will pep up after perihelion on Oct. 6.

Oct. 21

It seems to me it was about a million years ago that I wrote, "Nobody wants war. Nobody's mad at anybody."

Not true any more. War fever's got us.

You can blame it on the comet. Sounds crazy to say that, doesn't it? It *is* crazy. Yet in a way the comet's responsible.

The comet blazing in the daylight sky was hailed enthusiastically by the lunatic fringe as a sure sign of death. With the country in an acute state of war jitters people were ready to believe most anything. To avert a panic the government had scientists go on TV issuing soothing statements, there's no cause for alarm, don't listen to the prophets of doom, etc.

Then just when the situation was calming down what happened? The confounded comet changed from white to red—blood red. That did it.

Astronomers tried to explain how the blood color was due to red rays emitted by molecules of the coma. What molecules? Well . . . we don't know.

November 3

Mass hysteria is always hard to resist.

Comet Ikegawa still shows puzzling deviations from prediction. With so many observations available the orbit should be nailed down tight. Yet perihelion occurred about 30 minutes ahead of schedule.

How close is the comet coming on Nov. 7? You can take your choice. Forecasts range from 0.00091 au (Poulkovo) to 0.0171 au (UC at Berkeley).*

Nov. 7, 10:10 P.M.

This is the night. I'm here in my office writing this in a last effort to hold onto my sanity. The campus is dark. Everybody else has taken cover, I guess.

Poor comet! Supposed to reach its descending node in about an hour. It'll be all around us while we're passing through the coma.

If I could only do something noble for science on this historic

---

*85,000 miles to 1,600,000 miles.

occasion! Something great that would be retold in ages to come. Like Galois penning his theory of groups in frantic haste on the night of his fatal duel.

Nov. 7, 10:37 P.M.

Mob's awfully close. Once on campus they'll smash the observatory sure. Nothing I can do.

All right. I'm ready to die. I'm tired of this world. Glad to be leaving it. In this final hour I think of these words from my favorite poem:

> Out of the night that
> covers me,
> Black as the pit from
> pole to pole. . . .

1:20 A.M.

Dammit! I've changed my mind. I don't want to die now. Got an idea for a possible check on at a tie-in between the comet and Finch 17. Good old subconscious.

Got so absorbed in this idea forgot about everything else. Suddenly struck me after about an hour I was still alive and the world was still intact. Kind of disappointing. . . .

But no doubt SOMETHING had happened. It was so quiet. Not a sound anywhere. Maybe I was dead and didn't know it!

I unlocked the door and stole outside. (Somehow it didn't seem right just to "walk" outside.) The moon, a few days past full, was just rising. Never saw the campus when it looked so serene and peaceful. So still! Not a leaf stirring. The trees against the horizon might have been cut out of cardboard.

After my eyes got dark-adapted I could see the whole sky was filled with a fine mist, forming lunar haloes of radii about 29° and 53°, their inner edges red shading off to pale blue. The sky had a distinct cherry red tint in directions at right angles to the moon, as if the light was partially polarized. Evidently the mist had loaded the atmosphere, damping convection currents. Jupiter on the meridian was the only star easily visible.

The air, unseasonably warm earlier, now was cool and fresh. Stimulating, too, with an acrid odor as if charged with ozone. I filled my lungs with it. I couldn't get enough. With every breath I felt my worries and anxieties slipping away, dissolving into the mist. Never had I seen everything so clearly before. My problems were resolving themselves. (They really didn't amount to much.) All the tangled pieces were falling into place. . . .

Dec. 19

Here it is almost Christmas. Examinations are over, thank goodness. Time to bring the old diary up to date.

So much has happened since the last entry, it's a good thing I don't have to rely on my memory. What follows is a composite of excerpts from several tape recordings, which I have transcribed into one in the form of narration. As I recall, these TV interviews occurred in the weeks immediately following the transcendent events of November 7.

"Dr. Finch, how do people generally react when a bright comet suddenly looms in their sky?"

"Well, I would say their reaction is generally one of fear and dread. As we have just seen, people are prone to regard a spectacular bright comet as an omen of evil, a portent of wars and other disasters."

"Is there any scientific basis you know of for this belief?"

"Absolutely none whatever."

"Yet from the dawn of history to our supposedly enlightened times this dread of comets has persisted. Can you account for this irrational attitude on the part of the public?"

"Well, yes, I think I can. Let me emphasize, however, that I am not a psychologist and hence cannot speak with authority on such matters."

"Go right ahead, Dr. Finch. I am sure that any light you can shed on this question will be received with the greatest interest."

"Well, my feeling is that a spectacular comet provides us with a convenient object on which to project our own failings. All of us, I dare say, harbor sins and evil impulses which we would like to rid ourselves by transferring them to others. But this is not easy to do. For other people, instead of accepting them, are more likely to turn around and blame *us* for *their* sins. Thus as time goes on we become filled with a sense of guilt and frustration.

"Along comes this strange apparition in the sky, this comet. What is it? We don't know. But our natural tendency is to look upon anything outside our daily range of experience with dark suspicion. Thus in medieval times the mandrake plant because of its forked root was considered the work of the devil. The tomato won slow acceptance in the United States; as late as 1900 many feared to eat tomatoes, believing them poisonous. Is it surprising that we regard this ghostly intruder from outer space with dread and ascribe all sorts of evil to it? The comet can't defend itself. It's the perfect scapegoat!''

"Then there's no reason *a priori* for regarding a comet as an omen of evil?''

"Neither evil *nor* good. Or an omen of anything at all, for that matter.''

"But wouldn't you agree, Dr. Finch, that Comet Ikegawa was distinctly an influence for good?''

"No doubt about it. The history of the world was changed during the period of scarcely one hour that the Earth was passing through its coma. The gases of the coma induced in us an euphoric state of a type hitherto unknown in the annals of medicine. Thoughts of war and hate disappeared. They are nothing but dim memories now. We are like a woman after childbirth who is unable to recall the pains she suffered during labor.''

"Have they succeeded in identifying the structure of the molecule that gave rise to this euphoric condition?''

"Well, I understand there's a lot of work being done on that. They may get a clue from analysis of those bands in the red. So far there's nothing been established yet.''

"Do you have any explanation yourself for the presence of those red euphoric bands in the spectrum of Comet Ikegawa?''

"I think that Comet Ikegawa was something very special.''

"In what way, very special?''

"I am convinced in my own mind at least that the close approach of Comet Ikegawa was no accident. I think it was sent here for the very special purpose of saving us from self-destruction. Man is an organism of enormous complexity. The development of intelligent life was an event of fantastic improbability. The biologists declare it could not happen twice. That the Earth is the only place in the universe where life exists.''

Dr. Finch paused for a moment. Upon resuming he spoke slowly, choosing his words with the greatest care.

"I am afraid the biologists were wrong. I think it *did* happen twice. I think there *is* another world where beings exist probably exceeding ourselves in intelligence. In some way—don't ask me how—they foresaw years ago that a world war was inevitable. And so, lest they be the *only* world remaining where intelligent life exists, they sent this cometlike body across space to save us.''

"But could they from so great a distance—''

"Not *all* the way necessarily from their world to ours. I suspect they possess a technique for assembling molecules of Euphorium from atoms readily available within the solar system. Doubtless only atoms of common elements were required . . . carbon . . . hydrogen . . . oxygen and the like. Some such molecular assemblage technique was postulated as early as the 1960s."*

"Well, Dr. Finch, that's pretty tremendous. Can you offer any proof?"

"Not real proof, I'm afraid. Certainly not proof that everyone would be willing to accept."

"And now I see our time is almost up. Dr. Finch is there any last message you would like to leave with our audience?"

"Only this. That we owe a debt to the inhabitants of a certain planet, a debt that we never will be able to repay."

A summary of my results will appear in an early issue of the *Astronomical Journal*. This new orbit of Comet Ikegawa 1995g is based upon images which appear on plates of Finch 17 taken some ten years ago for proper motion. Extending the ephemeris back ten years I found, as anticipated, a moving object whose motion corresponded in direction and amount with that calculated for the comet.

These prediscovery positions yielded an arc much longer than hitherto available, enabling me to determine new elements of exceptional accuracy. After allowing for the perturbations of the major planets, it appeared that Comet Ikegawa was moving neither in an hyperbola nor parabola, but in an orbit definitely elliptical in character. Notice that *both* the longitude of aphelion and the aphelion distance agree closely with the position and distance, respectively, of Finch 17. We call attention to this circumstance without wishing to emphasize it.

Just opened my end-of-the-year letter from the bursar. I see they've promoted me to full professorship now. Also upped my honorarium by $1,700. Wonder how Wadstrom and Peabody made out? Not that it makes any difference. . . .

---

*Verhandl. Deut. Physik Ges., Berlin, Vol. 71, p. 217, 1963.

THROWBACK

Sydney J. Bounds

The Museum of Language soared pyramidally for thirty stories, its base enclosing an area of nine hundred hectares in City center; a warren of corridors and galleried chambers, each level interconnected, piled high with books, tapes, and microfilm that overflowed through attics and down into cellars. It was a place of gloom and dusty silence, visited in the rainy season and by children out for mischief. A mausoleum dedicated to, and completely filled by, words—written and spoken—from the time before the Great Change.

Into this silence came the padding footsteps of the Keeper of Language, a gangling youth of twenty years with tangled hair. Preceding him, like a mischievous echo, the scamper of tiny feet. These hushed as he came to a chamber signposted *Literature* and began to hunt among the shelves, a frown creasing his pimple-spotted face . . .

"Should be right here," he mumbled, "saw it two-three days back, know I did." He had a habit of talking to himself, unconsciously seeking to destroy the endless silence. Frown-creases deepened as his gaze traveled the shelves a second time. "Everything out of order . . . those damned kids again."

He turned, raging: "Come out and show yourselves! What have you done with my *History of Literature*?" The patter of racing feet echoed along the labyrinthine corridors, fading fast. He glimpsed fleeting shadows before they were gone.

180

He'd never catch them, knew better than to waste his time trying. Scowled and grumbled. "What's it matter? Complain to their elders and get promises it won't happen again. Till next time. You can't change kids—seems like their only fun in life is upsetting the Museum's filing system." He was past caring, but when he wanted to lay hands on one specific book in a hurry—for his weekly recital—it was infuriating.

Kids. Experience had taught him not to expect any contact with them. They spied on him constantly. Natural. He was a curiosity, to them a freak, but they shied off fast if he tried to corner one, talk to them.

A memory returned, racking him. He had been very young when his own elders decided to send him to Schooling: it had been in the nature of an experiment, but more than that for him. A trial. Sheer agony. He sat in their Circle, encased in sound, blank to their questing minds, children and tutor alike. He sweated even to think of it now. He'd just sat there, mouthing sounds into their silence. No contact at all. Except that they could see him, he might not exist. The experiment had been painful, lasted only a few days. Then his elders had taken him away and raised him on sound tapes.

He put the remembrance from him and reached down another book from the shelf, blindly. Glanced at the title: *Great Romantic Poetry.* He'd already decided on Literature this week, so it would do. *They* wouldn't know the difference anyway.

Sometimes he wondered why he bothered to go through with the farce. He could get out of it easily enough. They'd agree to cancel, he knew. They agreed to almost anything he asked. Kindness itself. But what would he have left?

Nothing.

His gaze, misting, rested on the wall chrono and he saw that he had less time than he'd thought. He took a down escalator and began to hurry through a maze of passages towards the recital hall, turning pages as he went. Forty minutes was his usual stint; in prose, two, or perhaps three, chapters. How many verses?

Calculating as he turned the pages, he was only vaguely aware of high tapping sandals ahead of him, a blur of figure, before he collided with yielding flesh. The girl turned, bewilderment writing a question mark across her face, eyes concentrated on him—and getting no answer.

He mumbled, "I'm the Keeper."

Her face cleared in understanding, and something else—the

question mark was replaced by pity. Her speech came slowly, uncertainly, each word formed with unaccustomed effort. "Of course, I should have realized—"

"But your sort knows without looking where everyone is, don't you?" His words snarled out, almost a shout, in reaction to her pity. She winced at the loudness and he regretted it. She was near enough his own age, with dark hair and luminous eyes, a hip-length dress tight across budding breasts. His pulse-beat quickened, the body not knowing it was useless, that biology no longer had the last word in mating. *Last word*, ironic phrase that, he thought bitterly.

The girl sensed instantly how she'd hurt him and tried to make it up. They all did, parrot-fashion; he could guess her exact phrasing, even before the slow words tolled.

"Variation is good for the species—"

"But torture for the individual!"

That startled her. They weren't used to him snapping back like that, but their pity was becoming increasingly hard to take. Her pity especially.

She said, slowly: "I am D'Arqeve. I am going to your recital. What is the subject, please?"

D'Arqeve . . . Dark Eve. Her name would be related to some mental aura they alone sensed, yet still it suited her.

"Romantic Poetry." Irony again. Here was the girl and he had the feeling. If only he were a poet, to put into words how good it was to walk beside her, observe the curve and sway of her body, distill her fragrance. He had few contacts with girls, yet with this one he felt at ease. Useless. It would be different if he were as they . . . but he knew a mating would never be sanctioned by the elders. He was the only one of his kind and they didn't want more throwbacks. . . .

They walked the book-lined corridors in silence, side by side, and he imagined her struggling to find lost words. *They* didn't need words any more. Words were obsolete when they had the perfect communications system, direct mind-to-mind contact. He couldn't even imagine what that was like . . . a tri-D picture perhaps, in color? A kind of super-empathy, with taste, touch, and scent thrown in? Whatever its form, it was a network linking them all, while he remained an outcast. A throwback. The one man who could not communicate their way.

D'Arqeve stopped suddenly, looked intently into his face.

"You have seen the sky? The strange brightness? You can explain it, perhaps?"

He stared back, confused. "I don't get out much." That was an understatement; he couldn't remember the last time he'd seen open sky. (No need to explain he avoided meeting them, the man who was not there.) "What are you talking about?"

She shrugged and moved on again. "I thought you might know—from your books."

"I can look it up," he said eagerly, grasping an excuse to see her again. There were books in the Museum, books about the sky. "Astronomy." He would make an effort to get outside and see what this was all about.

They reached the door of the recital hall and she stepped aside to allow him to enter first. Others were filing silently in, taking their seats. Someone worded a greeting as he passed down the aisle: "Good-day, Keeper."

He nodded back, climbed the few steps to the platform and took his place at the lectern; waited while the hall filled, the door closed.

He didn't need to count. There would be exactly the right number to fill the seats. This was their way of being kind to him, his weekly period of communication. He spoke words aloud and they listened with ears they no longer needed.

He was beyond caring, except for one. D'Arqeve. He hoped she would understand the words of long-dead poets, relate their longing to his own.

Silence, complete, and into it his words rasped harshly: "This week my subject is Romantic Poetry." He plunged straight into—

> "How beautiful are thy feet with shoes,
>   O prince's daughter!
> the joints of thy thighs are like jewels,
>   the work of the hands of a cunning workman . . ."

His voice thundered, shooting the words of Solomon like bullets among them. Was anything getting across? he wondered despairingly. Speech had atrophied, words lost their meaning. Could they translate crude sound into their own mode of expression? Were they receiving anything except "noise"?

His voice lifted, became harsher. How to penetrate this network of perfect communication? Were his words—beautiful,

golden words!—no more than the piping of a reed whistle to
their full orchestration?

D'Arqeve sat in the center front row, her luminous eyes
raised and intent on him. She became the focal point of his
recital, feeling for her Shakespeare's sonnet as he lashed the
silent air, filling it with thunder and roses . . .

> *"My mistress' eyes are nothing like the sun;*
>   *Coral is far more red than her lips' red:*
> *If snow be white, why then her breasts are dun . . ."*

Behind the glowing words, bitterness. Tolerated, an entertain-
ment for his successors. The history and literature of all mankind
to give them and he didn't exist. A void. He was wasting his
time, his life. They had no sense of time, of the past. Their
talent linked them inextricably to the present *now* even as it
linked them together, limited their experience to the immediate
moment of contact. At most they were aware of fading memory.
It was the price they paid.

The lack of any real feeling of communication filled him with
despair and he cut short his recital, not waiting for the mellow
tone of the gong to end his period. As he sat down there was
polite applause. Silently, they filed from the hall; all except the
few, as usual. Always a few remained to put their laborious
questions. D'Arqeve was one of these.

"The sky," she said. "Can you explain the sky to us?"

Startled, still immersed in his subject, it took an effort on his
part to recall her earlier question.

"It is daylight at night," she prompted. "Explain this,
please—we are afraid."

"I haven't seen this phenomenon," he answered. "I'd have to
read up on it. I can do that for you."

"Oh, yes, do that, please."

There followed other, literary questions and he dealt with
them mechanically, his thoughts on D'Arqeve; yet he was
aware of a restlessness among them that was unusual. Again,
someone asked him about the sky; it seemed to be preying on
their minds.

He wished he'd seen this phenomenon for himself. Must make
the effort, study the sky, read the Astronomy books . . . his
attention wasn't really held. He maneuvered to stay close to the
girl, talking at her with each answer he gave, preventing her

leaving. He succeeded. As, one by one, his audience drifted out, he found himself alone with her again.

It was natural that they leave together. Walking the corridors, he said: "Perhaps I can see you home?"

"To see the sky for yourself? *Oh* . . ."

Her face tightened as she looked at him and understood. Her smile vanished. Ice-cold now. "I am sorry. You must know, Keeper, that my elders would not approve."

She moved away, down a side passage, and he watched till she was out of sight. Variation of the species, fine, only he wouldn't be allowed a mate. An outcast, doomed to live out his days alone. Hands clenched, nails biting into palms, he walked the lonely corridors of the Museum. His Museum. He was trembling.

Silence.

He rode the escalator up to his apartment. He had the largest single building on Earth, given to him, a mausoleum of blank walls and artificial light, and books—milliards of books, filling shelves by the myriametre. He had lived here, alone, since his eighteenth birthday, shut in from them, from the sky . . . no point in going out to look at that now.

He reached his door and felt in his pocket for the key to unlock it: the only lock in the city. They respected privacy, but they didn't need locks to achieve it; they knew if one of their kind was inside. But they couldn't sense him; he wasn't on their net.

He dropped *Great Romantic Poetry* heavily onto the table; heavy as his own heart. "Can't bother filing it. Doesn't matter anyway. Kids'll only hide it."

He dialed for food and pecked at it, his hunger not of the stomach. Alone in a room filled with books, filled with the great thoughts of great men down the ages . . . yet he lacked one human contact. He stared unseeing at the shelves, remembering the past. . . .

After his fiasco at Schooling, his elders brought specialists home. There had been tests. Every conceivable kind of test, one after another. Encephalographs. Drugs. Surgical probing. And every conceivable kind of specialist. Psychotherapists. Hypnotists. Even, once, a faith healer. One and all had gone away defeated.

They had even put it into words for him to understand. "We are sorry, there is no hope. You are a genetic throwback. You can never belong to our society. You must learn to accept your handicap, adapt to solitary existence.''

It was then he had feverishly studied the history of the Great Change, the mutation of the human species. There had been books written about it, at the very beginning, before it spread through all humanity and the use of words atrophied. But nowhere could he find a clue to help him. He could not join the club, never get on their network. . . .

The memory faded and he sat staring at a wall of books, a wall effectively isolating him from human society. No hope, ever. No hope of a girl, friendship, a mating.

Nothing.

He listened to the silence, sniffed at dusty air, undressed, and slid into bed. Automatically, the room light flicked off. Sleep was a long time coming . . . restless, he thought of D'Arqeve, longing for her. Finally, he slept . . .

And woke again. Or was he dreaming? That sound, that dreadful ululation rising from the streets, surely that was the figment of nightmare? A wordless wail of terror that turned his spine to jelly and set his skin crawling.

He swung bare feet to the floor. Light came on. He was awake; yet the animal howl continued. It could only be the wordless ones. *What . . . ?*

He rose from his bed—sure now that something terrible was happening—and padded to a window. Shutters creaked as he raised them. Outside was the night, and night should be dark.

But *this* night was bright as day. He turned to study the wall chrono: three a.m. Yet the sky blazed with light. And he remembered D'Arqeve's questions as he stared down at the street.

Shocked.

The night street, arcanely lit, appeared violently alive. It swarmed and surged with an antlike mob. Panic-stricken, trilling their eerie cry, they writhed in knotted confusion. He stared down, mesmerized, watching appalled as they tore at each other's flesh, overturned street cars, smashed windows. Jagged glass. Blood flowing. Their fear pulsed out, insidious, communicating itself.

He felt himself affected and drew back. Suddenly understanding. Of course, panic would be a very special thing for them; fear in one mind, fear in all. Instant terror, spreading at the speed of thought. He was viewing the breakdown of society. Chaos.

His gaze lifted. Now the sky filled his window-horizon, a sky aglow with a band of eye-dazzling light extending half across it in a great scimitar-shape. A sunlike ball, flaming tail. Glowing brilliant as a torch.

He stared, awed by the apparition, his mind working only slowly. But still it worked, conjuring up the memory of a book, a picture seen. The ancients had a word for it: Comet.

Struggle to think clearly. Comets had highly elongated orbits around the sun, returned after long intervals. Years. Decades. And *they* had almost no memories, no sense of historical time, no stored knowledge to draw on. So they wouldn't know about comets. One up to him. Who was *Homo superior* now?

Wordless screaming vibrated the air, sent shudders through him, set his teeth grinding. He flung on some clothes and hurried along dusty corridors, no longer silent but echoing with disaster.

Searched shelf after shelf. "Astronomy . . . must be a book somewhere . . . those blasted kids." Finally he found a tome labeled *Comets and Meteors,* flicked the pages rapidly. A picture: the same. Satisfaction.

All he had to do was convince them the thing was natural, nothing to fear. Clutching the book to his chest, he rode the down escalator, made for the main entrance hall. The hair-raising wail was louder, closer. Sounds of wrecking. Beyond the door, a mob milled in blank-faced terror, fighting. Tearing sounds as someone tried to force a way through to him.

D'Arqeve. She saw him and cried out: "Keeper! You must help us."

He lurched forward, using his book as a blunt instrument, caught her by an arm and pulled her inside, slammed the door. He took her to a small room off the main passage, panting; opened the book and showed her the picture.

"What is it?" she asked, her voice small with fear. "The end of the world?"

"No, no. It's called a comet—just chunks of rock and stones, surrounded by gas. Goes round the sun, like Earth, only it swings out farther, takes much longer. Comes back years afterwards. Comets have been recorded many times, see—?" He showed her bewildering astronomical tables. "No danger at all. A perfectly natural phenomenon."

Slowly, she calmed. "I must inform the Council of this. Wait."

She stood rigid, face concentrated. Anxiety. She darted a

quick look at him. "It's no good. Fear-waves blank out everything. We must go to the Hall."

He gestured at the wall. "Out there? We'd be torn to pieces!"

"We must still try."

He guided her along more corridors, to a side door. The street was not deserted, but the mob was less dense. Shadows crouched in darkened corners, wailing eerily.

They started off under a sky bright as day, running, dodging. One terror-crazed group tried to stop them; he fought them off, ran on to Council Hall where tormented elders writhed in silent agony.

D'Arqeve shouted: "The Keeper can help—his books know all!"

Attention focused on him as he gulped air into straining lungs, opened his book. The picture held their interest. He recited words, quoted, expounded, and they strugged to grasp his meaning.

He kept repeating. "There is no danger. A natural phenomenon. It's happened before, and will happen again. Listen . . . the appearance of a comet in the sky was widely regarded as a portent of impending evil; catastrophes attributed to the influence of comets. Superstitious garbage!"

That hurt. *Homo superior* objected to being called superstitious. . . . A great calmness descended on the hall. Council elders relaxed visibly. Utter stillness as their minds united to dominate the panic and inform the people.

It could not have been easy but, after an endless time, the wailing died and again there was silence in the city.

The Council chairman rose, his face grave. "Truly it is said, variation is good for the species. We are grateful to you, Keeper. Your knowledge is of lasting value and must be made readily available to as many as possible. The ancient study of language must be resumed."

He paused, straining memory for unaccustomed words.

"Students—in particular the young—shall train under you in this forgotten art of communicating with words, in keeping records. I rename your museum: *workshop*."

Keeper felt D'Arqeve's hand slip into his, press warmly, and he was happy, knowing she would be the first to join him.

KINDERGARTEN

James E. Gunn

First day—

Teacher told my parent that I am the slowest youngster in my class, but today I made a star in the third quadrant of kindergarten.

Teacher was surprised. Teacher tried to hide it and said the solar phoenix reaction is artistic, but is it practical?

I don't care. I think it's pretty.

Second day—

Today I made planets: four big ones, two middle-sized ones, and three little ones. Teacher laughed and said why did I make so many when all but three were too hot or too cold to support life and the big ones were too massive and poisonous for any use at all.

Teacher doesn't understand. There is more to creation than mere usefulness.

The rings around the sixth planet are beautiful.

Third day—

Today I created life. I begin to understand why my people place creation above all else.

I have heard the philosophers discussing the purpose of existence, but I thought it was merely age. Before today joy was enough: to have fun with the other kids, to speed through endless

189

space, to explode some unstable star into a nova, to flee before the outrage of some adult—this would fill eternity.

Now I know better. Life must have a function.

Teacher was right: only two of the middle-sized planets and one of the little ones were suitable for life. I made life for all three, but only on the third planet from the sun was it really successful.

I have given it only one function: survive!

Fourth day—

The third planet has absorbed all my interest. The soupy seas are churning with life.

Today I introduced a second function: multiply!

The forms developing in the seas are increasingly complex.

The kids are calling me to come and play, but I'm not going. This is more fun.

Fifth day—

Time after time I stranded sea-creatures on the land and kept them alive long past the time when they should have died. At last I succeeded. Some of them have adapted.

I was right. The sea is definitely an inhibiting factor.

The success of the land-creatures is pleasing.

Sixth day—

Everything I did before today was nothing. Today I created intelligence.

I added a third function: know!

Out of a minor primate has developed a fabulous creature. It has two legs and walks upright and looks around it with curious eyes. It has weak hands and an insignificant brain, but it is conquering all things. Most of all, it is conquering its environment.

It has even begun speculating about me!

Seventh day—

Today there is no school.

After the pangs and labors of creation, it is fun to play again. It is like escaping the gravitational field of a white dwarf and regaining the dissipated coma.

Teacher talked to my parent again today. Teacher said I had developed remarkably in the last few days but my creation was hopelessly warped and inconsistent. Moreover, it was potentially dangerous.

Teacher said it would have to be destroyed.

My parent objected, saying that the solar phoenix reaction in the sun would lead the dangerous life form on the third planet to develop a thermonuclear reaction of its own. With the functions I had given that life form, the problem would take care of itself.

It wasn't my parent's responsibility, Teacher said, and Teacher couldn't take the chance.

I didn't hear who won the argument. I drifted away, feeling funny.

I don't care, really. I'm tired of the old thing anyway. I'll make a better one.

But it was the first thing I ever made, and you can't help feeling a kind of sentimental attachment.

If anyone sees a great comet plunging toward the sun, it isn't me.

Eighth day—

WEST WIND, FALLING

Gregory Benford and Gordon Eklund

He rested: floating.

Zephyr lay ahead—a black dot in Sol's eye, haloed by the soft light of the coma: red, methane orange, divine. The tail was only beginning to stream and twist now—they had crossed the orbit of Mars—but no one on Zephyr would see the threads of ionized gas dance as they poured from the head of the comet, their pace quickening as the sun neared; Zephyr was too close. The comet tail furled out for half a million miles, directly behind the rock in which Paul had lived all his days, and to be properly studied a comet must be seen from the side. Earth would get a fine view. If they cared.

His shuttle clicked, murmured, shifted under him; the mass sensors had locked on Zephyr and were dutifully considering the tumbling rock as a source of new metals. Any zinc, for ion exchange plates? *No.* Copper?—good conductors are always useful. *No, none.*

"Idiot machine," Paul said, and thumbed the controls over from automatic.

The sensors found nothing because the outer two miles were ice: water hydrates of ammonia, methane and sundry impurities (and *ah*, but the impurities tell the tale, add the zest). A snowball with a rock at the center: home. Zephyr.

The west wind; so said the dictionary when, at nine, Paul looked it up. Or: *something light, airy, or unsubstantial,* a second definition. (Why have more than one meaning for each word? he had thought. It seemed inefficient. But he was only nine.) Yes, the second definition fit it better now. Comets are unsubstantial; Zephyr was a lukewarm scarf of gas clinging to a jet black stone, all falling into the grinning sun.

Now it fit, that is. Twenty-seven years ago, when Paul was born, the billowing gas was dead ice drifting in company with the stone, exploring utter blackness beyond Pluto. It had been cold then even deep inside Zephyr, but Paul could not remember it.

His search was over. He nudged the shuttle into synchronization with Zephyr's rotation, found the main entrance tube and slipped the craft down it. The tube walls were rigid plastaform that transmitted some of the watery light of the ice mantle. The two miles passed quickly. He guided the shuttle into its berth, helped a lock attendant secure the pouch of metallic chunks he had found, and cycled through the lock.

The attendant came through after him. "Hey," the man said. "See it?"

"What?"

"Earth."

"Oh. . . . Yes."

"Well? What's it like?"

"Beautiful. White, mostly. Couldn't see Luna."

The older man nodded enthusiastically. Paul could see he wanted to hear more, but there just wasn't more to say. Earth was a bright point, nothing more. The attendant looked sixty at least; Paul thought he recognized him as the elder Resnick. To a man that old, Earth meant something. To Paul, born in Zephyr, Earth was a dull, disembodied voice which gave frequent orders and occasional help.

"That's all," Paul said, and turned away.

A corridor clock told him it was time for the meeting. *Feh*— more diatribes. He had been hearing them from all sides lately. Everybody had turned into a political theorist. Still, his position in the first family more or less required him to put in an appearance. And at the very least, Elias was worth a few laughs.

Down chilly passages with a low coasting gait; murmur of distant conversations; oily air—filtration sacs saturated (My *God*, was he going to have to speak to those dopes again?) and faint tang of cooking; slight lessening of apparent gravity as he trotted up three levels (inward, toward Zephyr's center); smile from passing friend; quickening pace; and he arrived at the meeting five minutes late.

Paul found an empty chair in the front row and flopped down in it. He looked around the room. There they were—the third generation—nearly fifty men, all younger than forty, and an almost equal number of women. Elias stood at the front, wrapped in his own dignity, and he smiled at Paul.

"We may begin now," Elias said, looking up. "Paul is here, and we all know how essential he is to our cause."

Huh, Paul thought, his attention drifting. He glanced idly at the girl who sat next to him. She was petite, with incredibly red hair—who in the second generation carried *those* genes?—and freckles that danced across her pale cheeks. Fitting a hand to his mouth, he whispered, "Aren't you Melinda Aurten?"

The girl nodded at him and he smelled his tenseness. She couldn't have been more than seventeen and he'd never spoken to her before. As he leaned over to say something more he felt a twinge of conscience. *One more time, eh? For practice.* Being an important man always had its advantages, whether one deserved them or not.

"I say we must make our demands *now,*" Elias was saying, his voice a shade too shrill. "And they must be *met.* We are the third generation. We have the most to lose, the longest to live. The first is too old—most of the best of them are dead. The fourth is too young."

To Melinda, Paul whispered: "Why haven't I seen you before? Is my luck always this bad?"

"I've been here," she said. "You just haven't . . . looked."

A girl's voice from the back of the room said, "Can we not wait to—"

"Wait," Elias said scornfully. "*Wait?* The ships from Luna will reach us within a month. *One month.*"

"Why?" said the voice. "Did Randall tell you that?"

"I'm afraid he didn't have the *time,*" Elias said with mock wryness. He glanced quickly down at Paul, who smiled back at him and reached over to clasp Melinda's hand.

"But there has to be some reason we're to be picked up on the inward slope of the orbit, instead of the outward as was planned," the girl said. Paul knew her—Zanzee, a brown-skinned girl he'd shared a room with seven years before. He remembered the bubbling way she laughed. Um. But then, there was Melinda.

"Randall says it was an administrative decision on Earth. They want our detailed data tapes for the whole seventy-three-year orbit. Randall *says* rendezvous on this side of the orbit is slightly cheaper, too. Can anyone check that?"

"I have," Paul said, his eyes still fixed on Melinda. She gave an up-from-under look, using the eyelashes. "Ran it through, just pure ballistics. It's cheaper, but not by much."

"So it's a blind," Elias said. "They want to get us away from Zephyr before we, the third generation, have time to organize. Randall knows our feelings better than we do."

Paul leaned close to Melinda, lips against ear, and said, "Let's get out of here."

"Now? But—"

"Now," he said.

Elias's voice had shifted to a warmer, more confident tone. "We have no alternatives. The question is really quite simple. Do we stay in this world which is ours, or do we go to our so-called mother world? I have my own answer to this question, but I cannot speak it for you. What do *you* say?"

Paul got to his feet, dragging Melinda up with him. A hundred pairs of eyes blinked and flashed.

"Paul?" said Elias. "Where are . . . You can't—"

Laughter.

"I'm tired," Paul said, turning and grinning. "Like an old log. Got to get to bed."

More laughter, and Elias blushed, dropping his eyes to the cold floor. As Paul moved up the corridor, right arm warm against Melinda's thin waist, he heard: *"Stay. Stay. Stay."* And he thought: Elias owns the mob; too bad he's such a plimb.

Within an interval which lasted one hour, twenty-six minutes:

"Do you have the measles?"

"No. Silly. You know."

"But they run all the way . . . down to . . . here."

"Ye—   Ah."

A pause, and

"Why don't you lie back down? Or are you . . . through?"

"No. Little nervous—"

"About us? I mean."

"Uh. Not likely. It *has* happened before, you understand."

"Well."

"No, relax."

"I wonder what Elias was planning to do?"

"Him? Nothing. He can't get his shoes on without a guide book."

"His speeches are—"

"A cataract of lies and omissions, as some poet said."

"I think he—"

"Let's see, this arm goes here; a leg there, and . . ."

For a while he wandered, corridors moving like slow glaciers, passing the viewing rooms; on impulse, he paused to watch. The mammoth 3D mounted on one wall had been scrounged out of spare parts several years after the Zephyr expedition was launched. Paul had spent hours here, watching Neptune sweep majestically by, or simply studying the stars. Now he looked instead at the void, letting its black hands clutch at his stilled senses.

This was the only way to see the void without going out in a shuttle. The life of the expedition depended upon the layer of methane and ammonia snow that sealed them into the rock. The snow itself was covered with a flexible plastaform coat that prevented most gas from escaping. The society inside the rock core melted the snow for raw materials—nitrogen, carbon, hydrogen, oxygen—that fed the hydroponics farms and fueled the fusion reactors. We live off the west wind itself, Paul thought. And the void feeds on us.

Paul turned to the image of Earth. Thick white clouds; past them, brilliant blue seas and glimpses of brown, barren land. Seeing it, he failed to understand. It was lovely, beautiful, shining with human life. But the 3D tapes he'd seen: people jammed together like dogs in a kennel; food rationed; wars and riots; shades of bleak, shades of gray.

Most of the people in the 3D room were first generation, and they looked at the screen with something that approached hunger. Paul watched them stare. Then he left.

Remembering corners and turns in the warren men had carved from rock. Places where he'd studied—friends made and lost— sweaty games with a first young girl. And hadn't she trembled when he'd touched her? And hadn't he trembled, too?

And here—yes—where Randall had faced down a mob of rebels, angry over the numbing hours required when the hydroponics tanks went sour.

The old days. As he lightly walked the corridors, he remembered them.

He rapped at the door and heard Randall's crisp voice answer.

He stepped into the large room (reproductions of the twisted hells of Bosch; green wallpaper with red tulips) and closed the door quietly behind him.

Randall was seated at a large desk, speaking slowly into a hooded microphone. When he finished, he turned, smiling, mass of white hair, eyebrows like fur, and said, "I think I remember you. Aren't you my grandson?"

Paul nodded carefully, grin concealed, and said, "And aren't you some sort of wheel?"

Randall laughed. "Where you been keeping yourself lately?"

"Here and there," said Paul. "You know how it is."

"I know," Randall said. "Or did, once." He reached inside a vest pocket and removed a damp, yellowed sheet of paper. He unfolded it tenderly. "Let's see what sort of mistakes you've been making."

"Snooping again?" Paul knew the paper was blank, but he was used to the game.

Randall smiled. "Why do you think I'm the First? So I can read about things in the news sheet, a month late?"

Randall scanned the paper, frowning, the rigid lines cutting deep into the rolls of fat in his cheeks. "According to this, you seem as popular as ever in some quarters. You do not often sleep alone. Tut."

"And you object?"

"Not if you continue to learn your duties as well as you have. You would have made a fine First. If I hadn't hung around this long, taking up space, you would be First already. But your training will count, even back on Earth." Randall smiled. The wrinkles of his skin almost concealed its paleness.

"Huh? Look." Paul took a ballpoint pen from the desk and let go six feet from the floor. It fell, tumbling slightly.

"Five seconds. On Earth it would be less than one second. There's not much spin on Zephyr, grandfather—our apparent gravity is about one twentieth Earth's."

"Well—"

"We can't live there. We probably couldn't walk down to collect our disability checks."

"I wasn't thinking of living *on* Earth—"

"So do I get a job as janitor in one of their orbiting labs?"

"Nonsense."

"There's more to it than that," Paul said. "Nobody in the third generation wants to go back to Earth."

"You?"

"I don't give a damn."

"You never have."

"And probably never will. Not—"

"Not while there are better things to do? Right. Politics is just a shouting contest, anyway. Wish your father hadn't misplaced a wire getting that booster ready for the tenth planet probe—he was a born talker. He could handle Elias and his Lib friends right now, and I could rest."

"Libs?"

"Sure." Randall raised his eyebrows over the coffee cup, looking at Paul. "You don't recognize it, do you? Same kind of yammering. Bunch of anarchists." He paused a moment. "Say, you don't suppose they've been transmitting to Earth, do you?"

"Not likely. Why?"

"Maybe they think there are still Liberationists back on Earth."

"After the Purge Year? Elias has seen the tapes, just like everybody. He knows."

"Well, I wonder. There was a lot of Lib talk when we were assembling the expedition—hell, the Libs even had a majority in some countries. Lot of gabble about breaking all functions down to the simplest level, no unified direction. It was just plain luck that I got the position of First in the expedition, despite all the Libs could do." Randall's voice pitched higher as he became more excited.

Randall waved a hand in dismissal. He got slowly to his feet, walked to a wall cabinet and opened the top door.

"Look," Paul said, "you decided to expend most of our probes on the tenth planet, when we came so close. And you dropped the programmed study of Saturn, even though it had been planned from the beginning. You had freedom to do things like that. Where am I going to get a job with that kind of elbow room in it?"

"You will adapt," Randall said mildly. "Coffee?"

Paul shook his head.

"You should cultivate a few bad habits. They can sometimes be very pleasant companions." Randall stood for a moment, staring blankly at the stained cup in his hand. A timer buzzed and he filled the cup with a brown, oily liquid.

"What's all this talk, Paul? It sounds like—say, were you at that kids' tea party of Elias's?"

"For a while." Paul unconsciously began to tap his knee with a forefinger.

Randall laughed. His skin wrinkled even more. He had a way of turning a laugh into a series of harsh barks that irritated Paul after a few moments.

"It's funny?" said Paul.

"Of course. My God, Elias must be the twentieth fool I've had to handle on this trip. On the way out, there were fifteen at least. Boredom, Paul, that's what does it. The only solution is to keep everybody hustling, keep their hands busy, so they don't have time to listen to idiots like Elias."

He laughed to himself once more and sipped some coffee.

"This trans-Pluto shot was the only good thing the Libs ever did—God knows why. Probably wanted to draw attention away from their regime; it was running into trouble even then. So we matched velocities with this comet, hollowed out living space in the core, set up converters for methane and ammonia—all that while the Libs were being sandbagged with problems they didn't have a prayer of understanding, the fools. And just when we got started out on the 67-year orbit, back on Earth the Libs lost their shirts. Ha!"

Randall slapped the coffee cup decisively on the table top, slopping some over the side to form a pool at the base. He stood there for a moment, staring into space, reliving dead victories—and then sat down.

"Probably a lot of Libs left in this rock, too. Passed the same garbage on to their sons, waiting to—well, doesn't matter. They haven't got any choice."

"No choice?" Paul said. He had heard the song and dance about the Libs before; it didn't even register.

"The tenth planet, boy," Randall said with a grin.

"Omega."

"Yes, Omega, end point—but that's not official, just a name we slapped on it. Have to let Earth do that."

"We found it, we name it."

"Maybe. It was just blind luck that we came so close to it. Too close, as it works out."

"Huh?"

"We lost orbital velocity when we passed through Omega's gravitational field. Zephyr isn't on its original ellipse any more. When we approach the sun this time, we're not going to make the turn out at Venus's orbit. We'll zip right in, past the orbit of

200   *Gregory Benford and Gordon Eklund*

Mercury. We'll be so close to the sun our ice mantle will boil away in one go.''

Paul leaped to his feet—and then, wonderingly, sat down again. He had felt a sudden, desperate loss, and for the life of him he could not understand why.

"Quite a change in the orbit," Randall went on.

"No moon," Paul said.

"Right, Omega had no moon, so there was no way to get a precise measurement of its mass. Without that, we couldn't estimate the angular momentum we'd lost with respect to the sun. It wasn't until we got a good referent on the Jupiter-Earth-sun triangle that we knew for sure."

"We'll fry," Paul said.

"Certainly. If we stayed." In the silence that followed Randall drained his cup, not noticing the rigid set of Paul's face. After a moment Paul relaxed and shrugged and said:

"So it goes. I guess I'd better sweep the corridors tonight. I'll need the experience."

"I've got good contacts on Earth, old friends. I'll get you a decent position. I've started looking into it already. The rest of the expedition might not do so well, but my own grandson will—"

"Yes, what about the rest of them? Why hasn't this been announced?"

"I don't want a panic. It's easier to deal with Elias and his crowd than it is to handle this rock when it's full of jittery people."

"Maybe so," Paul said. "I think I'll have some of that coffee now. And a cigarette, too—might as well pile it on." There was a note of tension in his voice. Randall, smiling, did not catch it.

Central Computing: three levels in, sensor heart, pulse-taker of a west wind.

Paul asked: DEFINE M, CATALOG SUBMATRIX, SUM RULE FOR PARAMETER RANGE ZERO POINT THREE TO ONE FOUR POINT FIVE, CALL SUBROUTINES ALPHA OVERGROUP THINE, PLOT HEMISPHERICALLY, DISPLAY, EXECUTE, CHARGE: ABLE BAKER CHARLIE.

The first time, he made an error. The silicon-germanium-tellurium gestalt cogitated, conjured, went back to his instructions to verify. Yes; wrong. The light green screen displayed, in typewriter script, SWIVE THEE.

Paul corrected the programming fault, entered it again. The question now read in English: "What is the mass of the solid, usable material within practical distance of Zephyr? Time average required for next month over all known orbits. Display the result as an integrated sum over a range of geometrical surfaces.''

The machine pondered, collected; the result came. Paul watched the neat hemisphere form and made a few notes. He logged the information and began to set up a complex rate equation, using the data already acquired.

"My, at work as *well* as play," Zanzee said. She walked down the narrow aisle between computer readout stations. (The room was among the first bitten out of the rock, done in a hurry, and thus crowded.) Her chocolate-colored skin looked freshly scrubbed. "Where *do* you find the time?"

Paul waited for a set of numbers to be punched out. He sat on a stool, legs awkwardly crossed. With elaborate casualness he looked up. "Haven't seen you for a while. How's it going?"

"As usual. Your own work?"—pointing and reaching—"or more—"

"Private," said Paul, scooping up the notes. "Self-education."

"Ah." She arched an eyebrow. "A grandson of the First takes time for research?"

"Not research. Amusement."

Paul moved to tilt against the console behind him—not a hard operation in low gravity, even on the sticklike furniture—and watched her. Her hips were even fuller than he remembered. *No freckles, a real sister, but, yes, very fine.*

"Want to share a room again?" he said. "I'm free." It was direct, but what the hell—

"I'm sure you are. I'm not." She looked away, at the next console booth.

"Get free."

"I'm getting pregnant."

"Dumb. You'll have enough trouble readjusting to Earth without a kid; your first, at that."

She turned abruptly, black hair swirling out and slowly falling back into place. Paul had always liked that hair; he had even liked the frown she made—it looked like a child's impression of an adult getting angry.

"We're not going back. You'd know that if—"

"Yeah, maybe we're not," Paul said languidly.

"You—" She stalled for a moment, the edge of her attack blunted. He had always enjoyed playing such games with her. "You'd *care* about it if you ever grew up. You weren't planning to settle here, ever. So you don't mind if we go back to Earth. It just means more territory for your—"

"Uh huh."

"*Oh!* Compared to you, Elias is a prince. He acts; he's not afraid."

"So Elias is going to be the father?"

"No!"

"Pity. That's just what Earth needs, more like Elias."

"But we *aren't* going—"

"Oh yes. Forgot."

"Paul." Zanzee's mood suddenly changed; the fire left her eyes. "We know each other."

"To say the least."

"No, I mean . . . emotionally, not the other."

He nodded, wondering why women—no, girls—never liked precise nouns.

"Your support would mean—"

Paul stood up, righting the stool. "Why, Zanzee"—he did a little two-step shuffle, waving his hands—"you know I don't know nothin' 'bout politics." He made a flourish, folded his notes and tapped them into his right breast pocket, and was gone.

Paul slept alone that night. And dreamed, so:

A corridor, endless. Above, it is raining. The rain slaps against the roof of the corridor, beating out little tunes, and the corridor leaks, and the rain deftly drips inside. There are buckets to catch it, but they are out of place, and the rain falls unimpeded to the floor.

His nose to the floor, wet and muddy, the black ghost prowls the corridor, sniffing. The ghost is thin, tall; a black veil covers his face and his hands are actually paws, like an African monkey seen in a frozen 3D scan, or a large ape.

The black ghost ripples, and looks for an end to the corridor. He has searched for many decades (perhaps seven), but the corridor is endless, as is the rain.

The corridor is saturated. Paint peels. Flakes of gray cling to the robes of the black ghost, and he breathes heavily.

The corridor ends.

Below is nothing; ahead, above: nothing. Warm comfort of the corridor behind. The ghost faces the void, staring, shivers. Rubs his eyes; Paul's eyes; back to ghost eyes, wet from the rain.

A red halo—
Central Computing—

For man can rhyme
The tick of time.

Black ghost, white ghost: grapple, tear gobbets from each other's bodies. Shriek in the tumbling darkness. Aged white ghost, spinning madly away with arms *wrapped*—

Opening his eyes, Paul rolled over. He faced Elias.

"What the hell do you want?"

"Paul, are you alone?"

"No. I'm playing cards with five Chinamen."

"I—"

"Well?"

"Your grandfather—he's called Earth. The ships are on their way and they have added boosters. They'll arrive in weeks, two weeks."

Paul rolled out of bed. His room was bare, naked; walls of slate gray, a single shelf of microfilm canisters the only decoration. The first three volumes on the shelf were: *Being and Nothingness, Soul on Ice, Swann's Way.*

Paul said, "And?" with a touch of weariness.

"We've got to stop him. This'll be the end of everything. He must've heard of our plans. Did you tell him? Not deliberately, I mean, just let it slip out."

"I didn't have to."

"Oh. Uh . . . well, we can't go back to Earth. We'll be nothing there."

"I will. Even Randall will, but he doesn't know it. They'll probably grant *you* a priesthood."

"Can't we forget—?" Elias held out his hands, and Paul was surprised to see they were quivering. "We have to—"

"What are your plans?" Paul picked up a box of dried apricots from the end of the shelf, sat down on the bed and began eating them. (*A dream: had it been about brown, soft Zanzee? Probably not. Too old for that kind of dream.*)

"I'm going to position my men around. We'll take the main points, the shuttle tube, hydroponics, internal maintenance, communications, computing. When the ships get here, they will have no choice. Either leave us alone, or wait for us to surrender. They can't get through a mile of ice."

"And only a few at a time can come up the tube," Paul said.

"Right," Elias said, forcing a harsh note into his voice.

"You'll kill my grandfather?"

"No, never! There's no need for that. We'll only, well, hold him. Until things are safe."

"Until he dies?" (*About Melinda? Brown freckles, red hair?*)

"No. Just until Earth decides to leave us alone."

"If you free him, you're a fool. Randall is still the First and he has a lot of support. The older people like him, and they want to go back. Hell, I like him myself. He'd make two of you. At least."

"Together, we can handle him."

Paul laughed then. He'd been saving it since he woke up, and now he laughed directly in Elias's face.

After a moment Paul said: "Randall asked me to keep this secret from you, but I guess I can't any more. We can't stay here. I know you don't understand things like orbital dynamics, but—well, Zephyr will come closer to the sun this time than before. The layer of ice will boil away. We'll have no more raw materials for our hydroponics tanks, no more fusion fuel, and we'll fry."

"Are you . . . sure?"

"Positive." (*White ghost? Black ghost?*) "I checked it myself."

"Then . . ."

"Then you'd better pack your bags."

Was Elias going to sob? The great prophets of the past had wept frequently.

Elias said, "It's not right. I—"

"Shut up," Paul said. (*The white ghost held the key—*)

"If *you* had helped—"

"Forget that." Thoughts swirled in his head. *Jesus, analyzing dreams, am I? It'll be Tarot cards next.* "Listen, follow through on what you planned. Send your men out. Put a lot at the table."

"I don't—"

"Move." Paul stood up, rubbed his eyes and began dressing. "What time is it?" He found his wrist watch. "Oh, middle of the night. Fine." Elias shuffled his feet, started to say something and then left.

Paul waited a moment, mechanically planning. The dream still bothered him—which was in itself unusual—but he was beginning to feel confident again. *The white ghost was Randall.* But then, he knew that anyway.

*   *   *

"Grandfather," Paul said softly.

"Uh?" A soft neon clicked on. Randall was stretched diagonally across the bed, eyes clouded from sleep.

"Get up. Elias has made his move."

"What?"

"He's got most of the important points already. Come on." He helped the old man out of bed and into a pullover. Randall took a long time to awaken.

Paul kept him moving with a stream of explanation and prodding, detailing the probable situation. Randall moved slowly, fumbling with his boots, stumbling, unable to believe what was happening.

"A coded signal," he mumbled, tying shoelaces. "I sent it to Earth, asking for a step-up in the rendezvous. They agreed; knew I could still think clear. Elias might do something, cause some trouble. But I never—"

"It's not over yet," Paul said. He'd never seen his grandfather like this—so weak and so old. "The picture isn't as bad as I've painted it. But we've got to move."

They moved, down Randall's personal elevator, silence clinging to both. Randall chewed his lips, muttering, waving hands awkwardly in the air. Paul used his mind, running over moves, checking, estimating the timing. The elevator stopped.

"Why here?" Randall said. His eyes darted fearfully. A small room; confined. Hard to breathe.

"We're close to the tube lock. And your suit is kept"—the door slid open—"here. Get into it. Where's a standard issue?"

Randall motioned at a paneled case on the other side of the room. He cracked the seal on his own suit case and began to pull it on. Paul took the standard suit and began adjusting it to fit his height and size. His personal suit was in a storage vault near the air lock. After a moment, he stopped.

"I can't do much in a suit like this. I'll—"

As he started to turn, Randall dropped a hand on his arm. "What's the point of all this?"

Paul looked down at his grandfather, seeing age shiver inside tired eyes. Guilt erupted inside him, but he fought it. The universe was too large to encompass emotions. "We're going to decompress the rooms with Elias's men in them."

"That's . . . murder."

"Only if they refuse to give up. We'll take the pressure down very low, but they'll live. I'd never kill anybody. You ought to know that.''

"I ought to," Randall said. He paused. "But couldn't I talk to them? I've always been able to control them before."

"No," Paul said. "It's never been this bad before."

Randall nodded. "But why suits for us?"

"Somebody's got to go in and get them, even if they give up. That'll be me. If anything goes wrong, I'll signal over radio, and you can pull the cork on the room. I'll live. If necessary, you can come in to get me."

"That's a good plan," Randall said. "I wish I'd—"

"Hurry!"

"Yes, right." Randall fitted the suit yoke over his shoulders.

"I'm going out to the lock," Paul said. "I'll get my suit and be back. Stay here."

"But—"

The closing door sliced off Randall's protest. Paul propelled himself down the corridor, scarcely touching the walls in a long, loping run. Once, he looked behind him, certain that he'd heard an awkward step tracing his own. But the corridor was empty.

He stopped at the entrance to the lock area. Had Elias's men moved into position yet? There was only one way to find out. He'd have to walk right in.

Opening the hatch, he poked his head through the hole and looked around. Two short-muzzled pistols were being pointed at him by men he recognized from the meeting yesterday. He grinned. The men stared at him a long moment, then lowered their weapons.

"Got some cord?" Paul said. The two men looked at each other. They clearly didn't work around the lock. "Never mind." Paul bounced over to a temporary storage chest, rummaged around, and found some nylon securing threads.

"Be back. Don't shoot me." He went back to Randall's private suiting room.

He opened the door to the room, keeping the cord out of sight, and found Randall looking at him through the view slot of his suit. Randall said something, and then realized Paul could not hear him. He reached for his decompression valve. Paul kicked away from the wall and slammed into Randall's side, throwing the old man against the wall.

Before Randall could regain his feet, stumbling awkwardly, unaccustomed to a suit after all this time inside, Paul was behind him and had pinned the clamp locks in the suit's wrists to each other. Randall could free them from inside if he remembered how, but Paul counted on his not remembering immediately.

He was right. Randall struggled to bring his arms around, but they were bound together behind his back. Paul slipped the nylon threads around Randall's arms. He criss-crossed them through Randall's legs, shouldering the man about as though he were a large toy, and in a moment had him completely bound.

There was no time for niceties. He scooped up Randall and thrust him out into the corridor. The old man must be getting a hell of a banging, Paul thought, but the suit would keep him from breaking any bones.

He propelled them both down the curving gray hall, breathing rapidly. *White ghost. Black ghost. Grappling.* The walls of the corridor seemed to close in upon him, and he moved faster, nearly stumbling in his haste. This is my grandfather who lies like a wet sack over my shoulder, he thought. My flesh; my blood. The man who raised me from nothing and made me into the kind of animal who could turn on his own. Mad laughter caught in his throat, and he slammed into the hatch.

He paused for a moment, catching his breath, counting to ten and reciting some Greek. Then he entered the room.

The two men stared at the bundle he carried; even through the view slot, they could see it was Randall.

"How—?" one of them said.

"Shut up," Paul said. "And hold this for me." He handed Randall to the men. He had to hurry; Elias would probably be here in a few moments. There wasn't any time to waste, but . . . *Forget that,* he told himself. He's just a man. You owe him nothing; it's his life or yours. He's old; you're young.

He had no trouble finding his personal suit. He slipped into it, and headed back to the central receiving area. Elias was waiting for him, standing over Randall.

"Elias," Paul said. "Send those men for a cradle of oxy bottles." Elias had brought two more men with him; Paul wanted them out of the way. "Now."

"What do you—?"

"Now!"

"Well, all right. Zabronski, Kanyen, do like he says."

The two trotted off. Elias pointed at Randall. "What—?"

"He's too much of a symbol. The older people will follow him anywhere. You don't want that, do you?"

"No. I—"

"Good. Then we're going to put him out of reach. I'll take him out with air and food and leave him on the surface of the ice. I'll hide him in a little valley somewhere, bound, with enough freedom of movement to replace his bottles and feed himself."

Elias frowned uncertainly. "This seems a bit drastic. Couldn't we—?"

"Are you afraid?"

"No." Elias shrugged. "He's your grandfather."

And that, Paul thought, was the key. "Open Randall's suit. I want him to hear us."

Elias did as directed. Randall's suit was orange-red, and he looked like a fat, grotesque lobster lying in the main bay of the airlock.

"Paul," he said, his voice soft, muffled.

"Randall, I—"

"Listen to my instructions," Elias said. "I am about to cast—"

"I don't have to listen to you." Seeing Elias had brought back Randall's strength. "If you kill me, you'll let anarchy loose on this world."

"Anarchy," Paul said. "And what's wrong with that?" The two men returned, wheeling a rolling cradle of bottles. They'd been listening: a case of food and water squeeze bottles rode on top.

Randall was glaring at Paul. "I don't understand," he began. "My own grandson. Paul, we could have—"

"I'm sorry," Paul said. "But it was meant to happen this way. I think you knew that all along."

Randall started to speak, but only nodded lamely.

"Didn't you ever wonder why you were chosen to be First on Zephyr when the Libs had a majority?" Paul said.

Elias looked strangely at Paul, and Randall again nodded. The other men stood silently, not following a word of the conversation.

"I think I know," Paul continued. "They had to throw a sop to the planners and bureaucrats and pencil-pushers, and you were it. But they knew you wouldn't matter, because they were right, in their way, about politics."

"They were criminals," Randall said, his voice far away, as if speaking from another time. "All of them."

"Probably so, before it was finished. By now, I'm a criminal, too. All men of action are criminals to somebody. The Libs wanted this trans-Pluto shot, but not for science or glory. They thought you'd be dead; they didn't reckon with low-gee and how long it can prolong life. They *did* know that freedom of the kind they dreamed about couldn't continue in that sardine can Earth was getting to be.''

''Ah,'' said Elias. Paul glanced at him. *Perhaps he's smarter than he seems*, Paul thought. *I'd better hurry this. A man who is dying deserves to know the truth.*

''The Libs sent Zephyr out, a small community, independent of Earth. They knew we wouldn't want to come back after the trip was over. As long as Zephyr was out beyond range of Earth's fast carriers, she was free. When she runs dry of nitrogen and oxygen, we'll find another comet out there, beyond the tenth planet. We saw enough on our first pass—next time we'll know what to look for. And as long as Zephyr is free, somewhere, *men* are free.''

''If Earth should destroy itself,'' Elias said slowly, ''we can go back to replenish it.''

Paul could see Elias already working out a role for himself in this new, unplanned drama. He would polish it, get the lines down right, and pretty soon believe it had been his idea all along. And convince the others, too.

But Randall didn't see it that way. Lying on the floor, his eyes closed, he began to laugh softly.

''What's funny?'' Elias said, irritation flooding his face.

''You are,'' Randall said. ''And Paul. You and your splendid plans. Going to replenish the Earth, are you? Well, haven't you forgotten something? You're not going to be in any position to replenish anything. After Zephyr passes the sun, neither of you will be anything more than a burnt corpse.''

Fear replaced the anger on Elias's face. He turned on Paul. ''What—?''

Paul shook his head. ''It's no problem. I catalogued the solids cruising in the same orbit as Zephyr, the junk that's followed us all the way around our ellipse. If we use every shuttle and work them constantly, we can collect enough to make a shield of rock. There might even be time to polish the surface, just to be sure we're safe. A hemisphere a few meters thick should do it.''

Randall laughed again, a bitter laugh. ''You have an answer for everything, don't you?''

''Just about,'' Paul said. He looked at his grandfather for a long moment, eyes meeting eyes, then turned to Elias. "Seal Randall's suit," he said. "We've wasted enough time."

He waited: floating.

"Can you reach the bottles and make the attachment?" Paul called down to Randall. They were connected by a talk pipe of metal that carried sounds between suits.

"I can."

"Well, let's hope Earth doesn't take too long to turn her ships back."

There was a pause. Then Randall said, "It's cold out here, Paul." His voice throbbed with the pain of antiquity. "So cold."

"You have extra power packs," Paul said. "Use them."

The milky light of early dawn on Zephyr's surface was filtering through the ice, refracted around the edge of the mantle and surfacing here. There was a somber orange to it that made Randall's suit stand out even more in the shallow hollow Paul had found for him. Down there, resting, the old man looked fragile, and very much alone. Like mankind in the universe, Paul thought. A tiny speck in the dark hollow.

"I'll die," Randall said. "You know I'll die. Look at me and say you don't know it."

Paul looked at his grandfather. "I know it's probable."

The void stood poised above them both, a vast empty devouring cloud.

"You're murdering me," Randall said. "And for what? For a *cause*. For a stupid, silly pointless cause."

"Not for a cause," Paul said, for there were no causes in his life. "For me. For my freedom."

Above, hard stars twisting in the void, shrouded by the brightness of the coma, turned slowly. In a moment, Earth would be visible, bright beacon of Man.

It calls not to me, Paul thought. Let it call to Randall.

"Paul—! Please—!"

I loved him once, Paul thought, and I've never loved anyone else. I worshiped his feet, kissed his every word. And now I've killed him.

Paul lifted the talk pipe away from Randall and attached it to the side of the shuttle. He stared down at the lone figure on the ice for a moment, then started the shuttle's jet. He did not wave. He did not look back.

The hollow that held Randall was twenty-five kilometers from the tube, but the trip was short. He flew over raw knives of dark ice, into the dawn. Paul clicked on his suit radio and called the lock.

"All secured," Paul said, his tone controlled. "Coming in."

There was a brief reply, from Elias.

Everything, from the start, had depended upon rushing Elias, keeping him moving, not letting him think. Randall wasn't the major obstacle, but he could have been if he'd stayed in Zephyr. It was Elias who would decide it all.

Paul moved the shuttle and dropped down the tube. The light around him dimmed and wavered, casting pale replicas of the shuttle's shadow. *Black ghost, falling.*

Paul remembered one line from the babble Randall had shouted on the trip out:

Do you really want to live under Elias?

Elias was the key. Once Paul gave him the idea of putting Randall in cold storage on the surface, what was more natural than the next step? Paul hadn't given a damn about the kindergarten politics Elias had played . . . but now things were different. And Paul was the only rival Elias had. Now, like it or not, he had to play the game.

He eased back on the jets and braked. The running lights had come on automatically and he maneuvered the shuttle into its berth. He felt a bit giddy in free fall; not enough breakfast. And what would he be doing now, Paul wondered, if Zanzee had slept with him last night, and he'd thrown Elias out when he'd come with the message? Paul grinned to himself, then laughed aloud. He didn't know. Events made the man. (And the murderer?)

He kicked off and approached the personnel air lock. The operational lights were normal; everything looked the same.

But if Elias seized his chance, he could seal Paul out forever, make him, too, a prisoner. In a moment, Paul saw it: he and Randall together and dying, with madness approaching, and hunger and thirst, and the terrible cold.

For an instant he cursed himself and his irrationality. He had done the job himself because—at last, he thought, are you going to admit it to yourself?—because Randall was his own blood. He could not send one of his own down that last dark path, alone. The act, in finality, had to be his.

Paul could have assigned this to another. He should be—now— with Elias, waiting for some lieutenant to return from the cold.

He should, said logic. But he knew that he could not, beyond all logics and all systems. To save any thread of dignity, the blade should come to Randall from one of his own.

Before he could catch it, some small voice in the turmoil of his mind asked:

And is that all? You did not know that a lieutenant, having done a general's job, will never truly be a lieutenant again? Are you sure there was no calculation?

Paul felt himself go rigid for a moment, blocking the thought. This, he thought, was what he had not expected. Once you begin to play the game and count the points, once that, things are not so clear. He would never really know for sure.

"I'm secured out here," Paul called over his radio. "Cycle the lock."

There was a pause. Paul put his hand on the lock hatch and waited. Seconds slipped slowly past.

Then it happened: A tremor, ever so slight, and the hatch came free.

Paul stepped through.

The gamble had worked. Elias hadn't thought quite fast enough. Paul was a free man. Once inside, he knew he could face down Elias and any of the men Elias had with him.

Paul breathed deeply of the oily air of the suit. It reeked with tension, death, and fear.

Do you really want to live under Elias?

No. He didn't intend to.

But why, he thought, *why am I crying?*

THE COMET,
THE CAIRN AND THE CAPSULE

Duncan Lunan

Three was the magic number in the design of the spaceship *Newtonian*. At launch, there had been three reaction mass tanks side by side in what older designers still called "Titan III configuration." A and B tanks had given their all to rendezvous orbit insertion and been jettisoned, taking with them the auxiliary thrust chambers and large segments of radiation shielding. (The turbines and as much as possible of the pump system were on *this* side of the shielding, and of course the helium feed tanks were right up *this* end, so EVA repair was at least possible, if needed.) There remained the sustainer motor, pile, shielding, C tank, then the service module and crew sphere, flanked by two modified lunar shuttles. One was topped by a capsule (Penetration Module), the other by a winged Earth Lander. When the Lander was sunward and its shadow fell on the crew sphere, it made the ship look like a ceremonial trident hanging in space.

Inside the ship, three was anything but a magic number. Paxton and Scherner had taken to sleeping in the Lander and Penetration Module, respectively, to get away from Sullivan and each other. It might be because, for the first time ever, they were traveling at a velocity which would take them out of the Solar System unless diminished; the psychologists at Mission Control had no other explanation for the unforeseen development; but the clash of personalities had arisen three weeks out from Earth, and escalated over the weeks following. In the last few days they had

213

been meeting only to collect their rations at feeding time, and had spoken only during routine checks.

It might, Scherner thought, have something to do with the visual aspect of what lay ahead. The comet was now putting on its full display, less than a week from perihelion, and the *Newtonian* was now very close indeed. The awesome spectacle of the tail, millions of miles long and beginning to curve as the nucleus gained speed, was foreshortened out of existence; they saw only the shock wave of the coma, spraying out from the bright spot of the nucleus, then pushed back by solar wind into a great plume against the stars. The ship's slow rotation wound the head around the forward window like the sweep of a celestial radar, but from the side windows only a faint mist could be seen, fading off into invisibility. Something so big but only seen from a distance was disturbing, as if the head too might vanish as they approached it.

By now, however, more detail was showing. They could see shells and smoky patterns in the gas coming off the nucleus, and the bright star of the nucleus itself had become a sunlike disk with spikes projecting from it. Behind the nucleus lay a tunnel of shadow, blurring away at its edges till it vanished into the glowing haze of the tail. Now the coma filled all the sky ahead, and was beginning to move across the field of view; it was time for the *Newtonian* to match orbit. Hyperbolic orbit, rare indeed, this comet was a stranger to the Solar System, and would never return.

The three astronauts strapped into their couches and got down to work, with a minimum of conversation. Mission Control, far enough away in any case to have little effect on the quarrels, was taking a business attitude—the mission had to go on, whatever the clash of personalities. The ship's rotation was halted, last refinements were applied to the burn computations, and the *Newtonian* turned away from the comet. The burn was a relatively short one at max chamber temperature, to boost the hydrogen jet past the comet altogether. If those superheated ions impinged on the coma, burning into those fragile shells, all the scientific objectives could be frustrated. There was no chance the crew would let that happen, taking out their resentments on the celestial body: each man's specialty was now taking absolute priority, as far as he was concerned.

They were much nearer the comet when Scherner saw it next, from the observation turret on the crew sphere, when the ship turned back to face it. The fuming gases around it seemed motionless, but after some minutes changes could be detected. The dazzling spikes around the nucleus were no longer sharp, but still too blurred overall by intervening gas and ice crystals for the telescope to resolve them. Probing with radar and laser beams, Paxton could tell even less about them; he was getting a general reflection from a layer about double the size of the nucleus, which by visual estimate was six hundred miles across. Scherner suspected that the spikes were internal reflections in a cloud of ice fragments orbiting the nucleus, but the changing light patterns he detected might just be due to the movement of gases out and back.

"At any rate," he reported, "I can't see any obvious hazards to Penetration."

"Radar seems to confirm that," Paxton broadcast. "The boundary layer I'm getting seems to be quite clearly defined. If we're following the programmed approach, we won't run suddenly into any problems."

They waited, still moving slowly toward the comet, for the signal to journey to Earth and the reply to amble back. A great deal of power was going into the *Newtonian* signal, to overcome their narrow separation from the sun. Interference had proved unexpectedly serious, and Sullivan's clamp-down on personal messages had been the first source of friction aboard. It wasn't as if they were overworking fuel cells, with power coming direct from the pile, and Scherner suspected that Sullivan, himself unmarried, was actively jealous of their daily hook-ups to their homes. Mission Control should have realized that a man without a wife and children could be most homesick of all and arranged someone to talk personally to the mission commander, but Scherner could hardly suggest that on open circuit with Sullivan right beside him. So Sullivan kept all radio time for business, and Scherner and Paxton lost a valued link with home.

The Mission Control bleep sounded. "Roger, no visible hazards. We agree that you should prepare for Penetration. Confirm launch readiness for final go/no-go decision. Over." *Bleep*.

"Okay, Dave," said Scherner, speaking directly to Paxton for the first time today. He didn't have much against Paxton, really, but he always felt he was talking across Sullivan when he addressed him. Perhaps the same feeling accounted for Paxton's incivility to *him*. "Why don't you move across into the PM, and I'll follow you through." He put the lens caps back on the turret instruments and stowed them for the next deceleration, then pulled himself feet-first back into the center section of the sphere. Sullivan didn't speak as he worked his way across, so neither did he.

Personnel selection had been almost wholly successful, he conceded as they checked out the Penetration Module. In space fiction (he'd never had time to read any, but he knew just what it was like) at least one member of the crew had to be a maniac, an agoraphobe, or something equally hard to detect, bent on aborting the mission five minutes after liftoff. But though the longest space flight yet had fallen down on compatibility, the conflict didn't even touch the mission program. After his unreasonable ruling on the signals, Sullivan had found it necessary to impose his authority in a string of minor matters, probably because he knew he had been unreasonable. He, Paxton and Scherner had worked up a real dislike of one another, but they weren't thinking of curtailing the flight.

There was a way to curtail the flight, but it was intended for more serious difficulty than this. After perihelion they had an "abort window," a chance to fire the motor and drop right back, returning to Earth three months later. Otherwise, riding outward with the comet as they studied it, they would make their separation burn not far from Earth's orbit and meet Earth itself nine months later. Fifteen months' voyage, or six; and they were going for fifteen, without hesitation.

There could still be a scientific payoff if they had to abort. The Lander's cargo space contained a payload at present, a much less sophisticated payload than the PM's. If Penetration of the comet proved impossible, they could launch a nuclear device which, hopefully sinking to the nucleus before detonation, would supply some of the data they hoped to get less violently from Penetration, and the experimental package—in effect, a complete space probe—they would leave behind.

The checks went through without incident, and they received a go for launch. They counted down the separation, and Paxton turned the craft for Sullivan's visual inspection. Then they moved out laterally, and Sullivan turned the *Newtonian* around once more. The final burn was gentle, the flaring gases missing the PM and the comet, bringing the spaceship to rest in the observation station it would hold for the next fourteen days. The PM traveled on with its original momentum, toward the hazed brilliance of the cometary nucleus.

There was no spectacle or sensation when they entered the

coma. Like the end of the rainbow, the smoky plumes of gas receded and dissolved before them. But little by little the glow around the nucleus spread above them and below, waxing brighter and separating into bars and columns like auroras. Now the spikes were breaking up, visually, into discrete sources—tens, dozens, hundreds—each one brilliantly reflecting the sunlight along spikes to its own. By the time the streamers of haze completely surrounded the capsule, the nucleus ahead was a lattice of light beams, with what seemed to be a second sun at its heart.

"We're going to slow the ship," Paxton reported, activating fly-by-wire. "Much of what looked solid from outside is separating now. There's a huge shell of ice fragments, probably orbiting in clusters, though gravity's so low you can't detect it. If the nucleus itself was more massive, we'd probably get a ring, like Saturn's. As it is, I don't see any problems in continuing Penetration. We can treat this stuff as weightless and stationary."

They burned their chemical motors to slow up; only briefly, for gravitational acceleration was negligible. Making less than five hundred miles an hour, the PM traveled into the three-dimensional ice field.

The "descent" was okay; they could see the solid surface they were making for, and bodies in their path separated visually and on radar in plenty of time to be avoided. Waves of sun-driven gases passed them from the huge bergs, too tenuous to affect visibility.

"By dead reckoning, we're two hundred miles inside," Paxton radioed. The PM's signals were being relayed through the *Newtonian* to Earth (another reason for the ship's sunward position), and they'd had loss of signal several times as they passed floating masses. "The concentration of material is increasing, and we're cutting speed right now with another thirty-second burn. As well as ice masses, we're now seeing dark rocky fragments, from which all the gases must have sublimed away. They're all of considerable size, up to hundreds of feet across. Our micrometeor counters have not registered any significant increases in impacts, and I'd deduce from that that the smaller rock fragments are being carried out into the tail by sunlight pressure and solar wind. This would seem to confirm the origin of meteors along cometary orbits."

"Roger, Dave," Mission Control said eventually. "We're happy with your fuel consumption, as indicated by Mike's last set of figures, but there's some anxiety here about your frequent use of vernier and braking engines. Your last burn should reduce the need for frequent restarts. Of course, each engine should be able to take several hundred separate burns, but we'd like you to keep to fewer, longer burns if possible.''

This was a problem they had foreseen. In a stronger gravity field, descending, they could keep the motors burning steadily at low thrust; but for such an approach to the comet, with the drawn-out Penetration through the rock and ice field, they'd have to come in much too fast. Conversely, if they'd started slowly enough to make the Penetration on attitude control jets, it would have taken far too long. But by now the situation had changed.

"We're nearing shoals, that's the best way I can put it," said Paxton. "There's a lot of loose stuff ahead, forming an inclined plane across our line of Penetration. I'd say it's material which broke away from the nucleus in the first major solar heating, before the coma began to form and scatter the incident radiation. This ahead of us is the lighter stuff, beginning to drift backward as the cloud of new fragments takes up a conical shape. Its transverse velocity is pretty well negligible, and we should go through without trouble. We're going now to continuous vernier burn.''

Tail-first, motors idling, they slid through the final barrier. Paxton held the ship confidently on fly-by-wire, turning the gimbaled verniers for brief bursts to avoid denser clouds of fragments. Visibility was poorer now, with so many reflecting surfaces around that they were back to the lattice effect, softened now by the greater density of gases. Then suddenly the jeweled reefs were above them, and they began their final braking.

"We're now in the lee of the stone nucleus, starting our final approach. The body looks to be loosely compacted chunks of rock and ice, with gravity very low. The streams of gas and pieces breaking away are all coming from the area under direct sunlight; the surface appears stable along a broad strip toward the terminator.''

"I'm getting a really bright radar echo from about two-thirds of the way up the terminator," Scherner added. "We have enough fuel to select that for our touchdown.''

Paxton began the course change. "If it's an anomaly, we'll want a look at that.''

The radar anomaly stayed conspicuous as the PM closed with it. "That's a bright echo," Scherner said. "It could almost be a metal outcrop.''

"I'll land as close to it as I can. There's a promising site right next to the thing. I can see it now. It does look like metal. Put the radar into landing mode."

"Landing mode activated."

The icy horizon came up around them as Paxton throttled back. Ignoring the feeble attraction of the nucleus, he was flying the ship all the way to the surface. He shut off the braking engine and let the remnants of their approach velocity take them down. Scherner was calling off the approach figures, so he didn't see the anomaly come into view.

Paxton did, and he interrupted the commentary. "Control, the anomaly is artificial. I say again, the anomaly is an artificial object. We are go for touchdown, well within fuel reserves. . . . Contact light!"

"Contact light is on," Scherner confirmed. "The PM has landed. Our inclination is three degrees, repeat three degrees. Fuel and oxidizer residuals as follows . . ."

They were through the landing checks and had given themselves go for a three-minute stay when the Earth reaction came back. "We're getting pretty bad interference on your signal now, especially in the final stage of descent. Repeat description of the anomaly, repeat description of the anomaly." *Bleep*.

"I say again, the anomaly is an artificial object, repeat *artificial*. Now here we go for the details." Turning to the right, Paxton could just see the thing from his couch. "It looks like the bottom half of a totem pole. I'd say there are three distinct sections, one on top of the other. The bottom one is gold, or covered in gold foil, cylindrical, with heat radiator panels projecting. The one above that is roughly spherical, black and silver, with solar cell panels on the surface and projecting antennas. The top section is hexagonal for three-fourths of the way up, then it becomes a straight cylinder of lesser diameter. It too is gold, and some of the panels of the hexagon have solar cells. There are connecting rods from it on one side, anchoring it to the bottom section. I don't think they touch the sphere at all."

"We have your landing status report," said Mission Control. "On the basis of that, we'll give you go to stay for twelve hours. Let us have your computer readout, and we'll assess status for the full mission." *Bleep*.

"Roger," said Scherner. "Secondary antenna is now deployed and locked on *Newtonian* for telemetry. Computer readout begins in three seconds—two, one, mark!'' He pressed the switch and the transmission light went on.

The reply to Paxton's description came back. "We copy the appearance of the object, Dave. Can you estimate the function or purpose of the device?" *Bleep*.

Paxton was still staring to the right. "The more I look at it, the more I think it's not one device but three. The three sections certainly don't add up to a unit like the three segments of the PM. Nor, I think, is any one of the sections a spacecraft in itself. I'd say ˙each of them is a scientific package like the one in our cargo compartment. Over.''

"We have your computer readout,'' said ˙Mission Control. "You are go to stay for the full mission.'' *Bleep*.

"Great. Now let me see this thing.'' Scherner pushed off his straps and sat up on his couch, then rose and turned to see out of the port. Paxton sat up more slowly. They both looked out in silence until Control came back on.

"Dave, we could accept that some other national group might have reached the comet some days ahead of us. But there hasn't been time for three complete scientific payloads to be landed even if three ships the size of *Newtonian* could be launched in secret.'' *Bleep*.

"Roger, Control, that confirms our assessment,'' said Paxton. Scherner glanced at him in surprise. "We're looking at objects from outside the Solar System altogether, like the comet itself. Sometime in the past, when this nucleus swung past another sun, there was another landing here—maybe more than one.''

"If that's true,'' said Scherner, "then the object might be millions of years old. This is a fast comet, but over interstellar distances . . .''

"Not less than a million years,'' Paxton agreed. "Well, let's eat.''

"Huh? Oh, yes.'' Their program called for a meal and then a sleep period. The discovery had knocked Scherner out of the routine, though he hadn't been thinking of going outside. The Penetration descent had left him fatigued, but he could have looked at the object a long time yet. "Okay, you break out the food packs and I'll get some pictures out of the window.''

He even took some shots out of the other windows, of the comet's surface, and the bright columns of gas rising past the sun's disk from over the horizon. The sublimation mechanism was his speciality, was what he'd come here to study, but it was taking place in his thoughts.

Next "day" they depressurized the command module, and Paxton made his way carefully down the side of the ship. Gravity was so low that effectively they were still in free-fall, but the exhausts had softened the surface enough for the landing legs to grip. Scherner waited in the hatch while Paxton collected a contingency sample from the surface, sending it back up on his line; then he opened up the cargo section and began passing down the research tools. After he descended himself, they were to start taking cores and putting down probes into the comet, but obviously that had to wait. Taking the cameras, they maneuvered on their jet packs toward the object.

It was roughly the same height as the Penetration Module, but all three sections were greater than it in diameter. Scherner had thought, in the capsule, it was somewhat smaller; but sizes and distances were hard to judge. The irregular horizon was close everywhere, but there was a big outcrop of ice behind the object; and light reflected from the crag lit up the side away from the sun, giving the structure a luminous ethereality. Close up, they could see that the bottom section was clear of the surface. In the shadow beneath it their torches found a great golden spike, driven deep into the frozen gases of the comet.

"Whoever put down the first one meant it to hold," said Paxton to Earth. "From the taper on the length we can see, which is about four feet, I would estimate that the spike would hold through at least one stellar passage even on the sunward side of the comet. Maybe the makers knew where the comet was going next, somewhere relatively close, and decided to use it as an interstellar probe. These radiator panels imply that there was a big power plant in here, enough to carry a signal over interstellar distances, maybe beaming its accumulated data once it got well out from the star again. It could be storing information to do that again right now, but the panels are at exactly the temperature of our surroundings, so I'd guess the pile's wholly inert. It's had millions of years to cool right down."

"Better say tens of millions, or even hundreds," Scherner corrected from above. "Once the probe was beyond use to its makers, it served as an anchorage for other people's. The spheroid was welded to its top, covering the antenna unit."

"And the top section added later still," said Paxton. "When I said the three didn't make anything in combination, I was wrong. What we have here is a cairn."

"Fantastic." Scherner was floating by the upper unit taking pictures. "These upper two could still be active, Dave, since they have solar cells. Maybe they're recording data on us right now."

"If the solar cells are still active after a million years in the interstellar dark, they're pretty good," said Paxton. "But if they have omnidirectional antennas, maybe we'll pick up something when we're tracking our own instrument package."

"That would be fantastic! If we could compare their transmissions with our probe's, we could maybe decode them. Then perhaps we could interrogate them about the planetary systems they originally passed through. It would be an interstellar probe for us—a time probe was well as a space one!"

"Great," said Paxton. "If we could get the second probe's recording of the *third* probe's system, we'd get some actual data about the people who put the third probe here."

But on closer examination, these were mere dreams. All three probes were inert, so thoroughly frozen that the ice crystals frosting them couldn't be brushed off. Scherner and Paxton didn't apply any force for fear that the whole structure would shatter; the metals must be nightmarishly brittle. There didn't seem to be any prospect of taking the probes apart, not even of removing data recorders that might be slowly warmed and interrogated. They couldn't find any access panels, not surprisingly; their own probe was a sealed unit, almost all solid-state, so its power would last as long as possible on the outward swing from the sun. They had no burning or cutting tools to force a way into the cairn; like their predecessors, they could only photograph the exterior and leave their own instruments in turn.

The work went on: studying the comet, as intended, as well as the unexpected marker it carried. Scherner ranged farther sunward day by day, taking rock and ice samples, studying the gas flow from the surface and the effects of the coma on sunlight and solar wind. Using a one-man jet platform, he penetrated the region where fragments were splitting off the comet, even landing there as the violence of the outbursts diminished. The comet was receding swiftly from the sun now, preceded by the vast length of the tail which would soon contract.

They were coming up to activation time for the automatic

station they would leave behind. One question remained to be settled, however. It seemed fitting to add the package to the top of the cairn, but it had been planned to anchor it to the ice—like the lowest unit of the cairn, though to less depth. In that position it was to "listen" for tremors in the comet as the sunward face stabilized, and obviously these would be affected by transmission through the cairn. It would also measure the rate of ice fall as the coma gases froze and their crystals were drawn back to the nucleus. That was less of a problem, because the precipitation on the upper face of the probe could be corrected for the height of the cairn, to give the values for the comet's surface. However, Mission Control had been holding up the decision.

When they did return to the subject, they had something very different in mind. "From the dimensions you've given us for the cylinder atop the cairn, it would be possible to grip it with the landing legs of the PM."

Scherner and Paxton looked at each other. Paxton raised his eyebrows. "That would be possible, Control," he replied. "We could lower the PM to the top of the cairn on the attitude control jets, and tighten up the jacks on the landing legs. We might even get a weld, with two metal surfaces pressed together in vacuum there; but I wouldn't expect the grip to hold if we tried to pull the cairn out of the ice."

"Surely that's not what they have in mind," said Scherner as they waited for the signals to course out and back.

"I can't think what else they want," said Paxton. "We couldn't use the central engine, but the four verniers could be angled sufficiently to keep the flames from impinging on the cairn. Maybe they want us to bring back the top section, but we haven't enough fuel even for that."

Scherner nodded. Neither of them put his own feelings into words; by now, they were of one mind concerning the cairn.

Mission Control replied. "As you may imagine, Dave, there's a big demand from scientists, and indeed from the public and their elected representatives, that the cairn be retrieved for study. The only way we can figure to do this involves sacrificing the backup capability of the PM and the Lander, so the final decision will rest with Bob Sullivan as mission commander. What we plan is for Bob to come down to you in the Lander and set the nuclear device in the ice at the edge of the current breakup zone. We calculate that an explosion at that point has the best chance of blasting the cairn out of the nucleus. Then we hope that you'd be able to get remote control of the PM and slow up the cairn with the vernier engines. With your present fuel reserves, it should return to the vicinity of the sun within a hundred years. We'd like to know whether you have any additional comments before we go to Bob for his decision." *Bleep*.

Paxton looked at Scherner. "You tell them," he said, looking sickened. "I can't."

Scherner swallowed hard. "Nothing to add, Control. Over."

After weighing up all the factors, Sullivan accepted the plan—surprising neither Paxton nor Scherner. His solo Penetration of the comet posed no real problems, because he knew what to expect. Only the landing might have been tricky, and for that he would have a talk-down. In due course they saw the bright flare of the Lander motors descending through the inclined belt of debris (bigger fragments now, more widely spaced), and with Scherner on the PM radar and Paxton outside, they talked him down without trouble.

Atop its booster, identical to the PM's, the winged Lander made an equilateral triangle with the PM and the cairn. Sullivan went through the routine checks, which took him quite a while on his own, then suited up immediately for EVA.

Paxton helped him out, and together they drifted across to the cairn. Scherner was already there waiting for them. They floated slowly up the structure, both scientists trying to read the mission commander's mind.

At the top of the cairn Sullivan cut his jets and hung there, sinking imperceptibly in the gravity of the nucleus. "I thought it might be an anticlimax," he said at last, "but that is absolutely beautiful. Not just in itself, though it has a strange unity of its own, but in all that it stands for."

"So it's got to you as well," Scherner said, inadequately.

"Yeah. Do you think it will survive disruption of the nucleus?"

"I doubt it." Paxton pointed to the ice bulk beyond. "That berg alone could crush it, just with the wallop it would pack tumbling over. That bomb is going to break loose everything on this side of the nucleus, maybe break the whole comet apart. I don't think we'll ever find the cairn again. There'll be nothing left of it to find."

"They only asked us whether it could be set up," Scherner said. "Not whether we thought it would work, or whether we should even *try* to retain the cairn. Earth wants, and Earth grabs. They'd sooner smash the cairn than let it go, if they can't have it."

Sullivan shook his head. Outside his helmet, the effect was just detectable. "Yeah. It's too bad."

"Come and see what Dave has been doing." said Scherner.

"What Dave has been doing?" Sullivan asked as they floated toward the PM. "Wait a minute. You fellows have been falling behind on the EVA program."

"I've been doing most of that lately," Scherner said wearily. "Sure it might have been a little risky, working so far from the ship on my own, but I stayed high enough with the platform to be in touch with Dave, except when I dropped to take samples. If I hadn't called again in thirty minutes, he'd have come for me."

The PM was before them, the four panels folded down from the cargo hold like the armored ruff of some giant reptile. Paxton hung over the first of them, indicating his painstaking work on the interior of the panel.

"I brought down the rendezvous laser, unshipped from its housing, and refocused it," he said. "We can't use it to cut into the cairn, because we haven't a long enough power line; but it can engrave these panels, before we blow them clear. We were going to mount them around our probe, on top of the cairn. On this one I've put the sun, the Earth's orbit and the comet's, and the *Newtonian's* path to the comet and back. I put the Moon beside the Earth so they could identify Earth in this second diagram at the side." He had shown the planets of the Solar System to scale, with their distances from the sun in astronomical units. "I've marked Earth E and the sun S, so ES is the astronomical unit, and I've put our numbers up to twenty-one along the bottom here so they can work them out. I couldn't figure any way to give them the actual distances, but at least they can chart the Solar System to scale.

"The next two"—he pointed across—"are star charts, north and south. I haven't put much stress on constellation figures because it'll be who knows how long before the comet goes through another inhabited system, but I've shown the relative positions of the Milky Way, the Galactic Poles, M-thirty-one, M-thirteen and other globulars, the Hyades, the Pleiades and the Magellanic Clouds. With those points of reference, people should be able to place where we are and when; even the open clusters should be good markers for a Galactic Year or so, provided they can be identified. That's for the scientists; the message is 'Here we are' and it doesn't matter that astronomical distances make it here we were.''

Drifting around the hull, Sullivan met him again at the fourth panel. ''This one should give them the identification. That's the Milky Way, with the cross in it showing our position now. There are the Magellanics, and there's Andromeda. I've started dotting in some globular clusters to show what they are, and then the Pleiades and the rest are obviously open clusters, by elimination. Then down here I'm going to put a stylized man, woman and child, to show what life is like on the Earth right now.''

''Dave, those are incredible,'' said Sullivan at last.

''I've put a lot into them,'' said Paxton. ''If you didn't feel as we do about the cairn, I might not have shown them to you. We could have blown them off and you'd never have known.''

''Nobody will ever know if we blow up the comet,'' said Sullivan. ''That's what you're trying to tell me. We have a chance here to add to what other intelligent races have begun, to make ourselves known to still others, perhaps, far from here in space and time. Or we can disrupt the comet and try to keep the cairn for ourselves.'' He fell silent for a moment, accepting that as mission commander the decision was his. ''Well, I've always heard that it was bad luck to break the chain. But at this stage if we don't plant the bomb we'll obviously be disobeying Mission Control. Can we get around that?''

''We could mount the PM on the cairn, as ordered,'' said Scherner, ''and take pictures to prove it. The ship will tell the next explorers of the comet still more about us. But before that, while Dave finishes the fourth panel, we tell Control that we're planting the bomb sunward, where they want it. But in fact we'll take it up with us for the first stage of the ascent, and cast it off when it has enough speed to leave the comet altogether. The excess fuel that we use for that first burn will cancel the excess we didn't use planting the charge.''

''All right,'' said Sullivan. ''You go back inside and tell Mission Control we're moving the Lander sunward. While Dave's finishing the panel, I'll take another look at that incredible thing over there.''

They moved the PM, instrument package and all, to hover above the cairn, and this time Sullivan talked them down. With the legs pushed inward to grip the top cylinder, the PM looked entirely right sitting up there—shiny and new, still to acquire the frost film of the lower components. They drew out the probe's antennas and instrument booms (the only frost-deposit record they would get this way) and activated the package. They were ready to tell Mission Control this was to get a clear location signal after the explosion, but they had lost touch with Earth. They could still hear the *Newtonian's* automatic beacon, but the high-gain antennas out there had drifted off the planet, the nucleus or both. Probably the nucleus sensors had wandered off along the illusory spikes. The brilliant lattice overhead was opening now, beginning to separate into discrete objects reflecting the sunlight.

Paxton and Scherner backed out of the capsule, bringing their few belongings. It was strange to come out of the hatch so high above the comet's surface; the original cairn was hidden by the bulk of the PM booster. "That's it, I guess," said Paxton with a last glance at his artwork.

"I guess so." Sullivan had been taking pictures of the new cairn, twice as high as before with the ship poised on top of it. "I wish I'd had more time here."

They gathered at the Lander hatch, pulled themselves through into the cabin. Sealing it up and pressurizing, they left ice and vacuum behind for the last time. Down through the prelaunch checks, without hitch to the moment of liftoff; a pause at low thrust, as with the PM, to free the landing legs from the ice, then up and away, through the roll maneuver onto course for the *Newtonian*.

Central engine at low thrust, verniers flaring one way and another, the Lander made its way up through the inclined plane of fragments. Beyond it, coasting outward, they let the bomb go. It drew ahead on its own solid charge, fast enough to separate entirely from the comet. Sharing all its outward velocity from the sun, by the time the comet next came to a solar system the device would be too far away to be associated with it.

"I wonder if we'll ever tell what really happened?" mused Scherner, watching it go.

"We might someday," said Sullivan. "Once people see the pictures we're bringing back, they may turn against the Space Agency for having tried to kill the comet. The administration may be glad to hear then that we didn't plant the bomb."

A floating iceberg was growing in their path. They started their second burn, the verniers pushing the ship aside to miss the obstacle. Threading a path through the satellites of the nucleus, the motors fired again and again, until one of them cracked.

A cluster of red lights came on, the warning buzzer sounded

and the ship was tumbled by the asymmetric thrust generated by the burn-out. Cutoff was automatic, and fly-by-wire brought the ship back into the burn attitude.

"Rate of approach to nearest hazard," Sullivan demanded.

"Distance one point four miles, three minutes to impact," Scherner replied smartly.

"Number three vernier has gone," said Sullivan. "We'll take a systems check on the others before we burn. Give me it from item thirty-one, Dave."

Out of touch with Mission Control, they had to get themselves through the emergency. They completed the check with a minute and a half to spare and made the next burn on the central engine alone. The approaching ice cliff, spread with gemlike points, slid past

Sullivan studied the reefs ahead. "We'll have to take some way off this thing," he declared. "Set up a twenty-second burn for the central engine, Dave." He drew back the hand grip for a 180-degree rotation.

"We're going to be late back to the *Newtonian*," said Scherner as they decelerated.

"Mission Control will sweat," Sullivan agreed. "They think an atom bomb's going off down here. But they won't tell your families until they do hear from us, I expect."

De-Penetration was much harder now. With one vernier out of action, more work would fall on the central engine and the three verniers remaining; so there was a greater risk of another chamber failure. Either they could angle the ship for each burn, loading work onto the central engine, or roll to bring the other verniers to bear when the missing one was needed. To conserve fuel in the attitude-control thrusters, in fact, they would have to use the verniers as much as possible; but with all those roll maneuvers, they could get off the *Newtonian* beam; and if they emerged low on fuel there was no one over there to come and get them. Control was a three-man job, and the team clicked smoothly together.

Scherner, on radar and communications, kept them headed in the right direction. They emerged into the coma in approximately the right place, and not long afterward the *Newtonian's* radio link locked onto them again. The Lander moved out toward clear space, the head behind them shrinking now as the new debris from the nucleus drifted into stronger sunlight and began adding its gases to the swelling tail.

"We were getting worried about you fellows for a while there," said Control. "But you should get back to the *Newtonian* and move out some way before the explosion." *Bleep*.

"Roger, Control," said Sullivan. "What will we tell them when there's no detonation?" he asked the others.

"No detonation," said Paxton.

"Right," said Sullivan, and they all chuckled, relaxed after the strain of the ascent.

Their hostility to one another was gone, Scherner realized; hadn't reared its head even after the stress was removed. The discovery of the cairn had overshadowed it and dissolved it. That was the reason—though it hadn't reached Earth yet—why the cairn had to remain intact, singing or silent, on its way between the stars. They had fulfilled the original objectives of their mission; and though photographs alone might never reveal the the secrets of the cairn, they were bringing back the big reassurance that man wasn't alone in the immensity of space and time—and that was payload enough.

SOME JOYS UNDER THE STAR

Frederik Pohl

In a few recognizable ways were Albert Novak—the man who stalked Myron Landau—and the Secretary of State alike, but they had this in common: they wanted. They each wanted something very badly and, as it happens, the thing that each wanted was not good by the general consensual standards of your average sensual man.

Let us start with the man who stalked Myron Landau or, more accurately, with Myron Landau himself. Myron also wanted, and what he wanted was his girl friend Ellen, with that masked desperation that characterizes the young man of seventeen who has never yet made out.

On this night of July in New York City the factors against Myron were inexperience, self-doubt, and the obstinacy of Ellen herself, but ranged on his side were powerful allies. Before him was the great welcoming blackness of Central Park, where anything might happen, and spread across the sky was a fine pretext for luring her into the place. So he bought her a strawberry milkshake in Rumpelmeyer's and strolled with her into the park, chatting of astronomy, beauty, and love.

"Are you sure it's all right?" asked Ellen, looking into the sodium-lit fringes of the undergrowth.

"Cripes, yes," said Myron, in the richly amused tone of a brown belt in karate from one of the finest academies on the Upper West Side, although in fact he had never gone into

Central Park at night before. But he had thought everything out carefully and was convinced that tonight there was no danger. Or at any rate not enough danger to scare him off the prize. Overhead was the great beautiful comet that everybody was talking about and it was a clear night. There would be lots of people looking at the sky, he reasoned, and in any case where else could he take her? Not his apartment, with Grandma's ear to the living-room door, just itching for an excuse to come in and start hunting for her glasses. Not Ellen's place, not with her mother and sister remorselessly there. "You can't see the comet well from the middle of the street," he said reasonably, putting his arm around her and nodding to a handsome white-haired gentleman who had first nodded benevolently to them. "There's too much light, and anyway, honestly, Ellen, we won't go in very far."

"I never saw a comet before," she conceded, allowing herself to be led down the path. In truth, the comet Ujifusa-McGinnis was not all that hard to see. It spread its tail over a quarter of the sky, drowning out Altair, Vega, and the stars around Deneb, hardly paled even by the lights of New York City. Even a thousand miles south, where NASA technicians were working around-the-clock shifts under the floodlights of the Vehicle Assembly Building, trying to get ready the launch of the probe that would plumb Ujisfusa-McGinnis's mysteries, it dominated the sky.

Myron looked upward and allowed himself to be distracted for a moment by the spectacle, but quickly caught himself. "Ah," he said, creeping his fingers toward the lower slope of Ellen's breast, "just think, what you see is all gas. Nothing really there at all. And millions of miles away."

"It's beautiful," Ellen said, looking over her shoulder. She had thought she had heard a noise.

She had. The noise was in fact real. The foot of the handsome white-haired gentleman had broken a stick. He had turned off the flagstone path into the shelter of the dwarf evergreens and was now busy pulling a woman's nylon stocking over his white hair and face. He, too, had planned his evening carefully. In his right-hand coat pocket he had the woolen sock with half a pound of BBs knotted into the toe—that was for Myron. In his left-hand pocket he had the clasp knife with the carefully honed edge. That was for Ellen, first to make sure she didn't scream, then to make sure she never would. He had not known their names when he loaded his pockets and left his ranch house in Waterbury, Connecticut, to go in for an evening's sport to the city, but he had known there would be somebody.

He, too, looked up at the comet, but with irritation. In his Connecticut back yard, as he had shown it to his daughter, it had looked pretty. Here it was an unqualified nuisance. It made the night brighter than he wanted it although, he thought in all fairness, it was not as bad as a full moon.

It would not be more than five minutes, he calculated, before the boy would lead the girl in among the evergreens. But which way? If only they would choose his side of the path! Otherwise it meant he had to cross the walk. That was a small danger and a large annoyance, because it meant scuttling in an undignified way. Still, the fun was worth the trouble. It always had been worth it.

With the weighted sock now ready in his hand, the handsome white-haired gentleman followed them silently. He could feel the gleeful premonitory stirrings of sexual excitement in his private parts. He was as happy as, in his life, he ever was.

At a time approximately two thousand years earlier, when Jesus was a boy in Nazareth and Caesar Augustus was counting up his statues and his gold, a race of creatures resembling soft-shelled crabs on a planet of a star some two hundred light-years away became belatedly aware of the existence of the Great Wall of China.

Although it alone among the then existing works of Man was quite detectable in their telescopes, it was not surprising they had not noticed it before. It had been completed less than 250 years before, and most of that time lost in the creeping traverse of light from Earth to their planet. Also they had many, many planets to observe and not a great deal of time to waste on any one. But they expected more of their minions than that, and 10,000 members of a subject race died in great pain as a warning to the others to be more diligent.

The Arrogating Ones, as they called themselves and were called by their subjects, at once took up in their collective councils the question of whether or not to conquer Earth and add humanity to their vassals, now that they had discovered that humanity did exist. This was their eon-long custom. It had made them extremely unpopular over a large volume of the galaxy.

On balance, they decided not to bother at that particular time.

What were a few heaped-up rocks, after all? Oh, some sort of civilization no doubt existed, but the planet Earth seemed too distant, too trivial, and too poor to be worth bothering to conquer.

Accordingly they contented themselves with routine precautionary measures. Item, they caused to be abducted in their disc-shaped vessels certain specimens of Earthly human beings and other fauna. These also died in great pain and in the process released much information about their body chemistry, physical structure, and modes of thought. Item, the Arrogating Ones dispatched certain of their servants with a waiting brief. They were instructed to occupy the core of a comet and from it keep an eye on those endoskeletal, but potentially annoying, creatures who had discovered agriculture, fire, the city, and the wheel, but not as yet even chemical explosive weapons.

They then dismissed Earth from their collective soft-bodied minds, and returned to the more interesting contemplation of measures to be taken against a race of insectlike beings that lived in a steamy high-G planet in quite the other direction from Earth, toward the core of the galaxy. The insects had elected not to be conquered by the Arrogating Ones. In fact, they had destroyed quite a large number of war fleets sent against them.

Nearly a quarter of the collective intelligence of the Arrogating Ones was devoted to plans to defeat these insects in battle. Most of the rest of their intelligence was devoted to the pleasant contemplation of what they would do to the insects after the battle to make them wish they hadn't resisted so hard.

While the handsome white-haired gentleman was stalking Myron and Ellen, the second person who wanted, the Secretary of State of the United States of America, was about a hundred miles north of and 40,000 feet above Central Park. He was on board a four-engined jet aircraft with the American flag emblazoned on its prow and he was having a temper tantrum.

The President of the United States was gloomily running his fingers between the toes of his bare feet. "Shoot, Danny," he said, "you're getting yourself all hot about nothing. I'm not saying we *can't* bomb Venezuela. I'm only saying why do we *want* to bomb Venezuela? And I'm saying you ought to watch how you talk to me, too."

"Watch how *you* talk to *me*, Mr. President" shouted the Secretary of State over the noise of the jets. "I'm pretty fed up with your procrastinations and delays and it wouldn't take much for me to walk right out and dump the whole thing back in your lap. Considering your track record—I am thinking of Iceland—I don't imagine you'd relish that prospect."

"Danny boy," snarled the President, "you've got a bad habit of digging up ancient history. Stick to the point. We've got to have oil, agreed. They have oil, everybody knows that. They don't want to sell it to us at a reasonable price, so you want me to beat on them until they change their minds. Right? Only what you don't see is, there's a right way and a wrong way to do these things. Why can't we just go in with some spooks and Tommy-guns, as usual?"

"But their insolence, Mr. President! The demeaning tone of this document they sent me. It isn't the oil, it is the national credibility of the country that is involved here."

"Right, Danny, right," groaned the President. "You can talk. You don't have Congress breathing down your neck at every little thing." He sighed heavily and opened another can of no-calorie soda. "What I don't see," he said, with a punctuation mark of gas, "is why we have to hit them tonight, with Congress still in session."

The Secretary said petulantly, "I have explained to you, Mr. President, that our communications system is malfunctioning. We've lost global coverage. There is strong dissipation of ionosphere scatter, due to interference from an unprecedentedly strong influx of radiation apparently emanating from—"

"Oh, cut it out," complained the President. "You mean it's that comet that's bollixed up our detection."

The Secretary pursed his lips. "Not precisely the comet, no, Mr. President. No such effect has ever been detected before, although it is possible that there is a connection. Doesn't matter. The situation before us is that we do not have total communication at this time. And so we have no way of knowing whether the Venezuelans are treacherously planning a sneak attack or not. Do you want to take a chance on the security of the Free World, Mr. President? I say preempt now!"

"Yes, you've made your point, Danny," said the President. He swiveled his armchair and gazed out at the bright spray of white light across the eastern horizon where Comet Ujifusa-McGinnis lay. "I've heard worse excuses for starting a war," he mused, "but I can't remember exactly when. All right, Danny. We'll do what you say. Get me Charlie on the scrambler and I'll put in the attack in two hours."

*   *   *

The watchers for the Arrogating Ones, hiding inside the pebbly core of the comet named after the two amateur astronomers who had simultaneously discovered it, studied the results of their radarlike scan of the Earth. This was routine. They were not aware that their scanning had damaged mankinds communications, but that was not their problem. Their only task was to spray out a shower of particles and catch the returning ones to study—this they did, and what their study told them was that the planet Earth had reached redpoint status. It was now well into a technological age and was thus an active, rather than merely a potential, threat to their masters.

The Arrogating Ones were no longer quite as effectively arrogant as they had once been. They had been creamed rather frequently in their millennia-long struggle against the insectoids. The score was, roughly, Arrogating Ones 53, Insectoids 23,724. The watchers, knowing this, were aware that at least their task would not under these circumstances involve the actual physical conquest of the Earth. It would simply be destroyed.

This was no big deal. Plenty of mechanisms for wiping out a populated planet were stockpiled in the arsenals of the Arrogating Ones. They had not worked very well against the insectoids, unfortunately, but they would be plenty powerful enough to deal with, say, mankind. The weapons for accomplishing this were readily available at any time, but not to the watchers, who were far too low in the hierarchy of authority to be trusted with anything like that.

Their task was much simpler. They were only required to report what they saw and then to soften up the human race so that it would not be able to offer resistance, even ineffectual resistance, to the clean-up teams when they arrived with their planet-busters.

Softening up was a technical problem of some magnitude, but it had been solved long ago. The abducted humans had died messily but not in vain. At least, from the point of view of the Arrogating Ones their deaths had not been in vain, for in their dying agonies they had supplied information about themselves which had enabled the Arrogating Ones to devise appropriate softening-up mechanisms. The watchers had been equipped with these on a standby basis ever since.

"Of course, from the point of view of the abducted humans the question of whether their deaths had been in vain might have had a different answer. No one had troubled to ask them.

At any rate, the watchers now energized the generators which would soften up mankind for its destruction.

While they were waiting for a charge to build up they looked up the coordinates and call signal for the nearest cruising superdreadnaught of the Arrogating Ones and transmitted a request for it to come in and finish up the job with a core-bomb. They then discussed among themselves the prospects of what their next assignment would be. It was not a fruitful discussion. Core-bombs are messy and there was not much chance that Comet Ujifusa-McGinnis's orbit would get them far enough away to be out of its range when it went off. Even if they survived, none of them had any idea what the Arrogating Ones' future plans for the watchers were. All they were sure of was that they were certain not to enjoy them.

We now turn to Albert Novak. He was in another four-engined jet, climbing to cruising altitude out of Kennedy en route to Los Angeles International. He was a crew-cut young man, with something on his mind. His neighbor was a short, white-haired, dark-tanned Westerner with the face of a snapping turtle, who offered his hand and said aggressively, jerking his head toward the window, "That confounded thing! Do you know the space agency wants to spend thirty million dollars of your tax money just to go sniff around it? Thirty million dollars! Just to sniff some marsh gas! Not as long as I'm on the Aeronautics and Space Committee. Let me introduce myself. I'm Congressman—" But he was talking to gas himself. Albert Novak had not accepted his hand, had not even met his eyes. Although the "Fasten Seat Belts" sign was still lighted in three languages, he unstrapped himself and walked down the aisle. Hostesses hissed at him and tardily began to unsnap themselves to make him return to his seat. He ignored them. He had no intention of ever arriving at L.A. International and when he wanted to talk to a hostess he would do so on his own terms. He carried a cassette recorder into a toilet and locked the door against everyone.

The cassette recorder could no longer be used to record or play. He had removed its insides the day before, replacing them with more batteries and a coil of fine wire, which he now carefully connected to 30 Baggies full of dynamite and firing caps he had sewn into the lining of his trenchcoat while his mother nearsightedly smiled on him from across the room.

Although Novak thought of himself as a hijacker, it was not

his intention to cause the jet to head for Cuba, Caracas, or even Algiers. He did not want the airplane. He didn't even want the one hundred million dollars' ransom he planned to ask for.

What Novak wanted, mostly, was to matter to somebody. As far as he had thought out his plan of action, it was to walk up to a stewardess with his hand on the detonating switch, show her the ingenious arrangement he had gotten past the metal detectors, be escorted to the flight deck in the traditional manner and then, after the airline had begun trying to get together the 5,000,000 unmarked twenty-dollar bills he intended to demand and the maximum of annoyance and confusion had been caused, to close the switch and explode the dynamite.

He knew that in destroying the airplane he would die. That was not very important to him. The one important failure that he regretted very much was that he would not be able to see his mother's face when the reporters and TV crew began to swarm around her and she learned he had been pushing around all kinds of people and thirty million dollars' worth of airplane.

The generators at the core of Comet Ujifusa-McGinnis were now up to full charge.

Disgruntedly, the watchers of the Arrogating Ones sighted the beam in on the planet Earth. They were quite careful to get it aligned properly, for they remembered very well what the consequences were for slipshod work. When it was locked in, they released the safety switch that allowed the contact to close that discharged the beam.

More than three million watts of beamed power surged out toward the near hemisphere of the planet. Certain chemical changes at once took place in the atmosphere and were borne by jet stream, trade winds, and the aimless migration of air masses all around the Earth.

The equipment used was highly directional, but the watchers who operated it were very close and large magnitudes of energy were involved. Some of the radiation sprayed them. There was some loss from corona points, some reflection even from the tenuous gases of the comet's halo.

As the radiation had been designed specifically for use against mankind, on the basis of the experiments conducted on the kidnappees of 2,000 years before, it was only of limited effect on the watchers. But they happened to be warm-blooded oxygen-breathers with two sexes and many of humanity's hangups, so that the weapon did do to them much what it was intended to do to mankind.

First they felt a sudden, sharp pang of an emotion which they identified (but only by logical deduction) as joy. The diagnosis was not simple, for they had little in their lives that would enable them to recognize such a state. But they looked at each other with fatuous fondness and, in their not really very human ways, shared pleasure.

The next thing they shared was serious physical pain, accompanied by vomiting, dizziness, and a feeling of weakness, for they were receiving a great deal more of the radiation than was necessary for the mere task of turning them into pussycats to receive the knockout blow of the Arrogating Ones. They recognized that, too. They deduced that they were dying, and doing it pretty fast.

They did not mind that any more than Albert Novak minded blowing himself up with the airliner. It was worthwhile. They were happy. It was what the ray was intended to do to people and it did its work very well.

And all over the near side of the Earth, as the radiation searched out and saturated humanity, joy replaced fear, peace replaced tension, love replaced anger.

In Central Park three slum youths released the girl they had lured behind the 72nd Street boat house and decided to apply for Harvard, while a member of the Tactical Patrol Force lay down on Umpire Rock and gazed jubilantly at the comet. At the park's southern margin the white-haired gentleman came leaping out at Myron Landau and his girl. "My dear children!" he cried, tugging the women's stocking off his face. "How sweet and tender you are. You remind me so much of my own beloved son and daughters that you must let me stand you to the best hotel room in New York, with unlimited room service."

This spectacle would normally have disconcerted Myron Landau, especially as he had just succeeded in solving the puzzle of Ellen's bra snap. But he was so filled with the sudden rapture himself that he could only say, "You bet you can, friend. But only if you come with us. Ellen and I wouldn't have it any other way."

And Ellen chimed in sweetly: "What do we need a motel room for, mister? Why don't we just get out of these clothes?"

Forty thousand feet directly overhead, as the Presidential jet sped back from the Summer White House near Boothbay Harbor, Maine, the Secretary of State lifted eyes streaming with joy and said, "Dear Mr. President, let's give the spics another chance. It's too nice a night to be H-bombing Caracas." And the President, flinging an arm around him, sobbed, "Danny, as a diplomat you're not worth a bucket of warm snot, but I've always said you've got the biggest damn heart in the cabinet."

A great bubble of orange-yellow flame off on the western horizon disconcerted them for a moment, but it did not seem relevant to their transcendental joy. They began singing all the good old favorites like "Down by the Old Mill Stream," "Sweet Adeline," and "I've Been Working on the Railroad," and had so much fun doing it that the President quite forgot to radio the message that would cancel his strike order against Caracas. It did not matter very much. The B-52 ordnance crews had dumped the bombs from the fork lifts and were now giving each other rides on them, while the commanding general of the strike, Curtis T. "Vinegar Ass" Pinowitz, had decided he preferred going fishing to parachuting into Venezuela in support of the bombing. He was looking for his spinning reel, oblivious to the noise on the hardstand where the 101st Airborne was voting whether to fly to Disneyland or the Riviera. (In any event, the Venezuelans, or those members of the Venezuelan government who were bothering to answer their telephones, had just voted to give the Yankees all the oil they wanted and were seriously considering scenting it with jasmine.)

The ball of flame on the horizon, however, was not without its importance.

Arnold Novak had released the armlock he had got around the little brown-eyed stewardess's neck and had begun to try to explain to her that his intention to blow up the jet meant nothing personal, but was only a way of inducing his mother to pay as much attention to him as she had, all through their lives, to his brother, Dick. Although he stammered so that he was almost incoherent, the stew understood him at once. She, too, had had both a mother and an older brother. Her pretty brown eyes filled with tears of sympathy and with a rush of love she flung her arms around him. "You poor boy," she cried, covering his stubbly face with kisses. "Here, honey! Let me help you." And she caught the cassette from his hand, careful not to pull the wires loose, and closed the switch that touched off the caps in all the 30 Baggies.

One hundred and thirty-one men, women, and children simultaneously were converted into maltreated chunks of barbecued meat falling through the sky. Their roster included the pilot, the co-pilot, the third pilot, and 8 other members of the flight crew; plus, among the passengers, mothers, infants, honeymooning couples, nonhoneymooning but equally amorous couples who did not happen to be married to each other, a middle-aged grape picker returning home after a 5-days-4-nights all-expense tour of Sin City (which he had found disappointing), a defrocked priest, a disbarred lawyer, and a Congressman from Oregon who would never now achieve his dream of dismantling NASA and preventing the further waste of the taxpayer's funds on space, which he held to be empty and uninteresting.

Whoever they had been when whole, the pieces of barbecue all looked pretty much alike now. It did not matter. Not one of the passengers or crew had died unhappy, since they had all been touched by the comet.

And deep inside the core of the comet Ujifusa-McGinnis, the device which was meant to display the wave forms signifying receipt of the destruction order for Earth remained blank. No signal was received. No one would have observed it if it had been, certainly not the watchers, but it was unprecedented that a response should not be received.

The reason was quite simple. It was that that particular superdreadnaught of the Arrogating Ones, like most of the others in their galactic fleet, had long since been hurled against the fortresses of the insectoids of the core. There, like the others, it had been quickly destroyed, so that the message sent by the watchers had never reached its destination.

It was, in a way, too bad, to think of all that strength and sagacity spent with no more tangible visible result than to give pleasure to a few billion advanced primates. Although this was regrettable, it did not much bother the Arrogating Ones. They had plenty of other regrets to work on. What remained of their collective intelligence was fully taken up with the problem of bare survival against the insectoid fleets—plus, to be sure, a good deal of attention given to mutual recrimination.

The watchers did not mind; they had long since perished of acute terminal pleasure.

And, as it turned out, they had not died entirely in vain.

Because the Oregon congressman did not live to complete his plan to dismantle NASA, all his seniority and horse-trading power having perished with him, the projected comet-study mission was not canceled. To be sure, the bird did not fly on schedule. The effects of the joy beams from the comet did not begin to wear off for several days and the NASA technicians simply could not be bothered while their joy was in its manic phase.

But gradually the world returned to—normal? No. It was definitely not normal for everyone to be feeling rather cheerful most of the time. But the world settled down, sweetly and fondly, to something not unlike its previous condition of work and play. So the astronauts found another launch window and made rendezvous with the comet; and what they found there made quite a difference in the history of both the human race and the galaxy. The watchers were gone, but they had left their weaponry behind.

When the astronauts returned with the least and weakest of the weapons, all they could cram into their ship, the President of the United States gave up his shuffleboard game to fly to the deck of the *Independence* and stare at it. "Oh, boy!" he chortled, awed and thrilled. "If that'd turned up two months ago Brazil would've had a seaport on the Caribbean!" But Venezuela went about its business untouched. The President was tempted. Even cheerful and at peace with himself and the world, he was tempted—old habits die hard. But he had several thoughts and the longest and most persuasive of them was that weaponry like this meant that somewhere there was an enemy who had constructed and deployed it and someday might return to use it. So with some misgivings, but without any real freedom of choice, he flew back to Washington, summoned the ambassadors of Venezuela, Cuba, Canada, the U.S.S.R., the People's Republic of China, and the United Irish Republics of Great Britain and laid everything before them.

Although politicians, too, were residually cheerful still from the effect of the comet, they had not lost their intelligence. They quickly saw that there was an external foe—somewhere— which made each of them look like a very good friend. Nobody was in a mood to fool with little international wars. So treaties were signed, funds were appropriated, construction was begun.

And the human race, newly armed and provided with excellent spaceships, went looking for the Arrogating Ones.

They did not, of course, find them. By the time they were ready to make their move, the last of the Arrogating Ones had gone resentfully to his death. But a good many generations later, humans found the insectoids of the core instead and what then happened to the insectoids would have satisfied even the Arrogating Ones.

FUTURE FORBIDDEN

Philip Latham

Dagny's policy for romance in married love was as deceptively simple (and successful) as the Bank of England's policy in finance: *Never apologize. Never explain.* As Bob (Dr. Robert Archer) had discovered long ago, verbal combat with his wife was simply energy wasted upon the suburban air. How could she explain something to him when she couldn't explain it to herself? Equally futile was his trying to withhold a secret. Given sufficient time she would always know. And Dagny had worlds of time.

It was early evening when Bob finally pulled in to his driveway. Dagny was feeding Margarit, their ginger cat. The two identified in many respects. They functioned by intuition, a means of perception much superior to ratiocination. Raising the lid on a tin of catfood, or opening a carton of milk, caused Margarit to materialize—sometimes, it seemed, from thin air.

Usually Bob was able to make the two hundred miles from Mount Elsinore by late afternoon. But the unexpected arrival of a Nobel prize winner at the observatory and the subsequent time required for Bob's plates to dry had delayed him. The Nobel prize winner he had managed finally to brush off. But his plates had been a different matter—he didn't like forced drying. Furthermore, he hadn't wanted anyone fooling with those particular plates but himself.

But at last—after twelve consecutive days and nights of exclusively masculine company on Mt. Elsinore—he was free and dirty and glad to see Dagny. Especially glad.

She deserted Margarit and followed him upstairs while he was having a shower and shave. Upon emerging from the bathroom he found her examining a slip of yellow paper in his record book.

Suddenly she exclaimed. *"Diabolique!"*

Dagny was native Russian but had moved early to Paris, where she had appeared professionally on the stage. Bob read French and could understand and speak it fairly well. This time she might as well have spoken in Russian, which he understood not at all. He leaped at her, snatched the paper from her nerveless grasp.

"Oh, God!" he cried. "To think you should have seen!"

"And why should I not have?"

"Because this is top secret—"

"So, scientists also have their secrets?"

Dagny, in her capacity as Official Witch of California, often received cryptic messages from fellow mystics. Occasionally it had been Bob's misfortune to have to take such calls. He faithfully recorded them, read them back, then passed the nonsense on to his wife without comment. He knew he could expect no reciprocity.

He stuffed the paper into his dressing gown. "Who said this was science?"

"What is it, then?"

He averted his face, scowling darkly. "Interpol. Mafia. Eskimo connection in Greenland."

"Robert, you are in danger?"

"It's nothing—nothing."

"They threaten you?"

Robert shrugged. To girls who liked him he was Robert, never Bob.

"I shall bewitch them," Dagny declared. "Destroy them with the blood of a lamb."

"Be kind of difficult, wouldn't it? Seeing you're a vegetarian."

"Perhaps a black turnip—"

Bob did a sudden changeover. His secret had to come out.

"Darling, forget the lamb's blood and the turnip. I might as well tell you—you've just discovered a new comet. Comet Dagny. This message is just the regular astronomical code for announcing a new object's position.

He smoothed out the crumpled yellow sheet.

DAGNEY COMET ARCHER 19501 30317 504—22376 11716-1124 20114 20001 75549 35216 ELSINORE

Dagny was completely bewildered.

"I discovered a comet? But who said so—"

Bob tapped his chest.

"I said. *Moi*. Me. That guarantees it will bear your name."

"You found it and named it for me? But how wonderful!"

Bob shook his head regretfully.

"Sorry, darling, but discovering a new comet doesn't amount to much. Anybody can find one—just by looking long enough."

"I still think it's wonderful."

"I didn't really discover it. Found it purely by accident. Thought I'd take a look at Mercury. Been several reports of conspicuous markings on the terminator. While we were getting set I spotted this fuzzy object. Looked suspicious. Managed to get a couple of plates before sunrise. No doubt about it—comet all right."

"Comet Dagny?"

Bob smiled wistfully.

"Other men give their wives and girl friends mink coats and diamonds. Me? Best I can do is a comet."

"My comet? We can see it?"

"Don't know. Probably not."

Bob opened his record book and did some rapid figuring.

"Hm—might at that. If my preliminary orbit's any good—which it probably isn't—this thing's pretty bright for an object beyond Mars. Ought to be down around magnitude sixteen by sixth power law. I'd say it's thirteen easy."

He took some dozen five-by-seven plates from his suitcase, each plate enclosed in a heavy manila envelope. He arranged them in chronological order, then stowed them away in his bottom dresser drawer.

"Comet Dagny," he said with some satisfaction, "safe and secure with my socks and shorts."

"But in the sky?"

"Somewhere in Aquarius the Waterbearer, I think. Mean anything in your astrology?"

Although Dagny had had no formal training in astronomy, from astrology she had learned the meaning of such elementary terms as right ascension and declination, hour angle, ecliptic, node, perihelion, etc.

She thought a moment before answering.

"I'd have to know where it's going first."

"General direction of Earth right now," he said carelessly.

He slipped into his bathrobe.

"Ah, does this old room look good," he sighed. "After that pad on the mountain." Then, at sight of Dagny's face: "Hey, what's the matter?"

Suddenly the light dawned.

"Oh, lord, I'll bet you've been seeing science-fiction films again! Don't you know that in popular science *every* comet, asteroid or thing-from-outside is inevitably heading straight for the Earth? Object coming closer. Situation growing desperate. President calls emergency cabinet meeting. Secretary of Education and Indian Affairs goes on TV. Keep calm. Have faith. Government has situation well in hand."

Dagny looked doubtful.

"Oh, hell, why did I ever mention it?" he muttered impatiently. He turned to a sheet in his record book. "See this sketch? The comet's path based on my parabolic orbit. N marks the ascending node. Circle's the Earth. You can see there's no chance of collision."

He fell back on the bed.

"For two weeks I've been working my head off on that damn mountain. Worst part about that clean ascetic life is you get to feeling so good. So good sometimes you can hardly stand it."

He drew Dagny down beside him.

"There's a conjunction coming up all right," he told her. "But not with any comet."

Dagny was a witch. If you had asked her she would have said so in the same matter-of-fact way she might have admitted to being a librarian or registered nurse. There was no secret about it. After her appointment as Official State Witch, of course, no secret was possible.

Bob and Dagny were "sexually compatible" and otherwise "mutually well adjusted," as the marriage counselors euphemistically phrase it. On one point, however, they differed profoundly. Bob was a professional astronomer, a man devoted to what he could observe and measure. As he was fond of pointing

out: no theory can ever *explain*. At most it can only *describe*.[1]
Bob was also a romantic, but a romantic with both feet on the
ground.

Dagny, on the other hand, was a mystic, a believer in astrology, parapsychology and occultism. Strangely enough, there
had never been any problem. Long ago they had taken a solemn
vow to respect each other's opinions. Bob shrugged off Dagny's
mysticism. Dagny accepted Bob's forthright pragmatism. It was
that simple.

Then, too, there was the very special nature of Dagny's
witchcraft. She had nothing but scorn for the famous witches of
old. Their powers were feeble, confined principally to grave-
yards and unrentable houses. Who ever heard of Medea beyond
the Aegean Sea? Had Morgan Le Fey ever made the headlines in
Hindustan?

Dagny maintained that witchcraft—truly valid witchcraft—
had no bounds. The speed of light is finite—that of thought,
infinite. Hence witchcraft, if good in Haiti, should likewise be
good in New York, on Mars or in the Andromeda galaxy, it
made no difference. She agreed with Conan Doyle that "A devil
with merely local powers like a parish vestry would be too
inconceivable a thing."[2]

Certain practical expressions of Dagny's prowess as a witch
had to do with the fact that she had never stopped acting. It was
the fragile "Marguerite Gautier," *The Lady of the Camelias*,
who beguiled the butcher into giving her an extra-choice cut of
steak. It was "Lady Macbeth" who prodded the landlord into
repairing the roof.

Occasionally she took part in some little theater production in
their neighborhood. Bob wished she wouldn't. Her "Laura" in
Strindberg's *The Father* had made "Martha" in *Who's Afraid of
Virginia Woolf?* look like a Sunday-school teacher at a wienie
bake.

Bob knew his preliminary parabolic orbit would be useless for
prediction after a few weeks. But to improve the orbit he had to

---

[1]The noted physicist, Ernest Mach (1838-1916) believed scientists
must exclude elements not perceived by the senses in arriving at
their results.
[2]*The Hound of the Baskervilles*.

extend the arc. And to extend the arc he needed additional observations.

To those unfamiliar with the operation of a large observatory this would seem easy enough. Just take the telescope and get them. But the observing time of a large telescope is jealously guarded, carefully rationed out to the various staff members according to their special needs, weeks in advance. Bob was all too well aware of the futility of requesting observing time for such an insignificant object as a comet. His only hope of getting more plates was to find some big-hearted individual who would squeeze him in for a few minutes. Bob had done such favors for others often enough. But he was forced to go from office to office as a suppliant, begging for that precious intangible quantity known as time.

"Be glad to oblige, but—"

"Sure sorry, Bob, but—"

"Remember how you saved my life once, but—"

Others simply shook their head or gave him a stony stare.

Of course, Mt. Elsinore was not the only possibility. Bob's wire to the Central Bureau for Astronomical Telegrams, Cambridge, Massachusetts had been broadcast to observatories all over the world. His comet was so near the sun, however, and so correspondingly difficult to observe that he doubted if any astronomers would care to make the effort. Time went on and on until Bob was forced to write Comet Dagny off as lost.[3]

Then, one morning, wholly unexpected good news came in the form of a handwritten letter from his old professor of Celestial Mechanics, Dr. William P. Killigrew, Director of the Killigrew Observatory, Dunedin, New Zealand. Not only was Dr. Killigrew the director of the institution that bore his name—he was also its entire observing staff, chief of public relations, science head and janitor. Its 12-inch Schmidt photographic being his own personal property, he could use it however and whenever he chose. The result was a dozen perfectly good positions of Comet Dagny extending the arc over another two months.

The new positions wrought some radical surgery on the orbit

---

[3]The Astronomical Society of the Pacific annually awards a gold medal to each discoverer of an unexpected comet. Ironically, the A.S.P. ran out of funds for gold medals the month Bob discovered Comet Dagny.

of Comet Dagny. The parabola was forced into a closed ellipse of orbital period 3.375 years, the shortest of any comet except Encke's.[4] A close brush with Jupiter had effected the shift.

Comet Dagny still missed Earth by a wide margin at the ascending node, N, where it "surfaced" from below to above the Earth's orbital plane. Bob had not earlier been much concerned about N', where Dagny ducked underground again. Now it was a jolt to him to discover that N' fell precisely on the Earth's orbit.

This fact alone, of course, did not mean that Earth and comet were doomed to collide. To collide, both bodies must arrive at N' simultaneously, a most improbable event. Yet a hurried calculation showed the comet had an excellent chance of scoring a hit.

Should he tell Dagny? He was undecided. He felt the truth never hurt anyone. And Dagny was not easily alarmed. The other side of the coin had to do with a direct blow to his ego—after his caustic remarks anent popular science writings and cosmic collisions. Furthermore, should the comet miss—as it doubtless would by a small margin—he would have himself look ridiculous a second time. But ego satisfaction should have no place in science.

Then he got another idea.

Few places on Earth can boast of such quick scenic changes as the great and tangled network of highways in southern California. Keeping an eye on one's surroundings while driving through is like watching a revolving stage. Start from the Los Angeles city hall. Head north toward the mountains. At the foothills follow the white line leading to Mt. Elsinore and at about 4000 feet park at some convenient wide turnout. Now you are in another world.

The time? Nine o'clock on a cool clear evening in October.

"Suppose we use that rock as our base of operations," Bob said, opening the car door. "You go sit down. I'll bring the lunch basket and blanket."

He waited until Dagny had reached the rock, then switched off

---

[4]Comet Wilson-Harrington of 1949 has a period of 2.31 years, but it has been observed at one appearance only and its orbit not well determined.

the lights and stumbled after her. Dagny began scanning the sky immediately. Bob was more interested in the lunch basket.

Dagny was frankly disappointed.

"The comet, it is there?"

"Some place in Aquarius—it's got to be." He came up with a couple of sandwiches. "Which would you rather have—cheese or tuna?"

"I see it!" Dagny cried. She grabbed Bob's arm. "There—over that pine tree."

Bob followed her gaze. The stars of Aquarius are faint and form no easily recognizable pattern. Bob, like most professional astronomers, was familiar only with the brighter constellations.

"That's her all right. Comet Dagny, a new female in the sky, along with Cassiopeia and Virgo and Queen Berenices' Hair."

Detail began coming out in the newcomer as their night vision sharpened. Bob found Dagny's hand under the laprobe. He wondered—how many men since the world began could boast of such an experience? The woman he loved the most by his side and her counterpart in the sky.

The comet did not correspond to the popular image of a comet, a hairy star with a beautiful long streaming tail. Instead it was an elongated blob with a stubby tail like a manx cat.

"It has no tail," said Dagny, disappointed.

"Sure it has. Sticking out behind it away from the sun." He scrutinized the celestial Dagny with a critical eye. "Wish there were a nice sharp nucleus in that big white coma. Makes it hard to get accurate positions."

"White?" Dagny asked. "Looks pale green to me, like something from the sea."

Bob turned his head slightly, trying to glimpse the comet by averted vision.

"It is pale greenish, isn't it? Probably emission from the Swan[5] bands of carbon. The C_2 molecule emits all through the spectrum, especially strong in the green." He chuckled. "Reason why women find candlelight so flattering. Emission from the Swan bands."

They watched the comet until it began to merge with the

---

[5]Named after Sir Joseph Wilson Swan (1828-1914), who first described this series of bands from violet to red. The nature of the emitting molecule was long in doubt.

branches of a pine. Dagny drew the laprobe closer. A chill wind was coming up from the west.

"Maybe we'd better be going," said Bob. "Must be getting on toward midnight."

They returned to the car. Bob drove carefully, as if lost in thought, his eyes fixed on the white line winding ahead.

"Imagine," said Dagny, "people fearing anything so beautiful."

Bob did not reply.

Predicted instant of perihelion passage for Comet Dagny was 1994, Tuesday, March 19d 13h 13m 47s UT = J.D. 2442126. 05124. Perihelion passage is a critical date for astronomers—it serves as a check on their calculations. Bob grew increasingly restless and abstracted with its approach. Not that anything particularly spectacular was expected: Comet Dagny was not a sungrazer like Ikeya-Seki of 1965, although it very probably would be visible in full daylight. Perihelion occurred as anticipated and was widely recorded.

By April Bob was going around in a daze. So completely had he identified with the comet that it had become more real than the world around him. Dagny appeared not to notice. She did not complain. She did not comment. She asked no questions. She had undergone such ordeals before. They always passed.

Then came a rainy evening in early April when Bob found his wife completely transformed. Gone was the quiet creature lolling on the chaise lounge by the fireside. Dagny made a point of always dressing for dinner. She cared nothing for fashion. Her taste ran to the thin transparent white Empire style gown of the early 1800s. Bob was scarcely past the door before she swung him around the room, her eyes shining, her voice husky, seductive:

> *The little apples man entice*
> *Since first they were in Paradise.*
> *I feel myself with pleasure glow*
> *That such within my garden grow . . .*

He was not as startled as might have been supposed. He had experience with Dagny's moods.

"Hey, let me get my coat off," he mumbled, trying to break loose. "I'm all wet."

Dagny fell back on the chaise, gasping and laughing. Bob mixed himself a drink and perched on the other end.

"Why all the merriment?" he inquired.

Dagny poured it out.

She had received an invitation from the International Grand Coven to attend its annual meeting during the last half of April in Bucharest. Owing to the rising interest in occultism, the IGC for the first time in its stormy history had wound up the year with a substantial surplus in its treasury. A special tour of Transylvania, the Dracula country, had been arranged. Grand climax was to be a performance of the Walpurgis Night scene from *Faust,* with Dagny playing Lilith, young witch "fair beyond compare."

"It's to be a real professional production with exotic costumes and special lighting effects," she ran on, unable to restrain her enthusiasm. "And guess what? They're paying all our expenses!"

"Sounds wonderful," Bob agreed, regarding his empty glass. "Sorry to be so late. Began raining and the windshield wiper wouldn't work."

Dagny surveyed him steadily

"So it started to rain? And the windshield wiper wouldn't work?" Her eyes never left his face. "That is all you have to say?"

"I said it was wonderful."

"Nothing else?"

"I'm very happy for you."

"Robert."

"Yes?"

"What is wrong?"

"Wrong? Nothing's wrong."

"Oh, I have known for months. Ever since that night on the mountain."

Bob had thought his wife could no longer surprise him. Now he had some doubts. There was an elegance about her at this moment, that compelling elegance which comes to some women after thirty and is born of absolute assurance in their poise and beauty.

"Madame Récamier," he said, grinning feebly.

He tried to turn away but her eyes refused to let him go. She had learned the art of catching the attention of an audience and holding it to some purpose, it seemed.

"Lose your slippers?" he said, glancing around the floor. "Your feet are bare."

"So were Madame Récamier's."

"That so? I never noticed."

"Robert, what is wrong?"

Bob reached for his glass.

"No!"

There was a long silence. Two minutes can be a long silence.

"This Grand Coven meeting," he began, "suppose it didn't happen."

"But I have the letter."

"I didn't mean that."

"No? What did you mean?"

"I meant—well, things occur that you can't control." He stood for several minutes, feet apart, head bowed. Suddenly he looked at her again. "Comet Dagny will strike the Earth. No doubt about it. Point of contact near Hawaiian Islands. Epoch is 23h 19m UT of May 21."

"But that's after the meeting," said Dagny.

Bob stared.

"You mean you'd go ahead with this witchcraft thing? With such a menace from outer space on the way? It's a big comet. No telling what may happen. Thousands—millions of people may die."

Dagny shrugged.

Bob was listening intently. He strode to one of the windows, cupping his hands against the glass.

"Come outside. Something I want you to see."

Then when she failed to stir: "Well, move!" he shouted. "Quick! *Vite! Stat!*"

They stepped out to the porte-cochere. The rain had stopped. The stars were dancing in the darkening sky. Bob seized Dagny by the shoulders and whirled her around to face a red glow low in the west.

"See that?" he demanded. "That's Comet Dagny."

"But Comet Dagny is green."

"Red now," he said gently.

They reentered the house. Bob threw another log on the fire. Dagny leaned back on the chaise lounge absently stroking Margarit.

"Why red?" she asked.

"Hard to explain in a few words," Bob said. "Comet's so much nearer the sun than when we saw it last October. Gases in the coma get so hot the molecules are torn apart into atoms. And oxygen atoms, for instance, emit red rays not ordinarily observable. 'Forbidden' rays we call them.''

" 'Forbidden?' '' asked Dagny. *"Tabou?"*

"Not absolutely forbidden. Rather—just highly improbable, let's say. So improbable that ordinarily we never see them.'' Bob hesitated, trying to think of a good analogy. "You might compare the oxygen atoms to a guy in a busy office trying to write a tough report. He can't get started because he's always being interrupted. So he switches to the graveyard shift. Now—no visitors or phone calls. He works straight through. Same principle applies to the oxygen atoms out in the vacuum of space. They're undisturbed and able to emit the red rays ordinarily too feeble to be observed.'' He smiled wryly. "Nice symbolism too. First comet's green—SAFETY. Red now—DANGER AHEAD.''

They sat for a long time gazing into the flames. Only Margarit kept on busily with her elaborate washing ritual.

Dagny spoke first.

"You said collision was impossible?''

"I said too much,'' Bob admitted.

"That was way back in the Paleozoic and was based on my parabolic orbit. Entirely new heresy now. Here, let me show you.'' He went to his overcoat, extracted a roll of paper which he spread out between them. "This oval's the orbit of Comet Dagny. Circle's the Earth's orbit. with Earth like a marble rolling around on top. The broken line shows where comet is moving below the Earth's orbit. Smooth line is where comet is moving above. This point, N, is the ascending node, where comet 'surfaces,' or moves from below to above plane of the Earth's orbit. Way off from Earth's orbit. Couldn't possibly have a collision. But look here at N', the descending node, where the comet dives under again. Falls smack on Earth's path. Dammit, never carried my preliminary orbit far as descending node.''

He gazed morosely at the offending point, N'.

"Of course, can't be a collision unless comet and Earth reach N' together. Highly improbable situation. But as it happens they will meet—right to the second. Like that traffic light I always hit on red.''

Such a one-in-a-million chance apparently didn't strike Dagny as so remarkable—she was familiar with the traffic light Bob had mentioned.

"Peut-être que oui," she murmured.

"Oh, we'll survive it," Bob assured her. "More crackpot ideas floating around! One they're pushing the hardest is a comet intercept probe. Looks pretty promising. We launch a rocket equipped with a thermonuclear warhead, probably sometime in April. We've already got the necessary instrumentation. The rocket zeros in on the comet. No chances for a miss. We give the command, warhead detonates, and comet's destroyed in a mass of bomb plasma."

"Comet Dagny—destroyed?"

"Afraid so. Arguments in favor are pretty strong. Nothing involved we haven't done before. They estimate fifty pounds of contaminant—"

"Never!"

Gone was the languid Madame Récamier. In her place was a defiant, imperious Saint Joan.

"Well, I'm resisting it," Bob hastened to add. "But then, hell, who ever listens to me?"

"It is I, Dagny. Official Witch of California, who speaks," she declared. "This collision is forbidden."

In previous crises Bob had discovered an attitude of passive nonopposition brought the best results. This time, however, he felt compelled to remonstrate.

"Remember, this orbit isn't any of my scribbling. It's based on data fed into a CDC 6600 computer with an n-body code. We took every possible gravitational force into account. Always with the same result—collision."

"No!"

"You still persist?"

Dagny replied with superb assurance, "Yes. In spite of everything."

Days passed.

The comet came on.

Bob took his coffee upstairs to watch the launching. Dagny refused to witness the disgraceful spectacle. Aside from giving Margarit an extra helping of gourmet cat food at twenty cents per fifteen-ounce can, she went about her household tasks exactly as usual.

"Well, perfect launching," Bob announced, joining Dagny at the breakfast table. "Funny thing," he remarked reflectively.

"Folks have been scared of comets for centuries. First time we ever took a shot at one."

Dagny did not appear amused. Bob decided not to press the subject. He glanced through the paper. Along with dire predictions should the mission fail, there was the usual routine list of floods, murders, hijackings, etc. Considerable space was devoted to a new outbreak of Exotic Newcastle disease, which threatened to double the price of eggs. (Associated in some obscure way with the onset of the comet.)

He laid aside the paper, poured more coffee, was about to comment on some household chore, then decided this was a situation demanding the direct approach. He went to his wife, put his arms around her, and kissed her. It was not a peck. It was a kiss.

"Don't take it so hard. Periodic comets generally peter out after a while. How much better a heroic end than a slow lingering death. Think! Comet Dagny will be a landmark in astronomy. Remembered in the annals of science as long as science itself."

Such intimations of immortality gave no consolation. As remarked earlier, Dagny already had worlds of time.

Slow fade to ten-second blackout during Bob's last impassioned outburst. Lights up revealing a nation, in home and cocktail bar, immobile, spellbound, awaiting the moment of truth. An expectant hush hangs over all. Only occasionally is the silence broken by the pop of beer cans and crackle of potato chips. All eyes are fixed, center screen, on the gleaming cylinder, hanging virtually motionless against the background of stars.

Flashback to mission control.

"The Space Intercept is now at rendezvous position with Comet Dagny."

But where was Comet Dagny? Millions of cubic AUs without a comet in sight.

The Comet Intercept was in the awkward situation of a rookie football player assigned to take out a certain opponent. He arrives at the designated position ready to carry out his assignment. Only his opponent isn't there. What to do?

Mission control after solemn deliberation decided to fire the warhead anyhow. Slow fadeout on $20,000,000 of bomb plasm.

Bob blamed it all on the stupid technologists in charge of operations. Never did trust those guys. No imagination. Well, wait till

May 21, the predicted date of collision. But the Earth passed the comet's descending node without incident, not even a piffling little meteor shower.[6]

A few billion beings breathed easier. There was much celebrating in the streets.

Soothsayers and the astrology-struck promptly began making fun of science and its predictions.

Evening of the day following the descending node. Dagny and Margarit reclining on the chaise before the fire. Bob restlessly pacing the room.

"Not the first time a comet's disappeared," he muttered. "Good evidence some comets are affected by nongravitational forces—Honda-Mrkos-Pajdusakova—Giac obina-Zinner. 'Erratics' we call them. But Comet Dagny's the first one that ever pulled a vanishing act right in front of us."

"Is it really so important?" Dagny said, absently stroking Margarit.

"It is to astronomers."

"But why?"

"Because it violates all our established laws of motion, that's why. Time and again we have questioned Newton's laws. Invariably the deviations have been traced to errors in observation or computation.[7] They survive the test of the experimental method. Not like astrology and that crap."

He flung himself on the chaise, his head in Dagny's lap.

"I'm sorry. Forgive me. Forgot our vow."

"You're so agitated about how comets go," Dagny said, after a pause. "Tell me, Robert, how do comets *come?*"

Bob pulled himself together with a masterful effort.

"That's harder than telling a kid how babies come. Why, the stork brings them. They find them on a rose bush or cabbage plant. As for comets—'they come from the everywhere into here.' "

He hesitated, trying to collect his scattered senses.

"Well, seriously, explanation most in favor is Jan Oort's comet cloud hypothesis. He postulates a spherical shell surround-

---

[6]An observer at the meteorological station, Kodiakanal, India, reported an unusually bright mock sun or sun dog.

[7]Bob, in his agitated state of mind, neglected the slight deviations due to general relativity.

ing the solar system 30,000 to 100,000 astronomical units thick. Comets originate from condensations in shell. A comet starts creeping toward the solar system. After millions of years finally makes it. Whisks around the Sun and heads back into deep space.

"Occasionally one like Comet Dagny has a close encounter with Jupiter. Poor thing's trapped. It's becoming a short-period ellipse like an asteroid's. All clear?"

Bob relapsed into gloomy silence. Margarit yawned.

"This comet cloud," said Dagny, "it forms how?"

"Easiest answer is by catastrophe. Body revolving between Mars and Jupiter blows up. Don't ask me why. Part escapes to the stars. Part goes to form the comet cloud."

"You have observed it?"

"Hell, no. We put it there."

"Ah, then you are like Margarit."

"Margarit?" Bob gave that ginger feline a suspicious glance. "How'd Margarit get into this?"

"You think your comets come from this cloud. Margarit thinks her food comes from tin cans. Why? Somebody put it there."

Bob pondered.

"Yeah, I get the point."

"Margarit sees me open a can. Out comes her food. She sees me open a cardboard carton. Out comes her milk. It always works. It's a law that never fails. Of course," Dagny said, "the creature's viewpoint is rather limited."

"Yeah, so's ours."

"I wonder," Dagny mused, "how many of our other ideas on life and the universe are equally limited? We think we peer so deep. But who can say? If we peered deeper might not we find a wholly new universe, utterly mysterious and incomprehensible?"

"Dagny, do you peer deeper? Is that what you're telling me?"

"Most cats, even, peer deeper. They discover mice—and thus seem sorcerers to such felines as our Margarit."

Bob gravely addressed the slumbering cat.

"Margarit, someday you and I will have a long talk about that." He rubbed her ear. She purred appreciatively.

"Little witch, I did hear you ban the collision. But surely you're not silly enough to . . ." Her proud stare stopped him. He could guess her thoughts. *Don't apologize. Don't explain.*

They both chuckled.

Then his jaw set firmly.

"But don't get me wrong. I'm still sticking with my same old stodgy ideas. All I believe is what I can observe and measure."

"*Quand même?*"

He nodded.

"In spite of everything."

THE DEATH OF PRINCES

Fritz Leiber

Ever since the discovery Hal and I made last night, or rather the amazing explanation we worked out for an acumulated multitude of curious facts, covering them all (the tentative solution to a riddle that's been a lifetime growing, you might say) I have been very much concerned and, well, yes, frightened, but also filled with the purest wonder and a gnawing curiosity about what's going to happen just ten years from now to Hal and me and to a number of our contemporaries who are close friends—to Margaret and Daffy (our wives), to Mack, Charles, and Howard, to Helen, Gertrude and Charlotte, to Betty and Elizabeth—and to the whole world too. Will there be (after ten years) a flood of tangible miracles and revelations from outer space, including the discovery of an ancient civilization compared to which Egypt and Chaldea are the merest whims or aberrations of infant intelligence, or a torrent of eldritch terrors from the black volumes between the glittering stars, or only dusty death?—especially for me and those dearly valued comrade-contemporaries of mine.

Ten years, what are they? Nothing to the universe—the merest millifraction of an eye blink, or microfraction of a yawn—or even to a young person with all his life ahead. But when they are your last ten years, or at the very best your next to last . . .

I'm also in particular concerned about what's happened to François Broussard (we're out of touch with him again) and to his ravishing and wise young wife and to their brilliant 15-year-old

son (he would be now) and about what part that son may play in
the events due ten years from this year of 1976, especially if he
goes on to become a spaceman, as his father envisioned for him.
For François Broussard is at or near the center of the riddle we
think (and also fear, I must confess) we solved last night up to a
point, Hal and I. In fact, he almost *is* the riddle. Let me explain.

I was born late in 1910 (a few months after Hal and before
Broussard—all of us, I and my dear contemporaries, were born
within a year or two of each other), too young to have been
threatened in any way by World War I, yet old enough to have
readily escaped the perils of military service in World War II (by
early marriage, a child or two, a more or less essential job). In
fact, we were all survivor types like Heinlein harps on (except
my kind of survival doesn't involve fighting for my species—
zoological paranoid fanaticism!—but for me and mine . . . and
who *those* are. I decide) and I early began to develop the
conviction that there was something special about us that made
us an elite, a chosen mini-people, and that set us apart from the
great mass of humanity (the canaille, Broussard had us calling
those, way way back) beginning its great adventure with democracy and all democracy's wonders and Pandora ills: mass production, social security, the welfare state, antibiotics and overpopulation, atomics and pollution, electronic computers and the
strangling serpents of bureaucracy's red and white tape (monstrous barber pole), the breaking loose from this single planet
Earth along with that other victory over the starry sky—smog.
Oh, we've come a long way in sixty years or so.

But I was going to tell you about Broussard. He was our
leader, but also our problem child; the mouthpiece of our ideals
and secret dreams of glory, but also our mocker, severest critic,
and gadfly , the devil's advocate; the one who kept dropping out
of sight from time to time for years and years (we never did, we
kept in touch, the rest of us) and then making a triumphant return
when least expected; the socially mobile one too, mysteriously
hobnobbing with notorious public figures and adventuresses,
with people in the news, but also with riff-raff, revolutionaries,
rapscallions generally, criminals even, and low-life peasant types
(we stuck mostly with our own class, we were cautious—except
when he seduced us out of that); the world traveler and cosmopo-
lite (we stayed close to the U.S.A., pretty much).

In fact, if there was one thing that stood out about François
Broussard, first and foremost, it was that aura of the foreign and

the mysterious, that air of coming from some bourne a lot farther off than Mexico or Tangier or Burma or Bangkok (places he made triumphant returns from and told us excitingly bizarre stories about, stories that glittered with wealth and high living and dissoluteness and danger; he was always most romantically attractive to our ladies then, and he's had affairs with several of them over the years, I'm fairly sure, and maybe one with Hal, it's just possible).

We never have known about his background at first hand, in the same way we do about each other's. His story, which he has never varied, is that he was a foundling brought up by an eccentric Manhattan millionaire (the romantic touch again), Pierre Broussard, but also called "French Pete" and "Silver Pete," who made his pile mining in Colorado, a lifelong secret crony of Mark Twain, and educated (François was) by tutors and in Paris (he's named his son by his young wife Pierre, the boy he told us would become a spaceman).

In physical appearance he's a little under middle height but taller than Hal and slenderer (I'm a giant), rather dark complected with very dark brown hair, though silvered when we last saw him in 1970 six years ago. He's very quick and graceful in his movements, very fluid, even in later years. He's danced in ballet and he's never motion-sick. In fact, he moves like a cat, always landing on his feet, though he once told me that gravity fields seemed unnatural to him, a distorting influence on the dance of life—he was the first person I knew to dive with aqualung, to go the Cousteau route into the silent world.

His style of dress has always accentuated his foreign air—he was also the first man I knew to wear (at different times) a cape, a beret, an ascot, and a Vandyke beard (and wear his hair long) all back in the days when it took a certain courage to do those things.

And he's always been into the occult of one sort or another, but with this difference: that he always mixes real science in with it, biofeedback with the witchcraft, Jung with the flying saucers, verified magnetism with Colonel Estobani's healing hands. For instance, when he casts a horoscope for one of his wealthy clients (we've never been his clients, any of us; for the most, we're something special) he uses the actual positions of the sun and moon and planets in the constellations rather than in the "signs"—the constellations as they were two thousand years ago and more. He's been an avid field astronomer all his life, with a real feeling for the position of the stars and all the wandering bodies at any instant. In fact, he's the only person I've ever known to look at the ground and give me the feeling that he was observing the stars that shine above the antipodes—look at his knees and see the Southern Cross.

(I know I seem to be going on forever about Broussard, but really you have know a great deal about him and about his life before you'll get the point of the explanation Hal and I discovered last night and why it hit us as hard as it did and frightened us.)

After what I've said about horoscopes and the occult, it won't surprise you to hear that our François made his living mostly as a fortuneteller. And in view of my remarks about mixing in science, it may not startle you all that much to learn that he was also apparently a genuine question answerer (I can't think of a less clumsy way to phrase it), especially in the field of mathematics, as if he were the greatest of lightning calculators or as if—this expresses it best—he had access to an advanced electronic computer back in the 1920s and 1930s, when such instruments were only dreams—and the memory of the failure of Cavendish's differential engine, which tried to do it all mechanically. At any rate, he had engineers and statisticians and stockbrokers among his clients, and one astronomer, for whom he calculated the orbit of an asteroid—Mack verified that story.

A queer thing about Broussard's question answering (or precision fortunetelling)—it always took him a certain minimum time to get his answers and that time varied somewhat over the years: ten hours around 1930, twelve hours around 1950, but only ten hours again in 1970. He'd tell his clients to come back in so many hours. It was very strange. (But we just mostly heard about all that. We never were his clients, as I've said, or members of his little mystic groups either—though we occasionally profited from his talent.)

A few more strange things I must tell you about Broussard while they're fresh in my memory, mostly unusual notions he had and odd things he said one time or another—a few more strange things and one vision or dream he had when he was young and that seemed to signify a lot to him.

Like Bernard Shaw and Heinlein (recalling both *Back to Methuselah* and *Children of Methuselah*) François Broussard has always been hipped on the idea of immortality or at least very long life. "Why do we all have to die at seventy-five or so?"

he'd ask. "Maybe it's just mass suggestion on an undreamed-of scale. Why can't we live to be three hundred, at least?—and maybe there are some among us (a long-life genetic strain) who do so, secretly."

And once he said to me, "Look here, Fred, do you suppose that if a person lived well over a hundred years, he or she might metamorphose into some entirely different and vastly superior sort of being, like a caterpillar into a butterfly? Aldous Huxley suggested something of that sort in *After Many a Summer Dies the Swan*, though there the second being wasn't superior. Maybe we're all supposed to do that, but just don't live long enough for the transformation to happen. Something we lost when we lost our empire or empyry—not, I'm just being poetic."

Another pet idea of his was a people living in and coming from space—and remember, this was way before earth satellites or planetary probes . . . or flying saucers and von Daniken either. "Why can't people live in space?" he'd demand. "They wouldn't have to take along all that much of their environment. There'd be perpetual sunlight, for one thing, and freedom from the killing strain of gravity that cuts our lives short. I tell you, Fred, maybe this planet was settled from somewhere else, just like America was. Maybe we're a lost and retrogressed fragment of some great astral empire."

Speaking of the astral reminds me that there was one particular *part* of the heavens that François Broussard was especially interested in and somehow associated with himself—particularly in the late 1940s and early 1950s, when he was living in Arizona with its clear, starry nights that showed the Milky Way; he had some sort of occult coterie there, we learned; he'd stare and stare at it (the spot in the heavens) with and without a telescope or binoculars through the long desert nights, like a sailor on a desert island watching for a ship along a sea lane it might follow. In fact, he once spotted a new comet there, a very faint one. Not very surprising in an astrologer, what with their signs, or constellations of the zodiac, but this spot was halfway around the heavens from his natal sign, which was Pisces, or Aquarius rather by his way of figuring it. He was born February 19, 1911, though exactly how he knew the date so certainly, being a foundling, we've never learned—or at least I never have.

The spot in the heavens that fascinated or obsessed him so (*his* spot, you might say) was in Hydra, a long and straggling, quiet dim constellation. Its serpent head, which lies south of zodiacal

Leo, is a neat group of faint stars resembling a bishop's miter flattened down. Hydra's only bright star, located still farther south and where the serpent's heart would be, if serpents have a heart, is Alphard, often called the Lonely One, because it's the only prominent star in quite a large area. I can remember thinking how suitable that was for François—"the Lonely One," theatrical and Byronic.

One other thing he had odd angles on, mixing the supernatural with the scientific, or at any rate the pseudoscientific, was ghosts. He thought they might be faintly material in some way, a dying person's last extruded ectoplasm, perhaps, or else something very ancient people transformed into, the last stage of existence, like with Heinlein's Martians. And he wondered about the ghosts of inanimate objects—or at least objects most people would think of as inanimate.

I recall him asking me around 1950, "Fred, what do you think the ghost of a computer would be like?—one of the big electric brains, so called?" (I remembered that later on when I read about Mike or Mycroft in Heinlein's *The Moon Is a Harsh Mistress*.)

But I must tell you about François' vision, or dream, the one that seemed to mean so much to him—almost as much as his spot in Hydra near Alphard. He's the sort of person who tells his dreams, at least his fancy cosmic or Jungian ones, and gets other people to tell theirs.

It began, he said, with him flying or rather swimming around in black and empty space—in free fall, a person might say today, but he had his dream and described it back about 1930.

He was really lost in the void, he said, exiled from earth, because the black space in which he swam was speckled with stars in every direction, whichever way he looked as he twisted and turned (he could see the full circle of the Milky Way and also the full circle of the zodiac) except there was one star far brighter than all the others, almost painfully glaring, although it was still just a point of light, like Venus to the naked eye among the planets.

And then he gradually became aware that he was not alone in the void, that swimming around with him, but rotating and revolving around him very ponderously, moving very slowly, were five huge, black, angular shapes silhouetted against the starfields. He could actually see their sides only when they happened to reflect the light of the glaring Venuslike star. Those sides were always flat, never rounded, and seemed to be made of some silvery metal that had been dulled by ages of exposure so that it looked like lead.

The flat sides were always triangles or squares or pentagons, so that he finally realized in his dream that the five shapes were the five regular, or Platonic solids, perhaps discovered by Pythagoras: the tetrahedron, the hexahedron (or cube), the octahedron, dodecahedron (twelve-sider), and icosahedron. A total of fifty sides for all five bodies.

"And somehow that seemed highly significant and very frightening," François would say, "as though in the depths of space I'd been presented with the secret of the universe, if only I knew how to interpret it. Even Kelper thought that about the five regular solids, you know, and tried to work it out in his *Mysterium Cosmographicum*.

"But oh God, those polyhedrons were *old*," he would go on. "As if very finely pitted by eons of meteoric dust impacting and weathered by an eternity of exposure to every variety of radiation in the electromagnetic spectrum.

"And I somehow got the feeling," he would continue, fixing you with those wild eyes of his, "that there were *things* inside those huge shapes that were older still. Things, beings, ancient objects, maybe beings frozen or mummified—I don't know—maybe material ghosts. And then it burst upon me that I was in the midst of a vast floating *cemetery*, the loneliest in the universe, adrift in space. Imagine the pyramids of Cheops, King's and Queens' Chamber and all, weightless and lost between the stars. Well they do make lead coffins and if the living can live in space, so can the dead—and why mightn't a very advanced civilization, an astral empire, put their tombs in space?" (Harking back to his dream in the 1950s he made that "into orbit," and we all remembered his dream when at that time some nut mortician suggested orbiting globular silver urns as repositories for human ashes.)

Sometimes at that point François would quote those lines of Calpurnia to Caesar in Shakespeare's play: "When beggars die, there are no comets seen; The heavens themselves blaze forth the death of princes." (Shakespeare was a very comet-conscious man; they had a flood of bright ones in his time.)

"And then it seemed to me," he would continue, "that all those ghosts were flooding invisibly out of those five floating mausoleums and all converging on me suffocatingly, choking me with their dust . . . and I woke up.''

In 1970 he added a new thought to his vision and to his odd notions about ghosts too, his eyes still wild and bright, though wrinkle-netted: "You know how they call the neutrino the ghost particle? Well, there are some even ghostlier and still more abstract properties of existence being discovered today. or at least hypothesized, by people like Glashow, properties so weird and insubstantial that they have names, believe it or not, like strangeness and charm. Maybe ghosts are beings that have no mass or energy at all, only strangeness and charm—and maybe spin,'' And the bright eyes twinkled.

But now in my story of François Broussard (and all of us) I have to go back to about 1930, when the neutrino hadn't been dreamed of and they were, in fact, just discovering the neutron and learning how to explain isotopes. We were all students at the University of Chicago—that's how we got together in the first place. François was living with (sponging off?) some wealthy people there in Hyde Park who helped support the Oriental Institute and the Civic Opera and he was auditing a couple of courses we were taking—that's how we got to know him. He was wearing the cape and Vandyke then—of fine, dark brown hair, almost black, that was silky with youth.

He'd come straight from Paris on the *Bremen* in a record four-day crossing with the latest news of the Left Bank and Harry's American Bar and Gide and Gertrude Stein. His foster father, old Pierre Broussard, the crony of Mark Twain, had been dead some few years (expiring at ninety in bed—with his newest mistress) and François had been done out of his inheritance by conniving relatives, but that hadn't taken the gloss off the grotesque incidents and scrapes of his childhood, which made old Silver Pete sound like a crazy wizard and François the most comically precocious of apprentices.

What with all his art interests he seemed something of a dilettante at first, in spite of also auditing a math course in the theory of sets (then groups, *very* advanced stuff at that time) but then we got the first demonstration of his question answering. Howard was getting his master's degree in psych, except that he'd gotten conned into doing a thesis that involved doing two semesters' paper work at least correlating the results of one of his thesis professor's experiments—simple enough math, but mountains of it. Howard put off this monstrous chore until there was not a prayer of his finishing it in time. François learned about it, carried Howard's figures off, and came back with the answers—pages and pages of them—sixteen hours later. Howard couldn't believe it, but he checked an answer at random and it was right. He rushed the stuff to the thesis typist—and got his master's in due course.

I was there when François passed the stuff to Howard, saying, "Three hours to digest the figures, *ten hours to get the answers*, three hours to set them down." (There turned out to be good reason for remembering that ten-hour figure exactly.)

Oh, but he was a charmer, though, François was, and in many ways. (Talk about strangeness and charm, *he* had them both, all right.) I think he was having an affair with Gertrude then. His rich Hyde Park friends had set him adrift about that time and hers was the wealthiest family of any of ours, though that may have had nothing to do with it. Yes, a thoroughgoing charmer, but much more than that—a catalyst for imagination and ambition was what he was. There we were, a small bunch of rather bright and fortunate young people, thinking ourselves somehow special and exceptional, but really very naive. Avid for culture on general principles. Just finding out about Marxism and the class war, but not seriously tempted by it. Social security was not yet our concern—the stock market crash of October end, 1929, had barely begun to teach us about social insecurity. Our heroes were mostly writers and scientists—people like T. S. Eliot, Hemingway, James Joyce, Einstein, Freud, Adler, Norman Thomas, Maynard Hutchins at our own university with his Great Books and two-year bachelor's degree, yes, and Lindberg, and Amelia Earhart and Greta Garbo. (What a contrast with today's comparable heroes and heroines, who seem to be mostly anti-establishment and welfare-state types; leftist social workers, drug-involved paramedics, witches and occultists, mystics and back-to-nature gurus, revolutionists, feminists, black power people, gay liberators, draft-card burners—though we did have our pacifists, come to think of it, but they were chiefly non functional idealists. What a tremendous change all that implies.)

Anyhow, there we were with our dreams and our ideals, our feeling of being somehow different, and so you can imagine how we ate up the stuff that François fed us about being some sort of lost or secret aristocrats, almost as if we were members of some submerged superculture—*slans*, you might say, remembering Van Vogt's novel of a few years later; tendrilless slans! (Several of us were into science fiction. I vividly recall seeing the first issue of *Amazing* on a newsstand—and grabbing it!—fifty years ago.)

I remember the exact words François used once. "Every mythology says that upon occasion the gods come down out of the skies and lie with chosen daughters of men. Their seed drifts down from the heavens. Well, we were all born about the same time, weren't we?"

And then, just about that time, there came what I still tend to think of as scandal and shock. François Broussard was in jail in a highway town west of Chicago, charged with a sex offense by a young male hitchhiker. (I've just been mentioning gay liberation, haven't I? Well, what I said about change and contrast between our times and then goes double here.) Hal and Charles went bravely off and managed to bail him out. To my lasting shame I dodged that duty of friendship, though I contributed some of the money. The upshot: almost at once, before I or any of the others saw him again, François jumped bail, simply disappeared, first telling Charles, who was dumbfounded by it, "Sorry to disappoint you, but of course I'm guilty. I simply couldn't resist the creature. I thought, mistakenly, that he was one of us—an imperial page, perhaps." And that grotesque and flippant answer was the end of the whole Chicago episode, leaving us all with very mixed feelings.

But as the months and years passed, we tended to remember the glamorous things about him and forget the other—in fact, I don't think we'd have kept in touch with each other the way we did except for him, although he was the one who kept dropping out of sight. Hal married Margaret, and his editorial work and writing took him to New York City, while mine took me and Daffy, married also, to Los Angeles and the high desert near it, where I got interested in field astronomy myself. The others got their lives squared away one way or another, scattering quite a bit, but keeping in touch through class reunions and common interests, but mostly by correspondence, that dying art.

It was Elizabeth who first ran into François again about 1950 in Arizona, where he was living in a rambling ranch house full of Mexican curios (he'd established dual citizenship) and surrounded by his artsy-occulty, well-to-do coterie. He seemed quite well off himself, she reported, and during the next couple of years we all visited him at least once, usually while driving through east or west (U.S. 40, old 66, gets a lot of travel). I believe Elizabeth and he had something going then—she's the most beautiful, it's the consensus, of all our ladies (or should I say the feminine comrades in our group?) and has perhaps kept her youth the best (Daffy excepted!) though all of them have tended to stay slimly youthful (conceivably a shared genetic strain?—*now* I wonder about that more than ever).

The visits weren't all our doing. After he'd been rediscovered, François to our surprise began to write notes and sometimes long letters to all of us, and pretty soon the old magic was working again. A lot had happened—the Great Depression, fascism, World War II, Hiroshima, and now the McCarthy era of suspicion, confession, witch-hunt, and fear had started—but we'd survived it all pretty handily. I'd just begun to think of us as the Uncommitted—with the double meaning that none of us seemed to be committed to any great purpose in life, nor yet *been* committed to a mental hospital, like so many others we were beginning to know or hear of, though we had our share of severe neuroses and were getting into our middle-age crises. But with François exerting his magnetism once more, we began to seem like aristocrats again, even to me, but not so much secret and lost as banished or exiled, standing a little aloof from life, devoted to mystery we didn't quite understand, yet hoped the future would make clearer. Someone once said to me. "Fred, you'd *better* live a long life."

I managed to stay with François three of four times myself down there in the desert. Twice Daffy was with me—she'd always liked his style, his consciously slightly comical grand manner. Once I was up to all hours stargazing with him—he had a four-inch reflector mounted equatorially. He admitted to me his peculiar interest in the Hydra area, but couldn't explain it except as a persistent compulsion to stare in that direction, especially when his mind wandered, "as if there were something invisible but very important to me lying out there," he added with a chuckle.

He did say, "Maybe that Lonely-One thing gets me about Alphard—a segregated star, a star in prison. Loneliness is a kind of prison, you know, just as real freedom is—you're there with your decisions to make and no one can help you. Slavery is much cozier."

He also had this to say about his point of interest in the heavens, that it hadn't started in Hydra but rather in the obscure constellation of Crater just to the east and south of Virgo—and now showed signs of shifting still farther west toward Canis Minor and the Little Dog Star Procyon and toward Cancer. "The mind is ultimately so whimsical," he said. "Or perhaps I mean enigmatic. Whatever walls of reason you put up, the irrational slips by."

He was still doing his question answering, making his living by it, except that now it took him twelve hours to get the answers. His slim face, clean-shaven now, was somewhat haggard, with vertical wrinkles of concentration between the eyebrows. His hair, which he wore to his shoulders, was still silky, but there were gray threads in it. He looked a little like a Hindu mystic.

And then, just as we were beginning to rely on him in some ways, he pulled up stakes and disappeared again, this time (we pieced together later) to dodge arrest for smuggling marijuana across the border. And he could hardly have run to Mexico this time, because he was wanted by their federal agents too. It appears he was one of the first to learn that they take equally stern views about such things, perhaps to impress the Colossus of the North.

Another twenty years passed, 1970 rolled or creaked around, and a remarkable number of us found ourselves living in San Francisco—or Frisco as I like to call it to the thin-lipped disapproval of the stuffier of its old inhabitants, but to the joy of its old ghosts, I'm sure, ruffians like Jack London and Sir Francis Drake. Hal and Margaret came from New York City to escape its uncollected garbage and sky blackened by all the east's industrial effluvia, Daffy (it's short for Daffodil) and I from Los Angeles to get out from under its mountainous green smog that mounds up into the stratosphere and spills over the high desert. More than half of the old crowd in all, from here and there across the country, as if summoned by an inaudible trumpet blast, or drawn by some magnetism almost as mysterious as keeps François' gaze fastened on the Lonely One.

We were no longer the Uncommitted, I told myself. Too many of us *had* been committed, or committed ourselves, to mental hospitals over the years—but we'd got out again. (It was beginning to be just a little remarkable that none of us had died.) I liked to think of us now (1970) as dwellers in the Crazy House, that institution in Robert Graves's *Watch the North Wind Rise* to which his new Cretans retired when they abdicated from social responsibility and the respect due age to enjoy such frivolities as pure science and purely recreational sex.

We (and Earth's whole society) were suffering the aftereffects of all the earlier good advances—the pollution and overpopulation that went with nearly unlimited energy, antibiotics, and the democratic ideal. (The only spectacular new advance during the past twenty years had been spaceflight—the beginning of the probing of the planets.) And we were going downhill into the last decade or two of our lives. In that sense we had certainly become the Doomed.

And yet our mood was not so much despair as melancholy—at least I'm sure it was in my case. That's a much misunderstood word, melancholy—it doesn't just mean sadness. It is a temperament or outlook and has its happinesses as well as its griefs—and especially it is associated with *the consciousness of distance*.

Do you know Dürer's wood engraving *Melencolia?* The instruments of work—carpenter's tools—are scattered about her feet, while beside her are a ladder and a strange stone polyhedron and a sphere and also a millstone on which sits a brooding cupid. On the wall behind her are a ship's bell, an hourglass, and a magic square that doesn't quite add up right. She sits there, wings folded, with a pair of compasses in one fist (to measure *distance*), elbow propped on knee and cheek on her other fist, peering with eyes that are both youthfully eager and broodingly thoughtful into the transmarine distance where are a rainbow and a bearded comet—or else the comet's "hair" may only be part of the glory of the setting sun. Just so, it seemed to me, we looked into the future and the sky, into the depths of space and time.

It was another work of high art that in a sense brought François Broussard back this time. I was in the great vault of Grace Cathedral atop Nob Hill, where in the clerestory they have the spaceman John Glenn and Einstein's $E = MC^2$ in stained glass. But I was looking at that one of the six Willett windows which in glorious glooms and glows both illuminates and enshrouds the words "Light after Darkness." The pavement scrutched, I turned, and there he stood beside me, smiling quizzically. I realized I was very glad to see him. He hair was grizzled, but cut very short. He looked young and nimble. He was standing on a patch of multicolored sunlight that had spilled through the glass onto the stone floor.

It turned out that he lived hardly a dozen blocks away on Russian Hill, where he had a roof (as I had and Hal too) from which to stargaze when Frisco's fog permitted. He still made his living answering questions. "Of course, they've got computers now," he said, "but computer time is damned expensive—I charge less." (And it took him only ten hours now to get answers, I learned later—things were getting brisker. While his odd point of interest in the skies was moving from Hydra toward Cancer, just as he'd thought it would.) And he was already in touch with one of us again—Charlotte.

And he was married!—not to Charlotte, but to her daughter, who was also named Charlotte. It gave me the strangest feeling about the tricks of time to hear that, let me tell you. And not only married, but they had a son who was already ten years old—a charming youngster and very bright, he turned out to be, who wanted to be a spaceman, an ambition which his father encouraged. "He'll claim my kingdom for me in the stars," François once commented with a cryptic little chuckle "—or else find my grave there."

Somehow these circumstances fired us all again with youthful feelings—young Charlotte and Pierre turned out to be charmers too—and it has stayed that way with us; only yesterday I was putting together an article on the many very young female film actresses who've surfaced in the past few years, girls even by feminist definition, a sort of nymphette runnel: Linda Blair, Mackenzie Phillips, Melanie Griffith, Tatum O'Neal, Nell Potts, Mairé Rapp, Catherine Harrison, Roberta Wallach. I wonder if this accent on youth, this feeling of some imminent rebirth, has any significance . . . beyond impending second childhood in some of its observers.

At any rate, we all saw a lot of each other the next months—the Broussard trio and the rest of us—and François became again our leader and inspirer.

And then, most mysteriously, he disappeared again and his wife and boy with him. We've never got the straight of that except that he was mixed up with people who were vastly anti-Vietnam and (how shall I say?) prematurely all-out anti-Nixon. Even old Charlotte doesn't know (or claims so most convincingly) what's happened to young Charlotte, her daughter, and François and their child.

But his influence over us has stayed strong despite his absence. Like the field-astronomy thing that's so symbolic of concern with distance. Last year, in spite of Frisco's fogs, I saw the moon's roseate eclipse in May, the close conjunction of Mars and Jupiter in mid-June, and Nova Cygni 1975 crookedly deforming the Northern Cross at August's end for four nights running before it faded down so rapidly.

And then last night Hal and I were talking about it all, as we have a thousand times—in other words, we were reviewing all I've told you up to now—and then an idea struck me, an idea that gave me gooseflesh, though I didn't at first dream why. Hal had seemingly digressed to tell me about an astronomy article he'd been reading about plans to rendevous a space probe with Halley's comet, due to return again in 1986 after its last visits in 1834 and 1910. The idea was to loop the probe around one of the big outer planets in such a way that it would come boomeranging back toward the sun and match trajectories and speeds with the comet as it came shooting in, gathering speed. It was already too late to make use of Saturn, but it could still be worked if you looped the probe around Jupiter, into its gravity well and out again.

"Hal," I heard myself asking him in an odd little voice, "where's the aphelion of Halley's comet?—you know, the point where it's farthest away from the sun. I know it's out about as far as the orbit of Pluto, but *where* in the heavens is it? *Where* would you look in the stars to see Halley's comet when it's farthest from Earth? I know you couldn't actually see it then, even with the biggest telescope. Its frozen head would be far too tiny. But *where* would you look?"

You know, it took us quite a while to find that out and we finally had to do it indirectly, although I have a fair little astronomy library. The *one* specific fact you're looking for is *never* in the books you've got at hand. (We found the aphelion *distance* almost at once—3,283,000,000 miles—but its *vector* eluded us.)

But then in Willy Ley's little 1969 McGraw-Hill book on comets we finally discovered that the perihelion of Halley's comet—its point of closest approach to the sun—was in Aquarius, which would put its aphelion at the opposite end of the zodiac—in Leo.

"But it wouldn't be in Leo," I said softly. "because Halley's comet has an inclination of almost eighteen degrees to the Ecliptic—it comes shooting in toward the sun from below (south of) the plane of the planets. Eighteen degrees south of Leo—where would that put us?"

It put us, the star charts quickly revealed, in Hydra and near Alphard, the Lonely One. And that left us silent with shock for quite a space, Hal and I, while my mind automatically worked out that even the slow movement of François' point of interest in the sky from south of Virgo to Alphard toward Cancer fitted with the retrograde orbit of Halley's comet. A comet follows such a long, narrow, elliptical path that it's always in one quarter of the sky with respect to earth except for the months when it whips around the sun.

But I'll be forever grateful to Ley's little book that it showed us the way, although it happens to have one whopping error in it: on page 122 it gives the radio distance of Saturn as thirteen and a half hours, when it happens to be an hour and twenty-five or so minutes—likely a decimal point got shifted one place to the right somewhere in the calculations. But the matter of radio distance has a bearing on the next point I brought up uneasily when Hal and I finally started speaking again.

"You know how it used to take François twelve hours to get his answers back in 1950?" I said, finding I was trembling a little. "Well, Halley's comet was in aphelion in 1948 and twelve hours is about the time it would take to get a radio answer back from the vicinity of Pluto, or of Pluto's orbit—six hours out, six hours back, at the speed of light. The ten-hour times for his answers in 1930 and 1970 would fit too."

"Or maybe telepathy also travels at the speed of light," Hal said softly. Then he shook his head as if to clear it. But that's ridiculous," he said sharply. "Do you realize that we've been assuming that Halley's comet is some sort of spaceship, some sort of living, highly civilized, *computerized* world in space— and that perhaps the memory of it comes slowly back to man each time it reapproaches the sun?"

"Or a space cemetery," I interposed with a nervous little laugh, almost a giggle. "A group of five mausoleums forming the comet's head—although you couldn't observe them telescopically as the comet approached the sun because they'd be concealed by the coma of warmed-up gases and dust. Remember what François once said about the ghosts of computers? Why mightn't computers, or the effigies of computers, be buried in the tombs of an astral empire?—and God knows what else. Just as the Egyptians put effigies of their servants and tools into their tombs, never dreaming that the great bearded meteor ghosting across their sweating, midnight blue Egyptian night every 76 years was another such ossuary.

"And remember François' cosmic dream," I continued. "That

intensely bright star in it would exactly describe the sun as seen from Pluto's orbit. And out there all the dust and gases would be frozen to the surfaces of the five polyhedrons—they wouldn't make an obscuring coma.''

"But you're talking about a *dream*," Hal protested. "Don't you see, Fred, that all that you're saying implies that there actually *is* some kind of elder cometary civilization and that we all are in some sense children of the comet?''

"The tail of Halley's comet brushed the earth in 1910." I said urgently. "Let's check the exact date."

That fact we found very quickly—it was May 19, 1910.

"—nine months, to a day, before François was born." I said shakily "Hal, do you remember what he used to say about the seed of the gods—or the princes of the astral empire—drifting down from the stars?"

"Just as Mark Twain (and maybe old French Pete too?) was born in 1834, the year of the previous appearance of Halley's comet, and died in 1910," Hal took up, his imagination becoming as enthralled as my own. "And think of those last two weird books of his—*The Mysterious Stranger,* about a man from elsewhere, and *Captain Stormfield's Visit to Heaven*—aboard a comet! Even that posthumous short 'My Platonic Sweetheart' about his lifelong dream-love for a fifteen-year-old girl . . . Fred, there *is* that suggestion of some weird sort of reincarnation, or mentorship . . .''

I won't set down in detail any more of the wild speculations Hal and I exchanged last night. They're all pretty obvious and maddeningly tantalizing, and wildly baroque, and only time can refute or vindicate them. Oh, I do wish I knew where François is, and what his son is doing, and whether a probe will be launched to loop around Jupiter.

I'm left with this: that whether he's conscious of it or not, François Broussard (and Hal and I, each one of us, to a lesser degree) has been mysteriously linked all his life to Halley's comet, whether diving around the sun at Venus' distance at 34 miles a second, or moving through the spaceward end of its long, narrow, elliptical orbit no faster than the moon drifts around Earth each month.

But as for all the rest . . . only ten years will tell.

THE FUNHOUSE EFFECT

John Varley

"Did you see what's playing at the theater tonight, Mr. Quester?"
The stewardess was holding a printed program in her hand.

"No, and I haven't the time now. Where's the captain? There
are some things he should—"

"Two old flat movies," she went on, oblivious to his protests.
"Have you ever seen one? They're very interesting and enter-
taining. *A Night to Remember*, and *The Poseidon Adventure*.
I'll make a reservation for you."

Quester called out to her as she was leaving.

"I'm trying to tell you, there's something badly wrong on this
ship. Won't anybody listen?"

But she was gone, vanished into the crowd of merrymakers.
She was busy enough without taking time to listen to the wild
tales of a nervous passenger.

Quester was not quite right in thinking of *Hell's Snowball* as a
ship. The official welcoming pamphlet referred to it as an asterite,
but that was advertising jargon. Anyone else would have called it
a comet.

Icarus Lines, Inc., the owners, had found it drifting along at a
distance of 500 AU. It had been sixty kilometers in diameter,
weighing in at about one hundred trillion tons.

Fortunately, it was made up of frozen liquids rich in hydrogen. Moving it was only a matter of installing a very large fusion

277

motor, then sitting back for five years until it was time to slow it down for orbit in the umbra of Mercury.

The company knew they would not get many passengers on a bare snowball. They tunneled into the comet, digging out staterooms and pantries and crew's quarters as they went. The shipfitters went in and paneled the bare ice walls in metal and plastic, then filled the rooms with furniture. There was room to spare, power to spare. They worked on a grand scale, and they had a grand vision. They intended to use the captive comet for sightseeing excursions to the sun.

Things went well for fifty years. The engine would shove the *Snowball* out of the protective shadow and, with the expenditure of ten million tons of ice and ammonia for reaction mass, inject it into a hyperbolic orbit that would actually brush the fringes of the solar corona. Business was good. *Hell's Snowball* became the vacation bonanza of the system, more popular than Saturn's Rings.

But it had to end. This was to be the last trip. Huge as it is, there comes a time when a comet has boiled off too much of its mass to remain stable in a close approach to the sun. *Hell's Snowball* was robbed of a hundred million tons with each trip. The engineers had calculated it was good for only one more pass before it cracked apart from internal heating.

But Quester was beginning to wonder.

There was the matter of the engines. Early on the fourth day of the excursion, Quester had gone on a guided tour of the farside of the comet to see the fusion engines. The guide had quoted statistics all the way through the tunnel, priming the tourists for the mind-wrenching sight of them. They were the largest rocket engines ever constructed. Quester and everyone else had been prepared to be impressed.

He *had* been impressed; first at the size of the pits that showed where the engines had been, then at the look of utter amazement on the face of the tour guide. Also impressive had been the speed with which the expression had been masked. The guide sputtered for only a moment, then quickly filled in with a story that almost sounded logical.

"I wish they'd tell me these things," he laughed. Did the laugh sound hollow? Quester couldn't tell for sure. "The engines weren't due for removal until tomorrow. It's part of our accelerated salvage program, you see, whereby we remove everything that can be of use in fitting out the *Icarus*, which you all saw near Mercury when you boarded. It's been decided not to slow *Hell's Snowball* when we complete this pass, but to let it coast on out where it came from. Naturally, we need to strip it as fast as possible. So equipment not actually needed for this trip has been removed already. The rest of it will be taken off on the other side of the sun, along with the passengers. I'm not a physicist, but evidently there is a saving in fuel. No need to worry about it; our course is set and we'll have no further need of the engines." He quickly shepherded the buzzing group of passengers back into the tunnel.

Quester was no physicist, either, but he could work simple equations. He was unable to find a way whereby Icarus Lines would save anything by removing the engines. The fuel was free; by their own admission whatever was left on the comet was to be discarded anyway. So why did it matter if they burned some more? Further, ships removing passengers and furnishings from the *Snowball* on the other side would have to match with its considerable velocity, then expend even more to slow down to solar system speeds. It sounded wasteful.

He managed to put this out of his mind. He was along for the ride, to have fun, and he wasn't a worrier. He had probably dropped a decimal point somewhere in his calculations, or was forgetting a little-known fact of ballistics. Certainly no one else seemed worried.

When he discovered that the lifeboats were missing, he was more angry than frightened.

"Why are they doing this to us?" he asked the steward who had come when he pressed the service bell. "Just because this is the last trip, does that mean we're not entitled to full protection? I'd like to know what's going on."

The steward, who was an affable man, scratched his head in bewilderment as he once more examined the empty lifeboat cradle.

"Beats me," he said, with a friendly grin. "Part of the salvage operation, I guess. But we've never had a spot of trouble in over fifty years. I hear the *Icarus* won't even carry lifeboats."

Quester fumed. If, sometime in the past, an engineer had decided *Hell's Snowball* needed lifeboats, he'd have felt a damn sight better if the ship still *had* lifeboats.

"I'd like to talk to someone who knows something about it."

"You might try the purser," the steward ventured, then quickly shook his head. "No, I forgot. The purser didn't make this trip. The first mate . . . no, she's . . . I guess that leaves the captain. You might talk to him."

Quester grumbled as he swam down the corridor toward the bridge. The company had no right to strip the ship before its final cruise. On the way there, he heard an announcement over the public address system.

"Attention. All passengers are to report to A Deck at 1300 hours for lifeboat drill. The purser . . . correction, the second officer will call the roll. Attendance is required of all passengers. That is all."

The announcement failed to mollify him, though he was puzzled.

The door to the bridge was ajar. There was a string spanning the open doorway with a hand-lettered sign hanging from it.

"The captain can be found at the temporary bridge," it read, "located on F Deck aft of the dispensary." Inside the room, a work crew was removing the last of the electronic equipment. There was the smell of ozone and oil, and the purple crackle of sparks. The room was little more than an ice-walled shell.

"What . . .?" Quester began.

"See the captain," the boss said tiredly, pulling out one of the last memory banks in a shower of shorting wires. "I just work here. Salvage crew."

Quester was reminded more of a wrecking crew. He started back toward F. Deck.

"Correction on that last announcement," the PA said. "Lifeboat drill has been canceled. The social director wishes to announce that he is no longer taking reservations for tours of the engine room. The second officer . . . correction, the third officer has requested all personnel to stay clear of the reactor room. There has been a slight spillage during the salvage program. Passengers are not to worry; this incident presents no danger to them. The power requirements of the ship are being taken over by the auxiliary reactor. The social director wishes to announce that tours of the auxiliary reactor are suspended. That is all."

"Is it just me?" Quester asked himself as he drifted by the groups of other passengers, none of whom seemed upset by any of this.

He located the temporary bridge, at the end of a little-used corridor that was stacked high with plastic crates marked "Immediate Removal—Rush, Urgent, Highest Priority." He insinuated his way past them with difficulty and was about to knock on the door when he was stopped by the sound of voices on the other side. The voices were angry.

"I tell you, we should abort this trip at once. I've lost the capability to maneuver the ship in the event of an emergency. I told you I wanted the attitude thrusters to remain in place until after perihelion."

"Captain, there is no use protesting now," said another voice. "Maybe I agree with you; maybe I don't. In any case, the engines are gone now, and there's no chance of installing them again. There is to be no argument with these orders. The company's in bad shape, what with outfitting the new asterite. Can you picture what it would cost to abort this trip and refund the fares to seven thousand passengers?"

"Hang the company!" the captain exploded. "This ship is *unsafe!* What about those new calculations I gave you—the ones from Lewiston? Have you looked them over?"

The other voice was conciliatory. "Captain, Captain, you're wasting energy worrying about that crackpot. He's been laughed out of the Lunar Academy; his equations simply do not work."

"They look sound enough to me."

"Take it from me, Captain, the best minds in the system have assured us that the *Snowball* will hold together. Why, this old hunk of junk is good for a dozen more trips, and you know it. We've erred, if at all, on the conservative side."

"Well, maybe," the captain grumbled. "I still don't like that lifeboat situation, though. How many did you say we had left?"

"Twenty-eight," the other soothed.

Quester felt the hair stand up on the back of his neck.

He peeked into the room, not knowing what he would say. But there was no one there. The voices were coming from a speaker on the wall. Evidently the captain was in another part of the ship.

He considered going to his cabin and getting drunk, then decided it was a bad idea. He would go to the casino and get drunk.

On the way he passed a lifeboat cradle that was not empty. It was the site of bustling activity, with crews hurrying up and down ramps into the ship. He stuck his head in, saw that the seats had been stripped and the interior was piled high with plastic crates. More were being added every minute.

He stopped one of the workers and asked her what was going on.

"Ask the captain," she shrugged. "They told me to stack these boxes in here, that's all I know."

He stood back and watched until the loading was complete, then was told to stand clear as the nullfield was turned off to allow the boat to drift clear of the *Snowball*. At a distance of two kilometers, the engines fired and the boat was away, blasting back toward the inner planets.

"Twenty-seven," Quester mumbled to himself and headed for the casino.

"Twenty-seven?" the woman asked.

"Probably less by now," Quester said with a broad shrug. "And they only hold fifty people."

They were sitting together at the roulette table, pressed into close company by the random currents of humanity that ebbed and flowed through the room. Quester was not gambling; his legs had just happened to give out, and the nearest place to collapse had been the chair he was sitting in. The woman had materialized out of his alcoholic mist.

It was nice to get back to gravity after the weightless levels of the *Snowball*. But, he discovered, getting drunk in a weightless state was less hazardous. One needn't worry about one's balance. Here in the casino there was the problem of standing. It was too much of a problem for Quester.

The casino was located at one end of a slowly rotating arm, which was mounted horizontally on a pivoted mast that extended straight up from *Hell's Snowball*. On the other end of the arm were the restaurants that served the passengers. Both modules were spherical; the structure resembled an anemometer with silver balls instead of cups on the ends. The view was tremendous. Overhead was the silver sphere that contained the restaurants. To one side was the slowly moving surface of the comet, a dirty gray even in the searing sunlight. To the other side were the stars and the main attraction: Sol itself, blemished with a choice collection of spots. The viewing was going to be good this trip. If anyone was alive to view it Quester added to himself.

"Twenty-seven, you say?" the woman asked again.

"That's right, twenty-seven."

"One hundred Marks on number twenty-seven," she said and placed her bet. Quester looked up, wondering how many times he would have to repeat himself before she understood him.

The ball clattered to a stop, on number twenty-seven, and the croupier shoveled a tottering stack of chips to the woman. Quester looked around him again at the huge edifice he was sitting in, the incalculable tonnage of the spinning structure, and laughed.

"I wondered why they built this place," he said. "Who needs gravity?"

"Why did they build it?" she asked him, picking up the chips.

"For him," he said, pointing to the croupier. "That little ball would just hang there on the rim without gravity." He felt himself being lifted to his feet, and stood in precarious balance. He threw his arms wide.

"For that matter, that's what all the gravity in the system's for. To bring those little balls down to the number, the old wheel of fortune; and when they've got your number, there's nothing you can do because your number's up, that's all there is, twenty-seven, that's all. . . ."

He was sobbing and mumbling philosophical truths as she led him from the room.

The ride in the elevator to the hub of the rotating structure sobered Quester considerably. The gradually decreasing weight combined with the Coriolis effect that tended to push him against one wall was more than an abused stomach could take. The management knew that and had provided facilities for it. Quester vomited until his legs were shaky. Luckily, by then he was weightless and didn't need them.

The woman towed him down the passageway like a toy balloon. They ended up in the grand ballroom.

The ballroom was a hemisphere of nullfield sitting on the surface of the *Snowball*. From inside it was invisible. The dance area was crowded with couples trying out free-fall dances. Most of them had the easy grace of a somersaulting giraffe.

Quester sobered a bit in the near-zero gee. Part of it was the effect of the antinausea drugs he had taken for free-fall; they also tended to reduce the effects of alcohol.

"What's your name?" he asked the woman.

"Solace. You?"

"I'm Quester. From Tharsis, Mars. I'm . . . I'm confused about a lot of things."

She floated over to a table, still towing Quester, and fastened him to one of the chairs. He turned his attention from the twisting bodies in the dance area to his companion.

Solace was tall, much taller than a man or a woman would

naturally grow. He estimated she was two and a half meters from head to toe, though she had no toes. Her feet had been replaced with peds, oversized hands popular with spacers. They were useful in free-fall, and for other things, as he discovered when she reached across the table with one slender leg and cupped his cheek with her ped. Her legs were as limber and flexible as her arms.

"Thanks," she said, with a smile. "For the luck, I mean."

"Hmmm? Oh, you mean the bet." Quester had to drag his attention back from the delightful sensation on his cheek. She was beautiful. "But I wasn't advising you on a bet. I was trying to tell you . . ."

"I know. You were saying something about the lifeboats."

"Yes. It's astounding, I . . ." He stopped, realizing that he couldn't remember what was astounding. He was having trouble focusing on her. She was wearing a kaleidoholo suit, which meant she was naked but for a constantly shifting pattern of projections. There seemed to be fifty or sixty different suits contained in it, none persisting for longer than a few seconds. It would melt smoothly from a silver sheath dress to an almost military uniform with gold braid and buttons to a garland of flowers to Lady Godiva. He rubbed his eyes and went on.

"They're salvaging the ship," he said. "The last I heard there were only twenty-seven lifeboats left. And more are leaving every hour. They're taking the electronic equipment with them. And the furnishings and the machinery and who knows what else. I overheard the captain talking to a company representative. *He's* worried, the *captain!* But no one else seems to be. Am I worrying over nothing, or what?"

Solace looked down at her folded hands for a moment, then brought her eyes back up to his.

"I've been uneasy, too," she said in a low voice. She leaned closer to him. "I've shared my apprehensions with a group of friends. We . . . get together and share what we have learned. Our friends laugh at us when we tell them of our suspicions, but . . ." She paused and looked suspiciously around her. Even in his befuddled state Quester had to smile.

"Go on," he said.

She seemed to make up her mind about him and leaned even closer.

"We'll be meeting again soon. Several of us have been scouting around—I was covering the casino when we met—and we'll share our findings and try to come to a consensus on what to do. Are you with us?''

Quester fought off the feeling, quite strong since his suspicions began to haunt him, that he was somehow trapped in an adventure movie. But if he was, he was just getting to the good part.

"You can count on me."

With no further ado, she grabbed his arm in one of her peds and began towing him along, using her hands to grab onto whatever was handy. He thought of objecting, but she was much better than he at weightless maneuvering.

"May I have your attention, please?"

Quester looked around and spotted the captain standing in the center of the stage, in front of the band. He was not alone. On each side of him were women dressed in black jumpsuits, their eyes alertly scanning the audience. They were armed.

"Please, please," the captain held up his arms for quiet and eventually got it. He wiped his brow with a handkerchief.

"There is no cause for alarm. No matter what you may have been hearing, the ship is in no danger. The stories about the main engines having been removed are lies, pure and simple. We are looking for the people who planted those rumors and will soon have all of them in custody. The chief engineer wishes to announce that tours of the engine room will be resumed—"

One of the women shot the captain a glance. He mopped his brow again and consulted a slip of paper in his hand. The hand was shaking.

"Ah, a correction. The engineer announces that tours will *not* be resumed. There is, ah . . . that is, they are being overhauled, or . . . or something." The woman relaxed slightly.

"The rumor that the main reactor has been shut down is unfounded. The surgeon has told me that there has been no spillage of radioactive material, and even if there had been, the amount was insignificent and would only have been a danger to those passengers with high cumulative exposures. The surgeon will be collecting dosimeters at 1400 hours tomorrow.

"Let me repeat: there is no cause for alarm. As captain of this ship, I take a very dim view of rumormongering. Anyone caught disseminating stories about the unspaceworthiness of this vessel in the future will be dealt with sternly.

"Lifeboat drill will be held tomorrow on A Deck, as scheduled. Anyone who has not as yet been checked out on his life

jacket will do so by noon tomorrow, ship's time. That is . . .
is that all?'' This last was addressed to the woman to his left,
in a whisper. She nodded curtly, and the three of them walked
off the stage, their magnetized shoes sticking to the deck like
flypaper.

Solace nudged Quester in the ribs.

"Are those women bodyguards?'' she whispered. "Do you
think his life is in danger?''

Quester looked at the way the women gripped the captain's
elbows. Not bodyguards, but guards, certainly. . . .

"Say, I just remembered I still have some unpacking to do,''
he said. "Maybe I can join you and your friends later on. I'll
just nose around, see what I can pick up, you know, and—''

But he couldn't squirm free of her grip. Those peds were
strong.

"May I have your attention, please? Lifeboat drill for tomorrow has been canceled. Repeat, canceled. Passengers showing
up at the cradles for lifeboat drill will be interrogated, by order
of the captain. That is all.''

On the way to Solace's room, the two were shoved out of the
way by a group of people in uniform. Their faces were determined, and some of them carried clubs.

"Where does that corridor lead?'' he asked.

"To the bridge. But they won't find anything there, it's
been—''

"I know.''

"I think we're being followed.''

"Wha'?'' He looked behind him as he bounced along in her
wake. There was someone back there, all right. They turned a
corner and Solace hauled Quester into a dimly lit alcove, bump-
ing his head roughly against the wall. He was getting fed up with
this business of being dragged. If this was an adventure, he was
Winnie-the-Pooh following Christopher Robin up the stairs. He
started to object, but she clapped a hand around his mouth,
holding him close.

"Shhh,'' she hissed.

A fine thing, Quester grumbled to himself. Can't even speak
my mind. He thought he was better off before, alone and puzzled,
than he was with this mysterious giantess towing him around.

Of course, things could have been worse, he reflected. She
was warm and naked to the touch no matter what his eyes told

him. And *tall*. Floating there in the hall, she extended above and below him by a third of a meter.

"How can I think of something like that at a time like this?" he began, but she hushed him again and her arms tightened around him. He realized she was really scared, and he began to be so himself. The liquor and the sheer unlikelihood of recent events had detached him; he was drifting along, rudderless. Nothing in his life had prepared him to cope with things like the black-suited man who now eased slowly around the corner in shadowy pursuit of them.

They watched him from the concealment of the alcove. Many of the lights in the corridor were not working or were mere empty sockets. Earlier, Quester had been alarmed at this, adding it to his list of ways not to run a spaceship. Now, he was grateful.

"He doesn't look much like a man at all," Solace whispered. And sure enough, he didn't. Nor a woman. He didn't look too human.

"Humanoid, I'd say," Quester whispered back. "Pity no one told us. Obviously the system's been invaded by the first intelligent race of humanoids."

"Don't talk nonsense. And be quiet." The man, or whatever it was, was very close now. They could see the ill-fitting pink mask, the lumps and nodules in odd places under his sweater and pants. He passed them by, leaving a pungent odor of hydrogen sulfide.

Quester found himself laughing. To his surprise, Solace laughed along with him. The situation was so grotesque that he had to either laugh or scream.

"Listen," he said, "I don't *believe* in sinister humanoid invaders."

"No? But you believe in superhuman heavy-planet Invaders like the ones that have occupied the Earth, don't you? And you haven't even *seen* them."

"Are you telling me you do believe that thing was an . . . an alien?"

"I'm not saying anything. But I'm wondering what those people were doing, earlier, armed with clubs. Do you believe in mutiny?"

"Solace, I'd *welcome* a mutiny, I'd throw a party, give away all my worldly wealth to charity if only such a normal, everyday thing would happen. But I don't think it will. I think we've fallen through the looking glass."

"You think you're crazy?" She looked at him skeptically.

"Yep. I'm going to turn myself in right now. You're obviously not even here. Maybe this ship isn't even here."

She twisted slightly in the air, bringing her legs up close to his chest.

"I'll prove to you I'm here," she said, working with all four hands and peds at unbuttoning him.

"Hold it. What are you . . . how can you think of that at a time like . . ." It sounded familiar. She laughed, holding his wrists with her hands as her peds quickly stripped him.

"You've never been in danger before," she said. "I have. It's a common reaction to get aroused in a tight spot, especially when the danger's not immediate. And you are, and so am I."

It was true. He was, but didn't like doing it in the hallway.

"There's not room here," he protested. "Another of those critters could come along."

"Yes, isn't it exciting?" Her eyes were alight by now, and her breath was fast and shallow. "And if you think there isn't room, you haven't done it in free-fall yet. Ever tried the Hermesian Hyperbola?"

Quester sighed, and submitted. Soon he was doing more than submitting. He decided she was as crazy as everyone else, or, alternatively, he was crazy and she was as sane as everybody else. But she was right about the free-fall. There was plenty of room.

They were interrupted by a crackle of static from the public address. They paused to listen to it.

"Attention, your attention please. This is the provisional captain speaking. The traitor running-dog lackey ex-captain is now in chains. Long Live the Revolutionary Committee, who will now lead us on the true path of Procreative Anti-Abortionism."

"Free-Birthers!" Quester yelped. "We've been hijacked by Free-Birthers!"

The new captain, who sounded like a woman, started to go on, but her voice was cut short in a hideous gurgle.

"Long Live the Loyalist Faction of the Glorious Siblings of the—" a new voice began, but it, too, was cut short. Voices shouted in rapid succession.

"The counterrevolution as been suppressed," shouted yet another captain. "Liberate our wombs! Our gonads! Our Freedom!

Attention, attention! All female persons aboard this ship are ordered to report at once to the infirmary for artificial insemination. Shirkers will be obliterated. That is all.''

Neither of them said anything for a long time. At last Solace eased herself away a bit and let him slip out of her. She let out a deep breath.

"I wonder if I could plead double jeopardy?"

"Insanity four, reality nothing," Quester giggled. He was in high spirits as they skulked their way down the dim corridors.

"Are you still on that?" Solace shot back. She sounded a bit tired of him. She kept having to hang back as he struggled to keep up with her supple quadridextrous pace. "Listen, if you want to get fitted for a straitjacket, the tailor's in the other direction. Me, I don't care how ridiculous the situation gets. I'll keep coping."

"I can't help it," he admitted. "I keep feeling that I *wrote* this story several years ago. Maybe in another life. I dunno."

She peered around another corner. They were on their way to the temporary bridge. They had stopped three times already to watch black-suited figures drift by. Everyone else they had seen—those dressed in holiday clothes—had ducked into doorways as quickly as they themselves. At least it seemed that the passengers were no longer in the holiday mood, were aware that there was something wrong.

"You a writer?" she asked.

"Yes. I write scientifiction. Maybe you've heard of it. There's a cult following, but we don't reach the general public."

"What's it about?"

"Scientifiction deals with life on Earth. It's set in the future—each of us creates our own hypothetical future with our own ground rules and set of assumptions. The basic assumption is that we figure out a way to fight the Invaders and reclaim the Earth, or at least a beachhead. In my stories we've managed to rout the Invaders, but the dolphins and whales are still around, and they want their allies back, so humans fight them. It's adventure stuff, purely for thrills. I have a hero called the Panama Kid."

She glanced back at him, and he couldn't read the expression. He was used to taking the defensive about his vocation.

"Is there a living in that?"

"I managed to get aboard the *Snowball* for the final trip,

didn't I? That wasn't cheap, but then you know that. Say, what do you do for a living?''

"Nothing. My mother was a holehunter. She made a strike in '45 and got rich. She went out again and left the money to me. She's due back in about fifty years, unless she gets swallowed by a hole.''

"So you were born on Pluto?''

"No. I was born in free-fall, about one hundred AU from the sun. I think that's a record so far.'' She grinned back at him, looking pleased with herself. "You made up your mind yet?''

"Huh?''

"Have you decided if you're the author or a character? If you really think you're crazy, you can shove off. What can you do but accept the reality of your senses?''

He paused and really thought about it for the first time since he met her.

"I do,'' he said, firmly. "It's all happening. Holy Cetacean, *it really is happening.*''

"Glad to have you with us. I *told* you you couldn't experience the Hermesian Hyperbola and still doubt your senses.''

It hadn't been the lovemaking, Quester knew. That could be as illusory as anything else; he had the stained sheets to prove it. But he believed in *her*, even if there was something decidedly illogical about the goings-on around her.

"Attention, attention.''

"Oh, shit. What now?'' They slowed near a speaker so they could listen without distortion.

"Glad tidings! This is the provisional captain, speaking for the ad hoc steering committee. We have decided to steer this comet into a new, closer approach to the sun, thus gaining speed for a faster departure from solar space. It has been decided to convert this vessel, hereafter to be referred to as the *Spermatozoa*, into an interstellar colony ship to spread the seed of humanity to the stars. All passengers are hereby inducted into the Proletarian Echelon of the Church of Unlimited Population. Conversion of all resources into a closed-ecology system will begin at once. Save your feces! Breathe shallowly until this crisis is past. Correction, correction, there is no crisis. Do not panic. Anyone found panicking will be shot. The steering committee has determined that there is no crisis. All surviving officers with knowledge of how to work these little gadgets on the bridge are ordered to report immediately.''

Quester looked narrowly at Solace.

"Do you know anything about them?"

"I can pilot a ship, if that's what you mean. I've never flown anything quite this . . . *enormous* . . . but the principles are the same. You aren't suggesting that we help them, are you?"

"I don't know," he admitted. "I didn't really think in terms of plans until a few minutes ago. What was *your* plan? Why are we headed for the bridge?"

She shrugged. "Just to see what the hell's going on, I guess. But maybe we ought to make some preparations. Let's get some life jackets."

They found a locker in the hall containing emergency equipment. Inside were twenty of the nullfield devices called life jackets. More accurately, they were emergency spacesuit generators, with attached water recyclers and oxygen supply. Each of them was a red cylinder about thirty centimeters long and fifteen in diameter with shoulder straps and a single flexible tube with a metal connector on the end. They were worn strapped to the back with the tube reaching over the shoulder.

In operation, the life jackets generated a nullfield that conformed closely to the contours of the wearer's body. The field oscillated between one and one and a half millimeters from the skin, and the resulting bellows action forced waste air through the exhaust nozzle. The device attached itself to a tiny metal valve that was surgically implanted in all the passengers. The valve's external connection was located under Quester's left collarbone. He had almost forgotten it was there. It was just a brass-colored flower that might be mistaken for jewelry but was actually part of a plumbing system that could route venous blood from his pulmonary artery to the oxygenator on his back. It then returned through a parallel pipe to his left auricle and on to his body.

Solace helped him get into it and showed him the few manual controls. Most of it was automatic. It would switch on the field around him if the temperature or pressure changed suddenly.

Then they were off again through the silent corridors to confront the hijackers.

At the last turn in the corridor before reaching the temporary bridge, they stopped to manually switch on their suit fields. Solace instantly became a mirror in the shape of a woman. The field reflected all electomagnetic radiation except through pupil-sized discontinuities over her eyes which let in controlled quanta of visible light. It was disquieting. The funhouse effect, it was called, and it looked as if her body had been twisted through another spatial dimension. She almost disappeared, except for a pattern of distortions that hurt Quester's eyes when he looked at it.

They reached the door leading to the bridge and stopped for a moment. It was a perfectly ordinary door. Quester wondered why he was here with this impulsive woman.

"Do we knock first, or what?" she mused. "What do you think, Quester? What would the Panama Kid do?"

"He'd knock it down," Quester said without hesitation. "But he wouldn't have gotten here without his trusty laser. Say, do you think we ought to go back and . . ."

"No. We'd better do it now before we think about it too hard. These suits are protection against any weapon I know of. The most they can do is capture us."

"Then what?"

"Then you can talk us out of it. You're the one who's fast with words, aren't you?"

Quester remained silent as she backed up and planted herself against the opposite wall, coiled and ready to hit the door with her shoulder. He didn't want to point out that skill with a typer and skill at oratory are not necessarily related. Besides, if she wanted to risk forcible insemination, it was her business.

Just on the off chance, he touched the door plate with his palm. It clicked, and the door opened. It was too late. Solace howled and barreled end-over-end into the room, reaching out with all four limbs like a huge silver starfish to grab onto something. Quester rushed after her, then stopped short as soon as he was into the room. There was no one in it.

"Talk about your anticlimax," Solace breathed, getting herself sorted out from a pile of crates at the far end of the room. "I . . . never mind. It was my fault. Who'd have thought it'd be unlocked?"

"*I* did," Quester pointed out. "Hold it a minute. We're sort of, well, we're being pretty hasty, aren't we? I haven't really had time to stop and think since we got going, but I think we're going at this the wrong way, I really do. Damn it, this isn't an adventure, where everything goes according to set pattern. I've written enough of them, I ought to know. This is life, and that means there's got to be a rational explanation.''

"So what is it?''

"I don't know. But I don't think we'll find it this way. Things have been happening . . . well, think about the announcements over the PA, for instance. They are *crazy!* No one's that crazy, not even Free-Birthers.''

Quester's chain of thought was interrupted by the noisy entrance of four people in life jackets. He and Solace jumped up, banged their heads on the ceiling, and were quickly captured.

"All right, which one of you is the provisional captain?''

There was a short silence, then Solace broke it with a laugh.

"Lincoln?'' she asked.

"Solace?''

The four were part of Solace's short-lived cabal. It seemed the ship was crawling with people who were concerned enough about the situation to try and do something about it. Before Quester caught all the names, they were surprised by another group of four, with three more close on their heels. The situation threatened to degenerate into a pitched battle of confused identities until someone had a suggestion.

"Why don't we hang a sign on the door? Anybody who comes in here thinks we're the hijackers.'' They did, and the sign said the provisional captain was dead. While new arrivals were pondering that and wondering what to do next, someone had time to explain the situation.

Someone arrived with a tray of drinks, and soon the would-be liberators were releasing their tensions in liquor and argument. There were fifteen pet theories expounded in as many minutes.

Now that he felt he had his feet under him, Quester adopted a wait-and-see attitude. The data was still insufficient.

" 'When you have eliminated the impossible,' '' he quoted, " 'whatever is left, however improbable, must be the truth.' ''

"So what does that gain us?'' Solace asked.

"Only a viewpoint. Me. I think we'll have to wait until we get back to Mercury to find out what's been happening. Unless you bring me a live alien, or Free-Birther, or . . . some physical evidence.''

"Then let's go look for it,'' Solace said.

"Attention, attention. This is the ship's computer speaking. I have grave news for all passengers. The entire crew has been assassinated. Until now, I have been blocked by a rogue program inserted by the revolutionaries which has prevented me from regaining control of operations. Luckily, this situation has been remedied. Unluckily, the bridge is still in the hands of the pirates! They have access to all my manual controls from their position, and I'm afraid there is but one course open to those of you who wish to avoid a catastrophe. We are on a trajectory that will soon intersect with the solar chromosphere, and I am powerless to correct it until the bridge is regained. Rally to me! Rise in righteous fury and repulse the evil usurpers! Storm the bridge! Long live the counterrevolution!''

There was a short silence as the implications sank in, then a babble of near panic. Several people headed for the door, only to come back and bolt it. There was an ominous roar from outside.

"... chromosphere? Where the hell *are* we? Has anyone been out on the surface lately?"

"... some pleasure cruise. I haven't even *seen* the sun and now they say we're about to ..."

"... pirates, revolutions, counterrevolutions, Free-Birthers, *aliens* for heaven's sake ..."

Solace looked helplessly around her, listened to the pounding on the door. She located Quester hunkered down beside an instrument console and crouched beside him.

"Talk your way out of *this* one, Panama Kid," she yelled in his ear.

"My dear, I'm much too busy to talk. If I can get the back off this thing ..." He worked at it and finally pulled off a metal cover. "There was a click from here when the computer came on the line."

There was a recorder inside, with a long reel of tape strung between playback heads. He punched a button that said rewind, watched the tape cycle briefly through, and hit the play button.

"Attention, attention. This is the ship's computer speaking. I have grave news for all passengers."

"We've *heard* that one already," someone shouted. Quester held his head in his hands for a moment, then looked up at Solace. She opened her mouth to say something, then bit her lip, her eyebrows almost touched in a look of puzzlement so funny that Quester would have laughed out loud. But the roof of the bridge evaporated.

It took only a few seconds. There was a blinding white light and a terrible roaring sound; then he was whisked into the air and pulled toward the outside. In an instant, everyone was covered in a nullfield and milling around the hole in the roof like a school of silverfish. In twos and threes they were sucked through. Then the room was empty and Quester was still in it. He looked down and saw Solace's hand around his ankle. She was grasping the firmly anchored computer console with one ped. She hauled him down to her and held him close as he found handholds. His teeth were chattering.

The door burst open, and there was another flurry of astonished passengers sucked through the roof. It didn't take as long this time; the hole in the roof was much larger. Beyond the hole was blackness.

Quester was surprised to see how calm he was once his initial shock had dissipated. He thanked Solace for saving him, then went on with what he had been about to say before the blowout.

"Did you talk to anyone who actually saw a mutineer, or a Free-Birther, or whatever.?"

"Huh? Is this the time . . . no, I guess I didn't. But we saw those aliens, or whatever they—"

"Exactly. Whatever they were. They could have been anything. Someone is playing an awfully complicated trick on us. Something's happening, but it isn't what we've been led to believe."

"We've been led to believe something?"

"We've been given clues. Sometimes contradictory, sometimes absolutely insane, and encouraged to think a mutiny is going on; and this recorder proves it isn't happening. Listen." And he played back the recordings of various announcements they had heard earlier. It sounded tinny in their middle-ear receivers.

"But what does that prove?" Solace wanted to know. "Maybe this thing just taped them as they happened."

Quester was dumfounded for a moment. The theory of a vast conspiracy had appealed to him, even if he didn't know the reason for it.

He played past the point of the computer's announcement and sighed with relief when he heard that there was more. They let it natter on to no one about crises in the engine room, spillage in the second auxiliary reactor, and so on. It was obvious that it was playing a scenario that could no longer happen. Because the ship had already broken down completely and they were headed directly for . . .

They seemed to reach that thought simultaneously and scrambled up toward a hole in the ceiling to see what was going on. Quester forgot, as usual, to hang onto something and would have drifted straight up at near-escape velocity but for Solace's grasping hands.

The sun had eaten up the sky. It was huge, *huge*.

"That's what we paid to see," Solace said, weakly.

"Yeah. But I thought we'd see it from the ballroom. It's sort of . . . *big*. isn't it?"

"Do you think we're . . .?"

"I don't know. I never thought we'd get this close. Something the captain said—no, wait, it wasn't the captain, was it? But one of the recordings said something about . . ."

The ground heaved under them.

Quester saw the revolving casino complex off to his right. It swayed, danced, and came apart. The twin balls broke open, still rotating, and spilled tables and roulette wheels and playing cards and dishes and walls and carpets to the waiting stars. The debris formed a glittering double spiral of ejecta, like droplets of water spraying from the tips of a lawn sprinkler. Bits of it twisted in the sunlight, cartwheeling, caroming, semaphoring, kicking.

"Those are people."

"Are they . . .?" Quester couldn't ask it.

"No," Solace answered. "Those suits will protect them. Maybe they can be picked up later. You see, when you hit something wearing one of these suits, you—"

She didn't have time to finish, but Quester soon had a demonstration of what she was talking about. The ground opened a few meters from them. They were swept off their feet and tumbled helplessly across the dirty white surface until they hung suspended over the pit.

Quester hit the far side of the rift and bounced. He felt little of the impact, though he hit quite hard, because the suit field automatically stiffened when struck by a fast-moving object. He had cause to be thankful for that fact, because the rift began to close. He clawed his way along the surface toward the sunlight, but the walls of ice closed on him like a book snapped shut.

For a brief moment he was frozen while the ice and rock around him shook and vaporized under the incredible pressures of shearing force. He saw nothing but white heat as frozen methane and water became gas in an instant without an intermediate liquid stage. Then he was shot free as the masses came apart again.

He was still frozen into a climbing position, but now he could see. He was surrounded by chunks of debris, ranging from fist-sized rocks glowing bright red to giant icebergs that sublimated and disappeared before his eyes. Each time the suit began to lose its rigidity he was hit by another object and frozen into a new position as the suit soaked up the kinetic energy.

In a surprisingly short time, everything had vanished. Every particle of the explosion was impelled away from every other particle by the pressures of expanding superheated steam.

But Solace was still clinging to his ankle. She was the only thing left in his universe apart from a few tiny flashing stars of debris far in the distance, tumbling, tumbling.

And the sun.

He could look directly at it as it swung past his field of vision once every ten seconds. It could barely be seen as a sphere; each second it looked more like a flat, boiling plane. The majestic, crushing presence of it flattened his ego with a weight he could barely tolerate. He found Solace in his arms. He looked at her face, which was endless mirrors showing a vanishing series of suns rebounding from his face to hers and back to infinity. The funhouse effect, so disconcerting only an hour ago, seemed familiar and reassuring now in comparison to the chaos below him. He hugged her and closed his eyes.

"Are we going to hit it?" he asked.

"I can't tell. If we do, it'll be the hardest test these suits have ever had. I don't know if they have limits."

He was astounded. "You mean we might actually . . .?"

"I tell you, I don't know. Theoretically, yes, we could graze the chromosphere and not feel a thing, not from the heat, anyway. But it would be bound to slow us down pretty quickly. The deceleration could kill us. The suits protect us from outside forces almost completely, but internal accelerations can break bones and rupture organs. This suit doesn't stop gravity or inertia from working."

There was no use thinking too long on that possibility.

They were hurtling through the corona now, building up a wake of ionized particles that trailed after them like the tail of a tiny comet. They looked around them for other survivors but could find nothing. Soon, they could see little but a flickering haze as the electrical potential they had built up began discharging in furry feathers of hot plasma. It couldn't have lasted longer than a few minutes; then it began to fade slowly away.

There came a time when the sun could be seen to have shrunk slightly. They didn't speak of it, just held on to each other.

"What are our chances of pickup?" Quester wanted to know. The sun was now much smaller, receding almost visibly behind them. They were concerned only for the next twenty hours, which was the length of their oxygen reserves.

"How should I know? Someone must know by now that something's happened, but I don't know if any ships can get to us in time. It would depend on where they were at the time of the disaster."

Quester scanned the stars as they swept past his field of vision. They had no way to slow their rotation; so the stars still went around them every ten seconds.

He didn't expect to see anything but was not surprised when he did. It was the next-to-last in a long series of incongruities. There was a ship closing in on them. A voice over the radio told them to stand by to come aboard and asked them how they enjoyed the trip.

Quester was winding up for a reply, but the speaker said one word, slowly and clearly:

"Frightfulness."

And everything changed.

I woke up and found out it had all been a dream.

The very first story I wrote, back when I was five years old, ended with words very much like that last sentence. I'm not ashamed of it. The thought was not new, but it was original with me. It was only later that I learned it's not a fair way to end a story, that the reader deserves more than that.

So here's more.

I woke up and found out it had *almost* all been a dream. The word "frightfulness" was a posthypnotic trigger that caused me to remember all the things which had been blocked from me by earlier suggestion.

I don't know why I'm bothering to explain all this. I guess old writing habits die hard. No matter that this is being written for a board of psychists, mediartists, and flacks; I have to preserve the narrative thread. I've broken the rules by changing to first person at the end, but I found I could not write the account Icarus Lines requested of me unless I did it in the third person.

"I" am Quester, though that's not my real name. I am a scientifiction writer, but I have no character named the Panama Kid. Solace's name is something else. It was suggested that I change the names.

I signed aboard *Hell's Snowball* knowing that it was going to break apart along the way. That's why so much of it had been stripped. They retained only enough to preserve a tenuous illusion that the trip was a normal one, then threw in everything they could think of to scare the daylights out of us.

We knew they would. We agreed to and submitted to a hypnotic treatment that would fool us into thinking we were on a normal trip and were released into the crazy world they cooked up for us. It's the first time they had ever tried it, and so they threw in everything in the book: aliens, accidents, mutiny, confusion, crackpots, and I didn't even see it all. The experience is different for each passenger, but the basic theme is to put us into a scary situation with evident peril of life and limb, shake well, and then let us come through the experience safe and sound.

There was no danger, not from the first to the last. We were on a stable, carefully calculated orbit. The life jackets were enough to keep us absolutely safe against anything we would encounter, and we were conditioned to have them on at the right time. As proof of this, not a single passenger was injured.

We were *all* nearly scared to death.

It says here you want to know the motive. I remember it clearly now, though I remembered an entirely different one at the time. I went on the Disaster Express because I had just sold a novel and wanted to do something wild, out of character. That was the wildest thing I could think of, and I could wish I had gone to a museum instead. Because the next question you want me to answer is how I feel about it now that it's over, and you won't like it. I hope I'm in the majority and you people at Icarus will give this thing up and never run another like it.

There used to be something called a "haunted house." One was led blindfolded through it and encountered various horrors, the effect being heightened by the unknown nature of the things one touched and was touched by. People have done things like that for as long as we have history. We go to movies to be scared, ride on roller coasters, read books, go to funhouses. Thrills are never cheap, no matter what they say. It takes skill to produce them, and art, and a knowledge of what will be genuinely thrilling and what will be only amusing.

You people had mixed success. Part of it was the kitchen-sink approach you took on this first trip. If you unified your theme the next time, stuck to a mutiny or an invasion, for instance, instead of mucking it up with all the other insanity you put in . . . but what am I saying? I don't want you to improve it. It's true that I was a little bemused by the unreality of the opener, but it was stark terror all the way when we approached the sun. My stomach still tightens just to think about it.

But—and I must cry it from the rooftops—you have gone too far. I'm basically conservative, as are all scientifiction writers, being concerned as we are with the past on Earth rather than the future in the stars. But I can't avoid thinking how frivolous it all was. Have we come to this? While our precious home planet remains under the three-hundred-year Occupation, do we devote ourselves to more and more elaborate ways of finding thrills?

I hope not.

There is a second consideration, one that I find it difficult to put into words. You hear of the "shipboard romance," when passengers become involved with each other only to part forever at their destination. Something of the sort happened to me and to Solace. We grew close on that loop through the corona. I didn't write about it. It's still painful. We clung to each other for two days. We made love with the stars at our feet.

We might even have remained involved, if our minds had been our own. But upon the utterance of that magic word we suddenly found that we were not the people we had been presenting ourselves as being. It's difficult enough to find out that one you care for is not the person she seemed to be; how much harder when it is *you* who are not what you thought you were?

It is a tremendous identity crisis, one that I am only now getting over. I, Quester, would not have behaved as I did aboard the *Snowball* if I had been in possession of all my faculties. We were tested, destructively tested in a way, to see if the injunction against discovering the underlying facts was strong enough to hold. It was, though I was beginning to see through the veils at the end. With a more consistent emergency I'm sure I would have had no inkling that it was anything but real. And that would be *much* worse. As it was, I was able to retain a degree of detachment, to entertain the notion that I might be insane. I was *right*.

The trip to the sun is thrill enough. Leave it at that, please, so that we may be sure of our loves and fears and not come to think that all might be illusion. I'll always have the memory of the way Solace looked when she woke from the dream she shared with me. The dream was gone; Solace was not the person I thought she might be. I'll have to look for solace elsewhere.

THE FAMILY MAN

Theodore L. Thomas

The first shadow appeared on the screen. Daniel Cranch leaned closer to be sure it was real. Then he touched the button that put him on manual and sat back with the controls in his hands. He checked the time. It would be eight minutes before Houston said to him, "Ah, *Siderite*, we see you have gone to manual before schedule. Explain reason, please."

"Well, he had eight minutes of peace and then another eight minutes before they could object to whatever he decided to tell them. In fact, they could no longer press him very hard. Even more than the distance, the cloud of ionized gases around him made it even more difficult to communicate with Houston, and his Earthbound teammates were just going to have to leave it up to him. Cranch settled back, palms dry, breathing even and shallow, more relaxed than he had been in a long time.

The shadow on the screen took on more substance, and it was larger than they had supposed. The nucleus of the comet must be one hundred and fifty kilometers in diameter. Unless he was getting a false reading, it must be about two hundred kilometers ahead of him, looming and quivering in the cloud of dust, sand, gravel, rock, and glowing gas through which he rode. Now that he was actually in the comet's tail, all of his instrument readings had to be treated with suspicion. But he had been right about one thing: he could hear through the insulated hull the thuds and the clunks as he worked his way through the cloud of debris at a relative velocity of about fifty kilometers per hour. He leaned to a porthole to see, and it was easy to resolve pieces the size of his fist as they went by. He bared his teeth. Those chunks, if they hit the Earth's atmosphere, would slash into it at some ten kilometers per second. All except the large ones would flare off into bright gases in a second or two.

He started to lean back, but a dark motion caught the edge of his vision. A dense stream of particles swept by the porthole, swirling, colliding with one another. One of the particles rebounded from several larger ones and lifted out of the main mass, turning slowly. Cranch could see it clearly. It was almost perfectly round, the apparent size of a marble. A vein of reddish material ran through it. It looked exactly like a child's marble.

"I'm off, honey. Jed Harris and I play in the semifinals in an hour, and I know how to beat him: play to his backhand and stay close to the net; I got the word from Gerry. Wish me luck, and I'll be home in good time for dinner."

Margaret was hemming a dress. She looked up and said, "Good luck. Don't be late. We're having . . ." Their young son came bounding in the front door, waving his arms, panic in his eyes.

"Mom, Dad. I got to play in the marble tournament, and I don't know how to shoot. Dad, will you show me?"

"Sure, Danny. Right after dinner we'll go out and I'll show you . . ."

"No, Dad. I got to know right now. Mr. Granger gave me the marbles"—he held up a transparent bag of aggies—"so I could play in the tournament this afternoon. You got to show me right now."

"Well, I'd like to, Danny, but I've got this match myself right now. You can enter the next tournament; there'll be another one soon."

Explanations don't reach eight-year-olds, and the tears welled. Margaret looked at Cranch, went over and put her arms around her son, and then looked at Cranch again. For a moment Cranch hesitated; then he put down his racquet bag and said, "Okay, Danny, let's go outside and I'll show you how to shoot right now." Danny smiled as Cranch phoned in his forfeit, and they went outside and practiced together for an hour and a half. Then Danny went off to the tournament and lost all his aggies.

* * *

Cranch studied the screen; the nucleus of the comet loomed closer. He narrowed the scanning beam to train it on the edges of the nucleus to determine rotation. He found no signs of rotation, and checked again, and then a third time. "Houston," he said, "the nucleus is not rotating. I repeat, not rotating. I've run three checks and it appears to have no detectable rotation. It's size now measures . . ." A message started in, and so he stopped transmitting and listened. It was the reply to his manual takeover.

"Ah, *Siderite*, we note manual ahead of schedule. Explanation, please." The transmission sounded scratchy, and it pulsed a bit. Cranch shook his head; communications were worse than predicted. They were wasting time with trivia.

"Houston, I'm in heavy debris. I'm having trouble receiving you, so start redundant transmission. I'm turning on analyzers now so you can get their output."

Cranch looked at his time. He was on schedule, but conditions were worsening. The glow around him had increased, and he could barely see the stars through it. If he had to slow down before he reached the nucleus, he might not have enough time to make it. Fuel was the problem; he needed enough to break out of the comet's orbit and find a safe, Earthbound orbit. Long hours had gone into the planning of the fuel requirements of this mission. By sending one man instead of two, they were able to add extra fuel in place of the second man and his life-support systems. Cranch touched his throttles a bit to add a kilometer per hour to his speed. At least they worried about his fuel.

"Margaret, I asked you to put gas in the car if you drove way over to that shoe discount store. It's empty, and I'm supposed to be at an infrared camera briefing in twenty minutes. Now I've got to get a cab, and I'll be late."

"Oh, I'm sorry, honey. I forgot. I'll take care of it right now." She jumped up and went to the phone to call their garage. Cranch had to wait until she was done before he could call a cab.

The warning horn let go, and Cranch cut in the crash circuits on the computer. Almost instantly the steering jets came on, turned the craft, and accelerated it on a changed course. Cranch then saw the object on the screen; it had been dead ahead. Before the computer control could cut the power to the new course, Cranch did it manually. He brought the craft to its original heading and gritted his teeth. The computer had moved the craft deeper into the cloud. It could just as well have turned the other way and avoided the object by moving outside instead of inside. Computers have no sense. Cranch leaned to the porthole to watch, and when the object went by, it was so close it startled him. It was an iron-gray block the size of an office desk, with rounded edges and corners, and it was streaked with grayish material that looked like dirty ice. It passed him twenty meters away, very slowly turning end for end, and then it was gone. Cranch transmitted a detailed description to Houston. Then he checked his time and fuel, and he saw that the maneuver had cost him dearly; an effective five minutes was lost. He shook his head. A couple more episodes like that, and he'd never make it to the nucleus.

"Ah, *Siderite*"—reception was even worse—"we hear you loud and clear. So it must be your reception. Your transmission is A-okay. Turn on all your analyzers, IR, UV, flame, gas, and gross. We are getting great data. We will report later." The words came to Cranch in short bursts, repeated, and he got it all as far as he could tell. He flipped all the analyzers on, wondering why they were so excited. Some of these analyses were supposed to be saved for the actual nucleus, but now they were using them early. The dusts and gases outside must show something unexpected. Hah. He thought he knew what it was. Exotic molecules, that's what. The stuff seen in interstellar dust and gas by the radio astronomers: methyl cyanide, methyl alcohol, formaldimine, lots of others. If those molecules were outside now, this comet might really be one of the outer solar-cloud-comets, instead of one of the dust-and-ice inner solar-cloud comets. Coming from many thousands of times further out than Pluto, this might be an outer comet that intermingled with the outer comets of Alpha Centauri. Here, right ahead of him, might be the interface of two stars. Cranch began to grow excited. The nucleus filled his screen now, even on small scale. Time, about ten minutes; fuel, about low-normal.

"Ah, *Siderite*, time-fuel ration below normal. Scrub all plans for extravehicular activity even if you find a place to put down." Cranch got it all, and he glanced ruefully at the EVA suit on the rack, ready to go. He had wanted to know, very badly, what it would be like to stand on the nucleus of a large comet. They had scrubbed EVA, and they had not even consulted him.

*   *   *

"Can I go, Mom?"

"Consult your father, dear. Whatever he says."

Their daughter, Lorraine, came swinging into the room where he was studying. At sixteen she was a rosy-cheeked image of her mother, except that the fine-spun golden hair swept halfway down her back. "Dad, can I go over to Hartford for the weekend? A whole bunch of the kids are going to see that musical version of *Hamlet*. We'll all stay at the Sonesta and we'll be back about noon Sunday. Can I go?"

"No."

"No? Dad, why not? I've got to go. I've got . . ."

"I told you, no more trips until you repaid me for the last one to New York City. You still owe me ninety dollars, and you've only got twenty in your checking account. Where's the money?"

Margaret came in. "Now, Dan. I don't think it's quite fair to hold her to that. Baby-sitting jobs have been scarce."

Cranch said, "Margaret, why did you send her in to ask my permission if you think she should go? Why didn't you just tell her 'yes'?"

"I didn't think you were going to forbid her."

Lorraine assumed her hurt and haughty posture. "It's all right, Mom. I did not know the money meant so much to him. Please put seventy dollars in my checking acount so I can pay him. That should take care of it." She went swinging out the door, her long hair flying.

There was no forward porthole in the ship, only the two on the sides. Radar showed a distance of four kilometers to the nucleus. So Cranch pressed his face against the side port and tried to look ahead. The glowing fog formed a huge tunnel around him, and the glow made it hard to see. Then, slowly, he realized that the great, looming background was an object, and not the mere dimming of light with distance. He said, "Houston, I have visual contact with the nucleus. It is big, fills all forward horizons. I see no irregularities. Preparing to fire retro rockets." He switched on the contact computer and sat back to monitor its actions.

He felt the surge press him forward against the restraining straps.

"Ah, *Siderite*, this will be the last transmission before you touch down. ETA four minutes. We confirm no time for EVA. You barely have time for touchdown. Now hear this. Make every effort to touch down and pick up raw sample from the surface unless you run out of time. You will have about one minute on surface before liftoff. All your transmissions are coming in loud and clear. Maintain voice description. Good luck, Dan.''

Cranch did not even notice that for the first time during the mission they had used his name. The forward straps pressed against him, harder now. All analytical systems aboard the craft functioned wide open. TV cameras scanned the entire area ahead of him, recording the images and transmitting at the same time. Eight different camera systems ran hundreds of stills per second up and down the spectrum. Gas analyzers pulled in ambient atmosphere, ran it through columns, and broadcast the results. Ion collectors, assorted dust collectors, particle collectors, pulled in samples, stored some and analyzed some. Magnetometers and gravitometers took measurements. The craft literally hummed from the huge consumption of power as the most advanced analytical tool yet devised by Man came within one hundred meters of the surface of the nucleus of the comet.

Cranch divided his time between the activities of the landing computer and the view outside. He described the surface he saw, emphasizing the grayness of it all, the wrinkled appearance in which a material of lighter gray seemed to fill the wrinkles. Gently rounded, low hillocks hundreds of meters in diameter gave a blistered appearance to the surface over a distance as far as he could see.

The impression he had was as if he were making a landing at dusk on a rolling, gray desert on Earth. The craft tipped and slowed and softly thudded to the surface. Cranch could hear the extension arms reaching out for samples. The one beneath the craft placed the charge and detonated it. The wave sensors placed on the surface awaited the return of the seismic vibrations.

In the cabin the one-minute gong chimed, then the thirty-second gong; and thereafter one note for every second. Cranch ensured all sampling arms were retracted and punched on the takeoff computer. At ten seconds he looked around, glanced back behind him out the porthole for the first time. Thirty meters behind him, on the surface, was a perfectly square depression on the surface, framed in a rim. A raised bar ran across the center of the surface of the square within the rim, and the bar had openings along its length. Openings, like handholes. As the next to the last note of the gong chimed, Cranch hit the ''abort'' button, and the craft wound down into silence. One at a time, Cranch reactivated the cameras and scanners, directing them to the square. He reported to Houston that he would be transmitting for the next few days and that they should give him details of any tests they wanted run. Then he removed the straps from the EVA suit and began to pull it on, humming happily to himself.

DOUBLE PLANET

John Gribbin

From Mars orbit the Earth-Moon system makes one of the most striking features of the Solar System—a double star with one component brighter than Venus seen from beneath the haze of Earth's atmosphere. But Frances Reese, riding herd on a comet, had no time to admire the beauty of the view.

The comet was a big one. A first-time visitor to the inner part of the Solar System, easing in on an orbit stretching back, past Jupiter and Saturn to the outer fringe of interstellar space. Even now, nobody knew for sure where such an object originated. Was it a fragment of interstellar rubble picked up by the Sun's gravity as it orbited around the Galaxy? Or maybe leftover debris from the formation of the Solar System itself, part of a cloud of forgotten fragments barely retained in the grip of the Sun's gravity, orbiting far out beyond Pluto for billions of years until some chance perturbation nudged it on its way past the planets. Nobody really cared about the origin of the comet. What mattered was the burden it carried, a million trillion tons of ice and snow, plunging on a course that would take it, thanks to the deflection caused by Jupiter's gravitational slingshot as it went past, within an astronomical hairsbreadth of that beautiful double planet.

A hundred years before, there would have been no prospect of human interference with the trajectory of such a monster. It was only in the 1980s, after all, that the first primitive probes had been able to rendezvous with a comet, on Halley's return in 1986. Reese's job still wasn't easy. With limited resources and a team hastily pulled together from other projects, she was expected to weld the great ice blocks—water ice, frozen carbon dioxide, ammonia and the rest—into some sort of coherent whole, dismantle the nuclear engines from most of the ships, and mount them to provide thrust on the cometary nucleus, using the virtually limitless supply of material from the ice itself as reaction mass. The resulting effect would be feeble compared with the gravitational forces that had set the comet on its way, but enough, by the time it crossed the orbit of the Earth, to nudge it a few hundred thousand kilometers from its present path. And since the computer projections drew that present trajectory right between the Earth and the Moon, with an uncertainty rather larger than the distance of the Earth from the Moon, a few hundred thousand kilometers could be crucial at that time.

Even so, it hadn't been easy persuading the politicians to make the attempt.

"A comet, Doctor Kondratieff, is hardly something to strike terror into our hearts in the 21st century, you know." The Secretary to the Council had smiled tiredly at his science adviser, preparing to dismiss another impossible claim upon the world's limited resources. Why couldn't these people understand that they couldn't return to the twentieth century, and that what effort could be spared for work in space had to be geared to practical ends? After the fiasco of the O'Neill colony, anyone could see that space was a waste of effort, even though the technology to reach Jupiter certainly existed.

"But, sir, allow me to explain." Kondratieff felt the sweat on his palms and tried to keep calm. It had been hard enough to get this audience, and on what he said now rested the only chance of deflecting the newly discovered comet from its path.

"You must appreciate, sir, the difficulty of predicting the precise fate of this object. The Earth and the Moon follow a complex path around the Sun, as you can see from this diagram. Most people think the Moon circles around the Earth, but it doesn't. The Earth and the Moon are more evenly paired in size than any other two planetary objects; the Moon is as big as Mercury, it's really a planet in its own right. Because of this, it's attracted by the Sun's gravity even more strongly than it's attracted by the Earth. To the astronomers, Earth and Moon are individual planets that each follow their own orbit around the Sun, each perturbed by the other. So both the Earth and the Moon follow wobbly orbits. All we can say about the comet's orbit is that, left alone, it will intersect this double orbit just when the two planets are there. It may pass harmlessly by. But it could very well strike the Earth.''

The presentation was faultless, Kondratieff was sure. The facts spoke for themselves, and the computer animation of the comet's orbit piercing the interwoven strands of the orbits of Earth and Moon around the sun was the icing on the cake. The probability of disaster might seem small, but as the report spelled out the effects would be immense. A small risk of an immense disaster; the only sane course of action had to be to reduce that small risk precisely to zero, whatever it cost.

''If this comet strikes the Earth it could be the greatest disaster since the death of the dinosaurs, worse than the nuclear holocaust we so recently narrowly avoided. We know the Earth has been bombarded from space over the eons, and we are pretty sure now that these bombardments explain why there are sometimes massive extinctions of life in the geological record. Sixty-five million years ago, it wasn't just the dinosaurs that died but hundreds of other species. And the best explanation is that the Earth was struck by a giant meteorite which wreaked havoc on the environment.''

''I know all this.'' The Secretary leaned back and waved a hand in dismissal. ''I may not be a scientific expert, but I do read the popularizations. That disaster was caused by a huge lump of rock, not a snowball. And it may have been a disaster for the dinosaurs, but not so bad for us, eh, since it opened the way for the mammals.''

Kondratieff, not for the first time, cursed inwardly the Secretary's habit of reading popularizations of science for light relief, and double cursed the writers who offered glib popularizations to a gullible readership.

''Of course, sir, I'm not suggesting a disaster on that scale. But this dirty snowball still has a mass of 10^{18} tons—that's a million, trillion tons of ice and snow. It's the biggest thing to come into the inner Solar System since civilization began.'' He had a flash of inspiration. ''And remember what happened in 1908. The Tunguska Explosion. Trees were knocked down all over Siberia. That was caused by a fragment of comet exploding in the atmosphere. If it had arrived a few minutes later, the rotation of the Earth would have placed Leningrad directly under the explosion. That's what even a small fragment of a comet can do, and we are dealing here with one of the biggest.''

Perhaps the popularizers deserve some credit after all. The Secretary certainly had heard of the Tunguska event, and his family came from Leningrad. By such silver-tongued persuasion did Science Adviser Kondratieff set the wheels in motion for the Reese expedition. If anyone except Kondratieff and Reese had known what the real purpose of the expedition was, however, it would, literally, never have gotten off the ground. After all, if you can nudge a comet *this* way as it moves through space, it is just as easy to nudge it *that* way, *toward* a collision instead of away from one.

From inside the hull of the *Sir Fred Hoyle* there would have been no way to admire the view of the Solar System's unique double planet, rapidly gaining in brightness ahead, even if anyone had had the time. With its engines removed, the command ship of the New Aeronautical and Space Administration's expedition just provided room for all the members of the expedition to gather and talk directly, face to face, without using radio. The seals that kept the compartment airtight were only patches, welded on after the engines had been removed, and everybody wore full suits and kept helmets at hand. The air they were breathing came from the comet itself, oxygen electolytically cracked from water. Chemically, the atmosphere was pure; emotionally it was highly charged by speculation about the reason for this unexpected gathering, called at short notice by Commander Reese.

"I've called you here to let you in on a secret." The buzz of talk stilled at the Commander's quiet words. "You know how much this expedition has cost NASA. Four ships out of the seven we came on won't be returning to Earth orbit, and three ships hardly constitutes a spacegoing fleet. We may be saving the Earth by this gesture—Bill, I know you think there's no risk to Earth, but hear me out—even if there is a risk, and we are saving the Earth, the losses might sound a death knell for manned spaceflight.

"It's all very well arguing that by proving the value of a spacegoing ability we're opening the door for increased budgets. You know as well as I do how the political mind works, and unless there are tangible risks or real benefits immediately visible, the political mind isn't going to do anything about space exploration."

"But that's what I said all along!" Bill Noyes could no longer contain his angry astonishment. "*You're* the one who persuaded us to join this crazy scheme, with your talk about how we'd be such great popular heroes the Council would have to let us have a crack at rebuilding Lagrange One."

"And I told the truth, up to a point. Sure, they'll let us have a go, with our pathetic three ships. But they won't give us the resources for more, and we can't do the job properly without. *But it doesn't matter*. We're going to give the Earth something better than Lagrange One, something to fire the imagination of all the people disillusioned with space, and make the Council sit up and take notice."

"You're not going to drop this iceberg on top of the bloody Council, then? That's the best thing you could do for the space program."

"No. We're going to drop it on the Moon."

Reese looked around the group. Floating freely, she had hooked one foot comfortably under a convenient pipe. Relaxed, her face spread into a smile as she watched the others wrestling with what she had said.

"The Moon!"

"What on Earth for?"

"She's crazy."

The noise of argument started to rise about her again.

"Do you really want to know why?" she asked quietly. Slowly the noise died down as they all turned toward her, wondering.

"Can't you make a couple of intelligent guesses between you? Take a deep breath and think hard." She resumed her impresonation of the Cheshire Cat.

Kristofferson saw it first. "It's the oxygen! You want to put an atmosphere on the Moon! But will it work?"

"Of course not." Noyes was checking through a calculation on his computer. "To keep an atmosphere a planet has to have an escape velocity at least six times the mean velocity of the molecules in the atmosphere. For oxygen, at about zero Celsius, the Moon couldn't keep an atmosphere for more than a few hundred years. Molecular weight's too low—only 32. Right, boss?"

"Up to a point, Bill. The one-sixth rule works for keeping an atmosphere for a *very* long time—billions of years. But as long as the atmospheric molecules have a mean velocity less than about one-fifth of the escape velocity it takes hundreds of millions of years for more than half the molecules to leak away. Jeans worked it all out, back in the 1920s. Still no good for oxygen, but even at about 100 Celsius the Moon could keep a respectable atmosphere of carbon dioxide for as long as any of us are likely to be interested. The extra mass means the molecules move just that much slower at the same temperature. The trick is to get the CO_2 there in the first place, which is where we come in.''

"So who wants a CO_2 atmosphere?''

"Come on, Dave, you know better than that. The Earth started out with a CO_2 atmosphere, and the odds are it got it from a comet, or several comets. Why do you think I chose this ship to lead the expedition? I knew the Council weren't bright enough to make the connection, but after all Hoyle was the guy who made that theory respectable. All the Earth's atmosphere, all the water—all the volatiles came in from space after the planet formed. The first volatiles had to come in at least one hard landing, but once *any* atmosphere formed it would act as a brake and slow down any other cometary chunks coming in from the outer Solar System. We're going to provide the Moon's hard landing. Once we've done that, we can lob any old bits of ice and snow in from the asteroid belt, and they'll stick. We can add material faster than it evaporates, and if we want oxygen to breathe we can keep it in domes or underground. We're riding 10^{18} tons of carbon dioxide and water. It won't exactly make a thick atmosphere, but it's a start. Add that to soil and you've got a pretty good basis for growing plants.''

"And you've got a perfect meteorite shield.''

"The temperature will stabilize out.''

"We're not talking about repairing a tin can in orbit; we're offering the world a second whole planet. They'll have to go for it.''

"Will it really work?''

"Well, we're going to find out. The problem is, we've got to make the orbit of this iceberg nearly circular, drop it in so that it just creeps up behind the Moon in its orbit round the Sun. Jupiter's done half the job for us, we have to do the rest. You've heard the good news, but there's more. It's going to be a lot harder than just deflecting the thing out of the Earth's path.''

*   *   *

The passage of the comet within half a million kilometers of the Earth turned the attention of six billion people upward and outward, away from their immediate problems. The return of the sole surviving ship of the expedition, with the five survivors from the 18 men and women under the command of the late Commander Reese, was the biggest media event of the 21st century. And when the First Secretary proposed to the Council that the only fitting tribute to the lives that had been sacrificed to save humankind would be to take up afresh the challenge of the new frontier, build a fleet to take advantage of the opportunity so strangely provided, and make the Earth and Moon forever a true double planet, no voice was raised in opposition.

"It's best this way, Kondratieff, but don't think I am fooled." The Secretary turned from his balcony, where the Moon, nearly full, was visible just rising above the horizon. "So we discovered that the thrust from four engines could not deflect the comet sufficiently, but six could do the job. Well enough to save the Earth, anyway, but not well enough, even with all that onboard control, to avoid the Moon. Thirteen martyrs, because those six engines had to be controlled until the last minute. I can understand that such a thing is necessary to hit accurately a moving target; not so necessary if all you want to do is miss the target. The military mind, you will appreciate, knows all about shooting at targets.

"So. You have given us the Moon, whether we like it or not. Within five years we'll have bases; in fifty we will be adding to the atmosphere so—fortuitously?— provided in that epic catastrophe. You expect me to be mad, to accuse you? To dismiss you even? Not at all. I'm not saying you weren't wise to keep me in the dark beforehand; the risk was too great. But now, there are opportunities."

"Opportunities? But, sir, you always dismissed the notion of opportunity for mankind in space."

"I dismissed the projects I was offered, Kondratieff, and with good reason. Tin cans in orbit, as far away as the Moon. What opportunity is there in a tin can? How many could Lagrange One have taken, even if it hadn't been for the accident? A few thousand, an elite, something for the masses to resent. The O'Neill colony was never more than an elitist concept, taking resources from the masses and building a plaything for the few. A whole world is different. You talk of the new frontier, and you speak better truth than you know. One sixteenth of the area of the Earth—one-fifth of the land area of our planet—is waiting there now for us to tame. It will take far longer than it took to tame the so-called new world here on Earth. But that's all to the good. The longer it takes the better, because when its done we'll only have to find another new frontier, to save ourselves from stagnation. Yes, indeed, Kondratieff, you have done well."

And, thought the Secretary, if the military mind understands how to hit a moving target, so the political mind understands how to seize an opportunity when it arises.

He turned back to the balcony, Kondratieff now at his side. The Moon was clear above the horizon in the still night. Unobscured by cloud, yet faintly indistinct, seen as it had never appeared before during human history; not quite fuzzy, yet not quite sharply outlined; a sister planet in the making.

PRIDE

Poul Anderson

Suddenly Nemesis exploded.

It happened just in time to quench an eruption within the watchful spaceship. The forces of violence had been gathering in men even as they did in the half-star. Mortal time-spans were smaller; but a pair of years, passing through darkness, had grown weary, and then months amidst strangeness and dangers laid their own further pressures on the spirit. Dermot Byrne crowed a boast, Jan Cronje could no longer keep silence, the hostility between them broke free and a fight was at hand.

Accident touched off the trouble, though something of the kind had been likely at some point during the years remaining before *Anna Lovinda* would come back to Earth orbit. Neither man was a fool. Since their friendship broke, they had tacitly avoided each other as much as possible. Maybe Cronje supposed Byrne was with Suna Rudbeck, in the cabin they now shared, or maybe—seeking to forget for a moment—he didn't think about it at all. He was never sure afterward. Whatever else was on his mind, he entered the wardroom to get a cup of refreshment and a little conversation, perhaps a game of chess or somebody who would come along with him to the gymnasium and play handball. At the entrance, he stopped. There Byrne was.

Several other off-duty people were present also, benched around the table or standing nearby. Conversation was general. Coffee and tea made the air fragrant. Music lilted out of speakers in

317

bulkheads softly tinted, where there hung scenes from home that
were often changed. Garments were loose, colorful, chosen by
their wearers. Folk needed every such comfort.

Not that they huddled away from the universe. As if to declare
that, a large viewscreen was always tuned, like a window on
space save that its nonreflecting surface left the scene clear
despite interior lighting. Stars crowded blackness, icy-bright and
unwinking. They streamed slowly past vision as the ship rotated.

Byrne was speaking. He was a slender young man, eyes
brilliant blue and features regular, very fair-skinned, beneath a
shock of dark hair, a Gaelic melody in his Swedish. A planetologist, he was lately back from his second expedition to the fourth
satellite of Nemesis, an Earth-sized world on which his had been
the first footprint ever made. "The wonder, the beauty, those
will never be coming through in our reports, no matter how
many pictures we print. Sure, and this crew ought to have
included a poet. But they have no imagination in Stockholm."

"They've got enough to dispatch us," laughed Ezra Lee, the
senior astrophysicist. "Oh, the Control Authority did begrudge
the cost—"

"Keeping world peace has not yet become cheap," murmured
engineer Gottfried Vogel in his mild fashion.

"Just the same, it took more politicking than it should have,
to get a few people out here," said Byrne. "Had not the probes
already told of miracles for the finding?"

Nemesis rose at the left edge of the screen. At a distance of
more than a million kilometers, it blotted out most stars with
hugeness rather than brilliance. Red-hot from the slow contraction of its monstrous mass, Sol's companion did not dazzle eyes
that looked upon it. Instead, that glow brought to sight an
intricacy of bands, swirls, murk-spots, sparkles—clouds, mael-
stroms, lightnings. God could have cast Earth into any of those
storms and not made so much as a splash. A moon glimmered
near the limb; a billion killometers from the giant, it was itself the
size of Saturn.

"Ah, well, we *are* here," Byrne went on. Happiness radiated
from him. "The scientific discoveries are only one part of the
marvel. This world where I've been—Suna wants to call it
Vanadis, and I Fand, but no great matter that, for each of us
means a goddess of love and beauty."

"A frozen waste," said Minna Veijola. But of course she was
a biologist, enraptured by the life (life!) on the innermost satellite.

"It is not," Byrne replied. "That is what I'm trying to explain to the lot of you. Oh, doubtless barren. Yet the play of light on ice mountains—ask Suna," he blurted. "That was what finally brought us together, she and I, after we'd first landed. The faerie beauty everywhere around us."

Jan Cronje stepped through the doorway. "I do not believe that," he said hoarsely. "You were sneaking and sniffing around her before the voyage was half over. You wheedled her into being your pilot on that survey, the two of you alone. Yes, it was nicely planned."

Silence clapped down. Through it, Cronje's boots made a dead-march drumbeat as he moved onward. He was a big man, and spin provided a full gravity of weight. Blunt of countenance, sandy-haired, ruddy-bearded, he had gone quite pale.

Byrne sprang to his feet. "It was not!" he cried. "It . . . only happened."

Cronje grinned. "Ha!" His Afrikaans accent harshened. "It was far on the way to happening by that time. If you had been an honorable man, you would have gotten another pilot for yourself. Me, for instance. I had not seen what you were up to. But no, it was my wife you wanted."

Byrne flushed. "You insult her. She was never mine for the taking, nor yours for the keeping. She's a free human being who made her own choice."

Cronje reached him. "I could stand that, somehow," he said. "Until now, when you started bragging before everybody." His left hand shot out, grabbed the other's tunic, hauled him close. "No more, do you hear?"

"Let me go, you lout!" Byrne yelled. His fists doubled.

"Jan, please." Veijola plucked at Cronje's sleeve. Although they were good friends, he didn't seem to notice.

Lee gestured at a couple of men. They left their places and moved to intervene, should this come to blows. A brawl, in the loneliness everywhere around, could have unthinkable aftermaths.

And then—it was mere coincidence. Providence surely has better concerns than our angers. But Nemesis exploded.

A yell brought heads around toward the screen. Shouts tumbled out of the intercom as crew throughout the ship saw, or heard from those who saw. The red disc shuddered. Cloud bands ripped apart, vortices shattered, waves of ruin ran from either pole until they met at the equator and recoiled in chaos. Then every feature vanished in rose-pearly pallor. Visibly to unaided eyes, the disc swelled. Star after star disappeared behind smokiness.

It was Lee, the astrophysicist, who lurched across the deck, stunned. "Already?" he gasped. "Just like that? The fire lit and—and Nemesis turning back into a star?"

Erik Telander, captain of *Anna Lovinda,* mounted the stage. With chairs set forth, the gymnasium became the general meeting room. A dozen faces looked up at him. Six more people were on station in case of emergency. Two, a pilot and a planetologist, had flitted off in one of the boats to yet another of the worlds that circled, like the ship, around the primary orb. Only such a pair ever went off on such a preliminary exploration. The unknowns were too many for the risking of a larger number. Twenty-one men and women were all too few at this uttermost bound of the Solar System.

Telander smiled. He was a lean, slightly grizzled man who seemed older than his actual years. "Well, ladies and gentlemen," he said, "we have had quite a surprise in the past several hours. And it appears that surprises are continuing. The task immediately before us is to decide what we should do. Although that decision must, of course, ultimately be mine, I want to base it on your knowledge and your ideas; for I am a single person among you, without the special knowledge and skills you variously possess. Frankly, my first impulse was to direct that we cut loose from *Gertrud* and blast off to a safe distance. Ezra Lee convinced me this was neither necessary nor even wise, at least for the moment. I would like him to describe the situation for you as he sees it. No doubt the data that the instruments have been—are—collecting will cause him to modify, already now, what he said to me." He beckoned. "If you please."

Lee rose. "You're all familiar with the theory, at least in general outline," said his flat Midwestern American tones. "I trust you're also aware how incomplete that theory is, how little we really know for sure about Nemesis. It could hardly be otherwise, across a gap of more than two light-years, when the object is so dim at best, and unique in human observation. Still, I suggest you take a minute to review for yourselves what you've been told. Get it as clear as possible in your minds. Then, if nothing else, you can ask me intelligent questions." He chuckled; teeth flashed against the dark brown skin. "Not that I guarantee to have any intelligent answers."

Humor died away. It was as if the silence that followed grew echoful of thoughts.

Nemesis, long-unseen companion of Sol, it was your murderousness that finally betrayed your existence to our species and made us search the skies for you. No, but "murderousness" is wrong. You are not alive; you are as innocent as a thunderbolt.

Yet every six-and-twenty million years your orbit brings you within 10,000 astronomical units of our sun. Passing through its Oort cloud, you trouble the comets there. Many fall inward, whipping around the star, perhaps for millennia, until their dust and ice are boiled off, the brightness is gone, only rocks that were in the cores remain. Some collide with planets or moons. Earth takes its share of that celestial barrage. Each cycle, one or more of those smiting masses is of asteroidal size. Continents tremble under the blow. Cast-up smoke and vapor darken the air for months. In such a Fimbul Winter, first the plants die, next the beasts; and when at last heaven clears again, the survivors begin a whole new order of things.

Thus did you slay the last dinosaurs at the end of the Cretaceous period, Nemesis, and with them the ammonities and . . . more kinds of life than endured. Thus did you kill the great mammals of the Miocene. And before these massacres there had been others, throughout the ages, but time has eroded their traces until they have become well-nigh as hard to find as you yourself, Nemesis.

That path of yours is not the least of the strangenesses about you. Neighbor stars should long since have drawn you away. Can they be what gave your track the form it has, so that only in the past billion years have you been launching your bombardments, and a billion years hence they will have ceased? Perhaps we shall learn the answer, now that we are at the end of a quest which took lifetimes of our evanescent kind.

A tiny, coal-red point afar, for which our finest spaceborne instruments sought through year after year before we knew . . . a flickering too faint and irregular for us to say more than that it takes about a decade from peak to peak . . . mass, as reported by our unmanned craft, slightly in excess of 80 times Jupiter's, which means well over 25,000 times Earth's . . . a family of attendants . . . tokens of a fire within, that kindles and goes out and kindles again, like the heartbeat of a man who lies dying . . .

Minna Veijola raised her hand. "Question!"

"Be my guest," Lee said. "Maybe whoever wants to speak

from the floor should rise, like me. We're too many for real conversation.''

The biologist obeyed. Jan Cronje, beside whom she had seated herself, came out of his sullenness enough to give her a glance that lingered, as did several other men. While small and somewhat stocky, she had the blond, slanty-eyed, high-cheeked good looks common among Finns. ''I don't want to be an alarmist,'' she said. ''I'll take your word that we are in no immediate danger. But this is quite out of my field of competence. Furthermore, you'll understand that I am bound to wonder and worry about effects on my beloved life-bearing satellite. Could you please explain what it is we have to expect?''

Lee shrugged. ''Yonder life doesn't seem to be hurt any by outbursts like this. After all, they've been going on for gigayears.''

''My colleagues and I have scarcely begun basic taxonomy and chemical analysis, let alone comprehend how evolution works there. I—very well, I'll say it, because it must be gnawing at others besides me. We're only a million-odd kilometers from Nemesis. If it's become a star again, even the faintest of red dwarfs, aren't we likely to get a blast of hard radiation from it?''

''I remember telling you, dear, rock specimens we've taken show no effects of anything but cosmic and planetary background,'' Dermot Byrne said.

''Why not? Ezra, you admit that what's happened was quite unexpected. How can you predict what will happen next?''

The astrophyscist ran fingers across the black wool on his scalp. ''I thought we'd been over this ground abundantly, both in training and in talk en route,'' he said. ''But, I suppose, on so long a voyage, in so cramped an environment, I guess everybody tended to get wrapped up in his or her main interests, and forget a lot. Certainly some of what you've had to tell me about your discoveries, Minna, has gone straight by me.

''And among the surprises was the timing of this event. Observing it at close range is a principal objective of ours, of course. Nevertheless, we've been caught pretty flat-footed. Past observations and theoretical studies indicated the system wouldn't go critical for at least another year. Well, it *is* a complex and little-understood thing, and we did know the periodicity is very far from exact. I'm afraid we're going to lose quite a bit of information we'd hoped to gather, because we weren't yet properly prepared.''

He drew breath. ''Okay. Please bear with me while I repeat

some elementary facts. It's just to identify those of them that I think are important in making the kind of short-range predictions you're asking about, Minna.

"We know Nemesis is the first example ever actually found of a so-called brown dwarf. Its mass is right at the borderline between planet and star. Gravitational contraction heats it—like Jupiter, but on a far bigger scale, so that the outer layers of gas have a temperature approaching a thousand kelvin. Near the core, heat and pressure naturally go higher by many orders of magnitude. At last collapse brings them to the point where thermonuclear reactions begin. The star-fires are lighted.

"But you can see how quickly this sends the core temperatures skyrocketing. This in turn makes the inner layers expand. Pressure drops below the critical point; the thermonuclear reactions turn off. The body as a whole expands for a while longer on momentum and interior heat, then starts falling in on itself again—and so the cycle recommences.

"I repeat my apology for rehearsing what everybody well knows, but I do believe we need to have information marshaled before us. You see, as usual, reality turns out to be more complicated than theory. That's why we're here, isn't it? To take a good, hard, close-up look.

"Now. You people surely remember that astronomical instruments and orbiting probes have shown rather slight variation in surface temperature or emission, and scarcely anything in the way of X-rays. Nor does Nemesis have a Van Allen belt worth mentioning, in spite of its terrific magnetic field. It's too far out to collect solar wind particles, and it puts forth scarcely any of its own. The reason isn't far to seek. That enormous mass absorbs everything from the nuclear burning. The fires never get intense enough to cause more than some heating and expansion of the outer layers.

"Because of that very expansion, and its cooling effect, the emission temperature—what we actually sense—doesn't increase much. In fact, we think that at maximum diameter Nemesis is actually a bit cooler than it was when this ship arrived. Granted, by then the fires have already gone out.

"That's why we're in no danger."

Veijola shook her head stubbornly. "Yes, I knew," she replied. "You miss the point I was trying to make. You did not expect this . . . this sudden outburst. Quite aside from its timing, the experts have told me—I do remember my indoctrination—

they told me expansion would be slow, and not begin until well after the nuclear reactions did. Therefore, could you please explain why you are so confident about the future?'' She sat down and waited.

A sigh went through the assembly. Telander himself threw Lee an inquiring glance.

The American's smile was rueful. "I truly am sorry," he said. "As flustered as I've been, I seem to've taken for granted that people in different lines of work were worse confused. Let me make what amends I can by giving you what new information my department has gathered.

"There is no doubt that fusion has begun at the core. Our neutrino detectors are going crazy. Just what is happening in there—what chain or chains of nuclear conversion—we don't yet know. We do have indications of an unpredicted quantity of metals, and this is bound to affect the course of events. I believe that when we have enough data, and have analyzed them, we'll also get an idea of why Nemesis pulsates so irregularly.

"As for that expansion—which some of you saw at the time and the rest of you, I'm sure, have seen on replay—as for it, yes, it was unforeseen too. Suddenly the apparent diameter of the body increased by about seven percent. Well, Mamoru"—Lee nodded toward his associate Hayashi—"soon came up with what I think is the right notion.

"When the core caught fire, it was like a bomb with yield in the gigatons going off. No, more likely several bombs, at once or in quick succession. Shock waves, powerful enough to tear Earth apart, propagated out through the mass above. The globe is flattened by its rotation, of course, so the shock reached the poles first, though it got to the equator only minutes later. It accelerated the outer layers of gas. They whoofed spaceward. Under Nemesis gravity, the pressure gradient in the atmosphere is so high that even this thinned-out topmost part looked opaque at our distance.''

Lee smiled. "Fascinating, isn't it?" he finished. "But not dangerous to us. As a matter of fact, which some of you have doubtless been too busy under general alert to witness—as a matter of fact, gravity has the upper hand again. That exploded shell is rapidly falling back into the main body. In other words, regardless of how astonishing, this expansion of Nemesis has been a transient phenomenon. Hereafter we can expect it will re-expand, but to a lesser distance and in a much more orderly fashion.

"I hope that puts your mind at rest, Minna. Naturally, our teams are going to be busier than a one-armed octopus, taking in what data we can. But given proper caution, we should survive to bring those data home." He looked around. "More questions?"

From her seat beside Byrne, pilot Suna Rudbeck jumped up. "Yes!" Her voice rang. "What about Osa?"

Men's gazes went to her more eagerly than they had gone to Veijola. Redbeck, was, perhaps, not intrinsically handsomer— tall, full-formed, with auburn locks framing sharply cut visage— but there was ever something flamelike about her. After an instant, the other pilot's lips twisted and he stared elsewhere. Not long ago, she had been Rudbeck-Cronje. She was not yet Rudbeck-Byrne, but these days he was alone in the cabin that had been theirs, and she shared the planetologist's. Veijola reached toward Cronje, then quickly, unseen, withdrew her hand.

Captain Telander raised his brows: "Osa?" he asked from the stage.

"The inner probe, in polar orbit," Lee explained.

Telander nodded. "Ah, yes, I remember now. Its nickname. I have never been sure why."

"No matter," said Rudbeck. "Listen. Ever since Nemesis went 'boom,' I've been thinking about Osa. Before then, in fact. We've been planning how to retrieve it. The information it carries is priceless, not so, Ezra?"

Lee swallowed hard and nodded.

"If gas expanded outward as far as you say," Rudbeck pursued, "Osa encountered a significant density, a drag. Its orbit will have decayed. What is its status at this moment?" Aggressively: "If you don't know, why don't you?"

"Oh, we do, we do," the astrophysicist said. "It was among the first things we checked. You're right. Osa's loss would be—is—terrible. I'm afraid, though—"

Rudbeck stabbed a finger in his direction. "*Is* it lost?" she demanded.

"Well, no, not precisely. Gaseous resistance did force it lower. The ambient medium is already much less thick than before, with density dropping fast as molecules return to the main atmosphere. However, a rough computation—I had one run an hour ago, Suna, because I'm as concerned as anybody—it shows that even if nothing else happens, Osa is doomed. Its new orbit is unstable. Variations in the gravity field—in local density and configuration of the geoid—will draw it farther down until it becomes a meteorite." Lee drove fist into palm. "Damn! But as I've been admitting, this has taken us by surprise."

"Osa," mumbled Cronje. The challenge posed by that thing had been talk whenever *Anna Lovinda's* three boat pilots got together. It stood now in the minds of everybody.

Years ahead of this manned expedition, the mother probe took station and launched her robot investigators. Osa was the innermost, in close polar orbit around the giant. For a while it transmitted back to Gertrud *that flood of facts which poured into its instruments—until the transmitter began to fail. Sufficient still came through, sporadically and distorted, to show how much more must be accumulating in its data banks, a Nibelung hoard of truth which might be forever irreplacable.*

Anna Lovinda *lacked the means to launch so gifted a satellite. Most of her capacity was devoted to humans and their life support. For she fared only in part to study Nemesis with the versatility of living intelligences, their capability of coping with the unforeseen. Her voyage was equally a test of whether humans could survive a journey across interstellar reaches, wherein speeds eventually neared that of light—whether the Bussard drive could indeed carry them as far as Alpha Centauri and beyond, on into the universe.*

"And now," Hayashi said as if to himself, though in Swedish, "now, when Nemesis has done this thing we did not await, it would mean a great deal to hear what Osa has to tell us. However—"

"No 'howevers'!" came from Rudbeck.

"I beg your pardon?" breathed Telander.

"Listen," she repeated herself. "You recall we had plans for retriving Osa in advance of Nemesis reaching star phase." She tossed her head. "Yes, I know, Captain, you were dubious, but the numbers showed it could be done." She laughed. "There was a bit of a quarrel over which of us pilots should get the glory of doing it. Well, Nemesis has jumped the the gun and time available has become short. But I think—Ezra, you'll not falsify the data; I put you on your honor—I think it can still be done, if we're quick. If I am!"

"No!" shouted both Byrne and Cronje, and surged to their feet together.

An unwonted coldness drew over Rudbeck's face. "Jan, I

claim the right by virtue of having made the proposal. Dermot, be still; you are not my superior officer."

"Hey, wait just a minute, hotshot," Lee protested. "Our margin of safety is thin at best. We can't risk one of our four auxiliary boats and their three pilots on a hairbreadth stunt like that."

Rudbeck's grin turned wolfish. "You just got through assuring us we are not in danger. Given adequate calculation and control, the mission should be no more hazardous than it would have been earlier; and we know it was feasible then." She swung toward Telander. "Captain, we're here at the end of the longest and most expensive haul in history. The knowledge in Osa is invaluable to science; and knowledge is what we're supposed to gain. But we must be quick. Let me go."

"I never claimed anybody can tell exactly what that damned monster will do next," Lee sputtered.

"Nor can you claim you will never fall over a beer bottle and break your neck," Rudbeck retorted. Eagerness blazed from her. "Captain, time is very short. What do you say?"

For pulsebeats that seemed to become many, Telander stood still. At last, slowly: "When we are on a frontier . . . with so vast an investment behind us, so much riding on what we can accomplish . . . how many megabytes of information is one life worth? If closer study proves the risk is within reason, I will authorize the attempt."

"By me!" Cronje roared.

"Let him go, let him go, and I'll pray for him every centimeter of the way," Byrne stammered.

Victory sang in Rudbeck's voice. "Jan, I'm sorry, you're a first-class pilot, but the uncertainties will be large, and you know my reactions test marginally faster than yours. Or Miguel's, not that he could get back soon enough anyway. Dermot, have no fears. I'll snatch Osa free, and we'll return to Vanadis together."

The boat, flamboyantly named *Valkyrie* by her pilot, eased from a launch bay in the ship, gained room for maneuver by a few delicate jet thrusts, and in the same careful fashion worked her way into initial trajectory. This was on autopilot, under computer direction, and Suna Rudbeck had nothing to do but sit almost weightless and gaze out the ports.

She kept the cabin dark so that her eyes could fully take in the splendor outside. Thus seen, space was not gloomy. There were more stars than there was blackness: steadfast brilliances, white, blue, red, golden. Among them, Sol at its distance remained the brightest, but barely more than Sirius. The Milky Way—in her native language, the Winter Street—swept in an ice-bright torrent whose silence felt like a mysterious noise, something other than the whisper of blood in her ears, filling the hollowness around.

As she drew away from the two large spacecraft, they became clear to her sight, starlit as heaven was. *Gertrud* (St. Gertrud, medieval patroness of wayfarers), the mother vessel of the unmanned pioneers, was a great metal mass from which instrument booms and transceiver dishes jutted. At the stern were simply linac thrusters, akin to those that drove *Valkyrie;* never being intended for return, only for getting around in the neighborhood of Nemesis, the robot ship had discarded her Bussard system upon arrival.

From her bow extended two kilometers of cable, a bare glimmer in Rudbeck's sight, no hint of the incredible tensile strength in precisely aligned atoms. The opposite end of the line anchored *Anna Lovinda*. That hull was lean, resembling the blade of a dagger whose basket-formed guard was the set of her own linacs. The haft beyond was mostly shielding against the Bussard engine, whose central systems formed a pommel at the top. The force-focusing lattice of that drive, extended while the vessel burned her way across deep space, had been folded back for safety, a cobweb around the knife.

The linked vessels, bearer of probes and bearer of humans, turned majestically about each other. Their spin provided interior weight without unduly inconveniencing auxiliary craft; one rotation took nearly three hours. At her slight present acceleration, Rudbeck felt ghost-light.

That soon ended. "Prepare for standard boost," came out of a speaker. The powerplant hummed, a low sound which bore no hint of the energies that burst from sundered nuclei, turned reaction mass into plasma, and hurled it down the linac until the jet emerged not very much less rapid than light. A full Earth gravity drew Rudbeck down into her chair. The boat could easily have exceeded that, but she herself needed to reach her goal unwearied and alert.

She turned on the cabin illumination, and her attention away from infinity, back toward prosaic meter readings, and displays on the panel before her. "All okay," said Mission Control. "You're in charge now, Suna. Barring any fresh data that come in, of course, or any calculations your inboard computers can't handle.

Her head jerked an impatient nod; no matter that no scanner was conveying her image. "I doubt that will be required," she said curtly. "What we have is a straightforward problem in vector analysis. Landing on one of those moons is a good deal trickier, believe me."

"Suna, don't get overconfident, I beg you. The velocities, the energies—"

"Velocities are relative. Or hadn't you heard?" Rudbeck realized she was being snappish. "Pardon me. But I would like a while to think, undisturbed."

"Certainly. We'll stand by . . . and cheer for you, *flicka*."

She did not at once devote herself to the figures, for her course was bringing Nemesis into direct view forward. It was impossible not to stare and wonder. Measurement, more than vision, declared that the body had fallen back into something like its former size; but that was enormous enough even seen from here. Measurement also told of gasps and quiverings going through it. The disc remained wan and well-nigh featureless, save when rents opened and the lower red glow shone angrily through, or where plumes leaped up, broke apart, and rained back.

—"Those shock waves are bounding about yet," Lee had diagnosed. "They reach levels where the gas is too thin to transmit them, and are reflected. Interference produces local calms and local eruptions. It'll take a long time to damp out."

Anguish had distorted Byrne's face. "What if—" he groaned, "what if . . . a geyser, or maybe a whole second expansion . . . happens just when Suna is passing by?"

"It's possible," Lee admitted. "I have not changed my mind about her effort being a bad idea. We've witnessed too many occurrences we don't understand, and haven't had any real chance yet to stop observing and start thinking. Those white clouds blanketing most of the surface, for instance. What are they? We still haven't managed to get a decent reading on them, spectroscope, polarimeter, anything, the way they churn around and come and go."

Byrne reached out toward the pilot. "Suna, darling, darling, I beg you, stay! Nobody will be scoffing at you, I swear."

She bridled. "Must I explain the kindergarten details to you?" she clipped. "Osa's orbital decay is now determined solely by gravity gradients. That means the path is completely predictable for a short term. Now suppose Nemesis does blow again when I am in the vicinity. The first time, it did not throw up enough gas to Osa's altitude to cause significant structural damage. At a second time, true, Osa will be lower. But the shock waves will have less energy. My orbit will be eccentric. A sudden increase in ambient density won't slow me much, nor heat my hull more than I can stand. I'll coast out into the clear. Or—worst case—if I must retrofire to avoid a plunge, or to avoid overheating, the linac won't be ruined. It can safely operate in a gas so tenuous, at least for the brief time I would need.''

Byrne stiffened. "If the danger is negligible, let me ride along with you.''

"Oh, nonsense." She relented. "But sweet nonsense." She moved forward and kissed him. The kiss lasted. "Well," she murmured, "the flight plan doesn't have me leaving for another hour. . . .''

—She had better review that plan again. It was only simple in principle; complex and subtle mathematics underlay it.

In its present track, Osa had velocity of some 180 kilometers per second. That fluctuated, especially when rounding the equatorial bulge, and *Valkyrie* must match it exactly. Given timing and related factors, this meant rendezvous over the north pole, with *Valkyrie's* path osculating Osa's. The former would be a long ellipse, but come sufficiently close to the latter near that point that Rudbeck should have time to make the capture. Immediately thereafter she must use her jets, first to equalize velocities—at such speeds, a tiny percentage differential could rend hulls or start an irretrievable plunge—and then to begin escaping. The delta vee demanded was approximately seventy-five kilometers per second, and the deeper in the gravity well that thrust started, the less reaction mass need be expended.

That was definitely a consideration. Given its exhaust velocity, a linac drive did not drain mass tanks very fast, but it did draw upon them, and the expedition had no facilities for refining more material. This wasn't a Bussard-drive situation, with a ship taking in interstellar hydrogen for fuel and boosterstuff after she had reached minimum speed—no limit on how closely she could approach *c*, how far she could range. The auxiliary boats were meant merely to flit around among planets. When their tanks were dry, *Anna Lovinda* must go home. Economy could add an extra year or better to the nominal five she was to spend exploring—could add unbounded extra knowledge and glory.

Rudbeck smiled and relaxed. She had about an hour of straight-line acceleration before the next change of vector. After that, maneuvers would become increasingly more varied, until in about four hours she was at Nemesis. There the equipment would cease carrying her as a passenger. She would be using it. Everything that happened would be in her hands.

Cronje sat alone in his cabin. It was not entirely his, though—only the pictures from home (his parents before their house, a kopje at sunset, breakers on a reef with the ocean sapphire-blue around them, a model-building kit, a closetful of clothes, the book he was screening without really reading). A bare bunk and bulkhead haunted the room.

There was a knock. "Come in," he snapped. As the door opened: "No. *Voetsack*. Get out."

Byrne twisted his hands together. "Please," he whispered. "Let me in. Listen awhile. Afterward do what you like, and I'll not be resisting."

Cronje considered. "Well, close the door, Speak. No, I did not invite you to sit down."

"She's . . . close to rendezvous."

"Did you imagine I do not know? This set will switch over whenever communication recommences. Go tune yours."

Byrne ran tongue over lips. "I thought . . . perhaps we might—" Facing the scowl before him, he mustered strength to plunge ahead. "Jan, Suna's dearest hope is that we two might be friends again. That may be too much to ask. But could we not pray for her together?"

"I am not a praying man. I doubt that my father's God would hear the likes of you."

Sweat glistened on Byrne's cheeks. "Well, will you listen a minute? This is hard for me. I've had to nerve myself to it. But when Suna is in danger—somehow it seems you should know about her. Know what an injustice you have been doing her."

Cronje's massive shoulders hunched forward. "How?"

Byrne straightened. Resolution began to resonate in his tone. "Think. You considered her such an idiot, so faithless, that my wiles lured her from you. But it was not that way at all, at all. How could it be? Nor would I have tried. Oh, I was in love with her almost from the time we departed Earth. But her nearness was enough." He sketched a smile. "We've unattached women without inhibitions abroad, as well you are aware, Jan Cronje."

"What? No, I never—"

"Of course you did not. But understand, you great loon, neither did she. She fought her feelings for me, month after month. If you had been more thoughtful of her, she could well have won that battle."

Cronje grimaced. "Was I ever bad to her? See here, we're both pilots, so naturally, as soon as we reached Nemesis, we were off most of the time on separate missions. But when we were together—" He snarled. His fist crashed on the chair arm. "Before God, I'll not drag our private life out in front of you!"

"You needn't," Byrne answered. "But she has needed to explain herself to me. She grieves on your account and wishes you nothing but well. Nevertheless, the fact is that she and I are . . . happier . . . than ever she— Well. No more. Today I decided my duty was to give her back your respect for her. Now you can send me away. Or if you hit me here where we are alone, I will tell the captain I had an accident."

Cronje slumped back. His jaw sagged a little. After a while he muttered, "Respect—"

The text on the screen vanished. Mission Control blinked into view. "We have a report from Rudbeck," the speaker said. Curbed emotions turned her voice flat. "She has visual contact with Osa. Parameters satisfactory. Except that an outburst is climbing ahead of her."

Valkyrie flew above Nemesis. Cold jets, microgravity, and all, no other words than "flew above" would do, when the sub-sun filled half of hurtling vision.

Right, left, forward, aft, the immensity reached, until eyesight lost itself. It was like an ocean, but an ocean of dream, where billows rolled and roiled—white, gray, pale red, deep purple— endlessly above furnace depths which glared through rifts and whirlpools. Here and there spume blew free, surf crashed sound-less, fountains spouted upward and arched back down. Haze overlay the scene, fading aloft into a blackness where stars gleamed untroubled. You could lose yourself, staring into that; your soul could leave you, drown in those waves, be scattered by them from horizon to horizon and there drift forever.

Rudbeck's gaze clung to the heavens. A twinkle onto which her radar had locked was growing into the satellite she had come to save. It seemed an unimpressive cylinder, with arms and steering rockets jutting at odd angles, the whole now crazily spinning and wobbling. But that was the mere shell around the few kilograms of crystals which encoded more knowledge than any human could master in a lifetime.

Beyond and below, a great ashen geyser was slowly rising out of the clouds. Its top faded off into nothingness, but already stars immediately above were dimming and going out.

"It's optically denser than I quite like, and will probably be opaque by the time I pass through," Rudbeck said. "I'm getting radar echoes, too. But you're receiving the readings directly. What do you advise?"

The transmission lag of half a dozen seconds felt like as many minutes. Telander's words came wearily: "Abort. Take evasive action."

"No!" Rudbeck argued. "Not after coming this far, with everything it means. I've been thinking. The optical density is likely due to nothing worse than water vapor becoming ice particles. The radar reflection could well be off ions. Neither appears sufficient to threaten my linac."

Time.

"Those are your guesses, pilot. Dr. Lee's team has not yet been able to ascertain what the truth is. . . . Well, pass by in free fall. You should suffer no harm from that. While your orbit is taking you around again, the situation may change for the better, or our understanding may improve, and you can make a second attempt."

"Skipper, I don't believe a second try will be possible. *Valkyrie* can bullet on through that cloud. I doubt Osa can. Too much drag, with such a low mass-to-surface ratio; and I'd anticipate eddy current losses too, because of what those ions must be doing to the Nemesis magnetic field. Before I can return, Osa will have slipped irrecoverably far down—to burn up—"

Rudbeck's hands tightened on the manual controls. "Sir," she said, "without being insubordinate, I remind you that the pilot of a spacecraft under boost is *her* captain, who makes the final decisions. I'm about to boost, and my decision will be to go ahead with the retrieval. I trust you will continue to provide support if needed. Now I have no more time for argument. Wish me luck, shipmates!"

She laughed aloud and became very busy.

An overtaking orbit was a lower orbit. With the help of

ranging instruments, computers, and jets, Rudbeck adjusted course
until the difference between hers and Osa's was measurable in
meters of space. She rolled her craft about, belly toward the
quarry. She pulled the switch that caused the cargo bay to open,
and another that extended the grappler arms. Like a single beast of
prey, stealing along on breaths of plasma thrust, Rudbeck and
Valkyrie closed in on Osa.

Peering at the scanner screen, fingers working with surgical
delicacy, she operated the grapplers. A shiver went through the
hull. Osa was captured. Rudbeck's touch on a button com-
manded an equalizing vector which a screen display counseled.
Weight hauled softly at her. The arms drew their burden into the
hold. Hatches slid shut.

The maneuvers, the momentum transferences had sent *Valkyrie*
sliding off downward. The atmospheric pressure gradient beneath her meant that she would become a shooting star within
minutes, unless she regained altitude. This was in the calculations. Likewise was the full-throated blast which was to make
good her escape from Nemesis. Rudbeck grinned at the cloud
ahead. It was weirdly like a fog bank on Earth. Her hands gave
their orders. The spacecraft leaped.

Abruptly the hull shuddered and bucked. A crash went through
it, the noise of a mighty gong. Rudbeck's body jammed against the
harness. An unbalanced thrust snapped her head sideways. Dazed
with pain, she hardly felt the weightlessness that followed. It
was not true weightlessness anyway, but a riot of shifting centrifugal forces. Like a dead leaf on a winter wind, *Valkyrie* tumbled
through space, borne wherever the cosmos cast her.

They were three who met in the captain's cramped little office:
Erik Telander, Ezra Lee, and Jan Cronje. They did not feel they
had time to confer with anybody else. Screens were tuned to
Mission Control and Observatory Central, but the sound was
turned low.

All three of them were on their feet. Lee's back was bowed.
"Oh, Jesus, I should have seen it, I should have seen it," he
moaned.

Cronje stood expressionless. "I gather you have established
the nature of that obstacle she ran into," he said. "Let us hear."

"With everything confused— But we do finally have clear
readings. We might have interpreted our data correctly earlier,
except that the conclusion is so utterly unexpected. . . ." Stop

maundering! Lee told himself. To the others: "The whitish material in the atmosphere, and in the plume she encountered, it's dust."

"What?"

"Yes, mostly fine silicate particles. I suspect carbon as well, possibly traces of higher elements—no matter now. I see with the keenest hindsight." Lee's chuckle was ghastly. "It's cosmic dust, from the original nebula that the Solar System condensed out of. Solid material, that got incorporated in the bodies of the lesser planets, in the cores of giants like Jupiter. And vaporized in Sol, of course. In the case of Nemesis, the parameters are special. Once the main mass had coalesced, more dust kept falling for a while, till the nebula was used up. The heat of Nemesis already served to keep it suspended in the lower atmosphere, though not to gasify it. It couldn't sink on into levels where the air was denser than it was, either. In other words, way down, that air includes a stratum of thick dustiness. When the fires turn on, the shock waves cast that dust aloft, till eventually it gets kicked into space."

Lee stared at his feet. "More and more is being coughed up," he mumbled. "The haze is getting heavier everywhere around Nemesis. Sure, it'll fall back, but fresh stuff will replace it. I expect that'll go on for weeks."

Cronje looked at Telander. "Have you any new information on Rudbeck?" he asked.

Anguish dwelt in the captain's lean visage. "Not really," he answered. "That is, obviously she hasn't managed to repair the radio transmitter that must have been damaged. However, we have no strong reason to suppose she herself has suffered serious injury. Doubtless the major harm was to the linac. Plasma bouncing off solid particles that did not flash into vapor as ice crystals would—plasma striking its electomagnetic accelerators at speeds close to light's— But I daresay the basic power plant is intact, and certainly the batteries should have ample charge. Life support ought to be still effective. Mainly, the boat is crippled."

"In a rapidly decaying orbit."

"Well, yes. Drag not only reduced eccentricity by a large factor, it shortened the semimajor axis. The period has become correspondingly briefer; and each periapsis, passing through those ever thicker clouds—" Telander stiffened himself. "But I am being weak. I want a message from her, a reassurance, which my mind says isn't really necessary, though my heart disagrees.

It *is* an eccentric orbit yet. Along most of it, the boat is in open space. The indications are that we have a day or two of grace before the final plunge.''

"And I can get there in four or five hours," Cronje responded. "Never mind precise figures beforehand. You can feed me those as I travel, and I'll adjust my vectors accordingly. My boat is fully in order. Have I the captain's leave to start?''

"You do." Telander hesitated. He raised a hand. "A moment. Let us spell this out. Your assignment is to match velocities at a safe point on Rudbeck's orbit, take her aboard, and return here. Nothing else. We can't afford a second gamble.''

"Bearing in mind I must exercise my own judgment. Let's not dawdle." Cronje turned to go. Impulsively, he seized Lee and hugged the astrophysicist to his breast.

"Don't you blame yourself, Ezra," he said. "Nobody could have done better than you and your staff. Damn few could have done as well. If nature isn't going to surprise us, ever, why the hell do we go exploring?''

Cronje left. In the passageway outside, he found Byrne waiting. Tears ran down the planetologist's face. "God ride with you, Jan." His words wavered. "If only I could. Bring her back. Afterward you can ask anything of me you want, and I . . . I will be doing my best to obey.''

Cronje wrung his hand, growled, "No promises," and hastened onward.

Crew were a-bustle around a launch bay airlock. Minna Veijola stood aside from them. When Cronje appeared, she ran to meet him. They went off together, out of sight behind a locker. Standing on tiptoe, she could take him by the shoulders. "Be careful, Jan," she pleaded.

A possible chuckle rumbled in his throat. "You know me, little friend. I never take needless risks. I don't even play poker. No doubt this is part of the reason Suna found me a dull sort.''

"You aren't, you aren't," she breathed. "Yes, I have come to know you—the voyage, the visits to my moon, oh, everything—" The slant blue gaze strained upward. "So I sense you have more in mind than what you are telling. Jan, don't do it! Whatever it is, don't do it! Only bring Suna back, and yourself.''

He stroked her hair. "A man must do what he must. And a woman, of course." A technician stepped around the locker to announce readiness. "Farewell, Minna." Cronje went to his boat.

*   *   *

Rendezvous could have been made when *Valkyrie* was at her farthest from Nemesis. However, that would have meant letting her swing another time through the clouds. Ezra Lee had been the first to confess that there was no telling—nothing but an educated guess—which of those close passages would prove the fatal one. The half-star was vomiting more and more spouts of dust and gas, in wholly unforeseeable fashion. Cronje was to meet Rudbeck at the earliest moment which was prudent. Her transferral should not take long.

Thus the vessels were cometing inward when they made contact. Nemesis filled the forward ports of *Kruger* with swirling, vaguely starlit smoke. Sometimes it parted for a short while to show crimson underneath, but mostly it was pearl-gray turmoil.

Against that background, *Valkyrie* gyrated helpless. Cronje could see how the webwork of her drive was twisted, partly melted, sheared across in places. It could be restored, but that required she be in space more calm than that toward which she fell.

Given his vehicle and his experience, approach was no problem. Erratic spin along the invariable plane was. Cronje spent an hour using his grapples, touch after finicking touch, to dissipate angular momentum between both hulls. At each stroke, metal shivered and cried out. At last he could lock tight.

He and Rudbeck had already exchanged optical-flash signals. She was uncomfortable but not badly hurt. When he had achieved a reasonable rotation and an embrace, she donned her spacesuit and jetted around from her airlock to his. He let her in. By then they were quite near Nemesis, and speeding ever faster.

They did not feel that. She hung weightless in the entry, surrounded by a bleakness of metal, and fumbled at her faceplate. He helped her unfasten it. She had washed the blood from around her nostrils but was still disheveled and hollow-eyed. Somehow the haggardness brought forth, all the more sharply, the fine sculpturing of bones, nose, lips. "Thank you," she said.

"My duty," he answered. "Are you okay?"

"Essentially, yes."

"But are you capable of work? Hard work, I warn you."

Her eyes ransacked his countenance. Behind the beard, it was like meteoritic iron. "What . . . are you . . . thinking of?" Pause. "Oh. Yes. Transshipping Osa. That must exceed your orders."

"Here I give the orders."

"Well—" A laugh rattled from her. "Why, my dear old cautious Jan! But I agree. It'll take a couple of hours. We'll have to pass periapsis again. Our orbit should not decay too badly, though. And this *was* why I came." She reached to catch his hands in her gloves. "Yes, let's get started. I'll help you on with your suit."

"My idea goes beyond that," he said. "It involves two or three close approaches. You realize the risk. Nemesis may cause us to dive. But I don't expect it, and judge the stakes are worth the bet."

She gaped. "Jan . . . you don't mean salvaging *Valkyrie*?"

He shrugged. "What else?"

"But—we do have a spare boat—"

"And who can tell what may happen in the future, what may be wrecked beyond hope?" he flung forth. "Not to speak of the reaction mass in your tanks. We can spotweld the hulls together. It'll cause awkward handling, but we need simply achieve escape— boosting in clear space, naturally. Miguel Sanchez has already been recalled from his expedition; he's on his way back to the ship; his boat can take us off, and leave a repair gang for ours. It will make an immense difference to the whole mission."

Afloat in midair, he folded his arms and looked squarely into her eyes. "Now this will give you no chance soon to rest," he said. "You're bruised and weary. Are you able? Are you game?"

Radiance replied. "Oh, Jan, yes!"

Everybody aboard *Anna Lovinda* was present to greet the return. Most stood aside, silent, more than a little in awe. Sanchez, who came through the airlock first, went to join their half-circle. Telander stood before it alone.

Cronje and Rudbeck appeared. There was nothing heroic about that advent. Perfunctorily washed and combed, exhausted, they shambled forth. When they stopped in front of the captain, they swayed on their feet.

"Welcome." Telander was quiet a few seconds. "I wish I could say that with a whole heart."

Indignation flared out of Rudbeck's fatigue: "Are you miffed that Jan's judgment proved better than yours? He did save not only me, but Osa and my boat. What this is worth to us, to humankind—"

Telander lifted a palm. "Certainly. But the precedent, the

example. You may imagine you have the law on your side. I doubt it. Captains, too, are obliged to follow basic instructions.''

Cronje nodded heavily. "I know," he said. "Do you want to bring the matter to trial?"

Telander shook his head. "No, no. People don't quarrel with spectacular success." He sighed. "I can but hope nobody else—nor you two—will feel free to ignore orders and violate doctrine. We are so few, so alone."

Rudbeck drew closer to Cronje's side. "You can trust him," she declared. "Believe me."

Byrne, who had lifted his arms toward her, let them fall and dropped his gaze.

Cronje disengaged himself. "Well," he said, "I'm off to sleep for a week."

Rudbeck stared. A hand stole to her lips. "Jan—?"

He barked a laugh. "Did you suppose I went out merely to rescue you? Or do you suppose, if the lost person had been anybody else, I would not merely have carried out my task? Think about it."

He started for the cabins. In that direction Veijola stood waiting.

Rudbeck spent a whole minute motionless before she joined Byrne. One by one or two by two, mute, folk went their various ways. Telander and Lee stayed behind.

The astrophysicist spoke low. "We have about twelve million years before Nemesis comes back to Sol's part of the System. Let's hope that will be time enough for a race like ours to make ready."

ABOUT THE EDITORS

Isaac Asimov has been called "one of America's treasures." Born in the Soviet Union, he was brought to the United States at the age of three (along with his family) by agents of the American government in a successful attempt to prevent him from working for the wrong side. He quickly established himself as one of this country's foremost science-fiction writers and writer about everything, and although now approaching middle age, he is going stronger than ever. He long ago passed his age and weight in books, and with some 330 to his credit threatens to close in on his I.Q. His novel THE ROBOTS OF DAWN was one of the best-selling books of 1983 and 1984.

Martin H. Greenberg has been called (in THE SCIENCE FICTION AND FANTASY BOOK REVIEW) "The King of the Anthologists"; to which he replied—"It's good to be the King!" He has produced more than one hundred of them, usually in collaboration with a multitude of co-conspirators, most frequently the two who have given you COMETS. A Professor of Regional Analysis and Political Science at the University of Wisconsin-Green Bay, he is still trying to publish his weight.

Charles G. Waugh is a Professor of Psychology and Communications at the University of Maine at Augusta who is still trying to figure out how he got himself into all this. He has also worked with many collaborators, since he is basically a very friendly fellow. He has done some sixty-five anthologies and single-author collections, and especially enjoys locating unjustly ignored stories. He also claims that he met his wife via computer dating—her choice was an entire fraternity or him, and she has only minor regrets.